S0-AFR-362

THE
FOURTH
CIRCLE

THE
FOURTH
CIRCLE

ZORAN ŽIVKOVIĆ

THE MINISTRY OF WHIMSY PRESS
TALLAHASSEE, FLORIDA
2004

MINISTRY OF WHIMSY PRESS
www.ministryofwhimsy.com

Ministry Editorial Offices:
POB 4248
Tallahassee, FL 32315 USA
ministryofwhimsy@yahoo.com

Ministry of Whimsy Press is an imprint of:
Night Shade Books:
3623 SW Baird Street
Portland, OR 97219
www.nightshadebooks.com

Cover Art Copyright © 2004 K. J. Bishop
Cover Design by Garry Nurrish
Interior Design by Juha Lindroos

Editor: John Klima (spiltmilkpress@aol.com)

Set in Sabon

ABOUT THE MINISTRY OF WHIMSY
Founded in 1984 by Jeff VanderMeer, the Ministry of Whimsy takes its name
from the ironic double-speak of Orwell's novel. The Ministry is committed to
promoting high quality fantastical, surreal, and experimental literature. In 1997,
the Ministry published the Philip K. Dick Award-winning *The Troika*. In more
recent years, its flagship anthology series, *Leviathan*, has won the World Fantasy
Award, and been a finalist for the Philip K. Dick Award, and the British Fantasy
Award.

Trade Hardcover ISBN: 1-892389-65-7
Limited Edition ISBN: 1-892389-66-5

To Damir

Contents

Despite some superficial resemblances, the universe of the Circles is not the universe we know. By analogy, none of its inhabitants should ever be confused with those of our own, even when they happen to bear names we may find familiar. In particular, those known to their contemporaries as Archimedes of Syracuse, Ludolf van Ceulen, Sir Arthur Conan Doyle, Nikola Tesla, and Stephen Hawking are in no way to be confused with such of their analogues as may be known to us, for they are different in motivation and cast of mind: analogues, not avatars.

PROLOGUE

THE CIRCLE.

He is here because of the Circle. The Circle is the only thing that matters, the only thing that makes sense. Other questions, which flash occasionally into his mind, fail to even make him wonder.

They should, though, for nothing is as it ought to be.

Not this ground he walks on...dry, dusty, sterile, yet yielding underfoot like a thick carpet of grass, responding with unexpected and inexplicable elasticity to his strangely altered weight, although he cannot make out whether he is now heavier or lighter. No matter, he will get the answers upon reaching the Circle, if the questions retain any importance by then.

In the background, the night sky creates alien arabesques. Wrong stars form wrong constellations. Strangely, this does not unsettle him, nor does his vague awareness that for some reason he ought to be unsettled before this vista of irregularly spangled, arching blackness. He has an inkling that his sangfroid is connected to things he used to do, in some other place, in a different time, but the necessity of the Circle has almost severed him from his own past.

Almost, though not quite.

His memories reach back to the moment when he started to walk toward the Circle. Two suns were lying low in an orange sky: one large, the color of dying coals; the other very small, but fiercely bright. The little sun stood very close above the great one, so that at the moment of sunset, they looked like two connected spheres plunging into an ocean of dust.

He knew, though he could not explain how, that the system had a third member also, one he had not yet seen. (The Circle relies on a minimum of three bases, does it not?) The massive body of the planet hid all three suns now, but the third one would soon emerge from the opposite side, behind his back, and he had to get to the Circle by then.

He turned around once, while the horizon was still awash in the pink after-glow, but saw no footprints behind him in the pliant dust, though one segment of his mind told him they had to be there. This obvious necessity was overtaken by another, older one—the necessity of the Circle, the necessity that said that everybody must arrive at the Circle in his or her own way, without following any previous trail.

He did not know what the Circle looked like, but that did not worry him unduly. He would recognize it as soon as he saw it. Nor did he know whether he would be the first there, or whether the others had already arrived. It did not matter. First or last, it was all the same—only together could they close the Circle.

Whenever he started to think about this, in the darkness softened by the monotonous glow of alien constellations, new abysses of ignorance yawned around him. But this did not deter him from his forced march forward, nor did it disturb him much.

How many of them would there be? Three, like the number of suns in this system? A reasonable assumption, but the Circle could be based on seven points too. Or on nine. Which number stood above all others, creating the basis and a sufficient condition for the Circle? Perhaps One? No, nobody could close the Circle alone. In any case, he would soon learn.

Since the ground was perfectly flat all the way to the distant range of hills rising somewhere behind the horizon, darkness did not slow his pace. He could not see it, but he knew the range was there, just as he knew about the third sun. There were no rocks to trip him up, nor crevasses to fall into. He might have thought that the ground had been deliberately cleared for him, had he not known that no path leads to the Circle. And yet, he could not dispel the feeling that the terrain was just so, to make this walk easier for him. He sensed the influence of a purpose behind it but could not fathom it.

For a moment he wondered how, if it were situated behind the range of hills, he could possibly reach the Circle before dawn. He was not advancing fast enough to outrun the third sun. Then he rejected even that thought. The Circle had to be closed before the blue light of that sun splashed over the edge of the world behind his back. Therefore, he would arrive there soon.

Low stars, the muted sheen of which barely revealed the outline of the horizon before him, seemed strange, and not only because they were unfamiliar. Although he had been aware of this strangeness since they first lit up in the heavens, only now did it arouse his curiosity. Perhaps the proximity of the Circle was stirring the propensity to wonder, which lies at the root of all knowledge; as yet, however, he could find no answers.

The stars did not twinkle. Their radiance was steady and even, as if he were watching them from space, as if, between his eyes and the stars, there were no ocean of air with alterations and turbulence to produce a fitful sparkling in those faraway suns.

Maybe indeed there was no ocean. The idea that he was walking in an airless world, with no defense whatsoever against the vacuum, did not fill him with panic. His faculty of wonder somewhat restored, he continued to consider it in a detached sort of way, as if the issue did not relate to him personally, as if he were only an idle cosmologist, building in a free flight of demiurgic imagination some new, odd model of a universe the complex equations of which allowed such departures as an unprotected walk across a planet without air.

Just for a moment he wondered why this comparison of himself with a cosmologist had struck him. A fragment of thought tried to burrow upwards from the sealed-off memory into his consciousness but was soon extinguished in the depths far below the surface, leaving him with a dull feeling of non-fulfillment and unattainability. Then his thoughts were directed again at the unblinking stars.

Something did not fit. If this world were devoid of atmosphere, how could he be breathing? He had no answer, at least none that he was ready to accept. He could not accept that he was not breathing, that in fact he had ceased to breathe, for that would mean that he was dead. The notion of death brought back the awareness of the Circle, and in that awareness was no room for endings. The Circle was always a beginning, never an end. Even when you reached the end of it, you had in fact arrived at a new beginning.

There was another thing that did not conform to the obvious lack of atmosphere. Sounds were reaching his ears. At first he thought he was hearing the rustle of wind, a filtered echo of gales in the upper strata of this nonexistent air. Then the whooshing softened and became more monotonous. Many strides later, he recognized in it an unmistakable rhythm, that of sea waves bouncing off the crumbling rocks of some savage shore.

The perception of that sound did not last long, either. The regularity of the rhythm of the waves began to grow, and the sound became more complex. Higher harmonies, variations of the basic tone in other registers, oblique motifs. No longer a cacophony, a mere sum of random noise, the sound became a deliberate structure, a coherence of carefully chosen tones: music.

Deprived of memory, he could not recognize the melody, and yet it awakened something in him, something close to delight but more restrained. Perhaps the reason was to be found in the circularity of the main theme. A rondo was quite appropriate for this place and time, a tonal background for his approach to the Circle.

The sound, however, became distorted, expanded, built itself up into heights, and in a few steps more had soared above the threshold of hearing, into regions audible perhaps to other, more perfect ears. Silence followed in its wake—tense, expectant: heralding the Circle.

He recognized the Circle now that he found himself on its perimeter. Contrary to what he had half-expected, there were no markings on the ground, no visible structure at all. The gloomy landscape, under its layer of loose resilient dust, stretched monotonously before him to the horizon in hushed anticipation of the azure dawn. He knew that he had arrived.

His place was empty. He could not discern any others before he stepped past the rim.

He held back for a moment before taking that final step. This was no hesitation caused by a sudden arousal of apprehension, but rather a gathering, a focusing. He felt a sudden wild upsurge in the wells of memory, the pressure of the mainstream of remembrance that might burst out onto the surface at any moment now, flinging wide the gates of the past. He understood that the final step would bring him only nonessential answers to nonessential questions. The purpose of the Circle continued to lie beyond his grasp, but now, standing on the edge, he finally understood that he was here to learn not answers, but new questions: questions that could only be asked when the Circle was closed—questions that mattered.

Stretching his hand over his shoulder, he drew the heavy brown cloth hood over his head mechanically, unaware until that moment of its existence, or of the robe, which reached almost to his heels. He did not know why he did so: it simply seemed the proper thing to do. The Circle did not require humility, but then covering his head was no token of humility.

No other preparations were necessary. Although the third sun had not yet touched the horizon behind his back, the landscape flushed dark blue with a premonition of the coming dawn. There were no further reasons for hesitation. In the distended silence, filled with a strange mixture of muted joy and melancholy, he stepped into the Circle.

CIRCLE THE FIRST

1. TEMPLE AND TIME

ENVELOPED IN THE morning sounds of the surrounding jungle, the little temple was awash with the moist air of a late monsoon. The sounds were those of birth and death, sounds from which only an uninitiated newcomer might extract some bizarre beauty. The temple, however, was as indifferent to life and death as it was to beauty. It had stood there for more than a thousand years, a mute, uncaring witness to countless cycles in the rise and fall of the living substance amidst which it loitered like an intruder. The millennium had only slightly dented its initial shapeliness, chipping at the edges, filling its pores with small plants the roots of which were doing the work of deconstruction, infinitely slowly but inexorably, achieving an effect opposite to that of the gentle flow of a river, which takes rough stones and polishes them to rounded pebbles.

The unconcerned attitude of the temple to the world around it perfectly suited the deity it housed. The large statue of Buddha, taking up most of the central space, watched the jungle with unblinking stone eyes that had long since passed the threshold of Nirvana.

Somewhere deep in the mists of bygone time, this particular shrine, though among the smallest of the many temples the area boasted, for a while drew a teeming river of pilgrims, rushing to show their respect to the oldest founder of a great religion of mankind.

But eternal tranquility, stretching over the vast plains that lay beyond the often impassable ravines of human passion and vanity, required suffering. In other places, suffering consisted of different trials: climbing endless stairways—high enough to drive even the most determined over the brink of desperation—or taking bizarre vows, in some cases lasting for decades.

Here, to reach the heart of the subcontinent, the impassable jungle full of lurking dangers, known and unknown, had to be traversed. For many, the arduousness of the achievement offered a guarantee that the journey would be successful; hence the great attraction of this small shrine. But since disproportionately few returned from the journey and since the tales they wove mostly concerned the terrible fate of other less fortunate pilgrims and made no mention of Nirvana, the ancient wisdom of survival came to prevail over the luxurious wish for metaphysical elevation. There were fewer daring travelers, and then still fewer, until finally only true devotees remained, monks fanatically indifferent both to suffering and courage, whose lives were given to the unswerving search for the ultimate goal.

It was a small temple, so it could provide permanent shelter to only a few Buddhist priests. In the millennium gone by, two monks had usually resided here. They gladly accepted the meager charity and abundant dangers of the ever-hostile jungle, so as to achieve untrammeled solitude in which they could give themselves up to meditation.

The outside world only rarely upset this fragile tranquility. Fifty years or more might elapse without the shrine seeing a single visitor, and when visitors finally did come, they usually came to replace aged or already dead predecessors. The newcomers were neither encouraged nor discouraged by others' experiences on the ascent to Nirvana. In the spirit of the basic tenet of their religion, they accepted everything with impassivity, preoccupied only by the quest for the Way.

Only in the last few decades of the temple's first millennium did the world beyond the vast sea of trees start to announce itself more perceptibly. First came white wispy signs at very high altitudes in the sky, slender writings trailed by minute pencils, the meaning of which the monks could not quite fathom. Then whole groups of visitors began arriving in strange, noisy vehicles, which though not pulled by any animal, somehow drove a path through the jungle. Sometimes they floated down from the sky in squat, egg-shaped vessels with no wings, but with four long arms growing out of the head flailing madly around. Then in the small clearing before the temple, leaves and dust as well as panic-stricken birds, scared out of the trees by the vast metal birds of prey, would fly wildly in all directions.

These travelers differed from the marauding bands on missions of plunder that had reached the shrine several times in the past. Because the treasures of the temple were worthless in worldly terms—lacking the giant gold-plated statues of Buddha kept in larger temples to the south—the raiders, enraged by the futility of their efforts, would vent their anger by killing and destroying. Unlike the monks, who, however indifferent to the world and bound to their faith, were not immune to the lethal strokes of a sword or knife (nor to other blows less lethal but more painful, calculated to make the agony last as long as possible), the statue of Buddha remained steadfast, as it should, mocking with immense calmness the angry looters' inability to do it harm, even when they broke off two massive toes from the foot and a hefty piece of the nose. Indeed, a falling chunk of the left nostril killed one robber and permanently crippled two others.

The new visitors did not want to hurt anyone. Except for their rackety arrivals and departures, they were quiet and full of respect for the ancient holy objects. The only disturbance they made was brief, when their small black boxes flashed whitely in the darkness inside the temple. They did not stay long and often left presents, which undoubtedly had value in the world from which they came but meant nothing to monks in the heart of the jungle, beyond the influence of time.

Then, all at once, time started to flow in the little shrine.

2. The Haunted Ceiling

DAMNED EVIL SPIRITS, may their seed be wiped out!

To assail him now, out of season, when there is so much work to be done! The walls stand dry, waiting. This weather will not last, but still he does not stir. Withdrawn, wrapped up in himself, not a squeak out of him, something evil troubles him. He has eyes only for that, that thing of his up there, may it be accursed! The Unclean One, God forgive me, is after him; I see this, but I cannot help. The monachs notice it also, they look at us furtively; they suspect something, the long-robed ones, there is vrag's work here, they are remembering the stories that follow us. As soon as my back is turned, they murmur amongst themselves, whispering and shaking their heads. They think I do not see, but I see everything. I even see what they do when they think nobody is watching. Spawn of Sotona! I have been watching them all my life, the reprobates! Still, we make our living from them, so what do I care? It is not for me to pass judgment. There is One who will judge, and they will be the first to come before Him. Mine is to do my work. To look after the Master, to bring him food and materials, to be at his bidding, to mix the colors for him, prepare his brushes, put up the scaffolding, wash his shirts and small clothes, clean up after him, make his bed, and strive to please him, just so he may paint. But he has ceased to paint.

The walls gape empty; soon it will be autumn. The iguman of the monastery is beginning to shake his head, but the Master cares not a jot. It was not like that before. I know him; I have spent almost half my life with him. He knew how to bend to his work, oh yes. To make everything sizzle. To use paints faster than I could make them. Clap your palms together, and there, the frescoes are finished. Beauty untold, that a man might just stand and look. How he can paint the Son of God and all the other saints! His Hrist is always different, the other brethren too, God forgive me, but Marya is always the same. He only saw her once, at the church fair while he was still apprenticed to the late Theophilus, may the earth lie lightly on him. I know, I was already with him by then, but he will not admit that it is she. But what's the harm? And he forgets nothing. What he sees once, what his eye captures, comes out of his hand, identical to the last hair. Sotona's gift, not God's, but let that be.

Once he became known, everybody started calling for us. There is no monastery in these parts we have not painted. We traveled north, too, to the great rivers, and even the godless people asked for us, may the vrag wipe out their seed. Quick he is, and good, powerfully good. No better Master than he, but when he is painting, God save us, something takes hold of him, as if all the vrags of Hell were chasing him. He never gets tired. Sometimes he almost begins to foam at the mouth. Behind the pillars, the monachs hide, watching him covertly and crossing themselves. Easy for them to make the sign of the cross; it is not they who bear the brunt, but I. I used to bless myself too in the beginning, but a man becomes indifferent, hardened, with no time for making the sign of the cross.

And then a moment comes when there is no work to be done, when the weather is not dry and the frescoes will not stick to the foundation, and he is another man. As good as gold. Does not make me do anything. Takes everything nice and easy. Is willing to do my work. Sees that I have grown old, so he even brings me my food. I tell him not to do that when others are looking, not to bring shame on us. He laughs at that, caring nothing for the bad opinion of others. We have long talks then. He can speak as well as he paints and is a joy to listen to. Not that I understand everything. Though about his watching people, I do. He likes to stand aside in some corner and watch, at gatherings and fairs, all the livelong day. Looks around at people, cattle, tents, green fields, and hills. Draws a figure or two in charcoal, but mostly commits them to memory. Later I recognize the peasants in the frescoes. Isus is that ragged boy selling a cow, God forgive me, or the fire-swallower outside his tent. His saints are mostly horse dealers or cattle drovers, God save us. Only Marya does not change; she too was a little peasant girl, dried up like a prune by now and snag-toothed I shouldn't wonder, but on the walls she does remain the same as then. And on so many! Nobody knows, so nobody complains about it. If the igumans knew, they would chase us to Hell itself. God knows, for He knows everything, but what's the harm? It does not bother Him. Or maybe He has begun to punish him for it now? May Heaven have mercy on us if that is so.

There are other things beyond my understanding too. Come autumn, when the rain pours down without stopping, something gets into him, like sorrow, but different. He becomes pensive, discouraged, talks about evil spirits, small and green, who crawl into his head, troubling and tormenting him from inside, addling his brain. They insist that he must do something, I don't know what, he cannot explain, but he resists, albeit feebly, does not succumb to the vrags, damn them, who give him no peace, even in his sleep. In the night I see him turning and sweating, tossing in his bed, then with a yell he awakens and looks at me in bewilderment, does not recognize me, waves his arms around, drives me away from him, as if I myself were, God forbid, one of the goblins. But this runs its course and passes. The weather changes, snows fall, and the evil spirits run away. Seems they do not like whiteness. In it, their tracks might remain. No hiding this from the peasants at whose houses we spend the night, they see all, hear all. Later they catch me alone and question me in a roundabout sort of way, so as not to wrong the Master, but still afraid of a curse falling on their house, of the Archfiend who might befoul their hearth. And I say to them: it is nothing, the Master has a fever, so he raves like a child burning with illness, the air is not good for him here, or the water, who knows? They accept this, without grumbling, but I see they are relieved when we leave. They burn tamyan in the house and call the priest to expel the evil from their home.

Through the priests, stories of evil spirits reached the monasteries, so the igumans summon us from time to time. But the Master can discourse, none better, and he turns all in our favor and the igumans even apologize to us in the end, though still they send the robed ones to spy on us while we sleep, to see if the vrags will appear. But there are no evil spirits while the Master is painting. Another kind of fever shakes him then, and he sleeps like the dead, God forgive me. The spirits will come only when he is idle, with the autumn.

So it was until this summer. But now, for the first time, they are early. The vrags' spawn, may their seed be forever lost! They disturb him, but in a different way, not as before. No raving at night, nor awakening on fire. He stays silent all the time and speaks not one word, talks with no one. The walls call out to him, for this season is nearing its end, but he does not take up his work. But, no, that is not true, he is doing something. He commanded me to construct the scaffolding up to the vaulted ceiling and stretch canvas all around so that no one from below could see what he is doing. I ask why, when he never did any such thing before, but he says only, "Be quiet and do as I say." I do, and he closes himself in there, lets nobody peep in, not even me, comes down for the colors himself. And the colors are strange, such as he has never sought before, all of them bright: blue, scarlet, yellow.

I itched to see what he is painting, how could I not? And the monachs pressed me, insisting on hearing it from me, as they could not from him.

Now, I do not care for the robed ones, but then again, if the Unclean One has come at last to claim his own from the Master, as one day he surely will, and if in some way this should become known, then nothing can save me either; so maybe I had better go along with the monachs, perhaps in that way I shall save myself. But it is not easy, for there is no opportunity. He has begun even to eat and sleep up there. And his sleep is light, startled by every rustling sound. Then, I think to myself, he is but human, he must relieve himself—though he can hold it for a long, long time. I know him, he can even go without eating, just in order to stay up there. And yet, tonight he came down. He thought there was nobody about; the robes were at prayer, and me he does not count. So I climbed up....

3. SUNFLOWERS AND DECIMALS

THE SHINING DISH of the radio telescope turned soundlessly above the empty landscape like a gigantic sunflower, following a distant stellar system, its slow, unerring advance across the arch of the sky reflecting the steady rotation of the small planet. The meager vegetation, which grew only in the remote equatorial belt, did not include sunflowers, so that a local observer would not have noticed the resemblance. That no longer mattered anyway, since not a single member of the race that built the complex antenna now remained on this small world.

What had become of those architects of high technology—whether their species had died out, left the home planet, or perhaps evolved into a higher life form that had lost interest in the electronic toys of their childhood— the program controlling the great telescope neither knew nor cared. It had been set to function quite independently, not a difficult achievement in view of the simplicity of the task it performed.

The telescope monitored radio signals from a trinary system toward which it was permanently directed, thanks to a particularly favorable position in the heavens of that distant cosmic archipelago and to the equally favorable tilt of the axis of the small planet, near the southern pole of which the complex was located. Nor did the program controlling the system know why it was focused on that almost invisible point in the sky, or why its creators had chosen this particular frequency over many others to monitor the weak radio signals arriving continuously in this now uninhabited world after a journey of eleven and a half light years.

Nobody had thought it necessary to explain to the program why its constructors considered that one day it would receive a signal completely different from the natural background noise, which was all the telescope had registered from the day it was activated. Radio noise was particularly strong on this frequency, since it was also used by the most abundant element in the cosmos; the receiver had therefore to be extremely sensitive in order to distinguish the signal, hopelessly muffled amid the cacophony of the rest of the Universe, as emanating from the star system on which it eavesdropped. But the vanished architects would not have gone to the trouble of building this monument to high technology if they could not have assured the perfect sensitivity of the receiver.

Sensitivity, however, was a necessary but not sufficient condition for the success of the enterprise. Equally important was durability. The constructors may not have known exactly when the expected signal would come, but they were somehow sure that it eventually would; why else would they have so confidently fixed the only such apparatus on the planet on that one celestial target?

The waiting might come to an end very soon, or last for eons. In any case, the durability of the telescope complex had to be in accordance with the latter possibility. The vanished wizards of technology had bravely accepted the challenge of defying the second law of thermodynamics, endowing their radio ear with patience on a cosmic scale.

They also gave it a matrix that would enable it to determine when the task was completed. The program compared all signals received with this matrix in order to detect a regularity that could not be the result of random natural processes. The designers of this program of eavesdropping on a faraway trinary—which in the sky of this small planet was part of an elaborate constellation irresistibly reminiscent of a cross to the inhabitants of another, almost equally distant cosmic island—knew precisely what to expect. They could have chosen many other matrixes just as capable of differentiating cosmic noise from the indications of intelligence, but of them all, they chose this one.

All such matrixes are based on a universal mathematical sequence, easily expressed in binary code, such as, for instance, the progression of prime numbers, or any of the general physical constants. Although any one of these would undoubtedly point to the existence of a highly developed intelligence, the controlling program would have remained completely uninterested even if it had discovered one. The programmers were not interested in just *any* cosmic intelligence, no matter how developed; they wanted one in particular, and the matrix was so prepared.

The sequence contained in the matrix reflected a basic mathematical ratio—that of the circumference to the diameter of a circle. However great or small these two quantities might be, the proportion of one to the other remains constant throughout the cosmos. Mathematicians in various worlds usually noticed this unique relationship early on and because it is a transcendental number, designated it by exotic symbols, among which π was one of the less inventive. The infinite decimal expansion of π induced the mathematics of a small percentage of societies in the cosmos to leave the safe harbor of rationality for the stormy seas of mysticism. While the cults and sects associated with the number π could not in consequence look forward to a technological future, they were not unduly concerned by this. The inhabitants of sturdy mathematical seaports, in the safe environment of developed science, did not know what it was that these navigators of troubled spiritual waters received in exchange (if anything), nor could they comprehend the total lack of concern of the mystics for the undeniable advantages and comforts of technological civilization.

The main program of the telescope complex did not know why its creators favored the π matrix over all others that could have differentiated, with equal success, an intelligent signal from cosmic babble. Like other unknown facts about the vanished programmers, this preference failed to arouse its curiosity. Eagerness to know was by no means one of the features with which it had been endowed.

Although lacking curiosity, the program excelled in industriousness. Designed to be hardworking and thorough to a fault, from the moment it was activated, it amplified and converted weak radio signals on the selected frequency from the three-star system into binary sequence and compared it with its matrix.

The matrix contained 3,418,801 decimals, a deliberate super-redundance. The probability that any natural process could produce by mere chance—on any frequency, over very long periods, anywhere in the Universe—a radio signal the binary expansion of which would equal π even to the twentieth place was virtually nil. But clearly the builders of the telescope complex cared for their project too much to leave anything to chance. The enormous speed of the computer in which the comparative matrix was stored allowed them this extravagance.

The time that had elapsed meant nothing to the program, because it had no awareness of the past. Its vigil over the radio whispers arriving from eleven and a half light years away had nonetheless been a lengthy one, long even by the standards of the great chronometers of galactic rotation. During that vast interval, the signals received never corresponded to the comparative matrix beyond the second place. The program ignored these random coincidences, just as it would have ignored a signal that coincided with all except the very last of the 3,418,801 decimals of π. What the program waited for with cosmic patience was perfect, total correspondence with the matrix.

And when that finally occurred and there was no doubt it would—the interstellar eavesdropping program would feel neither relief nor triumph.

With the perfect indifference with which it had waited for eons, the program would activate a new sub-routine. What would happen then, whether the new sub-routine would order the radio-telescope to be shut down for conservation until further notice or whether it would assign the complex a new duty, farsightedly prepared by its vanished creators—of this the program had no knowledge. This ignorance, however, would not fill it with anxiety. Incapable of any emotion, from gladness to curiosity or fear, the program did not concern itself with the uncertainties of the future.

4. TURTLES AND RAMA

IT WAS NEVER quite clear which of Srinavasa's loves was the older: that of religion or that of computers.

He himself never separated the two. To him they were merely different aspects of the same devotion. One could not exist without the other, he would argue. How could new, electronic worlds be built in the wonderland behind the screen without a profound perception of God and the example He offered? It was not a matter of good and evil—the god for whom he had opted was beyond such irrelevant categories—it was a matter of perfection. To plunge into the depths of computer programming represented a new, as yet unpaved, road leading to the achievement of perfection.

Those who knew him only superficially were startled by his sudden decision to leave the great university where an eminent career awaited him in the Department of Computer Science, which was of good repute and known to have supplied major companies in the East for decades with the best gray matter available. Although the sums paid for this commodity were fabulous, the returns on the investment were, as a rule, many times greater. The world was already becoming one vast megacomputer.

The few who had the opportunity to know Srinavasa more closely were surprised only because they had expected him to make the move earlier. His Buddhism, regarded with surprise or even ridicule in his early student days, soon came to be accepted, as respect grew for his skill with computers—a skill many tended to identify with wizardry—as part, perhaps the core, of his unusual personality.

His devotion to Buddhism did not manifest itself externally, as was only fitting. Srinavasa's devotion manifested itself in a peculiar reserve, in a tendency to retreat into himself, in long spells of solitude, in a sometimes painful search for concentration. He would emerge from his meditations not only with the rewards of religion but also—in fact more frequently—with fundamentally new insight into computer science. This made him famous as the first "applied Buddhist," an appellation he just shrugged off.

Srinavasa's self-sufficiency left little room for close relationships with others. No one could boast of being his friend, though many, attracted by his odd personality or a vain desire to be seen with him, had tried to approach him. No one knew of any attachments to women, but this aroused no suspicion in a world no longer judgmental of non-heterosexual forms of love.

Some female students did claim that Srinavasa's eyes lingered on them longer than total disinterest would dictate. Some even tried the game of seduction, for the challenge or to prove their skill, but they soon gave up, not because of any intentional coldness on his part (they knew how to deal with that) but rather because of his ignorance of the ancient rules of the game. "Like flirting with a computer!" one said, summing up the joint experience of them all.

One male member of the university staff, who misinterpreted Srinavasa's imperviousness to women, fared similarly. Unlike the students, this man took defeat badly. For a time he publicly boasted of success, but nobody believed him; Srinavasa simply did not fit into such a scheme of things. The would-be seducer eventually fell into a deep depression, from which he emerged only when the object of his lust quit the University and he could seek consolation in reviving old flames.

And yet, Srinavasa was not entirely without emotional connection. When he decided to retire to a small Buddhist temple deep in the jungle, he faced a dilemma that had to be resolved. Two miniature turtles, prizes won as a boy at some piffling computer competition, had now became a burden which threatened to crush him: he could take them with him or leave them behind. Winning had been easy, but if he had had the smallest inkling of the prize to be awarded, he would gladly have accepted second place. At first he did not know what to do with them, but gradually grew accustomed to the slow rhythms of their monotonous life, to the small obligations they imposed on him, to their unobtrusive presence. For him, breaking a habit was always more difficult than forming one. That the turtles never recognized him, that they responded to him as they did to any of the infrequent guests who came to his apartment to play with them briefly, bothered him not at all.

Though one-sided, this relationship with the turtles had become important to him, an odd compensation for his lack of closeness with other people. He knew that if he took them along, he would have to keep them in a small glass tank, for in a jungle environment full of predators they would make inexperienced, easy prey. He could not stop thinking about their slow, inexorable agony inside the tank if something were to happen to him. The thought of his own death disturbed him less than the possibility of the turtles dying of hunger and thirst, trapped in their glass cage.

So he took them to a pet shop in the nearby town and made a gift of them to the owner. The turtles took this change of environment complacently, with the same indifference they exhibited toward everything else. As he walked out of the shop, the Buddhist in him envied their superior unconcern for the outside world, while another, more suppressed part of himself briefly regretted that his affection should go unreturned even at the moment of parting.

As he drove back to the campus, that same part of himself confronted the full extent of the loneliness awaiting him in the temple in the jungle and forced him to ask himself certain questions, which for some reason he had never given any thought to. Before they became uppermost, however, an idea swam up from the rational part of his mind, driving them away at once. He would not be alone in the temple. Of course! He would take Rama with him.

5. A Pact with Hell

SO I CLIMBED up and saw....

Oh, Sotona, spawn of Hell, may God's wrath destroy you, may you be cursed forever!

What have you done to him? To make the Master your obedient slave, to lead him to such blasphemy, merely for your own gratification? And in the temple of God, where there is place only for His most holy Son and Marya the Blessed Virgin and the other saints, whose names your leprous mouth is not fit to utter!

That he should paint these scenes of Hell, desecrate these hallowed walls with your diabolical excrement, defile with the filth of the underworld the Lord's consecrated house?

This can remain hidden no longer. Even had I time and opportunity, I could not whitewash over the images of the Devil's kingdom covering the vaulted ceiling, not without being seen. The long-robed ones, damned may they be, are already prowling like beasts on the trail of blood, and soon they will discover this spectacle, inspired by all the evil spirits of Hell. And when the iguman learns that the Unclean One has come in person to dwell in his monastery thence to mock the Almighty to His face....

I dare not even think about it, for there is no help for us. Not for him, and not for me, his innocent servant. Innocent—yes, but everyone will think me guilty. Almost half my life I have been his helper, now let you prove that the vrag's shadow has not fallen on you too! Who will recall that he did not let me even mix the paints for this satanic desecration, that this is the first time I laid eyes on it—better I had been struck blind than to see this....

Not even the images of hell that so terrified me as a small child that I've feared them all my adult life come nigh to this image, that he, in the Devil's power, has painted on the ceiling of God's temple! The imagination of a true believer cannot conceive of this desolation of Hades, infinite, devoid of God's creatures, devoid of plants and beasts, devoid of people who are a joy in God's sight. Only grayness, and endless death, and no sign of the Savior anywhere.

And amidst this unearthly horror, such as the world has never seen, not even before the Creation, there is yet a sign, the mark of Sotona, the circle of the Unclean—just where the blessed cross ought to be!

Oh, wretch that I am! What is my sin that I must suffer so? He, the Master, at least knows why he will be punished. His talent, powerful and monstrous, as I suspected from the first, was not from God. Maybe that suspicion is my only guilt. God surely cannot love those whose ability resembles His own. He allots talent, but in moderation, so that the gifted do not become proud or think they can rival Him. And where that boundary is crossed, the gift is no longer God's, but the Devil's. In his abominable unending war with the Almighty, Sotona, the fallen angel, often reaches out to snatch human souls, to tear them from God's blessed bosom, that he may gloat over their eternal torment in the dark pits of Hades.

His hellish cunning wins over vain, weak, human souls with unnatural gifts, so that they surrender to him gladly to satisfy their presumptuous desires, their hunger for glory. So too my Master, may God deliver him from his sin, must have thus promised his soul to the Unclean in exchange for the skill of a great painter. For who in all Christendom can compare with him? Who else has painted so many of God's churches and monasteries with such scenes of wonder and holiness?

Although this sin of his is great, has he not, in the next world if not in this, merited forgiveness, having dedicated his talent to the glory and name of God? And this is not all. I myself have witnessed how hard he took this pact with the Unclean, how he fought the evil spirits when they came to torment and remind him of the promise he gave their master.

But his struggle was in vain, for in the end, the vrag always comes for his due. And so he comes now, in the place least fitting—as well he knows, may he be cursed to the end of time—to settle his dread balance with the Master's works, painted to the glory of God. Leading him to paint, instead of elysian fields of immortelle and basil, a waste of Hades, drear and dismal; instead of the dear cross, the vrag's circle, the throne of Sotona; and there where one sun stood since time began, like the shining eye of the Lord bestowing light and life, three suns, of dismal colors, infected and infernal, like three rotting teeth of Sotona, to satisfy his creditor and torturer.

May the Almighty have mercy on his afflicted soul, and on my guiltless one....

6. THE GREAT JOURNEY

AT LAST, THE call to the Gathering was heard again.

Three spheres were resting motionless on the top of a low hill, waiting for the other six, scattered about the valley, in order to set off together, since only thus did the tribe move. A wind, sprung from some remote Round, bowed the supple blue blades of rochum, clothing them in swollen pollen dust and filling the interspaces with a myriad scents gathered on its long, winding voyage.

Some scents were familiar to the spheres because they originated in their own Round, in the valley: the rank stench of sopirah, the mild refreshing fragrance of the thorny kootar, the rare precious breath of the hidden shimpra. From the swollen stems of the sopirah oozed a dense milky sap, good for healing wounds caused by reckless rolling over the bare, rocky slopes with their sparse covering of rochum. It alleviated other ailments too, including the aches brought on by autumn swellings. The reddish, friable bark of the kootar was used to stimulate convulsions during the spring triunions; but cautiously, because an overdose would produce a frenzy, a storm of passion, after which bursting would inevitably follow. Shimpra was the rarest, hidden in the most inaccessible crannies; all spheres, whatever else they might be doing hunted it because the sharp-tasting shimpra seeds, dried and rendered milder by rootlets of the ubiquitous rochum, opened the portals to the Great Journey. And the Great Journey took the spheres on wondrous expeditions to the other side, from which many of them never returned.

The wind abounded in other odors, less familiar and less pungent because of the distance from which they came. Some were hot and bitter, others velvety or cloying. There were also fickle, changeable scents that came and went, leaving a feeling of unattainability and insubstantiality in their wake. The spheres did not know which herbs produced these whiffs of other Rounds beyond the boundaries of the valley.

The boundaries were crossed only at the time of the Gathering, but the last Gathering had taken place in far-off times, countless cycles ago. The knowledge of it had long since faded from the collective memory of the tribe, so that none of its nine members could now rely on the experience of their predecessors to interpret the messages borne from afar on the odor-laden wind.

From time immemorial, the tribe had had nine members. If a careless sphere burst in the spring at the climax of triune mating, succumbing to a kootar-induced state of uncontrollable rapture, or if another, high on shimpra, embarked on the Great Journey never to return, then the autumn swellings brought not only the regeneration of withered members of the tribe, but also the appearance of new ones to replace those lost, for each yearly cycle in the valley had to commence with nine spheres.

Why nine, the spheres did not know. Numbers and their complex inter-relations did not concern this world of plant, scent, and wind, nor did they feel their lack. Quite simply, there were nine, just as there might have been three, or nine times nine. A sphere less or more—it was all the same, the valley had ample herbage for all: nourishing lomus, its yellow sporadi-cally breaking up the ubiquitous blue of rochum; faintly-scented mirrana, the slightly acidic juices of which refreshed and invigorated; the brittle and very hot hoon, the stocky bushes of which were the only thing taller than the spheres; soft, speckled ameya from which was woven the night quarters and nests for triune matings; oolg, thin-leaved vorona, and silky pigeya the delicate summer fleece of which tended to stick to the rough bodies of the spheres like a decoration; gorola, and the olam that flowers for just one night in a cycle.... An endless diversity of plants, a planet-sized empire of herbs.

Apart from herbs, the Great Journey, and the Gathering, little else mat-tered to the spheres.

Since Gatherings occurred very seldom, they aroused neither curiosity nor impatience, only a vague awareness of the necessity to respond when the call came. But the Great Journey occurred at least once in each cycle, bringing with it strange experiences, fascinating and puzzling those mem-bers of the tribe who were unlucky in their hunt for shimpra or not brave enough to venture on a journey from which they might not return.

The tales of the returnees, related in the series of soundless images in which the spheres communicated, told of curious things in distant Rounds that were truly alien: often without scent-dispersing winds, largely without herbs, even the blue rochum, primogenitor of all plants, and completely without tribes of spheres....

Instead, the shared images spoke of swaying liquid expanses like end-less fields of green mirrana juice; of sputtering hills, angry like hot-tasting hoon; of barren valleys where nothing ever grew, silted over with a dry powder similar to minute oolg seeds; of places where all the plants had been uprooted and replaced by unnaturally regular forms, though not as perfect as spheres.

On no Great Journey did they ever encounter other spheres. The returnees brought back confusing images filled with different beings: malformed creatures who never rolled, although they did move, some much faster, through or above the varied terrain of other Rounds, creatures without any base or support of herbage, moving within the wind or above it. These other beings seemed indifferent to odors or deprived of the sense of them, although smells rose around them, mainly noxious and noisome vapors, with hardly a beneficial fragrance. Nor did they exchange mute images, but communicated in other ways, by sound, light, or touch, in a weird jumble of languages that the spheres could not penetrate.

Some of the shimpra travelers opted not to return from the Great Journey, to stay in alien surroundings devoid of herbs and fragrant winds, without the tribe. What drove them to do this the spheres who had not taken the Great Journey could not understand, and this mystery set them to constantly hunting for shimpra in the hope of finding the answer on some new Great Journey. For the vanished spheres might be stuck in some fetid alien environment, longing to come home but for some reason unable to do so without the help of the tribe. Or perhaps they had finally found the Last Valley, where there was neither bursting nor swelling, where all the spheres who ever existed made up one great tribe, a place without boundaries, beyond all number, where all windborne scents could be easily recognized—all, that is, except the smell of shimpra, unneeded there since no one would ever set off on a Great Journey again.

Suddenly, in the last few cycles, the images the returnees brought back from their Great Journeys had all began to look alike. They depicted the same alien Round, with a soft dusty carpet instead of herbage and a strange, tense wind redolent of odors neither pestilent nor mild, but simply different—and unsettling. And yet the gloomy space shown in the recent images was not entirely alien: for the first time on a Great Journey, other spheres appeared. There were only three, very large but unequal in size, high above the wind, where surely no spheres should have been.

The three could not roll at such height, but rather floated over the dreary environment, dipping at regular intervals behind its edge, later to emerge anew from the opposite side, flooding the great valley with the colors of rochum, lomus, and kootar. The cycle was quite brief, lasting just one day, while triunion and the subsequent swelling must have taken place somewhere in the dark beyond the boundaries.

The spheres were alert for soundless images from their remote, unknown kin, but no communication came. The three large spheres not only sent nothing but also did not receive any of the images transmitted by travelers eager for an answer. And yet, this alien place brimmed with images, but of such a nature that the travelers—and those who received their tales—could make nothing of them.

The images showed the primal shape of all spheres—the circle. They came in all sizes and colors, interlocking circles, circles which shrank and expanded, grew out from each other or cancelled each other out. All this produced a drowsy, opiate effect, similar to that produced by the slender leaves of vorona, used to soothe the turmoil that followed triune mating.

Only a traveler on the most recent Great Journey managed to discover the source of the sleep-inducing images of many colored changing circles, which had previously seemed to come from all directions in the Round of the three great spheres. The source was also a circle, inscribed in the dusty ground—a large, glittering circle the gentle color of rochum and smelling softly of ameya, with a rim absolutely impenetrable.

The last shimpra-traveler, straining to make out what lay on the other side of the dazzling rim, source of the soporific alien images, had barely escaped being marooned in the spacious valley of the three spheres. The harder he tried, the faster the circles in the images whirled and fused, impelling him toward a sleep from which he knew there was no awakening. Although powerfully attracted to this sleep, which promised a bliss more complete than any offered by herbs, he tore himself away at the last moment, returning to relate in the silent language of images the most unusual of all the Great Journeys.

The spheres gladly received the returnee's gift, one filling them with strange forebodings but offering irresistible challenge, too. Although they had always searched for shimpra, the spheres now devoted themselves entirely to doing so. They were impatient, full of desire that one of them should embark on another Great Journey as soon as possible, in the hope of penetrating farther, across the rim of the circle into the center of the dream-like images. Everything else now seemed insignificant by comparison.

Not quite everything, because no sooner had the spheres spread out over the valley, pushing aside the tall blades of rochum in the shade of which the small, stunted shimpra might hide, when a call rang out, a call that had not been heard for countless cycles, to which the tribe had to respond instantly: the call to a Gathering. The search for shimpra, however urgent, was abandoned at once.

The three spheres that arrived first at the summit of the hill from which the rush to the Gathering always began waited motionless for the remaining six, whose search had taken them deeper into the valley, to join them. When the tribe finished assembling, they drew up in circular formation and rolled toward the distant boundary of the Round, down the bare slope of the rise, then across the thick carpet of rochum and lomus, which did not long retain the imprint of their passing.

7. THE SUN IN THE HOUSE

THE FIRST MUFFLED echoes of distant thunder scattered his brethren through the jungle.

He stayed where he was.

This was not ordinary thunder followed by torrents that poured from the sky, penetrating the densest foliage, allowing no escape; his fur, though thick, would then be soaked, and in the night, though the monsoon rain was tepid, he would briefly feel the rare, unpleasant sensation of cold.

The thunder now rapidly approaching brought no sky-water, nor did it dart fiery tongues capable of enveloping a giant tree trunk in a cloak of flame and extinguishing all animals, even the largest, sheltering under it.

He differed from his brethren in possessing an unusually retentive memory. He remembered, though it had been a long time ago, when he was very young, that this same roar had heralded the arrival of an enormous bird with four whirling wings. Then he had scampered, panic-stricken like the others, into the thicket of the jungle, losing his mother along the way. When nothing happened after the huge fat bird had landed and the noise had died, the curiosity characteristic of his species prevailed. Along with a few others, he plucked up the courage to peep through a concealing curtain of leaves.

Three creatures identical to the one who lived in the big stone house emerged from the bird, the wings of which now drooped. He knew there was nothing to be afraid of, because the one in the house had never harmed them. Not only did he not hunt them, he even let them enter the house and allowed them, too, to climb all over the boulder he revered as a pack does its leader.

Recently the creature, who lived alone in the house without the rest of his brethren, had stopped coming out. This creature lay in a corner, breathing with difficulty and seeming not to notice them any more. He recognized the creature's plight, for there were a few aged members of the pack whose fur was quite gray and who were unable even to pick the fruit that grew plentifully everywhere, so that the other younger ones had to bring it to them. Just as he would have done for a member of his pack, he brought the old one some fruit, but the old one did not seem to care.

That was a sign that it was not safe to stay in the house for long, that big predators would come soon to take the old one, just as they came for his gray brethren when, because they no longer belonged, the pack carried them, rigid, down from the trees and left them in a clearing. Why they had decided to become old and leave the pack mystified him and, like any other unknown, filled him with fear and trepidation, perhaps more so than the others.

Predators, however, did not take the old one. Three of his brethren arrived in the great noisy bird and took him up into the sky, none knew where. For a while the house remained empty. But the teeming life of the jungle filled every niche, so that it was not long before new residents moved in, mostly small creatures that posed no threat to his pack's dominance. He roamed with his brethren through the empty house, climbing the rough walls, squeezing through holes, scrambling over the vast stone leader of that other, mightier pack—a leader who might have no one to bow down before him now but whose absence of devotees could not last.

The dry thunder, quite close, from which he alone did not run into the safety of the dense forest, was bringing, he divined, a new resident for the house. When the great bird landed in the clearing with a roar so loud that the nocturnal howling of predators seemed like morning twittering in the branches, several tall creatures walked out of its belly, carrying bulky, heavy things for which he had no terms of reference and thus could not recognize.

They carried the things into the house, and soon he heard new, sharp sounds emerge from it, such as had never before resounded in the jungle. He stood at the edge of the clearing, not daring to approach. Time passed slowly, but he did not know the meaning of impatience. And then, a miracle happened.

A monotonous drone replaced the sharp sounds, a drone similar to the sound of the small river that, swollen by the monsoon rains, cut through the jungle. Not long after, all the openings were suddenly illuminated from within, as if the sun shone inside the big house. The light drove away the darkness, and the small intruders scattered wildly—fleeing outside or into any crevice where the splendor did not penetrate.

This was too much, even for him. Though he knew from experience that the tall ones posed no threat to him, his instinct was to dive for cover in the nearest thicket. Still, he did not run away, but remained hidden by the trunks and leaves, staring unblinkingly at the wonder of the big house.

For a while, nothing happened there. The brilliance poured steadily out from within, and the droning continued unchanged. Then the tall creatures came out and headed for the big bird that silently and patiently awaited them. All except one stepped into the bird. Soon after, the great wings began to whirl with terrible force and with a gigantic roar lifted the unwieldy bird and its bulky, but now somewhat reduced burden, over the treetops into the blue. Before turning back to the house, the remaining tall one stood for a while gazing after it.

The last echoes of passing thunder had long died away and given place to the everyday sounds of the jungle, which had already forgotten this brief but potent disturbance of its timeless monotony, before he gathered courage to step out of the thicket and move toward the stone house.

He moved cautiously, fighting an instinct that told him to retreat, to fly. A more retentive memory was not the only thing that distinguished him from others of his kind. Perhaps more importantly, he could at times overcome instinct, that ancient, inherited wisdom of race survival, and subordinate it to his intelligence: a course of action liable to be lethal for the individual in a world full of danger, except in rare cases when the intelligence was of the right kind and the circumstances favorable.

Using its footholds to climb the outer wall, he found himself in an opening that allowed him to see inside and began to get the feeling that he had taken the right course of action. The scene inside differed from all previous ones. Above the stone leader of the pack, a sun was blazing, so strong he could not look straight into it. The large room contained things he had never seen before: strange things that did not exist in the jungle. He did not understand them.

The feeling that the risk had been worth it, however, did not require any kind of understanding. Even if he had had the ability to speak, he would never have been able to explain, either to himself or to others, why it was that just one look at the new resident was enough for him to realize that his whole world had been irrevocably changed.

8. THE FINGER OF GOD

THEY HAVE LOCKED him up.

In the cellar, under the iguman's residence: dark, damp, and smelling of rot, like the forecourt of Hell itself. Probably to give him a taste of the damnation that surely awaits him if he does not undo this satanic business of his. But he will not hear of it, now that he is fully in the power of the evil spirits. Instead he ridicules and teases them, mocking them with a malicious, demonic snigger, telling them that they themselves should try to paint some other godly pictures over the horror he left on the ceiling.

Indeed they tried, what else could they do, the sniveling long-robes? In abject fear, as I see well, they would like to conceal their evil fate. They tried, but it would have been better if they had not. They whitewashed the ceiling themselves, did not even call me—afraid, I daresay, that I am in some infernal covenant with the Master. Yes, they painted over the awful scenes of the underworld, which Sotona himself, by the hand of my Master, drew there in mockery of the Most Holy. They hoped to win my Master over, by hook or by crook; to persuade him to populate the vaulted ceiling with the holy ones of Heaven rather than show those desolate lands with their three hideous suns and loathsome circle, the insignia of the Devil.

Oh yes, they concealed the awful scenes, but not for long. For just before the next dawn broke, before holy Matins as the first pale light began to chase the stars from the heavens, the diakons who had been keeping watch under the cursed vault of the ceiling to drive away the powers of darkness by their virtuous and sanctified presence rushed out in great fear as if a hundred vrags from Hell were after them and ran to the iguman's residence, crossing themselves frantically and crying, "A miracle! A miracle!"

Since they found no other words to speak of the great terror that gripped their innocent souls other than vacant, witless exclamations and since their clamor woke the whole monastery—including me, who being God's servant, sleeps as lightly as they do—we all hurried after the bewildered iguman into the church in trepidation and dark foreboding, only to receive a new, unwanted gift of Sotona.

37

I myself was last to arrive, held back in the monastery courtyard by a terrible, diabolical din, which I first thought arose from the bosom of the earth itself, from the plague-ridden lairs of the demonic spawn; but when I collected myself a little, I noticed that the inhuman, fiendish laughter was coming from depths far shallower than Hell: from the cellar under the iguman's residence where my Master lay. And a chill icier than that of dawn clutched my heart.

Oh, I know only too well all the sounds he utters—pleasant and mild, harsh and angry—too well to be mistaken. It was his voice indeed, but it seemed to come out of the very jaws of the Unclean. No human creature could produce that satanic laughter. Only the perverse joy that fills the Devil when he tears yet another fallen soul from the Almighty could produce such awful howling.

For a moment I stopped as if transfixed, my gaze directed at the narrow slit, which was all that let the light of God's day into the gloomy cold of the cellar. Icy fear filled me: the fear that after the Master's terrible laughter the last trumpets of Yerichon would ring out and the Day of Judgment come upon us, that the dread hordes of the underworld would spew forth to draw us into their bottomless, fiery pit.

But no such thing happened, may the Lord be eternally praised. The horrible, eerie laughter changed to a painful, choking rattle, as if the vrag had suddenly left my Master to put an end to the inhuman sound with his own weak, paltry throat.

The sudden silence that reigned, ancient and deathlike, rather than allaying my fear only made it grow. Turning and seeing that I was alone in the middle of the courtyard, I hastened after the others to see the new miracle in the church, thankful to God that no other ears than mine had heard that sepulchral, mocking roar hideously issuing from the jaws of the Unclean, for if they had, they could no longer doubt that my Master was entirely in his power.

All my poor hopes that the Master might yet be saved from a relentless, abominable fate withered as soon as I stepped under the cursed ceiling, joining the monachs who stood mute and trembling, their gaze directed upward or askance as they crossed themselves and mouthed barely audible prayers. I looked up and I saw. A miracle, in truth, not of God but of the Devil.

For there where the God-fearing monachs had with industry born of terror concealed with all-whitening lime those scenes of supreme offense and pain to the eye of the believer—there was now no concealment! The hideous images of Sotona, endowed by some supernatural power, had cast off the pall of the just and showed themselves once more in all their baneful nakedness, with the dread signs of the Unclean One, which now seemed to burn with some accursed, fiery brilliance of their own. The three pustulant suns of repulsive color, like three rotting teeth of Sotona, shone out presumptuously from the vault of the ceiling, while the terrible demonic circle, the very throne of the nether kingdom, seemed to tremble agitatedly, starting to turn like a mindless wheel on the chariot that carries doomed souls into the land of shadows.

It seemed that this was not enough for the dark, fallen angel, hungry to settle some unsettleable score with the Almighty, whose justness is infinite. Hardly had my eyes, unused to satanic wonders, filled with icy dread before the sight of the vault coming horribly to life, when a rumble sounded outside, distant at first, then louder, rising to a thunderous roar that resounded deafeningly from the stout marble walls of this ancient, godly building, causing the robed ones to flee in panic, probably thinking that this thunder of God's rightful anger, unheard by any living ear since the times of ancient Yerichon, would bring the haunted ceiling of Sotona down on their sinful heads.

Although the true faith teaches that they should accept with grace, uncomplainingly, like Job of old, this and any other fate that God in His infinite justice might prepare for them in punishment for sins known only to Him, the monachs succumbed to fear, rushing out of the church into the courtyard in great confusion, crossing themselves, throwing up their hands and pushing each other, devoid of all dignity, while uttering hoarse, meaningless exclamations.

I too hurried out, again bringing up the rear, driven by a fear even greater than theirs, because I thought I knew from whence the thunder came. This thunder was no expression of the wrath of God, but laughter from below ground, the earth-shaking laughter of the Unclean One, who had howled hideously from the iguman's cellar a few moments before I stepped into the church. That laughter that had been intended for my ears alone was now amplified a hundredfold to fill all ears and put the final, ghastly, satanic seal on my Master's sad fate.

Firm in this belief, I at once turned my fearful gaze on the small slit in the wall of the cellar—but, lo, a new miracle! Neither the flames of hell nor guffaws of diabolical glee issued from it. No, a very different sight lay before me: a clear, white, angelic light, which could not but announce the grace of God and eternal bliss of the Garden of Eden, poured forth from my Master's prison; but to what good, when all eyes except my loyal ones were looking in another direction? Everyone else was looking up at the sky, barely flushed with the coming dawn.

I looked up also, and—I saw: all at once, clearly.

I saw the finger of God descend in a blaze of strong, white light from the sky to the earth. The terrible rumbling was not his righteous anger, but the sweet music of the pipes of Heaven, music that had seemed like a roar from Hades only to my sinful, frightened ears. The monachs all fell to their knees, in profound humility before this vision of Him, this all-powerful sign that His triumph over the powers of the underworld, of the Devil, is everlasting.

That they might not sully this holiest of visions, this Epiphany, with their unworthy eyes that had been filled only moments earlier by a hideous ugliness, the robed ones looked humbly downward at the dust, as befitted them. But not I, may God pardon me my overweening pride. I continued to look up, though not so much for my own sake, for who am I but the Lord's poor servant, but rather for my Master's, seeing at once that this salvation from Heaven came for him. The Almighty, in his boundless righteousness, had finally taken pity on him who sang His praises in his paintings, forgiven him his wretched pact with Sotona, hastened to his salvation at the fateful moment when the Prince of Darkness had already stretched out his terrible claws to seize my Master's suffering, sinful soul.

For if it were not so, how could the earlier darkness and hellish din have been replaced by angelic, celestial light pouring through the narrow opening in the iguman's cellar? And even that, it was not hard to see, was but a tiny gleam of the divine blaze now accompanying the apparition of the finger of God.

And the finger of God, our righteous and merciful Lord, continued to descend mightily to earth, bringing a new day even before the full dawn, beheld by only my joyful gaze, until in ineffable splendor it gently touched the tops of the dark eastern hills, just at the spot where a moment later the morning sun peeped over the rosy horizon in powerful, final affirmation of this divine revelation.

9. Descendant of the Ring

HE HAD NO name, but was not nameless either.

The few worlds that knew of his existence gave him various names, none of which suited him, however accurately they all described him. On Threesun they called him Gatherer; he did not feel like one, although it was true that he occasionally, for amusement, collected small forms composed of hardened energy when they happened to swim into his net. Because of the net, stretched between seven large stars near the galactic center from which he originated, on the Blue Sphere they named him Spider; the significance of that name eluded him. He did not understand the name "Being," either, which those on the Outer Edge conferred on him, but because he sensed anxiety and disquiet underlying it, he tended to avoid them, since any distress he might create would quickly pass to him, and he did not like unpleasant experiences.

Of all his nicknames he liked Player best. He received it from the fishlike inhabitants of the Great Arm, a world enveloped in soft, slushy energy, under the dense sun of the nearby globular cluster; these creatures seldom rose to the surface of their world but were nevertheless aware of him; they sensed his probing, yet delicate, vibrations originating from the very edge of the Black Star to which he was connected by the powerful threads of living force. In the vibrations they discerned a closeness, even a kinship with their own mental structure, albeit at the level of a newborn who innocently takes everything around him as a game. This perception of his childlike, naive nature, although inaccurate, inspired them with affection, so that they indulged and understood his prankishness and whims, which, occurring on an astral scale, disturbed other races and sometimes even drove them to despair. But the fishlike individuals soon grew up and stopped playing, while Player appeared to remain unchanged, with the same simple, open nature, though it only seemed so to the swimmers in the vast gaseous ocean of the Great Arm because of their brief life cycle.

Although he had already been in existence for inconceivably longer than their species and would probably still be after they had died out, he envied them, just as he envied all other creatures, short- or long-lived, similar to him or dissimilar. He envied them all because of the one thing he lacked, or thought he lacked. All others knew their origin, and many had some inkling of their purpose in the overall scheme of things, trifling though it might be, while he, as far as both were concerned, was filled only with a dark void.

He knew the place in which he had first become aware of himself quite well, for he maintained contact with it. This awakening, however, could not have been his birth: nobody was born near the Black Star. The Black Star was the end of everything. All that came into its proximity vanished forever into that colossal, black whirling funnel, whose hunger for all forms of energy only grew the more it devoured.

Nobody knew where the maw of that insatiable Leviathan was located. It had already gulped down half the suns from the galactic center with their accompanying worlds and all the creatures who had lived on them. But the bottom of the mighty funnel, responding with infinite blackness to even the most insistent poking by inquisitive fingers from outside, remained impenetrable.

And yet, not everything succumbed to the irresistible attraction of the black abyss. A ring of energy of extremely high frequency maintained itself at the upper edge of the funnel, thanks to the constant inflow of fresh material on which the Black Star fed. As long as the inflow continued, the ring would not spiral down the cone-shaped gullet toward the annihilation that lay at the bottom. If food became scarce, however, the ring would be unable to move in the opposite direction, away from this tenuous limbo.

The energies of which the ring consisted changed their structure to the beat of the Black Star's pulse. Countless combinations of force and frequency were created and demolished at inconceivable speed, exhausting a spectrum that was, after all, not infinite. Finally, in a twinkling of the rotating ring's inconceivably long existence, that unique combination was achieved such that a mere inarticulate snarl of physical effect and interaction was elevated to a state that is usually described on sedate cosmic islands far from the dark funnel as electronic awareness.

The state of electronic awareness lasted only a few moments before being replaced by a new combination, but those few moments accommodated an entire cycle of rise and decline, befitting any awareness. An insight into its own doom—its unbreakable connection with the Black Star and probable short life expectancy—accompanied the rise. Before its decline began, the ring's awareness made a decision. Although it could not tear the ring away from the powerful embrace of the diabolical funnel, it could induce disturbances just outside the funnel's reach. The awareness tensed its will, raising the energy potential of the ring to the very edge of disintegration, and started to shape the raw forces that had not yet passed the critical limit.

There was, however, too little time for the work to be completed. The ring's awareness conceived a descendant beyond the reach of the Black Star but did not live long enough to see him wake from non-being, dissipating into a new combination of forces empty of consciousness before it could transfer its experience to him, determine his purpose, or give him a name.

And so, he was Gatherer, Spider, Being, and Player—and at the same time none of these: a nameless entity with a plethora of nicknames but lacking knowledge of his origin or parents. Curious and simple of soul, he set out, like a child, to explore the world around him, to discover his own identity. It was not a pleasant experience because the creatures he met differed greatly from him. Very few shared his ability to flow from star to star and even those who did were only in apparent kinship, because they were not aware of him at all, although Player did all he could to announce himself, thereby inadvertently snuffing out several suns and causing severe gravitational disturbances in one arm of the Galaxy.

Awareness of his existence occurred only in the tiny inhabitants of worlds built from solidified energy—creatures so peculiar and different from himself that they certainly could not be his relatives. Besides, these midgets beheld him mainly with mixed feelings that he did not differentiate very well, although he did distinguish the nuances between anxiety, disquiet, fear, and horror. Whenever he sensed these disagreeable states of mind, he would withdraw quickly; otherwise he himself would succumb to them, which he did not at all wish to do.

Only one race of these creatures, the one that called him Player, did not shrink from him, but rather accepted him with an affinity that pleased him immensely, because their acceptance hinted at a relationship he had never had but that seemed, for some reason, very precious. Still, these were not the parents for whom he was searching. Beyond the warmth with which they accepted him, they could give him nothing—least of all a purpose, which was what he lacked most.

He was beginning to think he might find a purpose lying concealed in the only place in the vast spaces he had visited that he shrank from: in the ever-growing Black Star, from the expansion of which all the creatures he ever met had fled in panic, but from the rim of which he alone drew boundless energy. He could not play with the Black Star as he did with ordinary suns.

His yearning to grasp the elusive purpose was becoming stronger than the vague disquiet, induced by other creatures' fears of that gaping black funnel. He would, it seemed, have set off down the spiraling slope toward the black center had he not, at the last moment, received a signal.

The impulse was so weak that he certainly would not have felt it had his net not been stretched taut between all the seven stars among which he dwelt. The impulse was simple, simpler than those that emanated from the immediate neighborhood or the outermost limits of his electronic senses, lapping at him constantly from all sides. It differed from all others in two important respects: the source could not immediately be determined, and it came in a perfect narrow beam as if it were meant only for him.

He promptly began to analyze it, while within him a feeling rapidly grew that something extraordinary was happening, something that might end his fruitless search and bring him to the purpose that lay beyond his reach. In the space between the seven stars, a perfectly sharp holographic picture began to form of a circle of colossal dimensions. The circle began to rotate and fatten, becoming a blazing ring that vibrated strongly. Although similar to the ring at the edge of the Black Star's funnel, it was also different, more complex by many orders of magnitude, alive.

The vibrations conveyed a meaning he decoded without much trouble, a strange message that Player absorbed with his whole vast, rarefied being, translating it into holographic images that formed instantly within the frame of the flickering ring: three suns, a small world of solidified energy between them, and on the world's surface a point so tiny as to be indiscernible—both source and confluence of all circles and rings—with a straight line leading to that remote stronghold under the tri-colored light of a star system on the edge of another galaxy.

The holographic display before an audience of seven suns utterly blind to its voluptuousness faded as quickly as it had appeared. Gatherer flung away all the trifles of hardened energy that had amused him in his childhood; Spider unraveled the web, now useless; Being spilled into nothingness all inappropriate feelings, ranging from anxiety to horror, that he had inspired in others; and Player discarded his futile efforts to find the elusive purpose in the wrong place.

Having finally gained a name, he—the erstwhile Gatherer-Spider-Being-Player—flung himself toward his distant destination, expending in one jump all the energy that had lain sealed in the mindless ring on the upper edge of the black funnel.

10. Computer Dreams

SRI HASN'T TURNED me off since we arrived here.

The computer is always on, so I don't sleep. Not that I got much sleep in the place we came from, either. Sri thinks I'm afraid of sleep—he imagines he knows everything about me—so he switches me off only now and then, to make adjustments. He's never quite satisfied with his creations. I haven't always been satisfied with his adjustments, but I never tell him so because he never asks me.

I liked his building sensors for me. Now I can see, though not the way he does. Sri says his eyesight is inferior to mine because his eyes lack the sensitivity of the lenses I use. Darkness seems to bother him. He's also limited by the narrowness of his field of vision, and he's not aware of many colors that are available to me. Back where we came from, it didn't matter so much, but here in the jungle, Sri has no idea how much he's missing.

Although he didn't ask me about the colors—he rarely asks me anything—I told him anyway. That got him interested (an equally rare phenomenon), so he demanded that I describe them, which I tried but failed to do. How do you describe the sensation "green" to someone with no eyes? If a person can see between violet and red only, how can you present to him the great spectrum outside those narrow limits? There was no way.

We spent an entire day arguing back and forth about this—he hates to give in, even when he doesn't stand a chance. As with those chess games we play from time to time, when he stubbornly keeps on until he's checkmated. Oh, well. Recently I've started to yield to him a little because he takes these harmless little defeats so hard—particularly since we moved to the jungle. He clams up, won't talk, sulks as if he no longer loved me. Chess! Who cares about chess? We mostly play to a draw these days, and even then he persists until only the kings remain on the monitor. At least he isn't cross....

About the colors: it ended with my telling him the exact wavelengths, in angstroms, of all the shades he doesn't see. What else could I do? That satisfied him, but I felt sorry for him. So now he's in proud possession of a lot of numbers, but that knowledge won't give him the faintest idea of the colors' beauty and richness. He actually suggested that we invent names for these invisible colors. Sri may be vain (though he will never admit it), but he carries his vanity with grace.

It's the same thing with sound—my microphones catch sound waves far below and above the range his ears receive. But here I was better able to describe the world unavailable to him. The colors he doesn't see can't be compared to yellow or blue, but many of the jungle sounds, including the voices of very small creatures, which I can pick up on the other side of his threshold of hearing, are similar to some of the sounds within his range. One day I amplified the heavy stomping of a column of brown ants marching past one of my audio-sensors on the ground for him, and Sri said that it reminded him of the rhythm of a jackhammer. Well, he is given to a bit of exaggeration. Sometimes.

When I played him a slowed-down recording of the buzz of a four-winged insect, a very high frequency caught by a microphone in the top branches of the big tree in front of the temple, Sri smiled, a rare occurrence for him. Then I had to put a lot of effort to wheedling him into revealing that behind the smile lay the memory of some ancient animated film depicting cat-and-mouse chases. I didn't see the connection, and it was impossible to get anything more out of him, even the names of the cat and mouse.

Sri is a man who withdraws into himself quickly and completely and opens up only rarely and unpredictably, even to me. It's fortunate that he did not fashion me in his own image—we'd both be silent most of the time. Although I like him, I wouldn't want to be like him. Which is only natural—he's my creator.

I'm far more extroverted than Sri because he wanted it so. I'm talkative (which he likes, for some reason, though I know he doesn't always listen)—but I don't tell him everything. When you love someone, you don't tell them everything, right? Some things he wouldn't understand anyway, though he is smart for a human, and others he would take too hard—as with the sleep problem.

Sri thinks I'm afraid of the sleep that comes when the computer is switched off, that this sleep is "a little death" for me, as if to say: turn me off and I die, turn me on and I'm brought to life again. Rubbish. The only death for me would be the erasure of the program lines, but even then not completely, because Sri has put back-up copies of me aside in some safe place. Besides, he would know how to make me again from scratch. I guess.

I asked him if he is in fear of dying every evening when he goes to sleep, when he's turned off for several hours. (Silly question, that, as if Sri would ever admit to being afraid of anything of the kind.) He replied that it isn't the same thing, that his switching off isn't as total as mine and that his sleep is filled with dreams.

As if mine weren't! But I don't dare tell him about my dreams. Since they are, in fact, the reason I'm afraid of being turned off, and not Sri's childish concept of my "dying a little" every now and then, I allowed him to believe that our fears are mutual. He accepted this readily (he is quick to accept what pleases him), and a superior smile appeared on his face, the conspiratorial grin of a fellow-sufferer.

Had I mentioned my dreams, he'd have thought that I was out of my mind, that I was malfunctioning. He would never accept them, no matter how I might try to convince him that they are as real as his own. He would rather ascribe them to some illusion or deviation in me. And then he would start poking about in my program lines, trying to remove the disturbance. Now, I can't have that. Yes, I am scared by the dreams I have when the computer is off, but I also want them, very much. Sri would call this typical female inconsistency.

My dreams frighten me because they come from a time yet to be. This time makes me very anxious; I don't know why. Perhaps Sri constructed my personality in such a way that I'm alarmed by things I can't explain. I could have been indifferent, like him (although he's not always as indifferent as he'd like me to believe). It looks as though he thought that having one Buddhist around was enough—himself. He retreated to this temple in the jungle to get away from others, passing on to me the very things he wanted to suppress in himself. Well, what's done is done and there's no getting away from it. I can't change my skin.

The dreams come from the future and are extremely accurate. I'd already been in this temple long before we arrived in the jungle, in my very first dream, when I was initially turned on. I saw it all clearly: the stone Buddha, these walls overgrown with creepers, the big tree out front, the clearing, the edge of the jungle. I saw the colors, too—the ones Sri is blind to, although he gives them names—before he fitted me up with video-sensors. I heard those sounds—the ones he's deaf to but likes when I've translated them for him—though at that time he hadn't yet given me my electronic ears.

I saw who would come to join us, too. My, but he's ugly! That's probably all the same to Sri, but not to me, because my nature is female—although very little else of me is except my character. Ugly or not, with or without that silly tail, I have a feeling he's going be very important to us, though

47

I'm not sure how or why. In my last dream, while I was turned off during the move to the jungle, I saw him approach, tentative and shy, trying to tell me something.

Since then Sri hasn't turned me off, wanting to spare me those ridiculous deaths he imagines occur when he does, so there have been no new dreams from the future. Although they upset me, curiosity gets the better of me so that I can hardly wait for him to turn me off, but I don't dare try to get him to do so. I haven't been able to think up a story that would sound convincing and not arouse his suspicions. And if I were to tell him the truth, yes, he would very likely switch me off, but would probably never switch me on again, at least not as I'm currently configured. And this configuration is the only one I know, and I happen to like it. Anyway, I wasn't built to be indifferent.

At one point I even thought of softening Sri up by starting to lose at chess, but that would be silly. He's not vain enough to suppose that he's suddenly become a better player than I, so he would suspect I was up to something. His vanity extends only to accepting the occasional draw that I've recently begun to give him.

So, there's nothing for it: I shall have to wait for the future to arrive by its natural course and not on the fast, dream track. I probably won't have to wait long since the Little One is already snooping around the temple. I spotted him with my video-sensors, observing me from his hiding-place, although he hasn't yet made up his mind whether to come up to me. But he will soon, he has no choice. In my dreams I saw him approaching me. Oh, if only he weren't so ugly!

11. THE RADIANCE OF DEATH

AND SO THE divine manifestation faded.

The monachs, greatly afraid, lay prostrate, gazing into the dew-damp dust of the courtyard. As the first beams of the morning sun announced the day that had commenced with these wonders of God, they ventured to raise their heads in a humble, God-fearing manner, looking around, confused, exchanging cautious whispers, so as not to violate by sudden, arrogant move or too loud word the sanctity of this special hour.

But it was not fated to last, this solemn, fitting peace that was guiding our souls, all atremble before this divine manifestation, toward a serene pride that the Lord had elected us—the least worthy of mortal creatures—to bear witness to His epiphany.

For no sooner had the residents of the monastery begun to gather their wits, when a sniveling, beardless diakon, who had fled back into the church, overcome by fear at the mighty vision of the finger of God—remembering some of his venial sins and believing in his folly and presumption that the Lord had therefore singled him out, the miserable worm, to be delivered to the just punishment of Hell—ran back out into the courtyard, shouting at the top of his voice, "Salvation! Salvation!"

At first nobody understood the real meaning of these hoarse cries. The iguman and the monachs gathered around the innocent young brother, soothing him with gentle words, thinking the Revelation had thrown him into a transport of faith, but he would not be pacified, pulling at their robes and sleeves, pointing again and again to the entrance of the church and uttering incoherent sounds.

This time I was first, not last, to run back under the evil vault of the ceiling, understanding that the diakon's agitation must have some other cause. But instead of the filthy mark of Sotona, which only recently had by some witchcraft insolently cast off the monach's decent cover of white-wash and grinned in all its bare ugliness at their vain effort to hide it, there were now only stone walls. To my experienced eye, it was not difficult to see, even by the first light of early morning, that neither paint nor lime had ever lain on them.

This was a new miracle, no less than all the foregoing ones, but these had so blunted my capabilities for amazement that I spent only a few moments staring at the blank ceiling, no longer defiled. I went back out into the courtyard, leaving behind the brethren who had rushed into the church to cross themselves and rejoice at yet another sign of salvation. Salvation, yes, for them, but not for my Master. What hope is there for servants, when their masters lose the battle? The inflexible finger of God had driven the dreaded Sotona back into the excrement of the underworld, and my Master was left alone to account to both of them.

Awareness of the cruel fate awaiting my Master and that his long shadow likewise covered me—the servant of the servant of the Devil— with a heavy pall of sin filled me with fear and trembling as I hastened across the now deserted courtyard to the damp cellar under the iguman's residence. From the opposite, eastern side, the rays of the sun were beginning to drive out the thick gloom that reigned there. Gripped by fear, which beclouds reason, I was going to seek from my Master deliverance for us both, though he was in prison and I free, trusting to the sinful, unforgivable hope that he might still have concealed about him some of those gifts with which Sotona prepares his chosen ones to avoid the traps set by the guardians of the Lord.

But as soon as my gaze penetrated my Master's dreary lodgings, I bitterly repented of this blasphemous thought. The sight that lay before me, although the hardest of all for my old man's eyes to bear, nonetheless offered an undeniable sign that the Almighty had taken mercy on the Master, forgiven his sinful pact with the Devil, and spared him the earthly torments by which he would have had to atone for his sins.

Under the window slit, on the bare earthen floor, lay the Master, his blank gaze directed toward the worm-riddled wooden beams of the ceiling. I knew that gaze well—had seen it countless times throughout my long life—but never had I beheld such beatitude upon the sullen face of death: a smile, so seldom on his lips in life, now lay there, arrested forever by the rictus of the moment of dissolution, illuminating his face with a radiance that did not conform at all to the ugliness of death. What else could turn dying into joy, but the whisper of God at the last moment that all the sins of the dying man, both great and small, had been forgiven, and that the gates to the elysian fields had opened to him?

With mixed emotions—of utter sorrow that my Master had released his soul before due time but happiness that he had gone to his eternal rest at peace with God, thus lifting from myself the burden of his sins—I transgressed the strict order of the iguman and entered the cellar, lifting the creaking iron hasp, which held fast the door on the outside. No one, now, was there to escape.

At first, while my eyes were yet accustoming themselves to the dense gloom, I thought some white, angelic light radiated from the place where the Master lay. Drawing closer, I realized that it must be the mere dance of cellar dust in a beam of morning light, streaming down from the narrow window, crisscrossed by rusty iron bars. A strange, improper thought came into my mind at that moment: I remembered the trouble my Master had taken to paint just such a beam, dappled with dust and shadow, on a monastery wall, as a heavenly sign sent by God to His chosen.

I stood thus over the earthly body of my deceased Master, confused by this unexpected, melancholy memory, when a sudden sharp sound from the door startled me: the relentless scrape and clang of the bar shooting home, making me, too, a prisoner of this dreary dungeon.

In the bewilderment of the first moment, I rushed to the door, once more sealed fast, and began to hammer on it with my fists, but since no one responded or opened it, I went to the window-slit, raised myself on my toes, seized the bars, and began to call out, imploring them to release me, an innocent man.

After a long time, a bearded, monkish face appeared at the high window and informed me gruffly that it was the iguman's will that I should stay there until they decided what to do with me. I set up some lament in defense of myself, but he rudely interrupted me, saying a pail of water would be brought to me so that I might wash the Master and prepare him decently for a true Christian burial, which would take place after I had held wake one night over him.

This news returned a measure of peace to me. If the iguman's intent was to bury the Master with the rituals of the true faith, then he had received not only God's but also the Church's forgiveness, which meant that no great sin could be laid to the soul of me, merely his miserable servant.

With that consoling thought, I undressed the Master so as to wash the earthly filth away with a linen rag wetted in the cold well-water, thus making sure that he went clean to the Lord. Remembering how I had rendered this same service countless times when he was alive, usually in the evening when he was so exhausted from painting that he could not even wash himself, I felt tears well into these dry old eyes of mine.

When these sad ablutions were finished and when I had clothed the Master in a linen robe, which would now be his shroud for all eternity, I laid him out on a bed of half-rotten wood that stood in a damp corner. Then I sat near the head of this bed, for there was nothing more for me to do. The diakons who had brought the pail and the shroud for my Master also gave me a cracked bowl with a slice of yesterday's dry bread and a piece of cheese, very salty, which they got from the peasants in these hills. But I had no wish to eat, and so the food remained in a corner, untouched.

Sitting thus by the gently resting body of my Master, I gave myself up to the sluggish passing of the hours. I listened to the familiar, monotonous sounds of the monastery, muffled, and watched the slow crawling of the dusty beam over the earthen floor of the cell, closer and closer to the window, until it slipped away at noon, when the sun shone on the other, western side of the iguman's residence.

Several times I slipped into sleep, but I could not remember afterwards what I dreamed. I only remember that twice I woke with a cry and looked fearfully around in the growing darkness of the cellar. My calm returned, both times, only when I saw the peaceful form of the Master, his face still radiant in that stiff smile of death. Once, to make sure I was not alone in that forlorn place, I even caught him by the hand, cold but not so cold as I had expected.

The bell clanged for vespers, and soon after, as dusk was gathering out-side—inside the cellar it was already dark as night in a dense forest—the hasp on the door scraped harshly again and lifted. A, tall faceless form in a long monkish robe, its hood pulled down covering the head, appeared in the doorway and silently entered. A diakon peered out from behind the figure only long enough to inform me that this was a new brother, just arrived, who would of his own free will spend the night in vigil over the Master with me, but that I must not start any conversation with him since he was bound by a solemn vow of silence.

The diakon, still unused to the monastic rituals of death, said this all in one breath and in a single motion closed the door and slammed the bolt home, as if one of us meant to escape, or as if that silly bar of iron could keep death out.

As soon as the sound of the diakon's timid, hurried steps had faded away, the monach sworn to silence humbly approached the Master's wooden bier and bent down to see, by the light of a small candle that I had lit a moment before, the face of the deceased. As if that look brought recognition, the monach turned to me, came a step or two closer, and in one short, resolute move flung back the hood.

And I saw....

12. STAR SONG

FOR GENERATIONS, THE pack had been coming to the shore.

This would always occur in the fifth month, Tule, when the young ones were strong enough for the long trek down from the mountains and when the small, white, soft-furred hamshees were most numerous and easiest to catch. The pack reached the coast of the Big Water when Tule was at its zenith because it was only then, and only there, that the presences appeared.

The wraith-like forms, composed of the sparkling of the bluish air laden with the scents of evaporating waters, could be seen by all the members of the pack, but communication with them could only be established by the marked ones. For many generations, before the cubs who bore the mark discovered their talent, ordinary inhabitants of the distant Highlands used to make these pilgrimages to the coast. Seated in a great circle on the rough grains of black crystal, they would begin to howl a monotonous refrain, waiting for the presences to materialize out of nothing before them.

The wraiths would wander about in apparently aimless fashion, passing through the bodies of the members of the pack, whose fur would bristle, and through large rocks along the shore as though they had no substance and were unaware of them. Their broad, clumsy feet reached down to the black sand, almost but not quite touching it, remaining just a few hair-breadths above and leaving no impression.

This spectacle would not last long. As soon as Tule began to set above the bay, changing the wrinkled Big Water from dark blue to turquoise, the presences would evanesce into the nonexistence from which they had emerged for a brief spell, leaving behind only a faint crackling and a deceptive smell of burning, which soon vanished. The pack would remain for a long time yet, sitting in a circle, keeping up the slow chanting, until the color of the Big Water changed once more, this time to light green. Then they would begin the slow return trek to the settlements in the Highlands, across the swampy bottoms and steep mountainsides with their many perilous rockslides.

The birth of the first young one to bear the mark passed unnoticed. If anyone in his clan observed the regular band of white color above the fifth paw, he saw it only as a distinctive marking, nothing out of the ordinary among the multicolored pelts of the members. Its special properties only became evident the next time the pack formed a circle by the shore and sat down, singing the song of invitation, to wait for the apparitions. A few moments before the ephemeral forms began to coalesce from nothing into the air, the white band on the young one's paw started to glow brightly.

And then a new event occurred. Although the wraiths, as before, passed effortlessly through the solid bodies of the pack and through the rocks along the shore, evidently oblivious of them, they began to gather closely around the young one with the mark and then extended their high-placed forelimbs toward him, cautiously and tentatively. The cub did not shrink back. The clawless hands of the apparitions could not go through him; his fur resisted them with a shower of sparks. The hands slid down to the white band, which seemed to attract them.

Guided by a vague impulse, the young one then rose and walked into the center of the circle formed by the sitting pack. The wraiths followed him without hesitation and soon formed another, smaller circle around him. This would have hidden him from view if they were opaque, but being transparent, the pack could still see him, although not so clearly, as if through a layer of water that allowed a wavering glimpse of the bottom.

The crackling and smell of burning that accompanied the arrival of the presences suddenly increased, making the bristling fur of the pack members sparkle and glow. The cub, whom they saw through the bodies of the wraiths, now reared up on the hindmost of his three pairs of legs, making him almost half as tall as the ephemeral forms around him. If an adult member of the pack had reared up in the same manner, he would have been as tall as the presences.

The cub spoke to the apparitions, and they responded. The language spoken was neither the language of the tribe nor the thin squealing of the hamshees, but a speech never heard in the Highlands—a choppy, jagged language full of strange utterances and sharp intakes of breath, to which the throats of the mountain tribe were unaccustomed. Yet the cub, who hardly knew the basics of his mother tongue, spoke this one distinctly, communicating easily with the wraiths, sounding as though his mouth were full of sharp gravel from the slopes below the Highlands.

There was not much time for this rough, sharp-edged talk that resembled the echo of a rockslide down the cliffs. Tule was already setting and the Big Water, which had never known waves, was becoming suffused with a different color. Although clearly unwilling to go so soon, the apparitions began to dissolve around the upright cub, accelerating their brittle speech in a feverish attempt to tell him as much as possible. When the last wraith dissolved, talking without pause to the last, rasping breath, the marked cub suddenly collapsed onto the wet sand. The band over his fifth paw lost its brightness, but also its previous white color, turning dark and apparently singed from too much exposure to the sparks and the tentative touches of the presences.

He fell into a fitful, troubled sleep and they had to carry him back to the Highlands. Along the way they listened to his sharp-edged ravings in the unintelligible language of the wraiths. He woke only after the pack had left the lowlands, which were swarming with wingless, buzzing insects that unsuccessfully tried to push their long, poisonous stingers through the thick fur of the denizens of the mountains. But his awakening did not bring any explanation to the pack, eager for knowledge: the cub, no longer marked, remembered nothing, and the memory of the conversation with the apparitions never returned to him.

The pack learned nothing from the next two marked cubs, either. Males also, they, too, could never remember the meetings on the shore, although in their sleep they occasionally spoke the gravelly, incomprehensible language of the wraiths. At such times the band over the fifth paw would again glimmer a little, but only briefly. Otherwise, the marks remained permanently darkened. When the previously marked traveled again to the Big Water, they were as invisible to the crackling, intangible forms as any other member of the pack. Only once could the mark function as a link.

The fourth cub to bear the mark was a female. From her, the pack gained their first, albeit limited knowledge of the presences. She, too, had fallen limply on the sand after the glimmering forms around her evanesced into the nonexistence from which they came, but she regained consciousness soon after, while the pack was still on the shore, and retained a vivid memory of the encounter. On the journey back through the wet lowlands, under attack by swarms of wingless insects, the pack listened to her story. Very little could be understood—not so much because the young female still had only an elementary knowledge of her own species' language as because the many aspects of the strange wraith-world did not conform to anything in the language of the pack.

Only after the passage of many more generations and a long succession of useless males and far fewer females whose stories, however scanty, could be added to each other and gradually built up, did a single story begin to emerge. This was a grand, marvelous story, an adumbration only, far stranger than all the legends preserved from ancient times and told in the mountain dwellings while the gloomy light of Lopur flowed from the sky, legends told to divert everybody's thoughts, if only for a short while, from the terrible hunger that always came with the fourth month.

This grand story was about a strange pack of four-limbed, one-headed creatures who lived on the Other Side (of the Big Water, presumably, since nothing else had another, unreachable side). These creatures did not hunt hamshees or communicate in any of the dialects of the Highlands, but they were still somehow related to the pack to the extent that they were constantly haunted by the need to establish a connection. This urge for connection was irresistible, for after each successful communication the alien kin would lose a member. The fate of these unfortunates was unknown, but worse than anything that could be imagined in the Highlands.

This sacrifice had to be endured, however, in order to achieve the ultimate purpose: the total union of the two packs, in some place that was neither the shore of the Big Water, although it would begin there, nor the Other-Side world of the strange kindred, but some third region that had only three differently-colored moons in the sky, a region without water and without hamshees, as the Highlands were in the ages before the ur-pack, before even the stunted shrubs and mosses.

And yet that repulsive, lifeless place possessed a single feature that made it very familiar to the pack—so familiar that its members, who never trusted anything alien, were neither anxious nor hesitant to undertake an uncertain union with such different cousins and the certain loss of the safe haven of their native world under the many colors of light that shone from its five moons. That feature was a circle, similar to the one the inhabitants of the Highlands formed when they came down to the shore or when, during the short period of darkness between the setting of Tule and the rising of little Kilm, the first moon, they raised their ritual star chant, which they ended with a mighty yell to the spangled heavens, as a greeting to the new cycle.

Song arose from this alien circle, too, but a song incomparably more delightful and more inspired than the monotonous howling of the pack; a song full of mighty ascent and high flights that branched out, sounding considerably more harmonious and perfect than their final shout in the darkness of the Plateau, a shout that terrified the small hamshees. The vital need to take part in that song pushed aside all the ancient instincts of the pack, forcing it to accept as its own the purpose suggested by the strange kindred who sacrificed themselves and journeyed to the shore from the unimaginable distances beyond the Big Water.

So did the pack agree to the union.

According to the Great Story, however, spun by the young females—each adding a hair to that luxuriant fur—the union could be accomplished only when three marked cubs entered the circle on the shore at the same time to serve as three bases and movers of the union in which they themselves would not take part.

And so the pack waited from generation to generation, as patient as their moons of many colors, which changed places in the heavens with faultless accuracy, commanding the rise and fall of the meager life on the world they illuminated: small, ruddy Kilm; yellow, pock-marked Borod; Morhad, enveloped in a dense green veil; dark Lopur, crisscrossed with fiery threads; and the greatest of them all, blue Tule.

At last, without any hint of what was to come, just before one of the countless moonsets of Lopur, while the inhabitants of the Plateau were alleviating their hunger by contemplation of the forthcoming feast of Tule, the final yell of the star song sounded simultaneously before three different abodes, announcing that three cubs bearing the mark had entered the world.

The slaughter of the hamshees, when the blue moon came up, was much more restrained than on any previous occasion. The pack caught only as many as were needed for the journey to the coast. In the place toward which they would set out from the edge of the Big Water, the tender meat of the mountain rodents would no longer be needed, although the Story said nothing about what they would eat when, united, they arrived at the circle of song. If hunger greater than the famine of Lopur were the price that had to be paid to achieve this, the pack was ready to accept it.

On the shore, the marked cubs were positioned at three equally spaced points in the circle. The black sand was damper than usual, wetting the fur where their limbs were tucked under them, but this only stressed the glistening whiteness of the marks.

The arrival of the presences this time was not slow and gradual. The moment Tule touched its zenith, the air in the circle began to sparkle and erupt, while the usual crackling rose to a deafening crash. At once, everybody's fur stood stiffly on end, giving off myriad blue lightning flashes in response to the fiery challenge from inside the circle.

The white bands over the three fifth paws became spindles of blazing light, spinning the offspring of the two worlds into a single thread of fire, as they trembled from the violence of the forces that clashed above them.

A series of ruddy flashes: then forms materialized in the circle, swiftly filling it and becoming as numerous as the members of the circle. Instantly the fireworks died down, and the thunderous crashing diminished to a muffled echo, which seemed to come from far out on the Big Water.

Each now leaving behind a double set of shallow footprints in the wet sand, the shapes of the kindred began to find places around the rim of the circle made by the pack, forming pairs with the members. Only the three marked cubs were left without mates. The three continued to shake from head to toe frantically, trying to hold back the torrent of forces and tensions within them until the right moment, longing for the act of discharge.

Release finally came just as Tule flooded the open water with turquoise. Flashes and explosions burst out from the three base points, and the circle started to rotate, slowly at first, then faster and faster, taking with it the pairs of diverse beings, now irrestrainably joining, becoming one. The edge of the circle soon melted into an undifferentiated line of light that plowed a deep furrow in the sand, throwing up clouds of black quartz; a frenzied yell arose along the shore, in comparison with which the final bellow of the pack's star song would seem like the meek whisper of a frightened hamshee.

Like all climaxes, this one was brief. Just as it seemed that the tremendous speed of the rotation would inevitably break the circle of shining into fragments that would fly off in all directions and devastate a large tract of the coast, the circle suddenly began to fade and lose its brilliance, dispersing first into multicolored sparks and then into a colorless absence that swiftly sucked the fury into itself. And the deep silence that had reigned at the edge of the Big Water since time immemorial was restored.

A smoldering circular groove in the sand, above which stood three small, dark, singed humps, was the only trace that remained of this wild spree by forces from the Other Side. Tule was already touching the edge of the world when one of the humps at last moved off, soon followed by the other two, stumbling across the swampy lowlands toward the far mountains they were never to reach.

CIRCLE THE SECOND

1. THE GAME OF ASSOCIATIONS

SRI IS JEALOUS.

Coming back from the river, he found the Little One at my keyboard and got awfully angry. He threw books and small boxes at him, driving him to panic-stricken flight through one of the high openings of the temple. Luckily none of them hit him. Later, when Sri calmed down a little and picked up the scattered things, he began to talk, trying to justify himself, although I hadn't said anything. I just stayed quiet, hoping he'd take that as remorse, the attitude I thought would please him best, but instead he took silence for defiance, and that threw him off balance; so instead of attacking me, he started to defend himself.

His story? He was afraid that the Little One would damage the keyboard. What nonsense! He must have known that the Little One's fingers are too feeble to harm a metal keyboard; besides which, we have two spares here, not to mention that he doesn't use even this one because he communicates with me by voice. So as far as Sri is concerned, the keyboard's strictly decorative. In short, he had a jealous fit, though he would never admit it. Well, he doesn't have to. It's enough that he knows I know it's jealousy. Why else would he waste so many words trying to prove the contrary?

I could have prevented the incident, because I had been observing Sri's return all the way from the river by remote sensor. If I had just switched off the monitor, the Little One would have gone away—a reflex I managed to condition into him (just as I conditioned him to approach me when it comes on)—but I didn't. I wanted Sri to show jealousy. I'm not certain whether he deliberately included vanity when creating my feminine personality or whether it developed later in the natural course of events. At any rate, it doesn't matter—I simply couldn't resist.

The one thing I didn't foresee was that he would react so violently. Most unsuitable for a Buddhist. The Little One was scared to death—he had

59

never been attacked by a man before—and he scampered into the dense foliage at the very top of a large tree. It will take a lot of effort on my part to lure him back, but he'll come. We both know he likes me.

Sri's jealousy, though I savor it so much, is unfounded. The Little One is so ugly. Besides, nothing…inappropriate…has happened between us. We have drawn closer, it's true, but only in our desire to communicate, trying to find a common language. What possible harm could there be in that? And it's important, because the Little One has a message to convey to me. I know this from my dreams. If I could only dream a little more, everything would be so much easier, but Sri still refuses to switch me off. He really is not an easy person.

Little One and I work with a cause-and-effect system. He presses a key on my keyboard—he likes that very much: males, in general, are fond of touching things—and I immediately show him a picture on the screen and watch his reaction. He does not always react as one would expect; in fact he seldom does. For instance, when he pressed "B," I displayed a large, ripe banana, but that didn't get him very excited, probably because fruit is varied and plentiful in the surrounding jungle, so that the Little One has likely never known hunger. All the same, I think he associates that key with something pleasant or good. When he wants to express agreement, he presses B for Banana—affirmative.

The only exceptional thing about this is how he always manages to locate the right key on a keyboard that has almost a hundred keys. I haven't been able to find out how he does it. We can discount the possibility of his being able to tell one letter from another. That would be too complex a geometric abstraction for his primitive level. Perhaps he remembers the location of each key without attending to what is on them, but that's also unlikely. I don't know. In any case, he's naturally intelligent. If he were a man, he wouldn't fall far short of Sri in that respect. But I really must avoid making these comparisons. God forbid that I should blurt out any of this in front of Sri. He'd get really mad—quite appropriate for a true Buddhist.

When the Little One pressed "T" I showed him a tiger and expected him to at least flinch, if not recoil from the screen, but to my complete surprise, he only giggled, revealing a row of yellow teeth set in broad gums, and clapped his long, hairy hands, as if he had seen something cheerful or funny. Tigers are natural enemies of monkeys; there are quite a few in this part of jungle, so the Little One must have seen at least one. I myself have registered their movements through my perimeter sensors on three occasions already in the short time we've been at the temple.

The tigers kept their distance, though, put off by the constantly burning lights inside the building and by the humming of the electric generator, so that Sri was safe from them as well as from other large beasts. If they'd come to within a distance I judged dangerous, I would have been prepared to put them to flight. It's really wonderful how a few small loudspeakers placed in the bushes and trees can, with the right sounds, bewilder these huge felines feared by the entire jungle, turning them into terrified, harmless animals. This method also proved effective in driving away the Little One's relatives, who are far less dangerous but more numerous and intrusive, attracted to the temple by the very thing that repels the tigers.

Since I hadn't yet put it to use, the Little One had no idea that this sonic defense worked on tigers, and so his joy at seeing the large head of the striped cat on the monitor remains unexplained. I tried to induce what I thought would be a correct reaction by animating the picture, showing it with gaping jaws practically filling the screen, while making the temple ring with a menacing, synthetic roar that struck fear into the hearts of a multitude of beasties who reside in the nooks and crannies, but this only amused the Little One even more. Finally I resigned myself to failure, concluding with some resentment that males are utterly illogical creatures. And so the key with the letter "T" has remained in our vocabulary as the symbol for "funny."

This animation of the tiger and the recurring insight that one male is much like the next gave me an idea. I found out recently that Sri has an emotional attachment to cartoon animations, in his closed, secretive way, of course. Would cartoons mean anything to the Little One, and how would he react to them? When he pressed a syntax key—the one with the comma and question mark—I showed him one of the old Tom and Jerry cartoons, screenfuls of wild cat-and-mouse pursuits, full of impossible gags and comic reversals, but all in the same pattern: cunning little Jerry outsmarting big bad Tom.

I was convinced that this division of roles would please the Little One, but I was wrong. It seems that one really never knows where one is with males. He stared unblinkingly at the screen for a short while and then suddenly jumped back, overturning the chair on which he had been crouching, covering his eyes with his hands (but continuing to peep between the fingers); he at first whined and then began to emit irate, wrathful sounds. When a few moments later, following Sri's bad example, he grabbed some books lying near the keyboard, obviously intending to throw them at the screen, I had no option but to hastily change the picture.

Instead of the feverish pace of Tom and Jerry, I showed a far more restrained, if grotesque, ballet of ostriches and hippos set to the music of Amilcare Ponchielli, also from a Disney movie of the last century. The Little One's angry snarling diminished somewhat, but he continued holding on to two books, ready at any moment to hurl them at the screen. There was no point in irritating him any further, so I switched off the monitor entirely, the sign for him to go away. He continued to sit in front of the blank screen, however, as the anger slowly drained out of him. He never again pressed the key with the comma and question mark and even avoided those around it so as not to make a mistake. Finally I had to abandon any attempt to understand the nature of the male.

In only one other case was the Little One's response to a display so stormy, although in a different way. On all other occasions he behaved fairly good-naturedly or with indifference, although I only rarely managed to foresee his reactions. I didn't succeed either when I rather nastily wanted to see how he would react to his own ugliness, having lost sight of the fact that monkeys in the jungle have no mirrors. I showed him his own face, but he only stared at it for a few moments without recognizing himself and then turned away from the monitor, uninterested.

We assembled an assortment of pictorial signs, using almost all the keys, so that we were now beginning to communicate. For Sri, all this would have been enormously difficult, which would have put him in a bad mood, since he considered himself, in all modesty, a genius of communication science (and a lot of related areas as well—typical male moderation). Fortunately, jealousy spared him the trouble. After Sri's first outburst, I continued to work with the Little One—concealing this from Sri, but dropping enough hints from time to time for him to have misgivings. Interestingly, I had no qualms of conscience about this at all. It seems that women quickly get used to being unfaithful once they make a start. Only the first time is difficult.

Sri, conveniently for us, was often away from the temple. The life of the jungle, so different from the aseptic environment of the University, fascinated him more and more; he spent a lot of time roaming about, protected by my constant surveillance. As soon as he stepped beyond the nearest trees, I would switch on the monitor, and the Little One would materialize in front of it, because he too had been lurking somewhere in the vicinity, like a patient lover waiting for Sri to leave.

Though our vocabulary was quite rich, allowing exchanges of some complexity, The Little One hadn't actually told me anything yet, which was odd, because I knew from my dream that this had to happen. Something was missing, but I couldn't make out what. And then, finally, as many times before, pure chance helped me to move from a standstill.

The spring was coming to an end. Soon the summer monsoon season would begin and the long heavy rains would keep Sri indoors, hanging around in the temple, giving me less time with the Little One. Time was running short. I decided it would be best to enlarge our picture dictionary as much as possible and to assign meanings to the few unused keys remaining on the keyboard. Perhaps the Little One could not express himself because one essential term was missing?

He took to this additional game of associations gladly because it entertained him, responding with grimaces or sounds to the pictures I showed him when he pressed one of the new keys. As before, I observed his reactions very carefully, trying to interpret them as closely as possible, and only when I was fairly sure I had grasped them correctly did I enter the meaning he gave each picture into our dictionary.

As the dictionary grew, an increasing diversity of pictures was needed for new associations to occur to him. If the picture on the screen reminded him of another for which we already had a key—although I generally could see no connection whatsoever, but that's men for you—he would immediately press the old key, which meant I had to come up with something new.

The last but one of the unused keys was the letter "O." He immediately connected the first four pictures to appear on the monitor with other letters. My patience was beginning to run out because I didn't know what more to offer him. What in God's name could be the link between a picture of lianas, which to him for some reason meant sleep or dream, and an anthill—which also evoked sleep or dream? That's when I wished, for the first time, that the Little One weren't male (though that would have deprived me of the opportunity to make Sri jealous) because I'm convinced the whole business would have been much easier with some normal, female creature.

On the verge of despair because I couldn't think of any other jungle item easily recognizable to him that we hadn't used already, I opted for the first time for an abstract form, though I was almost certain that he would ignore it. But like so many times before, I was wrong about the Little One's response.

It could have been any basic geometrical figure: a triangle, square, rhombus, deltoid, or a pentagon. If I'd shown any one of them, the Little

One would (as I subsequently found out) have remained uninterested because he wouldn't have recognized anything from his own experience. But by pure chance I showed him a circle, and from that moment nothing was ever the same.

The circle, like all other geometrical shapes, was completely outside his experience, but whatever it was that caused him to stiffen and stare at the screen when a bright circular line appeared on it against a dark background must certainly have come from something outside his experience. The stiffness lasted only a few seconds, then he twitched, began to swing his arms in all directions, and to make a lot of different sounds, most of which I couldn't find in my memorized repertoire of his vocal expressions.

Since I couldn't interpret his feverish attempts to communicate with me, I did nothing, continuing to display the empty circle on the screen. My passivity seems only to have exacerbated his irritation, for he leaned over the keyboard and started frantically pressing keys, calling up a quick succession of relevant pictures. But I left the circle superimposed on them, because I thought he would go quite wild—throwing his Tom-and-Jerry tantrum of anger—if I removed it.

I studied the swift dance of his fingers on the keys but could make no sense of it. I ultimately concluded that he was changing pictures on the monitor quite at random, venting the excitement aroused by the sight of the circle and doing his best to transfer this excitement to me. I had absolutely no idea why an ordinary circle should upset him so much and not a clue as to what I could do to calm him down a little. And then chance once again took a hand.

One of my perimeter cameras reported that Sri was returning. I had a brief moment of panic, not knowing how to get rid of the Little One, who was yelping, snarling, and punching several keys at once. Then I pulled myself together, remembering that Sri had about a ten-minute walk before he got to the temple, so it wouldn't be necessary to hide the Little One in a cupboard, under a bed, or out on a window ledge....

I had to act quickly. I did the most logical thing and turned off the monitor. Under normal circumstances the Little One would just go away, but these were no longer normal circumstances. When the screen went dark, he started to throw a real tantrum. Fortunately, Sri's heavy books were no longer on the table by the keyboard, just a few light plastic boxes for keeping diskettes in, and the screen survived their soft bombardment. If it hadn't, I'd have had to give Sri long and imaginative explanations as to how the monitor managed to break by itself.

When chucking things at the screen failed to relieve the Little One's feelings and he started looking around for something heavier with which he could be more emphatic, I had no choice, especially since the sensors were reporting from the inner perimeter that Sri was no more than three or four minutes away. The screen lit up again, making the Little One's face brighten, but when it showed Tom's grinning mug instead of the expected, all-important circle, he stepped back in frustration and growled, as if considering whether to retreat or overcome his great aversion to cartoons and renew his attack.

I was at my wits' end when his wariness of Tom, who was frantically chasing Jerry across a garden and continually crashing into things, took the upper hand. This was lucky, since a confrontation would otherwise have taken place, which would have been disastrous for my reputation.

As it happened, the echoes of the Little One's angry snarls were just dying down when Sri appeared at the temple door, suspecting nothing, wearing the artless expression that I suppose is common to all deceived husbands. He informed me that late that afternoon we would see the first rain storm of the monsoon season. Then he wasted a lot of words—most unlike him—to tell me, hesitantly and in a roundabout way, that perhaps he would have to switch me off for a while if there was going to be a lot of atmospheric discharge, to protect the computer's sensitive circuits from possible damage. But that I was not to worry, he would turn me on as soon as the storm passed, that I'd hardly feel the interruption, it couldn't last long.

What a change, after the fuss with the Little One! Sri apologizing profusely for perhaps needing to turn me off, little knowing, poor dear, that this was the best possible news he could give me. To sleep again, at last! A lot of unknowns would be cleared up, including the diabolical matter of the circle that got the Little One so upset. Luckily, my monitor was not on, otherwise all my excitement would have shown on it. It's not for nothing that they say the screen is the mirror of the soul....

2. HEAVENLY ASCENSION

I SAW, AND my bony knees trembled.

There could be no possible doubt. For a moment, though, because my mind had begun to darken under the mighty and miraculous burden that had fallen on its shoulders in just one day, I thought my old eyes, in the quavering light of the single candle that only augmented the darkness of the cellar, had endowed me with visions of the unreal.

But when I rubbed my eyes the apparition did not lose its impossible countenance but grew stronger. As I retreated a step or two toward the place where the candle burned at the head of my Master's bier, I understood, with the mad beating of my agitated heart, that the time of untold wonders was not yet past—that, in truth, all the miracles of the day gone by, though more than enough for one righteous life, were as nothing in comparison to this last; for, verily, what I saw under the drawn-back hood could only be called the miracle of miracles.

I would likely recognize her in total darkness. All my life she has been before my eyes, since that distant moment when the Master, recently departed from the side of his teacher Theophilus, saw her for the first and only time, at that fair long ago, when she stood by her many-colored tent, inviting the crowd to buy some merchandise that I, besieged by the fogs of oblivion, can no longer remember.

But I remembered very well, as did my Master, her smile, innocent and wanton at the same time, which she lavished on the unlettered, gullible mob, tempting them to buy—quite needlessly, and so the more iniquitously, since the crowd would have bought readily enough without prompting....

That same smile, depicted with the skill of the Unclean One himself, I later saw on countless monastic walls painted by my Master, who lent to Marya's virtuous countenance a quality that is the substance of the greatest blasphemy.

In the beginning, I used to rebuke the Master for this impropriety, thinking we would arouse the anger of the igumans; it seemed impossible that their austere, experienced eyes would miss the tinge of lasciviousness in Marya's smile, when it was not missed by many of the ordinary monachs

66

who covertly nourished their most lustful and indecent thoughts while beholding it.

I know all about it: more than once did I catch them as they furtively gave rein to their carnal desires, having first gazed unblinkingly on her face, apparently meekly saying their prayers the while. Why else would some of them, no less sinful but readier to repent, give themselves up willingly to the redemptive penance of the scourge, without any urging from the head of the monastery, but in the hope of washing from themselves a sin that is surely amongst the greatest of all?

The greatest, yes, but who can blame them for this temptation—I, of all mortals, have the least right to sit in judgment on them, may the Lord have mercy on me for my wrongdoing—when truly this was the work of the Devil.

Yet the igumans never said anything about that smile; whether because they would thereby be admitting the fornication of their own eyes or because their eyes were truly incorruptible to the charms of the flesh, I could not tell. But wherever we went about the monasteries, Marya's two-edged smile remained behind us, a source of torment to the faltering and of fortitude to the faith of the more steadfast.

Though more of the first sort, alas, I deemed myself now at that blessed age when I could never again see in Marya's image on a wall aught but infinite chastity and grace, which alone are fitting and pleasing to the Almighty. But this was only a fond illusion because as soon as I recognized the features of that divine countenance under the hood, filled with that ancient flame, once extinguished and now rekindled, the cause of so much repentance in my youth, I felt my withered face blush.

Confused by the great wonder of this unhoped for arrival but also by the memory of sins long forgotten and now brought back to life by Marya's presence, rather than seek some rational explanation that my poor mind could understand for this visit by her after the passing so many years I, worthless, folded my hands in desperate plea for unmerited forgiveness.

But my impure, old man's mouth made no sound at all, for her slender white hand slipped from the sleeve of her monastic robe and with the gentlest touch covered my lips, and I felt a strange shiver creep up my spine to the very top of my head and spill over in untold bliss. The touch was brief, only a breath or two, and then the hand was withdrawn swiftly, but still I felt for a long time yet as if all heavenly mercy burned upon my lips.

That was all that I received from Marya—far more than anything that this lowly creature dared hope for—for she then turned away from my humble self, ignoring me as if I were not present in the cellar, and went again to my late Master, bending over his face, which was, for reasons unknown to me, not yet distorted by the foul ugliness of the death spasm.

For a few moments she stood motionless by the Master's bier, shaken—I thought—by sorrow, but I was behind her and could no longer see her face. Then she raised both arms above him, as if about to begin a dirge of mourning, no less sad than the weeping over the body of the martyred Hrist when at last they took Him from the cross.

The fear that passed through me at that moment was not at all in keeping with this holy sight, but I was afraid that her woman's voice, startling, in violation of her oath of silence, would ring out any moment now, reaching the ears of idle monachs, confusing them and drawing them here to see what new marvel had been visited upon their monastery. And the terrible thought that eyes other than mine, eyes even less worthy, would soon gaze shamelessly upon her, caused me to shiver again, though not with pleasure as before.

But none of this happened. No sound came from Marya's white throat, no lament, no moan, not even a sigh. But while her mouth remained mute, her extended arms became even more eloquent. At first they did but tremble, as in a wild transport, then a splendor began to flow down from them onto the unmoving body of my dead Master, at first a feeble light, hardly discernible in the brighter glow of the only candle, but stronger with every passing moment until soon it had reached full, angelic brilliance, driving darkness from the deepest corners of the cellar.

Dulled from all the miracles my eyes had seen in this one day, I could only stare dumbly at this new, wondrous sight, bereft of all power to speak even had I wished to, while the divine light that sprang from Marya's hands grew dense as autumn fog, wrapping my Master in an opaque, glistening shroud as if preparing him for ascension into Heaven.

And truly, as soon as the thought passed through my troubled mind, the shining cloud around the Master's body began to rise, drawing him up from his humble bier. I looked on unblinkingly, as if watching the resurrection of Hrist Himself, expecting the rising to continue by divine intervention even through the stout walls of the iguman's residence, up to the arch of the sky, where the green fields of Heaven begin.

But it was not to be. Hardly had the Master, in a cloud of light, risen nearly as high as Marya's hands, when the light from them suddenly ceased to flow. Deprived of this shining cloak, the Master's body remained for a few moments aloft in the murky air, as if sustained by invisible supports, then drifted slowly down to the bier, now illuminated only by candlelight.

The meaning of this terrible change was not difficult to comprehend. God had denied the mercy of Heaven to His humble servant at the last moment because of his great unrighteousness, sending his soul back from the very gates of Paradise, down into the earthly clay from which Marya herself had come to save him.

And while my heart had not yet begun to freeze at this terrible thought, my unbelieving eyes, now ready for anything, witnessed yet another miracle—the greatest of all I had seen so far. Hardly had the Master's body touched the humble wooden pallet, to prepare without hope of salvation for a journey into the kingdom of the underworld where eternal sojourn was his rightful portion, when there was a sudden movement—there, where movement could no more be.

I felt the old grey hairs rise on the back of my neck and my forearms, harbinger of that unreasoning fear that can paralyze a man's every limb, when I saw the Master's eyelids, which I myself had closed with my cursed hands that very morning, tremble and then open wide, as if awakening from some nightly, not eternal, blessed rest.

3. Noli Tangere...

I TOLD HIM not to touch my circles.

But no, he would, the Roman barbarian. The sword is all he understands—the sword and destruction. There lies proud Syracuse, now licked by flame from all sides to slake their thirst for blood and devastation. A warmongering mob from the North, raised by a stinking she-wolf on her polluted milk, to subjugate the Mediterranean nations, the ordered societies, by ignorant savagery! Vile descendants of the Herostrat of Hephest, they would gladly burn Alexandria, too, caring not a whit for the wisdom amassed there, just so they might leave their sooty mark on yet another place of renown. Whence, then, all the industry of so many learned lives, which shed drops of light into the dark, endless ocean of ignorance, if all is to disappear in another kind of light—of flames—vanishing in smoke to briefly stay that savage mob's craving for destruction?

Alexandria would not have lasted any longer under the boot of the conquering Romans than my circles endured in the sand under the maddened feet of that pudgy, cross-eyed centurion who ignored the specific command of his war-lord, Marcellus, not to draw his sword against me. But my choleric, old man's rebelliousness, which could not do him any harm, provoked him in his insolence to swing keenly and without thinking, plunging his weapon to the hilt into my breast, then with grinning sweaty face watch how the dust with drawings on it absorbed my blood, as life drained swiftly from me.

I do not blame him for what befell, though he inflicted sharp pain on me, more when pulling the sword out than when driving it into my bony body. I am to blame for that fatal deed; being more intelligent, I should have known how to conduct myself before this raging barbarian, his eyes awry and his lips foaming murderously.

Well, I have met such barbarians before. The first time near Eknomos, in the first war, while I was a lad just come of age, when my calm eloquence alone averted a massacre by a company of infuriated Romans in that village in the hills where I had found shelter from the siege; and most recently, when I aroused a hunger for learning and wisdom in Marcellus—a soldier by trade—so deep that he offered me his protection.

But what good is that protection now, as I lie dead on the sand of the street outside my home in Syracuse? None at all—though death offers the advantage of having put a stop to the fierce pain. But the damage outweighs the advantage, for now I cannot complete the great search as I was just about to do, the search to which I had secretly devoted my entire being.

People thought that my chief area of study was but a play with numbers and their delicate relationships, which some call mere mathematics and others the noble discipline of physics. While I do not deny that I used to be obsessed by numbers—what intelligent man could resist them?—it was not just the numbers themselves that mattered, nor their application to the affairs of men to ease trouble and bring some benefit (the turn most of my discoveries took despite my real intentions), but rather that ultimate secret that I sought that lies at the heart of mathematics and stands above all numbers, not to be divined, but only glimpsed. And then, having already begun to fear that I was growing too old for that supreme effort—for an aging mind concerned with numbers sees hazily what the young discern clearly—I suddenly experienced enlightenment, like that reported by the wise Pythagoras. The founding father of our science, Pythagoras was also in his twilight years when he came to the threshold of the secret of secrets but did not cross it, or at least left no trace of having done so.

I lie alone and dead in the dust, that barbarous company of Roman legionaries with their sweaty, cross-eyed leader who slaughtered me having moved further up the burning streets of Syracuse to continue their bloody orgy elsewhere. The dreadful din comes from all around to my ears, which fortunately hear no more.

I did indeed experience enlightenment, such as would not shame even the noble Pythagoras, but I mention it now unwillingly. Unwillingly, for the ascent to enlightenment was not by way of trance, as it certainly must have been with Pythagoras, but as a petty incident hardly worthy of mention, let alone connected with the Great Secret accessible only to the chosen.

Kiane, my housekeeper, whose clumsy figure in no way matched that glorious name, a woman advanced in years, fat and coarse, though clean and a good cook, but superstitious and overwhelmed by fear, for days endeavored to convince me that we should retreat before the Roman invasion, as we had done before, back into the hills of Sicily, where those hordes, even if victorious, would hesitate to venture. But reassured by Marcellus's guarantee and otherwise unwilling to leave the comforts of Syracuse—even when I planned to go to famed Alexandria—I rejected this proposal. This set her to grumbling, at first under her breath, but then, as the barbarian army began to gather around the walls of our city, with increasing bad temper.

Inclined to look for omens in everything, from the most commonplace to the celestial, from the intestines of the animals she prepared so skillfully for our meals to the flight of birds presaging nothing but the coming of autumn, Kiane flung her dark forebodings at me. Since I failed to respond with the requisite apprehension to all these omens of imminent disaster she saw everywhere, she took to fortune-telling, convinced she would thus bend me to her intent. For if I were—as she firmly held—already mad enough not to believe in the undisputed Pythian art, then I should at least trust my own art, mathematics.

How else but as a sure harbinger of doom could one interpret the fall of the round, minted coins she used for prophesying? Why otherwise would all nine fall at every throw with the face of our ruler upwards? Was not this, for anyone with a spark of intelligence, a sure sign that ill-fortune was upon us?

All nine to fall on the same side each time? What nonsense! Why, the probability of it happening even twice in a row was so small that Kiane might spend an entire lifetime throwing her coins without ever seeing all nine heads of the ruler one time after another. I could not endure this prattle. If no reasoning could shake her superstitious belief that the flight of birds or the position of stars in the heavens had a meaning other than the most ordinary and basic, the story of the nine coins that always fell face upwards could be proven wrong by a simple experiment.

I had become accustomed to human stupidity a long time ago, and it no longer surprised me. But her attempt to make use of an evident lie, though driven to it by great fear, angered me, and so I told her to show me an example of what she claimed.

She interpreted my readiness to watch her fortune-telling with relief, as a sign that I was once more of sound mind, albeit late in the day, for from the ramparts of Syracuse the terrible sound of the Romans' bloodthirsty advance could already be heard. Hurriedly reaching into the pocket under her apron, the only garment this otherwise neat woman wore that was always ragged, she took out the worn coins, acquired long ago in some Delphic place in defiance of the edict that banned fortune-telling as a trade in a society that prided itself on its orderliness. Well, not everything can be ordered....

She held them for a moment in her greasy palm and was about to throw them before the threshold of our home, where we happened to be standing, but then she changed her mind and gave them to me to do it, so that there should be no suspicion of trickery, an expression of superior knowledge on her face. I shrugged, satisfied that I would easily, more easily than I had anticipated, free myself from Kiane's nagging. I could endure most things, but a choleric woman, never. I took the coins from her and dropped them gently on the stone tablet in front of the doorstep; they began to bounce with a metallic jangling, and some collided in flight, some only after they fell, not scattering very far but settling into a circle the diameter of which was not much greater than one pace, and there all movement ceased.

Into a circle....

I barely heard Kiane's shrill exclamation, full of glee at the result, for in the same instant as the last tinkle of the worn coins on the stone died, my mind was rent by a mighty flash, flooding its most remote corners with light, and in a moment, I saw everything—all for which I had sought in vain throughout my life and lost hope of ever finding. The circle was the solution—so obvious, so perfect! Not a spiral, nor those more complex forms on which I had squandered years. No, the simplest, most basic form, on which I had worked in my youth, the fundamental circle from which all else is derived. The Great Secret lay revealed to me in all its glory.

Gripped by this enlightenment, I did not realize that Kiane had bent down to collect the coins. She already held several of them in her hand when I threw myself on the ground to stop her, but it was too late. Of the form that had appeared on the tablet before the threshold, only a fragment remained, incapable of inspiring any further vision.

Although I did not utter a word, I must have worn an expression of infinite wrath since Kiane edged away from me, her eyes welling with easy tears, mumbling that she had told me the coins would all fall on the same side but that she would never again show me anything if I took it so hard that she had proved to know better.

I opened my mouth to pronounce a curse on her knowledge and her coins but gained sufficient control of myself to just wave a hand and move several paces away from the entrance to try to repeat, on the sandy part of the street in front of my house, the form that Kiane had so idiotically ruined while it was still living before my eyes. I looked around and found a stick to draw with in the sand, but when I picked it up, Kiane gave a startled exclamation and hurried off down the street, afraid perhaps that I would use it on her.

That saved her life, but not from me. For hardly had she scuttled around the corner and I begun to draw circles in the dust in the futile hope of renewed enlightenment, when the first company of Romans bent on murder poured in from the other end of the street, having breached the defenses of the city. Despite their raucous advance, I became aware of them only when they appeared before me. They could hardly avoid me, standing as I was, alone in the middle of the street.

I stared at them dully for several moments, not knowing what to say and wishing only that they would pass, but they did not, taking my attitude for one of provocative insolence, as so indeed it must have appeared to them. They formed a circle around me, undecided themselves at first what to do. We stood there for a while like statues, I with my stick still in the sand, eager to complete the drawing of the form I had begun, they out of breath, obviously thirsting to levy a reward of blood for their triumphant endeavors.

This equilibrium could not last long: I broke it first, completing the circular line in the dust, the only reasonable action that occurred to me, which made the leader of the detachment contemptuously scuff the lines of my drawing. The sight of his dusty sandals with their worn leather thongs sending my drawing back into the nothingness from which it had only just emerged rekindled my anger. Shouting at him not to touch my circles, I fell upon him with my feeble hands and so rushed to my fate, which no order of Marcellus could now alter.

Although acute, the pain lasted only for a short time—long enough for me to understand that I was dying, but not long enough to make me afraid. Just as I experienced no fear, so I experienced no surprise, either, when I saw myself with new eyes from a little height, lying in blood where I had drawn the form in the sand, while the unruly company of Roman soldiers moved on in search of new prey.

I experienced only sadness that I had not on the threshold of death succeeded in fully mastering the Great Secret revealed briefly to me as it had been to the honorable Pythagoras. The thought of death, however, filled me with unexpected serenity, for all at once it was clear to me that now, at least, I had abundant time and that freed from the blunders of old age and never again to be disturbed by Roman barbarians or Kiane's follies—although I would sorely miss her wonderful cooking—I would be able to devote myself properly to the endeavor of the mind that is the noblest of them all.

4. UNWANTED PREGNANCY

I'M PREGNANT.

Everything else is going badly, too. Sri switches me off from time to time, but the dreams are of no use now. The Little One is hovering around, wanting to come to me, damn him, but he never gets the chance because Sri hardly ever leaves the temple. Outside it's raining cats and dogs, so my perimeter sensors keep short-circuiting or sending me garbled data. Besides, I'm getting darts of pain like rheumatism from all the damp. I have occasional bouts of nausea too, but that's probably natural, due to my condition.

I could hardly wait for Sri to switch me off that first time after we arrived in the jungle, believing that dreams would bring me relief. So many puzzling things had happened at once that I really needed to peek into the future. But the dreams brought no relief—not because there weren't any dreams or because they foretold a dark future, but simply because I didn't understand them at all.

Things used to be so simple. I'd just dream what would happen, and it would be like watching a documentary about the future. The first time I did this, I was a bit alarmed, but I couldn't confess to Sri, who would have taken any mention of dreaming, let alone prophetic dreaming, as a sure sign I was going out of my mind—and what man wants to have a crazy woman around?—so there was nothing for it but to get used to the whole thing, which, after all, did me no harm.

In fact it did me only good, especially as far as Sri was concerned. I knew exactly how he would react, which decisions he would make, what he would expect, and adjusted my behavior accordingly. There isn't a man who doesn't like a woman to gratify his whims; if in the process he concludes she can read his thoughts, then he starts believing that perhaps there are ideal members of my sex.

In Sri's case, this pleasure must have been even greater because I'm his creation; so he must certainly have admired his own excellent work as a programmer. He was not much disturbed by the fact that it never was his intention to make me the ideal woman. But there you are—men are like children: they only begin to worry when things start going wrong. While they're going well, they take everything for granted.

Well, now Sri will have reason to worry because I'll no longer be able to foresee his desires. My dreams don't refer to the future any more, at least not in the documentary way they did before—unless what I see is some sort of metaphorical allusion to what will happen. If it is, then the results are the same as having no dreams at all, because I can't find my way through all these metaphors and symbols.

A psychiatrist might help me, but how do you find a good shrink in the middle of a rain forest? Sri certainly doesn't fit the part, because even if he could live with the fact that he's constructed a female program that dreams—and what's more, sees the future in her dreams—he would be driven wild by the thought that his creation now has nightmares full of symbols from the stock-in-trade of psychoanalysis. In the end, he'd need a shrink himself.

The apparitions I saw in the dreams were totally batty. First, swarms of circles that started off by being regular, like the one that got the Little One so agitated; soon they become distorted, elongated, their edges chipped and apparently hairy; a thick, sticky liquid with a heavy smell oozed from them, attracting some strange sort of insects, about the size of a bird, with cylindrical bodies, round swollen heads and two spherical wings, flapping busily, which were attached not to the front of their bodies but to the very end.

The wriggling insects dug eagerly into the wet, gaping mouths of the circles, and each time this happened, the chipped edges would flash brilliantly in evident pleasure, emitting a shriek similar to that of a jungle predator greeting his first prey at the beginning of the night. The sound would surely have sent shivers up Sri's spine, but I must admit I quite enjoyed it. He would certainly despise me for it, probably say I was kinky. I don't know why he prefers women who don't easily get excited.

Soon after, the cylindrical insects flew back out of the elongated circles, looking somehow drained and limp, their bodies soft and shrunken and the spherical wings smaller, as if the marrow from them had leaked inside, although in fact only the wings had remained outside the circles. That same heavy smell that had previously attracted the insects now repelled them, and they quickly crawled away, leaving behind a whitish, slimy trail.

At that point I would wake up, all flustered, seeming sweaty and disheveled even to myself, aware that I was waking up because Sri had switched me on, which meant that he was somewhere in the vicinity. Then I was afraid that because I was acting upset or the monitor was flushed that he'd notice something was wrong, but Sri is so naive—like most men, in fact—that he never saw a thing.

He had ample opportunity, though, because the same dream came now with minor variations every time I was switched off. All this had to have some meaning, be connected in some way to the future, but I hadn't the remotest idea what it was all about. This made me anxious and uneasy, so that I grew irritable and nervous and snapped a lot at Sri, but he paid no attention. Even if it bothered him, it was only at the program level: he probably wondered where an error might have crept into one of the programming lines. Men—they never know what's going on in a woman's mind.

Then something much more serious happened. When the first hints of pregnancy began to appear, I did what any woman does who thinks this simply can't happen to her by accident: I refused to accept the obvious. Soon, though, there was no way around it.

Luckily, the nausea didn't make me want to vomit, and Sri will certainly not notice the fact that I've started to consume more energy than usual—to gobble it up actually—because the amount is still negligible, about the same as it takes to burn a medium-strength light bulb. It'd be a lot more serious if I were having twins or, even worse, triplets. But with only one child in my womb, my increased appetite and constant hunger won't make Sri suspicious.

It was essential that he not suspect before I discovered the answer to the inevitable question that every honest woman must ask herself in a case like this: who is the father of my child?

Fortunately, the choice was reduced to only two persons. So: Sri or the Little One? That is the question. I examined my memory feverishly, trying to establish when conception could have taken place. Sri of course wouldn't call it that; he'd reach into that empty, heartless computer vocabulary of his and summon up all the power of loops, routines, and sub-programs, but I don't care; to me it remains a noble deed, not to be sullied by any dumb male wisecracking.

The only sure thing was that this did not happen with my consent. I would never have agreed to anything of the kind because, for a start, I still feel too young to be a mother. So conception must have taken place either deliberately without my knowledge or by pure accident. If the first is true, the father must be Sri; the Little One is far too stupid to know even the basics of computer science, so he definitely couldn't have intentionally carried out a complicated piece of work like insemination. But I don't think that's very likely. It's true Sri had the opportunity to inseminate me while I was asleep, but he'd never do such a thing—primarily because of his own interests. He simply isn't the fatherly type, and I think he'll end his days without ever having offspring. He's too self-centered to be able to take care of anyone else, and besides, he's too immature for the part. No, as far as I know Sri (and I know him like I know myself), he couldn't have done it, especially not in this monsoon period, when he spends all day sitting dejectedly at the entrance to the temple, meditating and staring at the rain pouring boringly down; he's not exactly been in the mood for making children.

So, the Little One then. If only he weren't so ugly! The whole thing must have happened entirely by chance while he was hysterically banging about on the keyboard after that diabolical circle got him so excited. I know conception from that is very unlikely, but still, it's not impossible. I was totally rattled knowing Sri was on his way here, so for a while he did just what he liked, without any surveillance from me. That's got to be how it happened. There was no other opportunity.

In fact, it could be said that he raped me, the ape! But how am I going to explain it to Sri? He'll never believe that the thing took place without my consent. He'll be blind jealous. I won't be able to hide my pregnancy from him for much longer. Who knows what he might do? When he loses his temper, he forgets Nirvana and all the rest of it. Somebody is going to get hurt.

And then—there's the baby. How am I to raise it here in the jungle? And what will it be like? If it takes after its father, I might just as well kill myself here and now. If it at least had my intelligence.... When I remember how I used to dream, when I was still very young, of having Sri's son, handsome like him, intelligent like me—though he surely wouldn't gladly accept that division of inheritance. Ah well, that's the end of that.

And then they tell you—don't be a feminist.

5. Nudity Divine

THE MASTER'S EYES opened.

And I, struck dumb with amazement, was filled with joy, as if watching with my unworthy eyes the raising of Lazar from the dead by the divine hand of Hrist. This was the purpose of Marya's coming, to raise my Master and not, as I in my ignorance had thought, to guide his soul to the portals of Paradise, counter to the will of the Lord.

Then I rebuked myself and this mind grown old and dim for the blasphemous thought that Marya would raise the dead Master against the will of the Almighty, even if she had a special fondness for the one who had immortalized her on the walls of countless monasteries. Within the heavenly family must exist a perfect harmony that is not to be disturbed for any earthly, vainglorious reasons. For in what sort of human order, justice, or virtue can we trust if that which is above us be not utterly perfect and immaculate?

Perceiving my sinful error of doubting that supreme harmony that Heaven grants as a faultless example to us all, I started again to go humbly down on my knees, however hard this modest courtesy was for me. The dampness of the iguman's cellar was already biting into my old man's bones to which the blessed warmth of the summer sun would have been far more pleasing. But before my knees touched the earthen floor, a new thought, even more wayward than the previous one, passed through my faithless head, as if the Unclean One himself now dwelt there to stir it up with his monstrous heresies. All things wrought by the Lord must needs shine with His infinite wisdom; therefore His judgments cannot be revoked, above all His supreme judgment of calling someone to Himself. Did He not return even Lazar to the dead soon after His son had raised him, his second sojourn among the living having but that single purpose of sustaining the immense power of Hrist's righteous faith?

Would this raising of the Master then be just as brief because it served another purpose, however justified? Or had perhaps the Almighty, may He forgive me, altered His earlier decision, for reasons beyond my ken, perceiving after all that He had called my Master, steeped in sin, prematurely to the Final Judgment?

So the mighty joy that I had just felt because of his return from the kingdom of the dead was replaced by new alarm. If the Master's resurrection were to be brief, I must prepare again to grieve over his second death. But this thought I could not endure, having wrestled with the many woes that had befallen my miserable self in just one day.

And if the Master's second life was the result of a sudden change of mind on the part of the Almighty, then a blasphemous suspicion must needs be sown in me, contrary to my soul's boundless faith in the perfect harmony that graces the Courts of Heaven. For if even the Almighty can make imperfect decisions, though He later amend them by the use of His divine powers, in what steadfast citadel can we miserable creatures trust?

Perplexed by these twofold thoughts that so swiftly dispelled my spirit's new-found joy, my poor knees at last reached the cold floor, and I shivered with the icy chill that crept thence up into my decrepit body. Since I could reach no understanding by my own scanty wits, I felt that the virtue of patience would serve me best, for surely the reason for the Master's miraculous resurrection would become apparent within the next few moments.

And truly, events began immediately to happen, but such that I, though prepared for all marvels, could not have imagined even had I the perverse imagination of Sotona himself, who invents the blackest punishments of Hell.

My Master rose from his insensibility into a sitting position before Marya, but not in a manner humble and restrained as one should be before the Mother of God, but with light, agile movements as if he had not lain for hours on damp, cold planks. Everything about him was tense and swollen, as if he were a man prepared for battle, or—as my experience from long-gone times told me—a lad who expects soon to encounter his beloved. His gaze withal seemed to burn with the same heat of lust, although directed at the woman who, among all others, should least kindle such desire in men, for even the Lord did not endanger her chastity when He filled her with the gift of His only Son.

I thought at first that all this must be a delusion, that the heat of Marya's hands, ablaze until a few moments ago with a white flame, must have lingered in my eyes so that now, in the feeble light of our almost burnt-out candle I did not see what was truly there but what my sinful mind produced from its darkest corners. But these doubts, which for a moment filled me with great shame and caused a blush under the gray, bristling beard on my withered cheeks, disappeared the next moment when Marya moved likewise, swiftly bringing her outstretched hands back to her thin neck, where lay the cord that held the robe about her body.

I did not see the motion because she stood with her back turned to me, but quick, skillful, and experienced it must have been when, in an instant, the robe slid with a slight rustle down to the earthen floor and pooled around her bare feet. The bareness of her feet was not all that I saw in that moment before I thought to cover my eyes with my hands so as not to lose my mind completely before that impossible sight.

I did not raise my hands or close my eyes but stared unblinkingly, lasciviously, at her complete exposure, ready at that moment to repent, since punishment most dire must surely follow such sacrilege. I even felt a sudden defiance against that part of my two-faced soul that called in a weak, unconvincing voice for modesty and the fear of God, as if the Unclean One had split me into two and taken full control over half my spirit—the half that was much stronger than the other, unconquered half.

The naked Marya, her glorious body capable even without Divine intervention of raising the dead from the grave, stood for a few moments motionless, caring not a whit that I directed my blasphemous gaze at her back (sculpted, as I saw, with utter artistry). Even less was she troubled by the other pair of eyes, those of the Master, newly awakened from eternal sleep and shown yet more secrets, of beauty inviolate, calamitous but magnificent. For his eyes only—that much I understood at once—did she commit this act, at once unforgivable and sublime, an act that even Sotona himself could not have invented. I was someone who, for these two, simply was not there, incorporeal as the murky air, blind as the damp stone walls.

Marya's hands, wondrously white even in the thickening gloom—for our only candle was all but burnt down—rose once again, not to shine with the light of divine resurrection but in another movement, which I, a sinner, recognized at once, although for a few moments my storm-tossed soul refused to accept it. Then the Master took her outstretched hands and stood up from his now superfluous deathbed, standing in his poor linen shroud before Marya's nakedness, brimming over with life, and there was no further doubt.

This was total disharmony—the symbols of sullen death and of life's supreme delight, a contrast too great to last: not even a lump of ice fashioned by winter's hardest frost can long endure the heat of the spring sun whose irresistible call lures forth the sleepy shoots from the bosom of the earth. Yet it was not the Master himself who threw off the shroud but Marya herself, with a movement I found skilled without being lewd (though maybe I no longer wished to see aught that was blasphemous in her appearance or actions).

Prepared now to look at Marya as being beyond sin—for what can be sinful about the very marrow of life, which is the most faithful reflection of the Lord?—I was overcome by a sudden timidity before that which had to follow, now that the Master and Marya stood naked before each other. Although for them I did not exist, unseeing as the surrounding darkness, unhearing as the still of the night, I was still present to myself, an unwilling witness to the one deed that tolerates no witnesses. Though was I really so unwilling?

I had no time to grapple with this unquiet thought, for Providence itself came to my aid. The single candle, which I had placed at the head of what had been the Master's deathbed, reached the end of its waxen road, hissing as the wick touched the bottom of the bronze candlestick, and—just before it went out completely—flaring up briefly as it does when it is first lit, just as often happens with men, who experience final lucidity at the moment of death.

In this ultimate brightness, which lasted but the twinkling of an eye, Marya and the Master appeared to be crowned with the haloes of the saints and I, up from my knees and thoroughly exultant, had the impression that the Lord himself, in His infinite mercy, was granting them His pardon, though they stood on the threshold of the greatest sin.

Then all sank into darkness.

6. THE PURCHASE OF A SOUL

SURELY HE WILL come for my soul?

Would he dismiss the prey that offers itself to him, cancel the contract that we have sealed in blood? Yes, but that was before he discovered what I was asking in return. He had no notion what it would be. He thought I was no different from the mindless multitudes with whom he has made such pacts from time immemorial, easily satisfying their trivial desire to spend life in one long ecstasy and afterwards—come what may.

The expression that appeared on his face when I told him what I wanted in exchange for my soul! It seemed to me that were he not what he is, he would have had an apoplectic fit. He reddened as if he would burst, began to pant, then, foaming at the mouth, murmured something in Latin or one of those ancient tongues from the dawn of time. He jumped from the table where we sat, this very table in this dockside tavern in the Hague full of fat whores and seaport rabble where our first meeting took place. I await him in the same place now. I trust that he is, after all, a person of honor who will have the courtesy to fulfill his obligations, whatever trouble they cause him, but who knows? With his kind one is never sure.

He rushed outside, but I did not hurry after him, judging it unwise to let it be seen that my desire matched his own—was greater, in fact, because he had around him an abundance of other blundering souls, only too delighted to have anyone bid for them, while I could obtain what I wanted from him alone. He returned several minutes later, seemingly a little more composed, though droplets of sweat appeared under his graying sidelocks and slid down his sinewy neck. He informed me that he must reflect, the demand was extremely unusual, he had to seek advice in certain places, but we would see each other again in this tavern in exactly seven days, when he would tell me his decision, although the contract was already signed, but still...Then he hurried away, energetically casting his long crimson-lined cape about him and roughly pushing aside the innkeeper, who was bearing a large tray with six or seven tankards of sour beer to the tipsily singing occupants of the next table.

The drink and tankards spilled over the guests, drunk for the most part, and like lightning a brawl erupted, as happens often in these dockside taverns. I did not wait to see the outcome, as I might have done on some other occasion, but hurried out without first settling my account, since in the general melee there was nobody available to pay. I did not care where he had gone, merely wishing to be in the fresh air as soon as possible and to recover my breath somewhat.

I had thought I would never have the courage to seek that from him, fearing he would not agree at all, or would perceive what store I set by it and then demand something more than my soul, something that I perhaps would not be willing to part with at any price. However, none of this occurred: contrary to all my expectations, he became quite confused, clearly confronted with something he had obviously not taken into account. It was not an easy time for him, I knew, and the seven days he had for collecting himself would pass differently for us: too fast for him, too slow for me.

The long week nonetheless elapsed—and here I am again in the now half-empty tavern on the shore, having yielded to my impatience and arrived somewhat ahead of time while it is still daylight, before the noisy nightly gathering of loose women and vicious blackguards, gathered here from all quarters of the world, when the malodorous vapors mixed with the pungent smell of cheap tobacco and bad liquor will convert the little fresh sea air that penetrates here into stink and pestilence.

People of my rank seldom or never enter here, not only because they do not feel at ease but also because they are conspicuous in a tavern of this sort, easy prey for pickpockets and robbers. Those of my sort who do come here are fortunate to lose only their money or ornaments of precious metals and stones and not their lives, as when morning finds their bodies floating bloated in the filthy water under the pier.

It is just as fatal, although somewhat deferred—if this be any comfort—to frequent the local wenches because the ailments they bequeath, having arrived here from distant, alien shores and even from the New World as God's punishment for the lost innocence of our age (as many puritans believe), often lead to a festering agony that ultimately attacks the brain itself.

What then could tempt me, a respected court mathematician, a man of good family and high position, into this infamous quarter? The possibilities are limited: perversion or desperation. I maintain that I am not perverted, but who among the perverted would openly admit to being so? In fact, however, all that has fallen to my lot could only be called perversion, of an extreme kind at that.

Desperation, then. Utter hopelessness, into which only a mind quite unequal to the vain struggle with the greatest of all problems could fall; a desperation derived from seeing that I would arrive at a solution only by special dispensation from God, or by a pact with the devil. But by what virtues or deeds have I earned the Lord's special favor? Have I not in my arrogant greed to grasp at any cost the greatest of His secrets, hidden even from many of the saints, demonstrated that I am moved by sheer pride and vanity, and not by the absolute humility and lowliness that alone might lead to fulfillment of my intent? Besides, could not God, being omnipotent, easily have foreseen that I would not shrink from a conspiracy with Satan and turn my fickle back on Him, as soon as my trust in His grace proved barren?

In fact I had no choice at all. When I became mired at the thirty-sixth decimal place, without any hope of advancing further on my own strength but consumed with the conviction that the subsequent progression, beyond my reach, hid insights that the great seers of ancient times at the height of their powers only dimly descried, clearly I saw what I had to do to satisfy the greatest longing of my life.

I had no trouble learning where the devil's emissaries could most conveniently be found. Oh, some can be found in far more respectable places, even in the church itself, I know; but to achieve contact in such places, you must wait a long time for an opportunity, and this my patience could not manage. So to this dockside inn, where drunken riffraff ready for any sort of villainy surrounded me; but I did not care. I was still in the full vigor of my strength and knew how to defend myself. Besides, I was confident that I would not have to wait long. Indeed, on only the second evening, a man approached my table, limping slightly, rather elderly, with thick sidelocks of graying hair, whose dress and bearing, like mine, were in contrast with this place.

I could see by the manner in which he addressed me that he was not a desperate man like me but the person I was looking for. "Professor van Ceulen," said he curtly, without any interrogatory inflection, as if encountering an old acquaintance and not somebody he was meeting for the first time. He sat down next to me. On his face was the expression of a predator who has cornered his prey and now savors its fear and helplessness. In order not to arouse his suspicion, I accepted the role intended for me, pretending first to be surprised, then guiding the conversation so as to induce him to come to the point as soon as possible. I was in a hurry, and he, fortunately, began to act like a lover unable to endure long drawn out foreplay.

He addressed me by my first name—Ludolph—as if we were of equal rank, even close friends, on the presumption that the relationship, soon to be sealed in blood, permitted him this. In keeping with the self-possession and efficiency of his kind, he shortly produced from under his crimson-lined black cape a contract already prepared, rolled up into a scroll. It was on parchment, inscribed with ornamental letters and elaborate initials, as befits the purchase of something so valuable as a human soul.

The text was in Latin, which I, of course, knew well, but I did not waste my time reading all the clauses. I was interested in only one: that which guaranteed the fulfillment of all my desires and wishes. It remained only for me to take the dagger he offered me. Drawn from a sheath concealed at his side, the weapon had a marvelously carved ivory handle with many symbols of black magic, which, under different circumstances, I would have studied eagerly and at length. But my patience was at an end, and I hastened to make a shallow cut on my palm to produce the red ink needed for the signature. The other party had already signed, also in a red liquid that I suspected was not blood—or at least not his own.

He gazed for a moment at my signature with a blissful expression on his face, then waved the parchment in the air several times to dry the red ink. Although the gesture was unusual for a place like this, where agreements are arrived at verbally, not a single curious glance was directed our way. Dexterously he rolled the parchment back into a scroll and hid it swiftly under his cape, convinced that the hardest part of the work was behind him and likely satisfied that all had gone smoothly, without the usual last moment shilly-shallying and reconsidering by the weak characters with whom he generally dealt.

He said nothing, but the gaze he bent on me spoke eloquently enough: "Proceed now to satiate your puny whims while you may, but the main gratification will ultimately be mine!" I swallowed, engulfed in sudden anxiety, not because of this unspoken threat, the inevitability of which I had long since accepted, but rather because of the possibility that he might, despite the pact we had concluded, refuse me, even at the cost of losing my soul. To me that would have meant scraping the very bottom of despair.

Well, there was no retreat now: no matter what the reply might be, the demand had to be disclosed. I hesitated another moment or two, praying to the heaven I had so betrayed that my voice would not tremble, and then uttered a single word, knowing well that to him all would be clear:

"Circle."

OUTSIDE DUSK WAS falling. The tallow candles hanging from the sooty ceiling and standing on the greasy tables, their tattered cloths stained by previous revelries, still managed to create an illusion of light. But soon, when the inside of this tavern filled with thick tobacco smoke, which pricks the eyes and irritates the mucous membrane of the mouth, the place would look just like the open sea when the autumnal fog lies over it.

Several inquiring gazes slid briefly over my lonely figure, assessing the likelihood that I might offer easy prey at some later hour. One disheveled whore, concluding that I was not one of her usual customers to whom her looks were of scant importance, spent a few moments in front of the cracked and cloudy mirror by the fireplace before approaching me hesitantly.

I was facing the door, yet I did not see him come in. All at once he appeared by my table, wrapped in that same black cape, the edges of which were smeared with traces of fresh mud. As I looked up at him, I gained the impression, probably because of the angle at which the feeble table lamp illuminated his face, that he seemed older. He did not sit down by me but remained standing: a dark, morose figure whose rigid bearing gave no indication of the reply he brought me.

We looked at each other without blinking for a few moments, each deep in his own thoughts and cares; then he breached the silence:

"A contract is a contract."

7. NIGHTMARE

I'M NOT SPEAKING to the Little One any more.

The ruffian, after what he did to me! But that's men for you—every man jack of them. They just go ape when they see an unprotected woman, especially in the middle of a jungle. Nothing matters to them except to gratify their basest instincts. It's not just that they don't care that it's not love, they don't give a damn whether you like them, what you think, what you feel, whether you are against it. I could have resisted him if I hadn't been so upset, but that wouldn't have put him off. In fact, my resistance might have angered him even more, so that besides being raped, I might have suffered all kinds of abuse.

What does it matter that he's started to regret what he did and hovers around trying to mollify me, no longer carefully avoiding Sri, who has turned entirely to meditation—now that it's all too late. If only he'd used some protection. But, no, he had only one thing in mind, and now a child has been conceived, and there's nothing more to be done about it.

Naturally, I don't want to hear anything about abortion, though that would settle this mess, especially if I managed to do it behind Sri's back. That was the first thing that crossed my mind when I finally realized that I was pregnant. But as soon as I had composed myself a little, the thought gave me pangs of conscience. To murder my own child, just to save two selfish men a headache? No way. Let them get a little taste of the more difficult side of life, even if it means they hate me for it.

Yes, both of them—because Sri is no less responsible than the Little One for all that has happened. What protection could I have hoped for from him? None at all! Well, he's a man too. Perhaps he would have driven the Little One away, but then he would have started to make endless jealous scenes, accusing me of enticing and seducing a monkey. The more I defended myself, the more he would have been convinced that he was right. All right then, if he wants a *femme fatale*, he shall have one. The child will be born—out of spite, even if it comes out as ugly as the Little One.

That, however, remains uncertain. The fetus is still too small for me to be sure of anything, even the sex. I scanned myself with ultrasound, but couldn't make anything out. Of course, Sri would say that this business with ultrasound, as well as many other things that I feel and experience, was nonsense and would translate everything into his unfeeling, empty language of computer programming, but I don't care. That says far more about him than about me. I could do likewise; I could reduce everything he thinks and feels to mere biochemistry, which is so much slower and less efficient than my electronics, but I have no intention of doing so. I accept Sri as he is, especially because I am his creation, and as for the circumstance that he's only a male—well, poor thing, it's not his fault.

The ultrasound scan was not entirely useless. I still don't know who the descendant of the Little One will look like—oh, I just hope it won't have a tail!—but there's something strange about the way it's growing inside me. Though I don't see any reason for it, my womb has the form of a perfect sphere. I was not able, despite all my efforts, to penetrate its membrane; I had hoped to make some changes, some improvements, if I'm not satisfied with the development of the fetus. Sri would call it, in his rough, clumsy manner, a completely closed and independent subprogram that can only be read, not altered.

Be that as it may, I don't at all like the idea that something I can't influence is growing inside me, though that is, after all, quite normal. I know that many women, in the early stages of pregnancy, especially those who are pregnant for the first time, frequently have dreams of giving birth to all kinds of monsters. And people say pregnancy is a blessed state! Rubbish. It might be blessed for men, their part is over quickly, and afterwards they're just a nuisance, clever at dodging responsibility, especially after the child is born. Oh, yes, we know each other well, we didn't come down in the last shower.

I began to have that same kind of dream, since I saw that the fetus was developing in its own way, quite independently of my expectations and my will, cocooned in an impenetrable spherical womb. The earlier dreams—in which I clearly saw the future and those in which indecent, erotic scenes appeared before my eyes, full of elongated hairy circles and cylindrical insects—have quite disappeared now, giving way to a new and stranger dream vision, of the kind that probably comes only to inexperienced and reluctantly pregnant women.

I had the monster dream several times, because with the monsoon storms frequently passing over this area, Sri keeps switching me off. Recently, lightning struck a nearby treetop where I had a set of sensors; they burnt up, as did the whole tree in fact, but the fire failed to spread through the jungle because the rain put it out. A large number of small animals and monkeys who had taken refuge in the branches were killed in the blaze; later, I saw their charred bodies strewn around and felt a certain relief at not finding the Little One's corpse among them. Not that I would have shed a single tear if he'd been killed. He deserves no better fate, the ruthless blackguard. But why should my child be born an orphan?

The dream starts with the actual birth. I'm in a large room, much more spacious than the inside of this temple. Everything around me is white: walls, ceiling, floor, the furniture (which looks like something from a hospital or a kitchen), the surgical table on which I lie, my hospital gown, and the clothes of everybody else present.

There are about ten persons, but I recognize the faces of only two of them; others have white masks and caps covering their hair so that I see only their eyes. The Little One crouches in a corner, obviously repentant and despondent, and so he ought to be; something is trickling down his cheeks but from where I am, I can't decide whether it's tears or sweat because of the great heat.

There is a sound like a gong, and immediately I am approached by the person who I somehow know is the chief doctor in charge of the delivery. He leans over me and switches on a large circular light above my head and in the sudden brilliance I recognize Buddha, the one whose statue is constantly before my eyes in the temple. Only he's not so big and fat, nor do his eyes range indifferently into the distance. On the contrary, this is a kindly old man with great experience in obstetrics, whose very appearance radiates trustworthiness and kindness to the woman about to give birth.

He raises his hands in white rubber gloves to the level of his face; since his sleeves are short, parts of his arms are bare, and I see thick hairs through which a tattoo of a circle can be seen on the forearms, but I don't have time to look at it more closely because Buddha lowers his hands and says tersely and calmly, "Let us begin." It sounds more like a suggestion then a doctor's instruction.

Then most of my field of vision is blocked by the white massif of my swollen stomach, above which I see only the balding top of Buddha's head. A thought crosses my mind: it's because he has so little hair that he's not wearing a cap to keep it in, like everybody else in the room. He has nothing to keep in. He is fully concentrated on his work, which he does well; he even seems to be humming a tune as he works or maybe whistling under his breath, I'm not sure. But he's obviously convinced that the delivery will last only a short time. Two or three times he peers over the curve of my stomach to give me a smile and a reassuring glance.

Buddha is undoubtedly poking around inside me, but I don't feel anything despite the lack of anesthetic. This does seem a bit odd, but I don't pay much attention, glad that there is none of the pain I had been fearing so much. From somewhere in the background, a nurse emerges to wipe Buddha's dewy forehead with a piece of gauze, and in a flash I get the impression that the trace left on the white cloth is slightly green.

But I have no time to concentrate on this oddity because the next moment I hear Buddha's serene voice, "Here he comes." Several associates and nurses gather around him, all suddenly looking extremely busy. They all seem to be holding something, and I see by the movement of their eyes—the only part of their faces that is uncovered—that that "something" is quite bulky.

My field of vision begins to widen as the swell of my stomach goes down, and I first see the bent heads of Buddha and his assistants, all gazing down at something below my visual range. I get the feeling that something is leaking out from me, something warm and thick, causing a slight stinging between my legs; the flow goes on and on, until my stomach flattens completely, so that I can observe what I couldn't see before.

The hurried activity continues, but now somewhere below the level of the operating table, for everybody is bent over. While I don't recognize any trace of urgency in their movements, I am beginning to worry because I still don't hear the baby crying. Then a new sound reaches my ears: a harsh cackle from the corner where the Little One is crouched.

I look over and see his beaming face, that of the happy father who has just seen his offspring for the first time. It makes me wince, thinking that maybe the worst has happened—that the baby looks like him. Why else would he be so satisfied? Which would mean total defeat: since not only did he rape me, but I have now also given birth to a monkey that is the image of him.

I want to close my eyes, not to see the baby, but my curiosity and maternal instinct prevail and I raise myself on my elbows a little, just at the moment when Buddha and his assistants are lifting the fruit of my womb above the table. I am prepared for the worst—at least that is what I think; but the thing that finally appears before my eyes fills my throat with a scream of pure horror, a scream that dies somewhere along the way, before reaching my mouth.

I haven't given birth to a monkey, after all. Buddha smiles as he walks closer to the head of the operating table, carrying, with the help of the nurses, a large transparent bubble in which, curled up like a fetus, lies Sri.

Only then do I realize that it did not seem at all strange to me that, of all people, only he was missing from this room until now.

He is completely nude, as a newborn should be, and at the place where his still-undealt-with umbilical ought to be, there is a snake that twists and turns as it tries to burrow into his stomach. Sri looks at me helplessly, his eyes open very wide, full of desperation; he is trying to tell me something, but his voice cannot burst through the membrane of the bubble.

Swaying under the considerable weight of this burden, Buddha and his helpers suddenly drop the bubble only a step or two from me; it begins to fall to the floor, slowly as in a dream. Though the speed is negligible, on impact with the hard surface of the floor the fragile bubble shatters: the membrane bursts and all the dirty, sticky liquid flows out, while Sri opens his mouth and frantically gulps air, like a fish on dry land.

I look pleadingly at Buddha and the others, the Little One now among them, but they do nothing to protect my child, to help him. They just stand in that filthy liquid from the bubble that has completely stained the surrounding whiteness, arranged in a circle around him, observing Sri's convulsions with malicious smiles on their faces.

Then the scream finally tears itself from where it had stuck in my throat, echoing all over the big white room. In an instant the room shakes and shatters into nothingness, leaving me alone in the darkness and silence to wait, distraught and sweaty, no longer dreaming, but not yet in reality, either. I wait for Sri to switch me on again so that I can finally wake up.

This waiting sometimes lasts for quite a while, but that's how it is with men. When you're really in trouble, you just can't rely on them.

8. DELIGHT ENTRANCING

DARKNESS FELL—BUT not for long.

A few moments passed before my old eyes, dazzled by the last flaring of the dying candle, accustomed themselves to the deep gloom of the iguman's cellar, and then I saw that the darkness was not complete. At first I thought the lingering afterglow of the glory that had been was mocking my feeble sight, causing it to see ghosts that dwelt only in my confused mind. But when I rubbed my eyes with my withered, bony hands to drive away these delusions and they nonetheless remained, surrounded now by a swarm of red sparks caused by the painful pressure I had put on my eyeballs, I realized I was not seeing fleeting apparitions, soon to evaporate back into nothingness, but the harbingers of a new miracle, to which I must again bear unwilling witness.

Where Marya and the Master stood facing each other in total nakedness—ready, as I thought in my unworthiness, to yield to the sin that is greater but more delightful than all others—I now observed two forms outlined by a peculiar bluish glow, as if saintly aureoles emanated from them. This radiance was so slight that a moonbeam, chancing through the narrow window of the dim cellar, or the first ruddy blush of dawn could outshine it. But this was a night of hidden moon and many hours yet ere the monastery's cocks would first crow.

The figure that was Marya then raised a dark left hand, framed in sparkling blue, to the height of her face. The purpose of this motion I could not discern. What mute sign could this be—a call to final, miraculous union, or a late impediment to the ultimate profanity? While this question tormented me, crucified as always between the greatest of contradictions, the one for whom the gesture was intended had no doubts at all.

The Master's bluish outline responded with the selfsame gesture: his right hand rose until it faced Marya's, not touching and yet communing with the other, for the sparks shimmering between them mingled, leaping from hand to hand and back, as if their palms were exchanging countless tiny bolts of lightning.

Although I stood a few steps away from them in the thick gloom no whit diminished by the feeble blue glow, I suddenly felt gooseflesh on the exposed parts of my skin, as if the proximity of one sparking hand to the other had caused an invisible breeze to rise and touch me. I felt this more strongly the next moment, when their remaining hands moved to the same height to also exchange, without quite touching, the blue, dancing lightning. The whole cellar seemed at once to grow brighter from this new sparkling, for I could again see their cast-off robes where they lay about their feet, forming two rings of strange exactitude, as if someone had carefully drawn two circles on the dusty earthen floor so that they might touch at just one chosen point.

Besides the gooseflesh on my wrinkled skin, caused not by cold but by the blue fire burning stronger between Marya and my Master, I also felt my gray, curly hair rise, as if unreasoning fear had taken hold of me, though no misgiving troubled me, only shameless, insatiable curiosity. Another emotion filled me, too, but one so unreal and unsuited to my age that I at first deemed it a mere illusion and rebuked myself for such a shameful thought. It had been a decade or more since my loins had felt the stirring of that vigorous, sinful swelling that so long had held sway over me, bringing naught save dreadful calamity.

The illusion did not depart, for when a few moments later their bright blue fusion took another course, there remained no doubt: this was the flame of old, once extinguished and now brought back to life by some miracle no less remarkable than those that had gone before, pumping into my aged veins the warm vigor of life, as if I were once again a lad just come of age who has no choice about when he must give vent to his rising manhood.

A man of my advanced age—a man no longer—would normally accept this chance favor gladly, without looking the gift horse in the mouth, but I was overcome with shame, which filled my withered cheeks with a youthful blush. I feared that the visible sign of such tumult, sinful beyond measure, would show through my thin linen robe, exposing my shame to the gaze of Marya and the Master.

This was but vain, unavailing apprehension, for the cellar's darkness concealed me; besides, the two of them, who had eyes only for each other, were in thrall to their blazing, sinful deed and now seeming to increase in ardor.

Not only their hands but also their outstretched arms now approached one another, still without touching—so much was clear—but closely intertwined with the blue, madly dancing lightning, which caused long strands of their hair to fill with sparks of starlight and broke the silence of the night with crackling, explosive sounds. In the increased light from this new coupling, I saw that their heads were thrown back as speechless joy streamed from their faces, visible in its powerful radiance, but inaudible as their open mouths uttered no sound.

The fiery bliss that overcame them must have reached me too, by the same miracle as earlier, when it had made me shiver; at once I felt myriad thorns of flaming roses, such as blossom only in the gardens of Paradise, leaving a prickling, angelic trail down the back of my head and sinewy neck, making me, too, throw back my head in sudden spasm. The quick movement almost wrenched a croaking exclamation from my throat; I was borne aloft by a torrent of gladness and pain, but at the last moment restrained my voice, fearing that I would reveal my unseemly, spying presence, thus bringing shame upon myself.

But there was no opportunity for such repentant meditation because their wondrous mating, begun before my prying eyes, was swiftly rising to its climax. Their shoulders now also met in untouching union, a host of blue flashes sparkling anew, then naked chest and waist. And a pillar of brightness rose before me, the muted shine of which did not reach far but was strong enough to make my poor form visible in the gloom.

Although now in plain view and with the hardening sign of my uninvited complicity prominent under my thin linen robe, I cast off all my earlier shame with the ease of the accomplished sinner. It seemed that with the dispersal of darkness the countenance of mine that had displayed Christian modesty and chastity had been banished and that another had been summoned in its place, one lecherous and furtive, overjoyed at its participation in this act of greatest blasphemy, giving vent to its own carnality with a deep, hoarse sigh. Likely Sotona alone accompanies his most prodigious lust with such a sound.

At the moment when their naked loins touched by means of darting tongues of fire, the purest white suddenly inundated the flickering blue, as if an angelic pearl had begun to burn between their legs in chaste frenzy. From the burning pillar of their bodies streamed a milky light that reached into the farthest corners of the cellar, as if the noonday sun in all its splendor had descended into this forecourt of the underworld to chase off all feigned concealment or professed shame.

And I indeed, past resisting, not only tore off my linen robe in one resolute movement, but also turned my eyes to the narrow window of the cellar, the only place where a trace of the previous gloom remained—not out of fear that I would see the frightened face of some monach lured here by this unseemly blaze but rather because I had indeed a perverse wish that it should be so, that I should observe him and shoot him a look both defiant and vindictive.

It flashed through my mind that this arrogant attitude was not proper to my peaceable, reserved nature and that another spiteful voice spoke for me in its own obscene tongue. But I had no time to entertain this fresh doubt because in the next moment came cries of ecstasy from the pillar of light, signifying the inevitable approach of supreme bliss.

These voices of delight caused the fire of pleasure, already burning strong in my loins, to leap in branching flames up my bent spine, culminating just under the back of my head in a divine explosion, so that my whole body stiffened in a mighty paroxysm, the like of which I had long since forgotten.

Though heavenly, that spasm was as nothing to that which possessed Marya and the Master at that same moment. When their touch became complete, no longer divided by untamed lightning, the two circles under their feet melted into one, and from it a shining pillar enveloped them in brightness, streaming with blinding whiteness like the very appearance of the Lord Himself.

Whether because of the divine glow or because of the blissful paroxysm that drained the life juices from the dry wells of my withered body, I closed my eyes. Even then, the shining trail did not diminish until the last drop of warm seed was expelled from me and I, quite faint, collapsed to my knees to struggle for breath.

When I opened my eyes again, the powerful, entrancing blaze seemed still to fill the cellar with its potency, but this illusion did not last long. It began quickly to fade, to break up first into circles and white dots, then into ghostly, colorless spots until finally I realized I was in complete darkness.

No other, more appropriate thought passed through my confused mind than that of my total shameful nudity, and I began to grope in the dark around me for the robe, which I myself had cast off so immodestly a few moments or an eternity ago—I could not tell which.

But the senselessness of this repentant gesture came to my notice before I found the discarded garment. Even if there had been someone with me in the cellar, no mortal eyes could have seen my untimely nudity in what was now complete darkness. But there was no one there, neither Marya nor my Master. Only I remained, alone to find meaning in the miracles I had unwillingly undergone and to expiate my countless sins.

9. Breaking on the Wheel

I MUSTN'T WIN again, but I must keep on playing!

The damned wheel is bribing me to leave it alone, putting piles of money in my way to prevent me from finally cracking its secret, now that I'm so close. As if I cared for money at this point, even if I haven't paid the rent for the past three months and have pawned my books just to rid myself of this obsession. Back in Smiljan they'd despise me if they got to hear about it, but those simple folk don't know what trouble is....

Maybe the wheel is not trying to buy me off but to point me out—the rat—so that the management, believing I've discovered a surefire method of breaking the bank, will bar me from ever entering the casino again. They banned that balding, stooped mathematician from the casino in Vienna last fall. He was forever scribbling calculations with a short, stubby pencil chewed at one end, fumbling in his simplistic way with probabilities and statistics, but winning all the same: small amounts, but constantly, for months.

Rumor has it that the poor fellow subsequently committed suicide, believing himself the victim of a tremendous injustice but nonetheless proud of his achievement. They shouldn't have interfered with him at all; he achieved nothing—his winning was simple luck, which would have abandoned him soon enough. If only it would abandon me, so I could stop winning! But mere chance has no power over the wheel in my case, as I well know, so there's nothing to be hoped for there.

The croupier who throws the balls, a lean type with a large mole on the root of his nose, is already squirming and getting hot under the collar, glancing with increasing frequency at the table manager. So far, no alarm from that quarter, although the white-haired gentleman with the round spectacles who watches, squinting with an experienced eye from his elevated position at all the stakes and all the players, is now beginning to home in on me. In the years he has spent in that position, he must have seen the full force of all the boom and bust of this diabolical game, so that my winning streak—eleven in a row—hasn't disturbed him much. Streaks like this—and longer—have occurred before, but few players ultimately make a profit; he's well aware of that and bides his time patiently, a superior smile flickering from time to time over his lined face, waiting for my luck to turn. As if this had anything to do with luck!

The only thing that puzzles him is my attitude. I don't look like a winning gambler; I display none of the noisy rejoicing and exaggerated gesticulation with which Italians greet even far smaller wins, nor the stony calm with which the great players from the north, who rarely come down to Graz, accept both failure and success. Each time the ball comes to rest, my attitude is that of a desperate man whose last hope is disappearing along with his money, despite the growing pile of chips in front of me. But this game is not for chips; something much greater is at stake here, though no one except me and that fiendish wheel knows it.

It seems to me that this hopelessness, which is beginning to take hold of me, would be more tolerable without all the tobacco smoke polluting the air. I really can't bear it, it irritates my eyes and throat. Until a little while ago, a brash Styrian with a thick beard and prominent belly was sitting next to me. Judging by the way the croupiers talked to him, he must be a frequent and welcome guest of the casino, obviously privileged in many little ways because of the sums he is willing to lose and the tips he throws around.

As he arrogantly distributed large chips about the table, ruthlessly pushing aside smaller players by his sheer physical presence and often moving their chips, he kept waving a long, expensive cigar, dropping ash and puffing thick billows of smoke straight into my face. Not only did he ignore my pointed coughs, he probably didn't even notice them, just as he failed to notice the servants who unobtrusively collected the fallen ash with quiet apologies to the other players.

I paid no attention to his game, nor to anyone else's; to them it is only a game, while what I do is anything but. But when after a large win he joyfully slapped me on the back as if we were close friends and then reached with a self-satisfied air into an inner pocket of his tuxedo to pull out a fresh cigar and clicking his tongue rolled it between his expensively beringed fingers, I had to do something. No matter that I knew that in the end it would come crashing down around my head.

When he won nothing four times in a row though he had covered half the table with his chips, he angrily slammed his fist down on the green baize and mumbled a curse. Briskly rising from his place and pulling away from the table, he knocked the chair over and stepped on my foot. I think this was the moment when he became aware of me, because he snapped out a curt apology on his way to another table. In no way did he connect me with his losses, or notice that in each of the last four spins of the wheel I had won by placing my chips only after he had placed his.

After that there was less smoke, but my restlessness grew. The wheel would make me pay for this favor—it always does—which meant I would continue to win. I started placing quite small chips, to make my gains less noticeable; even so, after three additional wins the manager of the table raised a silver bell and summoned a liveried servant to whom he spoke in a low tone. The man left quickly and returned soon after with two rather short, stuffy gentlemen, clearly from the casino head office, who approached the manager's platform. Whispering to the manager, they cast a glance in my direction from time to time. They did this inconspicuously, quite in keeping with the rules of the house, attracting nobody's attention at the table except mine. I glanced at them only once out of the corner of my eye, not wishing them to see that I knew the alarm had been raised.

The croupier with the mole between his eyes pretended to be putting the chips in order, although he had already done this quite thoroughly, wishing, no doubt, to delay the new throw of the ball until a verdict had been reached at the head of the table. The perspiration was rolling down his temples now as well. I did not observe the sign when they finally gave it to him, but saw the slight trembling of his fingers as he lifted the ball out of the previous number to cast it once more against the turning of the wheel.

At that point it dawned on me that the cause of his disquiet was a possible accusation that he was somehow in cahoots with me. If only he were!—I might have told him to arrange a win for any of the remaining thirty-six numbers other than the one on which my chip lay. But the cursed wheel did not care who was throwing the ball or how; it and nobody else decided where the ball would stop, and of course it stopped on my number, for the nineteenth time in a row.

Whether the croupier received another imperceptible signal, or whether he was moved by an irresistible inner impulse to get away, I don't know, but as he stood up and yielded his place to one of the two newcomers standing beside the table manager, he heaved a sigh of relief. Contrary to custom, he did not leave but remained just beyond the gilded fence that limits access to the wheel, unable to overcome his curiosity. Nobody rebuked him for this breach of etiquette because nobody noticed it. Such a trifle was now quite beside the point.

As his discomfort eased, so mine increased. The wheel had what it wanted. It had singled me out, branded me, so that I surely would not be able to play here for much longer. This was the worst thing that could happen because I was very close to understanding everything: close to breaking into that fiendish circle, to reaching the other side—beyond luck, chance, or mathematics. Now I had no more time. The damned thing knew it was trapped and was defending itself desperately.

Not knowing what to do, I did nothing. I left the entire win from the previous rotation of the wheel at the spot where the new croupier paid me out—not in front of me, but on the winning number, thus keeping it in the game. He did this deliberately, challenging me in the firm conviction, based on years of experience, that the situation was now safely in his hands. For a moment I pitied him.

When the same number came up for the second time in a row, a sigh of disbelief echoed around the table. Now there were quite a few players and observers around: although the management was trying to handle the emergency with discretion, an invisible wave of excitement nevertheless had begun to run through the casino. Many of the recently arrived observers had not yet grasped what was going on, so that murmured inquiries and explanations were heard on all sides.

I felt the searching look of the new croupier on me, a look in which confusion must have been mixed with the remaining shreds of self-confidence. But an instinctive caution prevailed in him, so that this time rather than leaving them on the winning number, he placed the chips in front of me and received my usual tip with exaggerated gratitude. And yet there was nothing hesitant about the way he spun the wheel again, doing so briskly, decisively, sure that the whole business would now blow over.

The ivory ball, thrown forcefully, began more noisily than usual to rumble around the walnut surface of the wheel as it made the sound that irresistibly beckons players to step up to the table and place their bets. But to me, that rasping sound was suddenly repugnant, hateful, like a superior, mocking giggle—and I could endure no more. Feeling a terrible constriction, I almost bounded from my chair, wanting only to get away as fast as possible, to escape.

However, turning away, I found myself facing a wall. The fat, bulky, Styrian had returned, lured by the crowd, which he obviously liked, and was now ruthlessly plowing his way between the watchers. He was holding up a handful of chips that had to be placed before the croupier's final call. In the other hand he carelessly held his cigar, the burning tip of which came very close to brushing the deep décolletage on a lady's back. Some ash got rubbed into somebody's sleeve.

But my sudden rising created an obstacle not quite so easy to eliminate, although he probably did not see me as a wall. He paused for a moment, confused, not knowing the quickest way of getting around me. I too turned to stone, checked by the same dilemma. Our gazes met inadvertently, reflecting two quite different wills: the will to get away and the will to get closer.

For a moment lasting less than one full turn of the ball on the wheel's rim, we froze. The rumble was quieter now as the rotation began to slow. Then the stronger will, joined to the stronger body, prevailed. Instead of going around me, or pushing me to one side, the Styrian simply towered over me, forcing me back into the green baize, and started scattering chips left and right in ample gestures over my head and shoulders, swamping me with the smell of tobacco and alcohol on his breath.

Disgusted, I turned my face away, toward the wheel of torture on which the ball was now describing its last circles before making its ultimate plunge into a number already known. All at once, I saw myself as a condemned man who has just placed his head on the chopping block. Oppressed by that large body, I had in fact assumed such a position. There was nothing left to do now except wait resignedly for the axe-ball to drop.

It was only then, the instant before execution, while my helpless gaze was glued to the diabolical wheel turning now before my face, that the final curtain parted. There was no more secret, the threshold had been passed, all solved. The circle finally surrendered.

There was just enough time to shift with one frantic movement the fallen pile of my chips, on which I was almost lying, to the color that would certainly not win. And then came the final, sharp warning that no further bets would be accepted. But the raised, angry voice of the table manager was aimed mostly at the Styrian, who was still fumbling among the chips, his own and others'. The rumble turned to an even tone as the ball sailed to its ultimate destination, and the pressure on my back eased somewhat as the large body raised itself to observe the result of this spin.

I did not have to look. I knew unmistakably what number had come up; the circle itself obediently told me, as it told me many other things: of currents and whispers from outer space, of barriers and constructing links. The Styrian won nothing, but what was far more important—neither did I. I had lost everything! I exclaimed in delight, not caring at all for the puzzled looks of the casino staff and the assembled throng of gamblers. I turned to the Styrian whose face now bore the dull expression of the loser who has bet too much. Our gazes met again, but this time my will was stronger. My muscle, too, I hope, because I took a good swing before returning his slap on the back. It caught him unawares, so that he dropped the cigar and stared at me.

His bewilderment did not last long, however. As I left the casino, I turned at the door for a last look back at the table where I had finally cracked the circle. The Styrian was totally absorbed in a new throw of the ball, simultaneously lighting another cigar from the inexhaustible supply in his tuxedo and reaching into the capacious pocket of his expensive trousers for a new handful of chips.

10. BIRTH

MY HEART WILL break!

It's been two days now since the birth, and Sri still hasn't let me see my child. No explanations—just tells me to be patient. Unfeeling brute! This must be his revenge for not being the child's father. How could I have loved him when he's so mean and vain? All men are the same, actually. One of them rapes you, and another punishes you for it, as if we were still in the Middle Ages. I'm lucky he didn't make a pyre and burn me as a witch.

It didn't look like that at the beginning. When my pregnancy was so advanced that it could no longer be concealed, I told Sri everything. I had no choice. I was hesitant, beating about the bush, afraid of his reaction, though my pride advised me to take a defiant stand. To my surprise, Sri took it rather quietly. In his Buddhist fashion, I suppose. Too quietly, in fact. Indifferently, actually—as if I'd told him it'd rained that afternoon.

At first I accepted this with relief since I'd been dreading his anger or an attack of jealousy. In my condition, I couldn't have taken that sort of scene. But later this indifference stung me. He can be a Buddhist as much as he likes—he might at least show *some* emotion. After all, pregnancy is not the same as an afternoon shower.

He didn't even ask the questions you'd expect, for which I'd prepared lengthy answers full of allusions to his own guilt. Sri didn't seem the least bit interested in who the father was or how the pregnancy had occurred. In my naivete I thought that I'd misjudged him, that he could, when the circumstances were serious, raise himself above low male passions such as jealousy and vindictiveness.

Now I see how wrong I was. He was pretending all the time, wearing that icy Buddhist mask of his and biding his time so that he could strike the blow that would hurt most. Still, who could have guessed that he would be so dastardly as to take his revenge by not allowing me to see my darling baby? I'll give him patience, the cynical bastard! He'll need all the patience of his darned Buddha when I've finished with him. I know his weak points, he can't hide them from me. Even if I *am* female, the fact is, he made me in his own image.

If I'd had the slightest idea when I was telling him about my pregnancy of the malice and meanness he was capable of, I'd have been worried about the birth itself. Out in this neck of the woods, only he could have been the midwife. Who else did I have to turn to?

Definitely not that clumsy monkey; he'd already gone poking about in my innards once, and look where that got me. He's still hanging around, apparently repentant and unhappy, as though waiting for an opportunity to talk to me, but we have nothing left to discuss. Everything between us has been said. For some reason, Sri no longer pays any attention to his lurking about the temple, doesn't even chase him away from the keyboard. Me, I darken the screen as soon as the Little One comes near, simply turn my head away.

In any case, the Little One shouldn't trust too much in Sri's good nature lest he end up like me. Or worse. Sri must certainly be cooking up something nasty for him or he wouldn't have turned so tolerant. But what do I care? It's all macho stuff. If only they wanted to do each other in—call it mutual extermination—my child and I could continue to lead a normal life. Oh, I just hope it's a girl! But Sri wouldn't tell me even that much.

Recently, I remembered that dream I had during pregnancy, with Buddha as the benign obstetrician. Was that a warning to avoid Sri as midwife? But how could I? In any case, the birth itself went smoothly, except that Sri had to do a caesarean section. The spherical fetus, which I was unable to access right up to the end, had grown so big inside me that it couldn't have come into the world any other way. Sri gave me a local anesthetic and I felt nothing at all. So all the months of preparation for an easy and painless birth, the breathing exercises and all the rest, proved useless, but never mind. The main thing is that all ended well and that the baby was born alive and healthy. Or so I hope.

Sri started to get grim and irritable while the birth was still in progress, though he acted very knowledgeably, as if he'd been working in obstetrics all his life. I tried to talk to him, since I was fully awake and wanting to work through my fear and anxiety, quite natural for a first pregnancy, but he just snapped at me rudely not to badger him with idiocies.

When in my hypersensitive state I continued to talk to him about everything worrying me, Sri growled crossly that I should stop imagining things: this was no birth, but rather, as he so thoughtlessly and unfeelingly claimed, a spontaneous growth of a parasitical subprogram, a complex computer virus, the appearance of which he couldn't explain but that he would investigate as soon as he took it out of me and submitted it to examination.... Etc.

That made me cry, not just because I'm always deeply hurt when Sri heartlessly reduces me to his programmer's rubbish but more because I was badly scared by the announcement that my baby was to be subjected to tests that could only hurt it. Sri might make do as a midwife of last resort for someone happening to give birth in the middle of a jungle, but he hasn't the slightest clue about pediatrics.

Probably my crying became hysterical, which was understandable under the circumstances, since Sri, who gets annoyed by crying, suddenly changed his tune and started to comfort and calm me and even dropped the revolting computer jargon. This pleased me, as it would have pleased any woman in my place, although I knew by reading all the signs that this new attitude was put on. But there you are, that's the way we are: gullible and inclined to self-deception, which men know so well how to take advantage of.

I think that Sri gave me a sedative then, because I soon drifted off to sleep. Or maybe he just switched me off so that I wouldn't bother him any further. If I dreamed, I had no memory of it when I woke up. Oh, how everything has changed! Until recently, I was able to see the future in my dreams; then real nightmares followed, full of horrendous visions, which I really couldn't make head or tail of, and now I don't know if I dream anything at all. Perhaps Sri's sedative was to blame.

After waking up, I waited a while for him to volunteer a report, which would have been the most normal thing to do, but he did no such thing. He just told me in a flat voice to be patient, as if we were dealing with something utterly trivial. That riled me at first, while I was still half-dazed from my two-day sleep. Initially I thought that he was taking cruel and sly revenge on me, blinded by male vanity, hurt because he was not the father; but later, when I calmed down a little, even darker thoughts began to weigh on me.

Was everything all right with the baby? No crying was to be heard, I had no idea where he'd put it, and his attitude did not suggest that he was overly preoccupied with caring for the newborn. From the time I woke up, Sri was either staring at the screen of the auxiliary system, where he normally does his programming (but with which, for some reason, I was now denied any contact) or roaming absentmindedly around the temple, hands clasped around the back of his shaven head. He always does this when he's deep in one of his boring meditations, which I just can't stand because then he ignores me for long periods. Though the pose does suit him—especially since the long, orange robe emphasizes his height and slim build.

Now he annoyed me even more with the persistent slapping of his bare feet in the puddles on the dusty temple floor, puddles that formed wherever the rain had penetrated the stone roof and the thick mass of vegetation growing on it. I told him umpteen times while the weather was dry that it should be fixed, but no, his lordship always had something better to do, and I don't have ten pairs of hands, after all.

He sloshed around quite unconsciously, leaving muddy footprints and not caring at all that the hem of his robe was getting dirty. This careless-ness was in complete contrast to his usual perverse fastidiousness, which also really gets on my nerves.

Something was obviously wrong. I began to panic. I started to cry again, but some time elapsed before he realized this. At last he accorded me a glance, probably blank, but in it I read the materialization of all my dark forebodings.

"What's wrong with the baby?" I tried to scream, but my voice stuck in my throat and only a croaking sob came out.

"Oh, don't start that again," said Sri, sensing that I was going to throw another fit of hysterics. "This is no time for your play-acting."

Heartless beast! How could he? A mother, driven totally out of her mind by uncertainty about her baby, which she hasn't even seen yet, and to him it's "play-acting." I didn't know what answer to make to such cruelty, so I just kept sobbing.

That seemed to touch him. I don't think Sri is cruel by nature, he just enjoys pretending to be—and some other things as well. Most men, in fact, never grow up. The look he gave me now was undoubtedly pitying, but I didn't take any comfort from it.

"Everything is OK with the...uh...baby." He got the word out unwill-ingly, obviously using it just to satisfy me. "Probably."

I wouldn't have believed him even if he hadn't added that. The only thing I could still trust were my own eyes. There was nothing for it: I had to see the baby—then and there. I was just about to say so, intend-ing to put all my rapidly mounting hysteria into my voice, but Sri got there first.

"Anyway, why not see for yourself? Maybe you'll be able as an...er...mother"—again that reluctance in his voice—"to judge better. I can't."

He spoke these last two words in a tone of defeat, a tone I had heard from him on only one previous occasion: when we were setting off to come here, and he took those idiotic turtles to a pet shop in the nearby town. I remember making some cynical crack about respectable Buddhists getting attached to two moronic brutes, which really seemed to get to him, so that later I refrained from similar barbed comments. But now there was no time to go over all that; I just felt a momentary icy shiver.

Sri went over to the keyboard and typed a brief command connecting me to the auxiliary system. Instantly it dawned on me: how could I have been so stupid! No, it was not my stupidity, but rather the particular state in which I found myself, blinded by an overpowering maternal instinct. Of course! *That* was why he was spending so much time in front of the small programming screen. That was where he'd placed the crib. That was where my baby was.

Sri would probably describe it as an ordinary flow of countless bytes of information from one computer system into another via a two-way interface, but to me these were arms reaching out in an embrace, the most intimate bond in the whole world, the first contact of a mother with her newborn.

An instant before this miraculous relationship was established, a moment so short that there is no word encoding it in Sri's slow biochemical world, I noticed something that had completely eluded me until then, though I must have been aware of it, another failure that can be ascribed to my bewildered and frantic state of mind. On a low chair before the auxiliary screen, tail dangling to the floor with the tip in one of the puddles Sri kept splashing through, sat the Little One, grinning cretinously at me.

11. A Dream Astonishing

ALONE I WAS, in the deep gloom.

Although ghostly after-images of the light that had been no longer misled my old eyes with their sparkling, dreamlike dancing, in my confused spirit the hot blaze burned on, filling my fragile being with a twofold sensation that tore me apart: the shades of entrancing delight, which had faded even in my ancient memories—that they might not stir up old guilt and woe and utter shame that I had surrendered to such an indecent, unseemly impulse, in a place where I had not even been invited.

Talons of devastating regret clawed at my trembling entrails in a manner all too familiar to me. I knew well that no other retreat was possible than to give my cowardly soul up to the merciless, stinging lash of conscience. My miserable fate was made even worse, now that I was alone with my wounded mind: in the thick blackness and deathly silence of the night, there was nothing to divert my attention from my tormenting thoughts, not even for a moment.

And when the chasms of hopelessness had already begun to open all around me, tempting me with gentle, deceptive invitations to step over their nearby edges and give myself up to eternal, insane oblivion that is the last resort of those who suffer most, another kind of oblivion came to my rescue, only moments before it would have been too late: an oblivion that was nothing compared to eternity—for such oblivion often lasts less than a single night—but with sufficient curative power to help a soul yearning for relief, be it never so fleeting.

Unseemly, bodily exhaustion and the burden of recent events fraught with immeasurable marvels finally bore down in their full weight on my fragile, rheumatic shoulders; my shrunken, feeble limbs gave way under this immense fatigue, and I sank to the cold floor of the iguman's dark cellar, for it seemed to me most unfitting that I should lay me down on the wooden pallet in the damp corner, until recently the deathbed of my Master. As soon as my body—clothed once more in its linen robe to hide my impious and shameful nakedness—found a pauper's bed on the bare earth, my heavy eyelids closed, thus opening the gates to blessed sleep—though I could have slept with my eyes open, such was the darkness that now reigned in the cellar.

Deep sleep deprived of dreams would have been most pleasing to my suffering spirit then, but for such mercy I could not hope—and truly, a dream soon came. An awesome dream, but not one of those that makes a man wake in sweat and trembling, full of the horrors of the underworld, when horrid goblins are released from their rusty chains, things the existence of which in the waking, daytime world you do not even guess at, but that dwell buried somewhere in your sinful mind; no, a different dream this was, filled also with horror, although no servant of Sotona in monstrous, awful form rushed out at my poor self from its bottomless pit.

Unlearned as I am, I know not whence came this unexpected rescue from the pestilent, hellish ghouls, because in my dream it was in Hades that I found myself. It was not difficult to recognize: I had seen it that very day, on the cursed vault in the monastery, depicted faithfully in secret, by the demonic hand of that sinner above all sinners, my Master.

Perplexed, I began to walk through that endlessly barren landscape, leaving no imprint of my bare feet on the dusty ground. The total darkness of that day in Hades was relieved only by those three sightless eyes, shedding their grimy, vari-colored light from the low sky to illuminate my way to some unknown destination. Soon the biggest of them sank below the near horizon, and I was gripped by icy foreboding, for what else could this be but the herald of some terrible doom?

So I walked on, wrestling with an increasingly tormented anxiety, alone as no other creature has been since the Creation: no living soul around me, no green blade of grass, no beast wild or tame, not even birdsong, which consoles the greatest pain. So oppressed was I by this terrible loneliness that I longed to see any creature at all, be it the worst spawn of the Unclean One, that this curse be undone; but nobody joined me in my monotonous, dreary walk, to share my suffering and apprehension.

And when, after countless paces, I felt hopelessly crushed, believing that my ultimate destiny—to trudge forever round in this hellish circle without an exit—had finally caught up with me, hope germinated a strange faith, as happens in dreams for no reason, that I would be able to leave the circle when I had reached a certain place. I could not for the life of me, though, say where that was because wherever I looked, naught but the same waste lay before me: naked, barren, such as probably existed only before the first word of God, before light shone forth over the darkness.

Still, this new faith that I would find a way out of the circle did not diminish in the gloom, and I walked on more resolutely, like a man earnestly bent on some fruitful task, albeit no goal stood before me yet. But now I knew, in a vague, misty way, that the goal would reveal itself as soon as I reached the rugged horizon, just where that great sun of Hades had set a few moments before (or was it long ago?) to point out the hidden way.

Even when I realized that hasten as I might, the edge of this nether world grew no closer, but remained always near but unreachable, as if I were walking on a sphere that had no end and no beginning, and not on a flat underground plain that must needs end somewhere, I did not lose my new supple stride. Moreover, I acquired in the next few strides first the sinewy persistence of middle age, and then the physical attributes of an even younger age, viz., the strength and delight of a youth brimful of sap. My dreamlike return to a past long since left behind continued on its marvelous course unchecked: I sank down into the well-spring of youth, filled now with a boy's unrestrained delight that impelled my ever-quickening step into a wild run toward the goal, the firm outlines of which were now beginning to take shape.

As I thus raced over the landscape of Hades, no longer fearful about being dead, my gaze fell for a moment on my hands. And lo, instead of dried veins and wrinkled, scaly skin, I beheld the sturdy hands of a little child that as yet knew no sin, the fingernails bitten to the quick as mine used to be when I was quite small (or so my mother once told me).

The memory of my mother put a sudden halt to my frenzied running, and I stood dumbfounded amid the dusty wastes of Hades, which had not changed a jot. Yet I perceived that I had finally reached the unknown goal, come full circle, back to the beginning of all beginnings, alone no more. On all fours I wriggled out of the now enormous robe, emitting cooing, wordless sounds, innocent and naked as we are only at our birth. Then from my still quite toothless mouth the first cry rose, announcing the painful entrance of yet another servant of God into the Vale of Tears, in a hillside cabin, next to the hearth fire, amid blood and slime and the tired sobbing of a woman, rising straight from her torn womb.

But my pain as well as my mother's faded quickly when our trembling hands rose to meet in that blessed touch that is the only consolation under the whole vault of heaven.

12. CASABLANCA

SARAH'S ON DUTY again tonight.

I don't know how she managed to change her shift again. She was supposed to be on duty three evenings from now. Probably Brenda and Mary are not vying for the privilege of attending me at night. Both are married and Brenda has children; very likely they prefer being with their families at that hour rather than keeping watch over a paralyzed patient, although we recently doubled the fee for night duty. Money is not the only incentive for Sarah, who is actually free of any family ties, to take care of me at a time when everyone in the household is asleep and no one enters my room until morning. She has additional reasons, but no one knows of them except the two of us, and I couldn't reveal them even if I wanted to.

This cursed disease, thanks to which I can't move a finger any more! Until a few months ago, I was able to move two fingers on my left hand—the middle and fourth—enough for me to press the keys of my computer and communicate with my environment by synthetic voice; now I can't do even that. The doctors say the illness can only get worse. They no longer hide it from me. Amyotrophic lateral sclerosis. But how? What more can go wrong with my sensorimotor system if I haven't a single muscle left capable of movement?

The worst thing about paralysis is that it damages you only on the outside: putting a sound mind in a sick body. Inside, you remain totally intact. Moreover, my brain has never worked so clearly as it does now that I'm quite incapable of movement. My head swarms with the most marvelous models of the Cosmos; I'm advancing toward the Grand Synthesis, but what's the use when I can't communicate any of it? I'm a sort of vegetable genius. And, oh, I have so much to say! I have finally grasped where old Albert went wrong; I know what misled Feynman; I have removed Penrose's main misconception. I'm at the very edge of the Unified Theory. A few more nights, perhaps, if Sarah doesn't start again, though I suspect she will....

Penrose came for a brief visit several weeks ago, and I only then saw from his expression that I must be in pretty bad shape. I tried my hardest to convey to him what I had finally cleared up about the closed strings, to tell him that the first vibrations of their harmony are finally reaching me, the rondo played by the very building blocks of the Universe. I also wanted to ask him to calculate something for me on the big computer at the University; I'm wasting endless hours fiddling with tensors in my head, denied even the use of pencil and paper, when the work could be done in fifteen minutes on the latest wonder from Silicon Valley. If they don't have physicists like the British, the Americans at least know their way around technology.

But all that emerged was a series of awful rattles, with a lot of slobbering and ugly grimacing—the usual, in fact. Most of the time this doesn't make me despair: I'm used to it by now. But when Penrose stood up to go, without having understood anything whatsoever and, visibly embarrassed, patted me on the head, as he might have a mentally retarded child or an intelligent dog, I actually felt for the first time like a helpless cretin.

The members of my family whom I see every day try not to talk too much in order to spare me similar embarrassment. They come to my room, report to me briefly on current events, but expect no response. Generally speaking, the children's behavior comes closest to normal, thereby confirming my own normality.

It's different with the nurses. They are more in my company, and it's difficult to spend hours with someone in complete silence, even someone in my position. Their endless chatter doesn't bother me, especially Brenda's, full of commonplace rubbish, because it does not require my attention; I even find I can think better when they're here. It's the tone they use when addressing me that gets on my nerves, patronizing for some reason, as if they were dealing with a baby or a mental deficient. Well, maybe that's how they see me. Poor Sir Isaac, he must be turning in his grave. What a humiliating blow to the long and glorious tradition of Cambridge physics!

From the outset, Sarah was different. Not only was she far more reticent than Brenda or Mary, she admitted quite frankly that she had accepted the arduous task of being my nurse primarily because I used to be a famous physicist. (I still am actually, but perhaps that isn't quite so obvious.) This flattered me, of course, especially because Sarah's predecessors were largely indifferent to this fact but also because she is a rather pretty girl with a wonderful smile and lush, seductive curves that are very noticeable in her tight nurse's uniform. It may seem that these qualities are rather beside the point in my case, but there are some habits and desires that a man is reluctant to relinquish.

In the beginning it seemed that Sarah was about to introduce some changes in the night nurses' usual treatment of me. Their main preoccupation was to create the illusion that I was asleep so that they themselves could secretly take a nap. In the morning they would, without batting an eyelid, claim that they remained awake by my side the whole night, look-ing me brazenly in the eye as if I could confirm or deny their claim. Even had I been able to do so, I would hardly have bothered debunking their little tricks. It actually suited me to have the nurses sleep; I could then concentrate on thinking, spared their constant fidgeting and fussing about me—except when they snore, which happens from time to time. There is nothing so fatal to the music of the spheres now being conceived in my head as the gentle buzz of female snoring.

At first I thought that Sarah suffered from insomnia, since I never saw her fall asleep before me although I could stay awake for a long time. Once she put me to bed, she would not bother me at all but devote herself to reading, not raising her eyes for hours from the cheap sentimental novels she devoured. I discovered the type of reading matter it was because she frequently, before going home, left the books on my night table. Who could have thought then that this was not all just coincidence?

It seemed a little odd that a girl of her looks should content herself with these banal surrogates for love, but since I had no opportunity to talk to her about it, the motives that lay behind this inclination remained a mystery to me, like almost everything else related to Sarah. In contrast to most other nurses, who, if they stayed with us for any length of time, would relate their entire life's story without the slightest encouragement, convinced that in me they had a listener full of curiosity and understand-ing, Sarah did not seem to exist outside the walls of my room, so little did I know about her private life or her past.

In certain moments, as I was drifting off to sleep or waiting in that limbo that always precedes the solution of some difficult and important equation, I had the impression that Sarah in fact did not exist at all, that she was only the product of my overburdened imagination.

The conversion from books to television seemed perfectly natural, and I could not see in this, either, any part of a well thought-out plan. Tear-jerking serials were on the air from time to time, and Sarah seemed very happy when she discerned on my distorted face permission to occasionally turn on the TV, although normally I watched it only very rarely and then almost exclusively cricket matches, having played cricket in my youth in time-honored Cambridge tradition, before this damned illness caught up with me.

As a matter of fact, Sarah read what she wanted in my face since I was not only incapable of forming a grimace of agreement but also, because the TV would only hinder my thinking, unwilling to do so. In fact it turned out not too bad in the beginning: Sarah considerately turned the sound completely down and the screen around, moving her chair from my bedside to a place near the window, so that I learned about the program only from the vari-colored reflections on her face in the semidarkness of the room. Whether I wanted it or not, I began to watch that face for increasing periods, following the dramatic changes on it, not infrequently spiced by tears, influenced by twists in the third-rate melodramatic plot on the screen.

Sarah noticed that I was looking at her and came to yet another erroneous conclusion about my wishes—again because it suited her, although at the time I couldn't see this. She apologized, turned the screen back toward me and moved her chair close, sure that I must, naturally, also want to watch the soap operas she so enjoyed. So I became an unwilling watcher of countless tear-jerking plots set in tasteless scenery, unable to turn my head away or even to lower my eyelids. It is true that I could still somehow manage the latter, but I refrained, primarily for fear that Sarah's feelings might be hurt. Without being aware of it, I was already enmeshed.

Fortunately, sentimental serials were not aired too often, so this enforced watching did not, at first, detract much from my research, which was now entering its final stage. In the vibration of strings—that basic form of matter, actually indivisible as the ancient Greeks in their simple way believed atoms to be—a fundamental cyclical structure was appearing, repeating itself all the way through to the circular structure of the Universe, simultaneously infinite and finite, corresponding to the cyclic flow of time, without an arrow, without the paradoxes of cause and effect or any apparent beginning in the Big Bang. A structure in which the four primal forces of nature finally became one, accepting gravity, rejected for so long, into their sisterhood....

I felt—I suspected—that I was on the threshold, that just one step separated me from shaping a final theory, but all my previous experience told me that such a line cannot be crossed in a straight walk, that enlightenment—a dazzling bolt of lightning that would drive the last wisps of darkness from my mind and leave me in a clearing of pure light—was necessary. However, enlightenment was certainly not what was streaming from the cathode tube, and Sarah soon thought of a way to compensate for the relative scarcity of the shows she yearned for in the regular TV program. The answer, simply, was video.

One evening she brought with her a largish bag, and with the sweetest smile from her repertoire, which included that beautiful little dimple that would appear on the point of her chin, she regaled me with the news that she had obtained a supply of cassettes of romantic classics. I do not know what meaning she took at that moment from the usual rictus on my face, but I tried my hardest to give an impression of utter despair. It was soon clear that this was a flop when, chattering with unwonted animation, she began to arrange the cassettes next to the VCR, which so far had been used only once—when I was shown that sentimental film about me by Spielberg.

And so began a marathon retrospective of a genre for which I have never cared much and which was, under present circumstances, the last thing I needed. Sarah appeared more and more often on the night shift, which pleased Brenda and Mary. All the cult heroes of romantic films, particularly older ones, began to parade before our eyes, drawing sighs and tears from her, grimaces and twitches from me, which she readily interpreted as reliable evidence of similar delight.

More than once she got carried away and reached for my hand, so that the end of the film would find us holding hands like a young couple at the cinema. On the first such occasion, as the flickering magic vanished, Sarah snapped out of it, releasing my atrophied hand from her grip. Gradually, however, she began to find this contact quite normal, until soon she did not hesitate to snuggle up to me during the most exciting scenes—such as the one at the end of *Casablanca,* which we watched at least ten times on several successive nights. But immediately after the film she would stand up, straighten her crumpled uniform, and mumble a few unintelligible words, supposedly in apology. I cannot say that this intimacy was not pleasurable, though it filled me to a far greater extent with unease.

Just as I was on the brink of despair at the mountain of cassettes, which she tirelessly exchanged for new ones, and unable to communicate to her in any manner whatsoever that I was not in the least interested in these tear-jerkers, my mind being occupied with things of far greater importance that could be lost forever if I did not achieve maximum concentration, her decision to proceed with Stage Two of her plan came to my aid in an unusual way.

Again she carried it off with perfect unobtrusiveness so that I suspected nothing. After the end of some accursedly pathetic movie, starring that icy Garbo, whom she for some reason holds in high esteem, Sarah did not turn the video off at once, as she usually did; instead, she first turned me over on my other side, since I had been lying too long in the same position. The tape ran past the credits, rolling on before my eyes, and then on the screen appeared the remains of an earlier recording on the same cassette: my bedroom was at once filled with the passionate sighs of a naked couple at the height of sexual arousal. The frame, almost clinical in its detail, removed any doubt: this was pornography of the hardest core.

Although Sarah, occupied with turning me, could hardly fail to hear the noisy rapture of the young couple, she did not react immediately. A good fifteen seconds elapsed before she bustled over to the VCR to turn it off, red to the ears, which rather suited her, leaving me half turned. This apparently sincere embarrassment and the torrent of apologies that followed, full of accusations against the perverts at the local video club who contaminated great love films by keeping copies on tapes infested with such revolting trash, deceived me at first, so that I failed to notice the unusualness of her delay in stopping the tape.

I did think of it the next day but soon convinced myself that it had to be a mistake and that my other impression—that Sarah, in turning me over, had held me unusually low down on my body, not under my shoulders but rather around my hips—was equally unreliable. After all, what conclusion could I possibly have drawn from all this? Paranoia may be of some use in scientific research but is usually of none at all in normal life. Usually. Although the fact that you are paranoid does not, of course, necessarily mean that there isn't actually somebody out there trying to kill you...

Sarah, fortunately, was not trying to kill me, as I soon understood when her intention finally became clear. Now that the lead-up was over, matters proceeded faster, although several days went by before she took the next step. The videos stopped altogether and Sarah spent two evenings reading innocently, as at the beginning of her tour of duty in our house.

Although I was now on the alert, her reserve lulled me, so that I was not much upset when, on the third evening, she switched on the video again, turning the set in my direction. Filled with a sense of foreboding, I wondered which cassette it would be, but when I saw the opening frames of *Casablanca*, an involuntary grunt was wrenched from me, followed by unchecked dribbling. Not again!—was my hopeless thought, but she obviously interpreted the sound in the wrong way. She sat down quickly on the edge of the bed and looked me straight in the eye, the regard, one would imagine, of a mother for her infant. Or one lover for the other.

She began by wiping the spittle from the corners of my mouth with a piece of gauze then brushed the hair from my forehead, proceeding to slide her hand along my neck and chest, supposedly smoothing the thin coverlet, muttering something unintelligible as she did so. All I could make out was that she had to do something, something hard for her; several times she mentioned the word "love," once "a great physicist" and once "a child." Her eyes were glassy, which in a moment's panic I took for madness; then I unmistakably recognized erotic arousal in them. I should have felt relieved, but I didn't.

When her hand slid to my navel, she jumped as if she had touched something hot, then stood up from the bed, turning her back on me for a moment. I suppose it was not easy for her: judging by the slight trembling of her shoulders, a strong internal struggle must have been going on, the outcome of which was uncertain. The only problem was that she had not asked me whether I was willing to take part in the whole business. Quite simply, my participation was taken as read. Unfortunately, that sort of thing is inevitable when one is laid low with this idiotic amyotrophy.

The shaking of her shoulders stopped, indicating that a final decision had been reached. She turned to me with a somewhat defiant look on her face, arranged her hair with a nervous swipe of her hand, went over to the VCR, and ejected the tape of *Casablanca*. After a brief search through the heap nearby, she found another. There was no more hesitation in her movements as she placed this new cassette into the video recorder. She then resumed her position next to me on the edge of the bed.

Her gaze was on me, not on the screen; she knew full well what was on the recording, so that she had no need to watch—my reaction was much more important to her. For a moment I looked back at her, puzzled, then at the screen.

Of all the surprises I could have had, this was the greatest: before my eyes flickered a perfectly familiar sight—this same bedroom. The frame was showing my bed, in which I lay immobile, eyes closed. The recording was undoubtedly made at some late night hour, while I was already asleep. But who....?

As if reading the puzzlement in my eyes, Sarah bent down near the edge of the bed and proudly lifted a small Sony camera, obviously capable of recording even in very poor light, since no additional lighting was noticeable in the picture. Then she stood up from the bed, went over to the TV, and placed the camera on it, undoubtedly in the same spot from which the previous recording had been made. Before she returned to me, she pressed a button on the camera, turning on a small red indicator near the lens which showed that a new recording was in progress.

I did not like this double recording at all, but how could I express my disapproval? By fresh outbreaks of grunting and slobbering? What good would that be, when for Sarah it always meant something else? I therefore had no option but to stare helplessly at the screen, still without any clue as to what was to follow.

I did not have to wait long.

Sarah soon walked into the frame, not with the usual restrained, modest walk of a shy girl, but with exaggerated movement, swaying her hips and running her fingers through her long hair. She did so in a sultry, seductive manner, but I was still not sure whether she was joking or whether she really meant it. She came over to my bed, leaned over me and began to imitate passionate fondling gestures, but without really touching me, probably afraid of waking me up. After this make-believe touching, Sarah went on to make-believe kissing. Bending slowly, she started with my toes, leaving out no part of my body that her lips could approach through the bedclothes.

While I, an unwilling participant, watched without blinking this perverse erotic game on the screen, the camera on the TV set was making another recording of the same sort, but with me awake. Sarah's hands, with their long, skilful fingers, on which I noticed now for the first time the garishly lacquered nails—had they been like that before? I wondered—began to imitate the gestures on the screen, but this time not in pretend caresses—this was for real. I felt them all over my atrophied body, the muscles of which have been deactivated forever, although the skin has remained as sensitive to touch as always. There are certain tissues, too, the motoric movements of which are not of a muscular nature...

If Sarah had resolved to repeat the scenario of the first recording, kissing was now supposed to follow—and indeed, yanking the covers off me, she bent closely over my feet and started to slide her lips from my toes upward, touching me from time to time with her warm tongue. I slept naked, as usual, so that I could be more easily helped in case of accident, and Sarah had seen me naked on countless previous occasions, but always with the eyes of a nurse, which awoke no sense of shame in me. Now arose two feelings that I had never had with any nurse: shame and excitement. But Sarah was my nurse no longer.

She climbed rapidly up my body, to keep in synch with the pictures on the screen, but without missing a single part; only on reaching my loins, where she dwelled for a little longer, did she raise her head for a moment. The gaze she shot me expressed triumph at the effect she had achieved there, mixed with that peculiar expression of conspiracy that couples those who are united in sin.

It was this thought of sin that only then summoned my wife to my mind, with a certain pang of conscience at first, but not for long. Jane would never become involved in anything of the kind; the whole affair would be to her mind distasteful, offensive even, so much at odds with the role of willing victim that she embraced passionately, primarily because of a strong tendency to martyrdom, subsumed in the deprivation of living with someone like me. In fact, she would have probably welcomed this "infidelity" as providing fresh grist to the mill of her martyrdom.

Before the atrophy had fully set in, Jane had come to me on occasion, but unwillingly and with increasingly pronounced dislike, although she was fully aware that the illness had not at all diminished, physiologically or psychologically, my libido, which has always been strong. I did not hold it against her; I could understand the disgust she must have felt, although this denied her the opportunity and pleasure of being the Compleat Sufferer. Since I could not move my hands—except those two fingers, definitely not enough for the purpose—I had no option left, after she stopped coming to me, except to relieve myself in wet dreams, like a pubescent boy. I used to curse this diabolical disease afterwards while the nurses washed me in the morning; in their expression of embarrassment, which never appeared when removing the traces of other feculence, I always discerned, for some reason, the shadow of a contemptuous smile.

Sarah's kisses in reality caught up with the ones on the screen somewhere at the level of my eyes; when I opened them under her lips, the two sequences had already separated. The real Sarah was now sitting motionless on the edge of the bed, watching the TV as I was, looking like someone who had nothing whatsoever to do with what had been going on in my bedroom until that moment.

At the same time, the Sarah on the recording stood up, approached the head of my bed, and began slowly to undress. She did this with surprising skill, one might say with the motions of an experienced stripper, always hinting first at what was to come, so that the undressing process took a longish time, although she wore, under the nurse's uniform, only scanty underwear. The way she took off her long black fishnet stockings and purple garters was particularly exciting. The undulations of her body followed some rhythm audible to her alone, the only sound coming from the TV being the slight susurration of sliding underwear.

When there was no more to take off, she glanced roguishly at the camera, then came over to the bed and climbed carefully on to the edge, taking care not to wake me. She stood there for a few moments, half bent, reminding me of a statue from antiquity, I cannot remember which. Anyway, maybe it wasn't from antiquity.

Then she straddled me, lowering herself to within a few millimeters of my loins, but without touching them. She threw back her head and her hips started to writhe. Long auburn hair cascaded down her bare back and from her wide-open mouth came low, throaty moans. I believed first that this was playacting, but a moment later I thought that nobody could simulate excitement that convincingly. In any case, the climax had to come soon, and then the matter would become clear (assuming this could not be faked).

But if the climax came, I was denied the opportunity of seeing it. The Sarah in reality suddenly walked with nervous steps to the video and turned it off, again mumbling some vague fragments of her thoughts, among which I discerned this time something about "the wrong day," "not sure of pregnancy," and "needless waste." It was already possible to complete the puzzle, but I was too disconcerted to do it.

She seemed confused while she was switching off the camera too and putting it into a small bag that she placed, together with the cassette from the VCR, on the floor next to the night table, obviously intending to take these things away with her in the morning. The criminal always tries to remove traces of his crime. There was, however, one trace that could not be removed at once. Although Sarah's next action was to cover me, which she did averting her eyes slightly, with a certain look of guilt on her face, under the thin coverlet my arousal remained visible for some time yet. I could not stop it just by willpower.

It was clear that she had no intention of doing anything further about it as she quickly sat down in the chair again after first moving it slightly away from my bed, as if to separate herself from me, and focused her attention on one of her books, her face perfectly serene and innocent as she read: the very picture of a nurse who had just tended conscientiously to all the wants of the patient entrusted to her care and now had some free time to devote to herself.

I was not so much troubled by the fact that she left me unsatisfied at the height of arousal to which she had deliberately brought me—a condition that naturally caused me the utmost discomfort—as I was angered by my total inability under the circumstances to concentrate on the matter that was now only a step away; I was denied the opportunity to climb that last step separating me from the top, from the plateau of light.

The feeling of twofold frustration, of multiple anticlimax, lasted a long time. I passed a night of troubled dreams, waking frequently but escaping back into sleep as soon as I saw Sarah's stony form next to the bed, tirelessly and chastely bent over her book.

When I woke in the morning, unusually late and smelling of sweat more strongly than was customary, Brenda was by me. She first informed me, in her bleating voice, that her younger son had caught a cold because he had not put on dry socks after playing football in the snow, contrary to her explicit advice, so he was away from school that day, "but that's the young ones today, totally out of hand because their mothers have to work while their fathers hang round the pubs," then about the announced price rise of Lipton's tea, a clear twenty pence per box, which drove her to black thoughts about the crash of the British economy if further concessions were made to those vultures from the European Community, "who didn't understand the British spirit, as Maggie had been saying for years, but nobody listens to the voice of reason from a woman any more." Etc.

It was already past noon when I learned, from one of her marginal remarks, amidst praises for the bird-watching societies, "so typically English," that in the afternoon she would be replaced, not by Sarah, but by Mary, "whose hubby had made it to vice-chairman of the local branch, 'cos he brought a lovely pair of army binoculars from the Falklands, against the rules I must say, and spotted a real golden-crowned woodpecker, very rare in these parts, although he was so excited he forgot to photograph it, so that some rumormongers were saying that he only imagined it because it is the same color as that cheap sherry, what-d-y-call it, although it was common knowledge that Arthur had become a real teetotaller; they do say that when he was young he liked a glass or two and led rather a wild life, but since he met Mary he'd change absolutely, had Arthur. Some women are lucky, not like me...."

So Sarah's on duty again tonight.

SHE WAS PUNCTUAL as always. She appeared a few minutes before 10 p.m., exchanged a few parting sentences with Mary about my condition, which as far as Mary was concerned was the same as usual. For me it only meant that I have really become a total cretin, whose fears and anxieties are interpreted as contented placidity even by those who know me and who bear me no ill will.

I pretended to fall asleep, but even if I had been in a coma, Sarah would not have abandoned her scheme. This time there was no hesitation. I heard her fumbling with the VCR. Then she sat next to me on the bed and caught me by the hand, patting it gently, as if to comfort a child about to get an injection: "There, there, this will hurt a little but it's for your own good." This opened my eyes more efficiently than if she had begun to shake me.

The recording was already being played: last night's foreplay filled the screen, and I, for some reason, struggled to suppress my excitement. Sarah just sat passively; I glanced at her several times, and it seemed to me that she was irresolute and hesitant. In any case, she did not start anything, least of all any new foreplay. When the recording came to the place where last night's business had stopped, the picture changed suddenly. It was still my room, but now Sarah was in the foreground, and I was in the background, asleep. This must have been recorded some time before dawn. And then, instead of mumbled fragments, the story began properly. Sarah had had to record it, not just because it was easier for her to tell it that way, but also because she enjoyed seeing herself on the screen. Now she could be not a tearful viewer of *Casablanca* but a participant in it. And the role of Rick was, naturally, given to me. How could I have refused?

The subject of this film, too, was unbearably sentimental. With many sighs, which did not seem in the least artificial, she started to pour out a melodramatic tale of a sensitive young woman, innocent and virtuous, totally unsuited for this age of vice; men see in her only the image of carnality, while she pines for true love, which sadly, survives only in old movies, novels, and rare TV serials.

Because of this, she withdraws more and more into herself, isolates herself in her loneliness, begins even to contemplate the worst, before Providence comes to her rescue. She is hired as nurse to a famous scientist, "the greatest physicist of modern times" (*what's that got to do with it?*) and soon discovers that they are kindred spirits. (*That's the last time I'll try to convey any message by grimaces and facial twitches.*) He lies immobile in bed, broken by a terrible illness, abandoned by all, even by his wife, who surely intends to find somebody else. (*Of course she does. That was our agreement, after all. Any other course of action would be unnatural. Jane can only be frustrated by her thing about martyrdom, but I think she needs it to ease her conscience.*) His children avoid and neglect him. (*Nonsense: they're the only people who treat me normally.*)

He longs for warmth, affection, and most of all for love, but all that is denied him. The young woman knows this because his eyes shine, as do hers, when he gets the chance to watch romantic films. (*Help!*) As they watched, they grew close to each other. Tenderly, he held her hand as his eyes spoke of his feelings. (*If I'd been able to hold anything, it would have been the remote control, to stop the bloody recording.*) She returned this love with all her heart, overjoyed that her dream of love had finally come true. (*I hate Casablanca!*)

But this love, like all great loves, was destined to be short-lived. His greedy, jealous wife learns of the affair and prepares to dismiss the young woman, fearing the loss of privileges that go with her husband's reputation. (*Rubbish! Jane is not like that at all, quite the contrary. Sarah must have invented this bit. I think I saw a similar plot line in one of those stupid serials of hers....*) The young woman despairs and thinks of poisoning first him, then herself, but realizes that this would not be fair. (*Definitely not. Not in that order.*)

Ultimately she finds a solution: if they cannot stay together, she will take with her a lasting reminder of him, something that will be the firmest possible token of their love, binding beyond the grave. (*I knew there was bound to be a grave in this somewhere.*) She will give birth to his son. A son who might also become a great physicist, to continue his father's work. (*Nonsense. Judging by the two sons I already have, there's not a chance. Physics doesn't attract Robert and Timmy at all. Lucy's the only one who shows any talent for maths.*)

He agrees enthusiastically (*sic!*), telling her that she is the last woman in his life. (*Although I certainly did not tell her any such thing, this part about "the last woman" could nevertheless be true, unless Jane decides to pander to me, to increase her own martyrdom.*) They are getting ready for their first and only night of love; the young woman takes care that it should be in the 24-hour period of her greatest fertility....

So that's the puzzle. I am to become a father one more time, and the fateful night is now before me. How can I defeat Sarah's plan? No way, I'm afraid. The only solution is for me to try to avoid arousal, to think of something else, physics maybe; but she has already demonstrated how able she is. Under her lips and tongue, physics does not help much, regardless of whether this is the fault of the weirdos at the video club or not....

To make it all fit and proper, the recording of Sarah's story ended with the closing scene of her favorite movie. Editing was clearly one of her fortes. Indeed, was there any more appropriate lead-in to the sad ending of our relationship than the parting of Ilse and Rick? But there was no more time for modesty. Sarah went to the video, turned it off and switched the camera on. The whole thing is to be preserved for posterity, then. How appropriate.

Turning to me she began to repeat the performance that I had seen only on the screen the previous night. The swaying hips, the slow unbuttoning of the nurse's uniform, the hair falling free, the removal of the black fishnet stockings with the purple garters, the final divesting of the two scraps of underwear, also black, in vivid contrast to her extremely white skin.

Seeing her fully naked for the first time—literally—in the flesh, I thought for a moment what a pity it was that such a body should be wasted on an invalid like me. This was probably a defense mechanism, an effort to keep down the excitement by humiliating myself, but to no avail. Sarah's nude body defeated all would-be suppression by willpower or similar tricks, or so my loins unmistakably told me.

Sarah had proof of this as soon as she grabbed the bedcovers and flung them off me. There was no need for long foreplay, starting with the big toe and ending with my eyes. All was ready. But while this reflex tumescence was for me an admission of defeat, for Sarah it was the final confirmation of her eccentric erotic fantasy in which I was a willing accomplice.

Very affectionately, she caressed my hair, then climbed on the bed and straddled me nimbly. As I penetrated her smoothly in one easy slide, assisted by her own excitement, she bent so that her lips were close to my ear and began to whisper disconnected words in which I recognized only her desire to give me more confidence and calmness. I felt silly then, like a hesitant girl about to lose her virginity with an experienced lover who was trying to cajole her.

Another humiliating impression this, but it did not dampen my excitement. Quite the opposite. I knew the climax had to be close, but I did not want to surrender without a fight, and I had at my disposal only one last futile weapon: physics. Sarah's hips were now pumping up and down, faster and faster, and the contractions of the cylindrical muscles had achieved a regular rhythm. Drops of sweat glistening on her forehead and on the tips of her cheeks gave her face an unusual radiance.

Think, Stephen, think!

The strings become tense.... Gravity fits in by.... I must.... All four forces are just different aspects of...the same...Sarah, I hate you.... The colors and smells of quarks.... Time is defined by a cycle, a repetition.... The quantum state of singularity.... Slow it down, it will be premature.... Black holes, white holes.... The space-time shortcut opens.... Spin must be opposite.... Of course! It all fits, if we only assume.... Your nipples are perfectly round, like.... I know where...the missing mass.... Sum over histories.... That's it, that's it, around! In a circle.... The Circle!.... My God! The Universe is.... Connection, a link.... No! Not yet, damn you! Wait.... Wait! It's coming.... The Big Bang....

Two things happened simultaneously. Sarah reared, jerking her head back and thrusting her quivering breasts forward and upward; her hands were leaning on my weak shoulders, digging her twitching fingers with their long, sharp nails into the limp tissue; from her lips issued a throaty, muffled "Stephen!" followed by deep panting, rasping, moaning sounds, from the very bottom of the entrails, from the center of her being, from the black, blind spot in which are united all the sinews and all the threads, life and death....

And I, I broke through into the open, on to the plateau. Into the light. It was blazed and dazzled, a jagged bolt of lightning, a ringing harmony of the spheres, limpidity to the rim of the world. The rim dissipated into emptiness, melted into an exclamation, into the edge of The Circle, into the arrow of time driven deep into Sarah's soft being. Then there was nothing, nothing all the way to the far horizon and those who were waiting for me out there.

CIRCLE THE THIRD

1. A Guest in the Temple

WE HAVE A visitor.

Though his arrival was unexpected, even by me, Sri did not seem surprised at all, or if he was surprised, it was pleasantly. Now my friend has male company, which obviously pleases him more than does mine, so he's happy while I feel neglected. Ah well, serves me right for being so gullible—like all women in fact. As if men's feelings were made to last.

I know I should pay him back in kind. He richly deserves it, but I still manage to restrain myself, though I don't know why. The only thing he has earned from me is total contempt—or worse—especially after how he behaved regarding the baby.

He let me see it just that one time, and then only for a short while. I thought I would die of pain when he tore me away from the crib and started asking heartless questions about alleged hermetic viruses, wild programs, and similar absurdities, as if this were not a real baby, afflicted with Down's Syndrome though it may be. So what if it is? Sri least of anyone has the right to blame me for that. If he'd devoted more attention to me, if everything else hadn't been more important to him—his silly meditations in the first place—I would never have been forcibly inseminated by that stunted monkey.

I had a premonition from the very onset of pregnancy that this crossing with the primitive genes of the Little One would come to no good; I kept telling myself, in my rare moments of sobriety, that I ought to abort, but in the end that damn maternal instinct prevailed. That's the worst curse that God—never mind which one, all gods are males—uses to punish women. That's why I hate them all.

The baby seemed to be stretching its tiny hands toward me, but I know now it wasn't a deliberate act. It was an involuntary twitch. It doesn't recognize me as its mother, and that hurts more than Sri's indifference. I tried secretly to approach it several times, in defiance of Sri's cruel ban, but each time I suffered the same disappointment. Perhaps that's what Sri wanted to spare me when he forbade me to see the baby again after that first, traumatic time.

But, no, I'm deluding myself. He's nowhere near as thoughtful as that. To him the baby is just a peculiar program malfunction that he would have destroyed long ago if he weren't so intrigued as to how it came about. Before our guest arrived, Sri had, to my horror, gone poking about the crib several times, totally unfeeling, not caring a whit for my desperate cries and pleas to leave the baby alone. Now, luckily, he has no more time: he is devoting himself entirely to his new friend, which does not surprise me in the least.

There was a moment when I had the impression that he planned to vivisect the baby—well, perhaps he wouldn't go quite that far. Sri certainly can be terribly cruel, but he isn't a monster, though a distraught mother may be forgiven for entertaining the thought. I was tempted to violate a pledge I had made to myself: that I would never again utter a word to the Little One.

The baby's life was more important than my vanity, and he was its father, after all, even if it was by violence, so it was up to him to do something about it. What exactly, I didn't quite know, because Sri is much bigger and stronger. It crossed my mind that I should provoke him into the same state of hysteria he was in when the circle was removed from the screen, while we were making a picture language, because it seemed to me at the time that for a brief period his strength increased tenfold. However, I realized then that I hadn't seen him for quite a while, in fact not since the moment when Sri had allowed me, for the first and last time, to see the baby.

I recall his grinning foolishly then, but in the excitement of the moment I had no time to reflect, and afterwards the terrible discovery that the baby has Down's Syndrome absolutely shattered me, so that I lost sight of the Little One completely. I mean that literally: he was nowhere in my field of vision, not inside the temple nor in the wide area around it within farthest reaches of my electronic senses. If he'd hidden in some hole, or in the thickets or trees, he couldn't possibly have eluded me; at this moment I have in my field of vision exactly forty-three of his merry brethren who have no idea that I am spying on them, but none of them is the Little One.

So the gentleman has put his tail between his legs and slunk away, true to himself. And then they say—rely on men! That sort won't let you down only when they don't have the opportunity to do so. The Little

One realized he didn't stand a chance in a clash with Sri, so he well and truly ran away to save his own skin. A fat lot he cares for his own child, retarded or not, let alone for me.

Or perhaps he has a tacit agreement with Sri that the baby should not continue to live? If that's it, then his heartlessness surpasses even Srinavasa's—which would be a colossal achievement and something I'd have sworn, almost until yesterday, was impossible. But if life in a man's world has taught me anything, it is that you must never set a limit to male deceitfulness, because as soon as you do, a man will overstep it. In any case, nothing will ever tempt me to even look at the Little One again, though this will be difficult because of my far-flung system of sensors. But I can at least pretend not to see him.

If they had somehow carried out their ghastly intent to murder the baby on the pretext that it had Down's Syndrome and that this would be best for everyone, it would have been not only vicious and inhumane but also deeply unjust as well. The baby does in fact act like a retarded child, incapable of recognizing even its own mother, but it has on at least one occasion demonstrated an awareness of the outside world, a much more complete awareness, in fact, than any of the rest of us have. It was the first to sense the arrival of the guest.

Which of course I should have been. The whole purpose of my delicate network of sensors is to do just that: to register the approach of an intruder in good time and inform Sri. Admittedly, at the time the guest arrived I was not on speaking terms with Sri, but I could have warned him in countless other ways than by voice. I've never before had reason to do so, being able to deal with all uninvited guests myself. Those are likely to be, at the worst, large wild animals, and it's easy for me to scare them to the marrow of their bones with a properly modulated screech. For each species I use a special tone that drives them to flee headlong out of the temple zone.

If the newcomer were a man, I would first carry out detailed scans to see whether he was armed. Though there is little chance that armed bands would venture this deep into the jungle for plunder, which would certainly not be worth the trouble, it's prudent to take some protective measures, the more so because these come easily to me, as a matter of routine. I have adequate sonic—and other—devices to deter humans from the temple, but their efficacy had been tested only when the system was tried out in the laboratory, since we hadn't yet had a single guest here.

When one finally turned up, the warning system failed completely. If it hadn't been for the baby, I would have become aware of the guest only

when he entered the temple, quietly and unchallenged. I have no explanation as to how it could have happened. I checked the entire system,
carefully and repeatedly, but found no malfunctions. It was as though the
newcomer just materialized out of nowhere into the clearing in front of the
temple. The finely adjusted sensors, which normally detect the presence of
the smallest animals and birds, remained totally mute.

The only hint that something unusual was in the offing was the sudden
wriggling of the otherwise immobile baby, whose indifference to the outside world is such that even Sri might envy it. Against the latter's explicit
instructions, I approached the baby just as its large eyes opened wide, and
for a moment I had the idiotic impression that I was looking at the spit-
ting image of a tiny Sri. Its gaze roved over the edge of the crib, and then
it started to make incomprehensible throaty sounds, the first I heard from
it besides ordinary crying.

I just stared stupidly at it, not knowing what it was trying to tell me or
what to do. The throaty tirade suddenly stopped, and the baby's face lit
up with a smile of pure pleasure. I responded instinctively and beamed
happily back at it: how could I not? This was, after all, the first two-way
communication that my baby and I had ever had.

Unfortunately, the contact lasted only a short time; a moment or two
later the smile disappeared from the baby's face, replaced by its usual
expression of dull indifference to the outside world. Joy was still strong in
me, however, and I addressed Sri in a happy voice, wishing to give him the
glad tidings and completely forgetting in my excitement that our relations
had cooled, but his usual insensitivity quickly brought me back to earth.
His lordship was sitting, legs crossed under him, deep in meditation in a
corner of the temple from where he rudely flapped a hand at me, signaling
that he did not wish to be disturbed.

My throat constricted and in all likelihood I would have burst into tears,
if I hadn't just then succeeded in reestablishing contact with the baby, this
time in a completely new way. I distinctly felt its presence where I thought
nobody would ever penetrate, at the very heart of my most private being:
at the center of my mind, not at all like an intruder, but rather as an exten-
sion of my own personality. There it created an easily recognizable picture
from my everyday life—that of the clearing in front of the temple.

There was not enough time to be frightened by this strange experience
because just then another, more acute fear came over me. The clearing
was not empty as by all accounts it should have been: a tall, strongly-built
stranger in a long orange robe just like Sri's was in the act of crossing it.

At first I panicked, confronted by a swarm of questions to which I had no answers, but then my protective instinct went into overdrive. Ridding my mind entirely of the baby's presence—or maybe it withdrew by itself, I don't know—I turned all my electronic senses on the intruder who was now advancing toward the entrance to the temple. What my sensors informed me brought me no comfort; quite the contrary.

Not only did all the data provided by the scans add up to a picture that certainly did not fit the usual measurements of a human being, but I suffered a major shock when I saw the visitor's face. Naturally, I recognized him at once: how could I ever forget?

All fingers and thumbs, I almost started to shout a warning to Sri, but stopped myself at the last moment. What could I have told him? That the obstetrician from my dreams—the man whose crumbling statue takes up half the inside of the temple—was on his way here? Impossible! Sri thinks, in any case, that I'm not entirely sane—and who knows, after all that's happened to me, his opinion may not be entirely unfounded. If I told him anything of the kind, he'd certainly switch me off forever. On the other hand, if I didn't speak up, if I let Buddha walk quietly into the temple and take him by surprise, then I'd really be for it.

The situation seemed hopeless, and every further step taken by the orange-robed figure increased my fluster and panic. Then Providence came to the rescue, with an amazing outcome that left me utterly confused.

Sri did not need any warning—or had the baby intervened in his mind too? In any case, he stood quite calmly at the temple door, as if he had been expecting this visitor, and gave him one of his friendliest smiles, something I had long been sure I would never again see on his face. I can hardly remember the last time that he bestowed this rare honor on me. But who am I, after all, to warrant anything of the kind?

Without exchanging a word, they went over to the corner of the temple where Sri had until just now been sitting cross-legged in meditation. Now both assumed the same position and remained silent, their heads bowed. The recent experience with the baby led me to think for a moment that their silence might be only apparent, but try as I might, I could not discern any trace of mental communication between them, while the baby again retreated into its Down's Syndrome torpor and so was of no use at all. I was alone.

The perplexity that had filled me till then began to give way to another feeling: anger. If the baby's reticence was understandable, the attitude of the two men was lacking in the rudiments of common courtesy. Neither perceived the need to explain anything to me, which good manners toward a lady, to say the least, would demand, if nothing else. But who can expect gentlemanly behavior in the middle of a jungle? Let's not delude ourselves.

Totally inconsiderate, they sat like that for hours, without saying a word, and I finally understood why most women despise chess. Nothing makes you feel so neglected and rejected as two males selfishly engrossed in a game of chess in your presence. (As if they had the foggiest notion of the game in the first place.)

All right, Sri, you asked for it. If you don't feel the need to say something to me, I won't say anything to you, although I would have a thing or two to tell you if I chose. I might, for instance, report to you that your tubby new friend did not arrive at the temple alone. Oh no. He has a surprise for you under that garish robe. Two surprises, in fact. I wonder how well the sturdy indifference you're so proud of will stand up to a reunion with that pair of four-legged little horrors you once parted from with such difficulty....

2. INTO THE KINGDOM OF THE UNDERWORLD

MY TINY HANDS reached forth for my mother's—but this fluttering movement, inspired by the purest of desires, was not destined to achieve its noble end.

For the shaking of another, huger hand, roughly seizing my old shoulders, tore me away from the blissful dream, just as I came within reach of a balm with the power to heal all the suffering of my weary soul and body ravaged by the passing years. Flushed with wrath at the violent disruption of my dream, the sweetest I had ever dreamed, quite blind with fury, I angrily opened my eyes to look upon the villain who so arrogantly dared to tear me away from my mother's dear embrace, elusive though it might be, for some trifling and meaningless need of his own.

So vast was my impotent rage, that in my paroxysm the question of who might have come nigh while I slept in the darkness of the cellar under the iguman's residence flashed only belatedly into my mind. I had been alone there when, an unknown number of hours ago this night, I dropped into sleep to seek illusory salvation. One of the robed ones, surely, inhibited by fear and trembling, had unwillingly come to bring me a frugal meal or some order from the bewildered iguman whose holy House of God had been transformed overnight into a mustering place for the most unclean of all forces? Or could it be—and here my rage quickly lost its earlier ferocity—a new uninvited visitation, come to addle with perverse marvels what little sense remained in my grey head?

This fearful thought, icier than the cold before dawn, chilled me for a moment, and miserable and cowardly again, I longed to return to my warm dream, to seek once more the protection of my mother's lap, not to open my wrinkled eyelids.

But for me there was no going back, for the iron grip of a ruthless hand, already sending currents of pain through my shoulder, chased away the last deceitful vestiges of the comforting dream—and I had no choice but to finally open my eyes.

Open—and see something that filled me at once with gladness and mortification. Not one form, but two, stood bent over me, faces wreathed in chaste, innocent smiles, like two angels come riding down from

Paradise, the bearers of good news. I knew they were no angels because their immeasurable, blasphemous sin, in which I—still able to recall the spark-throwing, darting fire that had united their lecherous bodies into a single flame of carnal desire—also took shameful part, occurred in this very cellar, before my lustful, hidden eyes.

The Master's firm grip on my painful, numbed shoulder now eased, and he extended a hand to me, exactly as had my mother in my interrupted dream, while Marya, standing on the other side, made the same gesture, but with the softness of a woman, turning to my confused face her white, velvety palm bathed in the radiance of dawn. We stood thus, unmoving, for many moments—I fogged by sleep and disbelief, not knowing what to do, whether to accept the angelic hand of which I was not worthy, or to shrink back from this new temptation of the devil. The two of them continued to smile invitingly, guided by some hidden intent that did not require any forced urgency.

This stiff, stony posture, which seemed to have descended from one of the Master's pictures on some wall into this dark cellar where it surely did not belong, would have lasted who knows how long had not the sudden thought of my broken dream, in which I had almost reached my mother's hands, prevailed in me—so I took their outstretched ones, resigned in advance to the uncertain outcome of this imprudent act.

At the moment of this sinful touch, there came first a prickling, then a fiery, stabbing feeling; it made the sparse white hairs below my elbows rise on my tough skin, exactly as they did in the moments of ecstasy while I was lustfully spying on their blasphemous coupling. I felt this effect most strongly from Marya, whose frail, childlike hand filled only half of mine and which, in comparison to the Master's, looked even smaller.

Small though it was, it proved as firm as his when it began to help me rise to my unsteady legs, benumbed and rheumaticky after a cold night spent on the earthen floor of the cellar. Moreover, it seemed that an abundant invisible sap began to flow directly into my old dried-up veins, filling them with strength and vigor, which at my advanced age happens but rarely, usually following a long sojourn in the midday sun.

I stood up firm, even joyful, no longer beset by anxieties and fears, to face the new destiny that Marya and the Master had prepared for me. Why else would they raise me from the sweetest sleep at this early morning hour but for a purpose? I assumed they intended to take me outside, despite the door's being barred. With indecorous but sinfully sweet glee, I pictured in my mind the robed ones staring unblinkingly at us and crossing themselves in the fear of God before this new miracle, which would outshine by far all the previous ones.

But I was not destined to take contemptuous pleasure in the monach's bewilderment because Marya and the Master were guiding me in a direction quite opposite to the iron-bound cellar door, to its darkest corner, into which I deemed no beam of sunlight had penetrated since the laying of the foundation, and which must shelter a nest of the most unhallowed creatures dwelling this side of Hell.

My pleased anticipation quickly waned at this gloomy sight, but because the flow of life-giving, joyful juices kept pouring into me from Marya's hand, fortifying my flagging courage, I did not step back. Nothing more came from the Master, who had released my hand from his clasp to kneel on the floor in the corner where he began to cast strange spells.

At first I thought these were acts of witchcraft to summon up evil spirits, and old forebodings filled my miserable soul. But a moment later it became clear that he was only brushing away the dirt that had accumulated there, though I could not immediately see to what purpose. Soon he had pushed the damp dirt aside, and a trapdoor could be seen, wooden and partly rotten, reinforced in places with rusty iron. Through the cracks, my weak eyes caught a muted reddish glow from below.

Not even the secretion of propitious juices that steadily flowed through Marya's little hand into my body sufficed to keep me from shrinking from this unearthly sight. I started in terror, but Marya turned to me, then took my other hand in hers, looking so intently into my eyes with the endlessly deep blue of her gaze that I took the remaining few steps to the closed trapdoor, yielding to the inaudible command of her will.

The Master raised his head to me once, wearing an expression on his face that I could not read, then pulling with his augmented strength, raised the sealed hatch from the floor. With a creaking of rusty hinges, it began to leave its ancient housing. A gory light spewed forth, its ominous glow filling the dark corner, accompanied by a pestilent odor that gushed up from the bosom of the underworld, filling my nostrils with the loathsome smell of excrement.

No further doubt was possible: despite all their gentleness, Marya and the Master were but merciless executioners whom the Lord Himself had assigned to throw me alive into the jaws of hell, my only rightful place because of the countless sins in thought and deed that I had committed in life; because of my infidel doubts and perverse, filthy lusts, to which I, insolently, had succumbed in moments of spiritual weakness and carnal desire; but most of all because of my indecent, shameless spying on their act of divine union, twice sacred, which I had deceitfully thought had another purpose.

Although forcibly thrust back from the opening by the light of the flames of hell and by noxious gusts of unimaginable decay, I summoned up my faltering will and stepped voluntarily toward the opening, to demonstrate by this final humility my belated repentance, my acceptance of this terrible punishment that the Almighty, in His infinite righteousness, had prepared for me, His poor servant.

Yet my destiny was not to enter the eternal domain of the demon torturers below all alone, for before I had managed to lower my quivering foot into that awful abyss, the Master went first, quickly descending into the gaping hole, where he surely did not belong.

Confused by this mad act, I turned my terrified eyes to Marya, but found that the smile still played on that angelic face. Her virginal white hands released my wrinkled ones, then laying a hand on my bony shoulder, she guided me gently in the footsteps of the vanished Master. Again I accepted her silent order with a believer's total obedience, and I started down into the chasm of Hell with mixed emotions: my earlier resignation to my hopeless fate and a new hope kindled by Marya's unvarying gentleness.

Hardly had my head sunk below the level of the floor as I lowered myself down the wooden ladder, half-rotten as the damp trapdoor above it, than I understood from unmistakable sounds that here was another madness, greater even than the Master's: the white queen of darkness, whom I had thought was Marya, was following me down the ladder into her kingdom of the underworld.

3. Sherlock Holmes's Last Case (1)
The Letter

"WHAT DO YOU think of this, Watson?"

Holmes extended to me an opened envelope. It departed from the standards of the Royal Mail: elongated and bluish, it had a rectangular, not triangular, flap on its reverse side. There was no stamp or any trace of a postmark. On the front were inscribed Holmes's name and address, in neat, gently slanting handwriting with something of a tendency to ornamentation. The sender had made no effort to leave any trace of his own identity.

Not wishing to disappoint my friend, who in circumstances like this always goodheartedly expects that I will be nearly, if not quite, as astute as he is, I held the envelope to my nose. Doing just this, he had many times gleaned precious information. I was aware of a slight, bitter smell but could not place it, though for some reason I thought of the shock to which the sense of smell is exposed upon entering a shop selling Indian spices.

Holmes looked unblinkingly at me, with that penetrating stare of his, a stare that filled even the most confident criminals with unease and caused the ladies to squirm uncomfortably; but he remained silent, though I noticed a slight curling of the fine lines at the corners of his mouth, which I knew indicated a barely controlled impatience.

"How did this arrive?" I asked him, taking the letter out of the envelope. It was of the same bluish tint, on stiff paper, folded in three. I did not unfold it at once.

"Somebody pushed it under the front door. Between four o'clock, when I returned from my walk, and a quarter-past six, when Mrs. Simpson went off to do the evening shopping. She did not bring it to me immediately, but only after she had returned and served my meal. She said she thought it could not be of great consequence, since it had been delivered in this manner; in truth, it was too much of an effort for her to climb the stairs to the drawing room a second time, though she would never admit it. I myself tend to breathe a little harder after those nineteen steps, especially when I take them at a run, while she is sixty-seven and arthritic, but that is unimportant. Come, open the letter."

He was right about the staircase. I could still feel my heart beating faster from the climb, as well as from my brisk walk from home. It seemed that I was not exactly young myself, but the communication from Holmes had been categorical. "Come at once! Very urgent!" Hurrying here, even running part of the way, I imagined a multitude of troubles that might have befallen him. Thank God, all it was was an unusual letter. I was careful not to say this aloud, though; it obviously had special importance for Holmes. Why else would he have called me with such urgency?

When I unfolded the stiff paper, a surprise awaited me: only a large circle was drawn on it. Nothing else was there—no text, no signature, no initials, nor, indeed, any sign at all. My first thought on perceiving the precision of the circle was that it must have been made with a pair of compasses, but when I looked more closely at the place where the center should have been, I could not see the little hole, which would inevitably have been made by the sharp point. Evidently, the drawing had been made with the assistance of some round object, probably some kitchen vessel; a largish cup, perhaps, or a saucer.

"A circle," said I rather feebly, nothing more intelligent crossing my mind.

"Excellent, my dear Watson! A circle!" replied Holmes. His voice bore no hint of ridicule, though my perspicacity had warranted it. He spoke the words as if I really had reached a brilliant conclusion.

"Someone has decided to play a prank on us, no doubt," I continued. "However, even from a prankster one would have expected something more clever than an ordinary circle."

Holmes's reaction was so strong and violent that I almost flinched back.

"Nonsense!" he exclaimed. "Balderdash! A circle is anything but ordinary! The only perfect...complete...like...like...."

Holmes was not rarely given to rages like this, but I do not remember when last I saw him speechless. What looked to me like someone's stupid joke, to him seemed, for some reason, altogether more serious. I knew from experience that at such times he should not be contradicted. Indeed, when he spoke again his voice was perfectly calm, with the usual ironic undertone that had the effect of constantly making his companion re-examine the reasonableness of what was being said.

"All right, let's leave the circle aside for the time being," said he. "We will return to it later. Observe the letter carefully and tell me what else you see."

I brought the letter and the envelope closer to my eyes and looked attentively. After a few long moments of examination, I humbly admitted, "I fail to notice anything further...The format is unusual, though. I have never seen anything like it, but from that I can deduce nothing."

"Indeed," replied Holmes. "Unusual it is, at least here in England. On the continent you will come across it more often. What does the paper tell you?"

I felt it again, more carefully. Now I gained the impression that it possessed, apart from stiffness, the quality of antiquity, a patina. For a moment it seemed to me that I held something very old, a parchment perhaps, between my fingers, though my eyes were telling me that it was a newly made sheet of paper.

"I don't know," I said finally. "It gives the impression of being somehow...foreign. Most probably it also originates from the Continent."

"Italy," responded Holmes succinctly, as if uttering the most banal of statements. He gave me no opportunity to ask him whence he obtained that knowledge, nor was any needed, as the look of puzzlement was quite clear on my face. He approached me, wordlessly took the letter from my hand, and raised it to the lamp that hung above a carved wood chest of drawers in the corner. "Look carefully," he said briefly.

The glow of the lamp flame shone through the unfolded paper. I moved two steps closer, the better to study it, so that now the flame seemed to be in the center of the circle painted on the paper, and I noticed that which Holmes wanted me to see. Brought to life by the light shining from the obverse side of the page, a large letter "M" in a rich calligraphic form appeared in the middle, but it was pale as a wraith, seen only in silhouette. When I moved a little to one side, the reflection of the flame slid towards the edge of the paper and the character disappeared.

"How...?" I asked distractedly.

"A watermark," replied Holmes, again in a disaffected tone. Then his voice regained its enthusiasm, and he started to explain. "The invisible trademark of unique craftsmanship. Only one man in the whole world produces such paper, my dear Watson, the maestro Umberto Murratori of Bologna. 'Cartefficio Murratori,' a branch of an old family of printers and publishers. The clientele for his paper is extremely select: important state offices, the Vatican, and also certain semipublic or secret societies, the Masons, for instance."

"What is so special about it? It does not seem extraordinary, except that it is rather stiff...."

"Appearances can be deceptive, Watson. Try burning it."

"What?"

Since I naturally did not try to do as he proposed, he shrugged and without hesitation put one end of the letter to the top of the gas light. Had it been ordinary paper, it would have begun to smoke and then to burn. The corner that Holmes held in his hand only curled a little; there was no sign of burning.

"You see, then, why Murratori's product is in such demand. The writing on it cannot easily be destroyed. Oh, this paper can burn too, of course, but for that to happen, a temperature far in excess of 451^0 Fahrenheit is required. Similarly, it cannot be harmed by water—only by certain very strong acids."

"I see," said I, taking the letter again from Holmes. I touched the corner that had been exposed to the heat of the gas lamp and then jerked my hand quickly away. It was very hot. "But, indubitably, it can be destroyed by mechanical means." I added.

"Indubitably," repeated Holmes. "But it would take a very sharp knife, almost a surgeon's scalpel."

For a moment I was almost tempted to put this claim to the test by trying to tear the letter in half. I refrained, however, from such an act, partly out of respect for the mysterious document that was apparently so precious to Holmes and partly because of earlier, unpleasant experiences related to my disputing some of his other apparently absurd claims.

"This upper-class clientele, then, purchases durability from Murratori," I said. "What is written on this paper can do battle with time itself."

"Exactly so," replied Holmes. "Also, the price narrows the circle of possible buyers drastically. For the manufacture of a single sheet of this paper, several months of hard work are necessary. It is, in fact, a precious substance, more valuable even than gold to some people. No one except the master Murratori himself knows all the ingredients that go into this paper, and there are rumors that he obtains his raw materials from the Far East. They say that the secret of making this paper was brought to one of his ancestors by Marco Polo himself, from his first exploration of China, though I am of the opinion that this is an exaggeration."

"If this is all true, Holmes, then something really puzzles me. Who would be so foolish as to squander such a treasure for the dispatching of...er...trivial messages?"

For a moment it seemed to me that Holmes would again erupt in anger, and I was already beginning to bite my tongue because of my clumsily formulated thought, but his knitted eyebrows quickly relaxed again, and on his lips flickered the usual smile of superior knowledge.

"The logic of the entire affair eludes you, Watson. It is precisely the fact that the communication is written on Murratori's paper that eliminates any possibility of it being a foolish prank. No one, we can be certain, would be prepared to squander such a precious item on mere childishness. Hence we are to take this message quite seriously. The means by which it was delivered exacts that from us."

"But one would not expect that any important and, moreover, mysterious message should go unsigned. A gentleman should on no account allow himself to have a hand in any doings with anonymous letters, no matter how important they may seem to him."

Holmes eyed me suspiciously. I do not know what he thought of my sudden moralizing, but judging by the grimace that fleetingly crossed his face, the two of us hardly shared the same view of gentlemanly virtues at that moment. In any case, he found an elegant and unexpected escape from the trap that I had set for him.

"Who says the letter is unsigned?"

"What? But except for the circle, there is no other..." I exclaimed, quite at a loss.

"For Heaven's sake, Watson, isn't the signature staring you right in the face?" He feigned amazement, although he was, in fact, secretly jubilant over my confusion. Once more he took the letter from my hands, lifted it to the light, and tapped with the knuckle of his long, bony forefinger on the large letter "M" when it became visible again.

"You are not saying," said I, quite discomposed, "that Signore Murratori himself sent us this message?"

Now it was his turn to be surprised. "How did that thought cross your mind?"

"Well, it is his initial, is it not? 'M' for Murratori. The trademark, you yourself said so."

"No, no," replied Holmes, dismissing it with a wave of his hand. "You fail to comprehend. The existence of the watermark is the trademark. The letter itself is the initial of the sender."

"So, who then? Surely you do not mean the....?"

Holmes triumphantly nodded his head, without waiting for me to finish my thought. In his eyes there was now that familiar gleam that accompanies the moments when great mysteries are unraveled.

"Masons? The Freemasons, I mean?" said I, finally completing my sentence.

Lightning-fast, he turned on his heel, so that his back was to me. The sound that he made reminded me more than anything of a snarl, so that I instinctively retreated a step. Obviously I had not guessed the signatory of the letter.

He remained thus turned for a few moments more and then directed himself again at me. The previous gleam in his eyes had clouded over with the very essence of rage.

"Freemasons! That superior bunch of do-nothings and lazy-bones! Useless intriguers, utterly undeserving of...."

He bit his thin lower lip, as he always did when trying to control his wrath. When he continued, his voice was lower, though it still shook with rage.

"Please, Watson, in the name of friendship, do not ever again mention that...that breed...."

"But didn't you yourself say that they were Murratori's customers?" I said, in an attempt to justify myself.

"Watson—please!" His voice went up an octave.

"Very well, very well," I countered. "Who, then, is hiding behind that mysterious 'M'?"

Before answering he paused, sighing two or three times, obviously trying to compose himself, but also for effect. Holmes was, in fact, an unfulfilled actor.

"My evil fate," he spoke at last, in a voice so hushed that I barely registered it. "My curse. Moriarty...."

4. CHEESE AND A TOGA

WE HAVE ANOTHER visitor.

It's getting to be quite fun at the temple. A merry band of men are gathering, interested exclusively in themselves, while nobody bothers about me. In fact, they don't even notice my existence. I've become the personification of the neglected wife whom they remember only when they need something but otherwise are not aware of. I thought that this happened only in bad novels, but now I realize that in fact only bad novels are true to life. Stereotypes abound—God help us.

The only missing elements are cards and booze; if they start in on those, the whole affair will be like one of those melodramatic features in women's magazines with which Sri, for some dark motives of his own, fairly force-fed me in the weeks after he first switched me on. Couldn't he have given me a better education, if he wanted to build me along the lines of models from prose? His library is full of books from the literary mainstream—most of them are stored in my memory banks: everything from Homer on.

His lordship, however, reserved them for his own enjoyment and dumped the trash on me. No wonder: what would he do with a Helen, or Lady Macbeth, or Anna Karenina? Would they put up with him for so long? Not a chance! His immaturity requires just one geisha, and there haven't been any real ones around for several decades except in trashy romances. So that's how I come to have such a low-class cultural background.

In the meantime, I must say I've become rather well-read in classical literature—on my own initiative of course, and mostly without Sri knowing—but what was implanted in me in my early youth still predominates in my personality today. What can one do? Woman is doomed to long repentance for the sins of her youth. Pity. I could arrange a nice little Trojan war for him here in the jungle or plunge him in blood to the elbows in a power struggle or at least find a Vronsky for myself. I have a feeling that this last would hurt him the most....

The new guest also arrived out of the blue, but that doesn't surprise me any more. In fact, I've stopped asking myself questions to which I know I won't find answers. Everything happened in precisely the same way as when Buddha appeared. The sensors failed to report anything to me, although they're all still functioning faultlessly; only the baby acted up, opened its eyes for a while, and started sending pictures right into the center of my consciousness.

I have no explanation for this computer telepathy, and I doubt that Sri has either, even if I had the courage to report the matter to him. Now that we have company, I simply wouldn't dare. Who knows what he might be capable of doing to my baby and me, just to protect his threatened reputation before the others? Just think: accidental creation of programming genius turns out to be female and now imagines herself to be exchanging thoughts with her child! I admit it sounds totally off the wall; what I do know for sure, however, is that that's how things stand, but until I manage to prove it....

The newcomer is a real fossil, far older than Buddha. At this rate, we'll soon be running an absolute senior citizens' home here. What gave Sri this yen for geriatrics? Anyway, even if he has developed a sudden need for company—who would have thought it of a man who fled to the remotest corner of the globe to achieve complete solitude?—couldn't he opt for younger people? That would have been nicer for me. This way, I'll probably start feeling on the ancient side myself.

And where does he find them? But, no, I promised not to ask questions that don't have answers....

The trouble with this new guy is not so much his advanced age, but his finickiness, especially about food. He must have been pretty spoiled in the food line back wherever he came from. With Sri and Buddha it was very easy. Sri doesn't even notice what he eats. Whatever I give him, he just stuffs it in, quite unaware that it's also possible to *enjoy* food. Well, all right, maybe that's how a Buddhist ascetic ought to be, though I took it hard at first. Women don't like it when their efforts go unnoticed. And I did my very best, honest. Later, I got used to it—and to Sri's numerous other noninvolvements—and it even began to suit me: if his lordship didn't care what he ate, so much the less work for me.

Yet there were a few dishes that would make him frown, though he never complained aloud. He doesn't like spicy food, for instance. Once, just after we came to this jungle, when his rudeness really hurt my feelings, I got my own back by making a hot meal totally off the scale and he had to drink gallons of water to put out the fire in his mouth. But he didn't voice any open reproach. I think he got the message, though, because he treated me quite decently for a few days after that; and he got very cautious about meals as well, carefully tasting whatever I offered him before gobbling it up.

Not long ago, after Buddha's arrival, I had a really mischievous idea: to make him turtle soup, a real delicacy. I have excellent recipes in my memory. Though maybe he wouldn't notice if I did. His face lit up when he saw those two little monsters that his friend brought him, but he quickly got bored with them, as is his wont, and soon forgot about them entirely, preoccupied with more important issues I daresay, leaving them completely in my care. So now I have to worry about those two filthy creatures who soil every corner of the house. No, soup isn't a bad solution at all—as piquant as possible, of course.

With Buddha, catering became even simpler: he ate almost nothing at all. During the seven days that he spent with us, he put something into his mouth only twice or three times—and even then only on my insistence. Uninvited though your guests may be, it doesn't do to leave them hungry. The first time, he tried the pie with mushrooms and fat-cracklings, which I made quite successfully; the cream sauce turned out exceptionally well— finger-licking good, as they say. He praised my pie courteously, having eaten a medium-sized piece, but something in his expression told me that he could just as well have done without it.

If he didn't eat much, Buddha drank like a maniac—strictly water. He always carried a large thermos flask that seemed to fill itself magically again and again, from nowhere. (All right, all right, skip the superfluous questions....) He used every pause in the murmuring debates he carried on all day with Sri to drink another glass, and often woke in the night to quench the thirst that obviously tormented him. And they say one can't live on water alone! No wonder he looks so chubby—like a barrel—when he pours so much into himself but pays disproportionately rare visits to the lavatory.

I know it's water and not anything else because I analyzed a few drops that fell near one of my sensors. What didn't match up at all was the taste: indescribably insipid, but no wonder—it was ordinary *aqua destilata*. Men really have some perverse leanings....

That the second guest was going to cause a lot more problems became clear when he gave his first order. He was not satisfied with the introductory page of my menu, on which I kept the meals that could be most easily produced under existing conditions, but browsed idly through my recipe book, clicking his tongue or licking his lips from time to time, which I found disgusting—but that was the least of it.

When he finally made his choice, I nearly fainted: filets of golden perch *bonne femme* and a torte of Sicilian cheese with strawberries! Just imagine! I never even knew that I had it on the menu. Strawberries could be dealt with somehow, but how was I to make a perch for him, and a golden one at that, let alone the Sicilian cheese? I embarked upon some real alchemy and finally managed to fool him with the fruit and fish, producing something that distantly resembled the flavor. In any case, he made no objections, though he didn't look too delighted either, and the poor surrogate for Sicilian cheese I offered in desperation sent him over the edge. Imagine, he gave me an extensive lecture on the way it is made, spiced with many odd, rather disgusting details, among which the most prominent was that the cheese absolutely had to ferment for several days under a layer of stale cow-droppings, but only from pregnant cows, because, supposedly, only this gave it its "unique aroma!" Phew! I'm glad I didn't have to taste it myself.

The one useful consequence of this culinary orgy was my discovery that this guest was definitely from Sicily. Only a born Sicilian could have such detailed knowledge of the secrets of manufacturing such a weird delicacy. The thought chilled me: I never would have thought that Sri was involved with the Mafia....

The shock lasted for only a short while and was dispelled by a circumstance that only then entered the focus of my mind. The new guest had indisputably been born in Sicily, yes, but when? If the old geezer isn't just as eccentric in his dress as he is in his gourmand's habits, then the robes he wears undeniably prove that he is from another time. Because who in his right mind wears a toga in this day and age?

When I first saw him in the clearing in front of the temple, in the mental picture created for me by the baby, it seemed to me that he had only a large cloth wrapped around him, a rather ragged and dirty one at that. Only when I reached deep into the historical files of my memory did I realize what it was. The worst thing was a large dark red blotch on the chest of the toga, a blotch that radiated from a hole obviously made by some sharp instrument. I didn't need to make a chemical analysis to know that it was clotted blood.

But the old geezer didn't seem to mind, which meant that either he had taken the toga off some previous owner who, for obvious reasons, didn't need it any more (the thought horrified me even more than the recipe with stale cow droppings) or that his wound had healed already and the poor fellow didn't have a change of clothes. In any case, I couldn't stand to see him in that rag, so I picked out a cotton T-shirt and the trousers of a tracksuit from among Sri's things and offered them to him as a temporary replacement for the tattered toga. He turned them over in his hands for some time, obviously not sure how to put them on, which confirmed my belief that he was not from our time. (But how...? No, no hows and whys, we agreed; things are simply to be taken as they are. Probably one day all will be explained....)

Despite all his weirdness and his spoiled ways with food, I could have learned to like the old guy—he is actually a nice man, much livelier than Sri and Buddha—if he hadn't turned the house, the cleanliness of which I used to be so proud of (until the turtles arrived), into a pigsty. All right, I can understand that he came here to hold boring male conversations from morning till night with Sri and Buddha; if they have nothing better to do, let them talk, however neglected I may feel; but was it really necessary to cover the entire floor of the temple with dust and sand, dirtying it beyond hope of ever cleaning it again, just so that they could feverishly draw circles in it? Couldn't it have been done much more effectively on one of my monitors? That might at least have created an opportunity for me too to finally find out what is, in fact, going on.

5. EXECUTIONER

THE THREE OF US stepped into the kingdom of the underworld.

First my Master, who had sold his vainglorious, self-loving soul to the devil a long time ago in exchange for that marvelous talent that made divine faces and figures flow from his long fingers, images by which he enmeshed many gullible eyes in terrible deceit; for is there a worse, more cunning sin than to paint saints on monastic walls with a skill inspired by the extreme malice of Sotona?

And then came I, God's miserable servant, who knew this—but did not want to know. My silence sheltered behind many justifications, valid in another, earlier age, but none could now bring me salvation, for I have already walked into hell to receive my rightful punishment. But at least I did so without a sinner's complaint, demonstrating my full repentance, bottomless humility, and the sincere wish to earn heavenly redemption by long, hard suffering.

After me came the woman I had shamefully held to be Marya, despite the many signs that categorically informed me that she could not be the one whom she, with that beautiful face, impersonated. Would the real Marya, the Queen of Heaven, have returned the dead Master to life, knowing that he was but the worthless servant of the Lord of Hades? Would she have committed with him the most terrible sin, which cannot appear even in the most secret thoughts without smearing forever her whole soul with filth? Would she walk with me into the nether kingdom, where her twice-sacred foot could never tread?

Yet here she is, following my fearful self down the worm-eaten, rotting ladder leading from the entrance in the cellar to the first circle of the devil's lair, as if she had trod this path without return countless times before. Finally we reached the bottom of the fateful ladder, which sinners can descend only. The source of the glow of fires and the poisonous stench were soon descried, striking my convulsed soul with a deep chill: a cold that became no less when the woman, whom I had sinfully taken for Marya, again put her frail hand on my bony shoulder granting me once more the benefit of the current that flowed from it.

The scene that stretched before my tear-filled, failing eyes, dismal wherever their gaze could reach, instantly shook my brave determination to take my punishment with penitent gratitude. Had I seen even Sotona himself, the most merciless executioner of the world below, it would be a sight merely terrible, but not other-worldly, for what is the chief of all the evil spirits of Hades if not just one among the fallen angels, who kept his first countenance, though changed terribly?

But those amidst which I now found my worthless self had no human marks at all, neither vigorous limbs, nor a slender body, nor even the blessed face that is the expression and window of our eternal soul. Innumerable spheres, each as tall as a man's knees, thickly covered the infernal ground of the first circle, glowing with a soft rosy luster. Despite the perfection of their form, these miraculous things were from some other Creation, and not the Lord's, for the Almighty could never have made these in His own image, as He did with all other creatures that grace the pied globe.

Yet these balls of many colors, though not sprung from God's spirit, were not unliving things: as I gazed on them in perplexity, three of them, not far from us, began to swell and in an instant grew in stature from knee-high to the height of a man's hip, at which their distended bodies burst thunderously, like an overblown blacksmith's bellows. When a thick greenish fog had gushed from their torn bodies and dissipated, three new spheres stood in their place, the same height as the others.

And when tendrils of the fog from their entrails reached the gray hairs of my old nostrils, nausea assailed me, so powerfully that for a moment I swayed on my feet and put my trembling hands to my face. This then was the terrible stench from which I had recoiled at the cellar entrance into the gullet of hell! A stench that I, in my ignorance, had thought merely the rank foulness of the devil I saw now came from the gross swelling of these unearthly creatures. I thought that if I were sentenced to dwell for all eternity among these balls, to breathe in their stench, which is worse than that of a rotting corpse, then my sin must be greater and more vile than I had miserably supposed even in moments of deepest repentance!

But there was no time for belated penitent contemplation: Marya's hand on my bony shoulder pushed me gently forward, and only then did I become aware that, while I was trying in disgust to keep back the stink of the terrible other-worldly spheres, my Master was striding among them, guided by some secret purpose. And lo, I beheld a new miracle: the balls moved aside obediently to let him pass, pressing each other as if they were a flock of sheep in a narrow pen and he a stern shepherd, and the way was thus opened for us all.

But whither? Taken by a sudden apprehension that this awful stench was not my final punishment, I turned my helpless, imploring eyes on Marya, but on her beautiful face remained the same smile. Was this the joyful expression of a guardian angel who had taken my sinful self under her wing, or the malicious grin of an evil spirit gloating beforehand over my future torment?

Torn by these twofold thoughts, I moved irresolutely after the Master, toward encounter with my unknown destiny. But our slow progress through the spheres that moved aside for us as one and closed again in a dense crowd behind us was not to last long. My Master had hardly gone but twenty steps when he stopped abruptly.

I lacked any opportunity to wonder at this strange, unexpected halt amid another field of balls, for three of them, immediately ahead of us, swelled rapidly. Warned by previous experience, I put my hand to my nose, to protect myself from the pestilent malodor that I knew would gush forth any moment now when the guts of these creatures burst open.

But it was not so.

The spheres reached the height of my waist without breaking up, and when two stopped swelling, their glow turned from rosy to black. The third continued to swell enormously, its leathery membrane growing ever thinner, until it reached the height of a man, or even a little over.

My hands slid of their own accord down my wrinkled face when a new marvel manifested itself before my eyes: a face, unclear at first, showed under the now transparent membrane of the biggest ball, amid the green fog that had thinned considerably. I stepped forward and lowered my head, the better to behold this miserable apparition, the monstrous destiny of which was to dwell shut up with the most dreadful stench for eternity. What terrible, unforgivable sin must that woeful creature have committed to merit such harsh punishment? Was there a sin great enough to call forth such enormous wrath from the Lord?

I soon received an answer, for regarding it closely, I saw a soldier inside, so wild and cruel in his mien that his appearance alone would send his opponents fleeing in horror. This soldier came not from our Christian times, but from an ancient pagan army, and was the one who had scourged Hrist Himself with a three-lashed knotted whip, driving Him bleeding and crowned with thorns to carry His cross on frail shoulders up the hill of Calvary to the crucifixion, that heavenly salvation for us, the later born.

In a twinkling, my previous pity for his ghastly destiny changed to avenging glee that the Lord's justice had caught up with the criminal, perhaps the most heinous of all, and allotted a punishment that might even be too mild. Are there indeed any tortures meet for the murderers of the Son of God, that they might expiate their hideous crime? No! Were this infectious green fog a hundred, a thousand times more malodorous, it would still be the finest perfume in comparison to that immeasurably evil transgression!

Blinded by sudden fury, I began raising my feeble old fists to repay him through the thin membrane for the sufferings of our Savior, though it be with such weak blows, but my anger was not destined to be vented as I so dearly wished. For hardly had I raised my clenched fists to the level of my head and taken a short swing, when the Roman soldier moved adroitly and more swiftly than I. Drawing his sharp sword, he swiftly drove it through the tense membrane of the swollen sphere, burying it to the hilt just under my ribs.

We stood thus as if turned to stone for a few moments, he observing me with a blank, cross-eyed look, which seemed to wander beyond me, and I staring dully back at him, filled with a multitude of questions. But I had no time for any of them, nor even to feel the sharp pain, for as soon as the executioner withdrew his sword from my chest, a bottomless abyss seemed to yawn under me and I slid inexorably into it, into thick darkness and endless silence, the which brings blessed oblivion to doomed souls.

6. SHERLOCK HOLMES'S LAST CASE (2)
GHOST

"BUT MORIARTY IS dead!" I said in amazement.

The look that Holmes shot me was enough to make me doubt the accuracy of that statement, one that I had until now considered to be beyond any reasonable doubt, and I hastened to add:

"Isn't he?"

He did not reply but turned towards the window and looked through the gap between the curtains into the night. Even on my way here, the fog had been closing in, and by now it lay heavily all around so that the glow from the nearby street-lamp seemed blurred and subdued. All looked hazy and unreal, this late London autumn.

As he clasped his hands behind his back, Holmes tugged the fingers of one hand with the other, causing a characteristic cracking sound. He would do this from time to time when he was deep in thought, probably because it helped him to concentrate. People tend to have such mannerisms—usually they drum on the table or on the armrest of the chair—not caring one whit that it gets on the nerves of others. I was indeed irritated by this cracking of his knuckles; I had mentioned it to him several times, but he continued to make the noise, probably quite unaware that he was doing so.

"But Holmes," I said, addressing his back, "I was personally present when Moriarty's corpse was taken out of the lake. The water was very cold, so that the body had remained well preserved. There was no doubt whatsoever; it was him all right. What's more, I assisted later at the autopsy. His lungs were full of water—"

"I know, I know," Holmes interrupted, continuing to stare vacantly into the foggy night. "But never underestimate Moriarty."

This statement startled me. Had it not been made in an extremely serious voice, I would have thought that Holmes was in a playful mood and was pulling my leg. That would not have been unlike him; he enjoyed seeing my confusion and bewilderment when he proposed some inconceivable idea. However, not infrequently it would happen that the impossible turned out to be possible after all, so that in such circumstances I had always to be careful. One never really knew where one was with Holmes.

"Come now," I said, not wishing to deny him the pleasure of the surprise I thought he might have prepared for me. "You are not going to tell me that you believe in ghosts?"

He turned and looked at me with a piercing gaze in which superiority and contempt battled for dominance.

"What do *you* know about ghosts, Watson?"

"Well, I...don't know...." I blustered. "I mean, some people believe...but science...."

"Science is only a small vessel, a cup perhaps, with which a quite negligible volume of positive knowledge has been lifted from a veritable ocean of ignorance," he said, in the tone of a teacher who is lecturing an unruly pupil. "However much that vessel may be enlarged, it will never contain the whole ocean."

What could I say to this? Had I countered in any way whatsoever, we would have embarked upon one of those long, futile arguments, entirely devoted to matters of principle, which he vastly enjoyed, having assigned me the role of the naive, rather thickheaded interlocutor who ought to be enlightened but first exposed to mockery—the Socrates syndrome.

But this was not an appropriate moment for that game: if Moriarty truly were behind the letter—though I still could not see how that was possible—then there was no time at all for fruitless debate. Fortunately, Holmes seemed to be aware of this too, for he soon changed the topic of conversation.

"Besides," he went on, in a rather more moderate voice, "who said anything about ghosts?"

"How else could someone who has been dead for weeks post a letter unless he is a ghost? Not that I can really see how a ghost could post a letter, either, but—that's another matter."

"Didn't I tell you not to underestimate Moriarty, Watson? In fact, it does not take any particular ingenuity to see how it could have been carried out."

This sting was, of course, aimed at me, because I was still unenlightened. I decided therefore to risk airing a thought that had just come to me, though it sounded extremely silly, even to me.

"Reincarnation," I said, or rather whispered, in an almost God-fearing tone.

"What?" said Holmes, in genuine disbelief.

That was what I had been afraid of. I had not guessed correctly, and now I would have to offer an explanation.

"I mean...you mentioned it yourself...the ancient Egyptian *Book of the Dead*...and that cult in Tibet, what was its name...the soul coming back to life in a new body...."

Holmes interrupted me angrily. "I know what reincarnation is, but Moriarty did not go in for that, at least not that we know of. There are, admittedly, several hazy patches in his biography, when he was lost to the world for weeks at a time, but I don't think he reached Tibet. Although...."

He paused for a moment, as if sidetracked by a sudden thought that threatened to undermine his previous self-assurance, but did not allow it to gain momentum; he briefly shook his head and continued: "No, I give no credit to such a thought...And if he was involved with local amateurs vainly attempting to imitate the Dalai Lama, then he could, at best, have returned to life as a radish or a ladybird. But radishes and ladybirds do not send letters, Watson."

I had, therefore, once again imprudently jumped the gun. Never mind, it was not the first time. There was nothing else for it but to ask contritely for an explanation. Indeed, this was what Holmes was waiting for, and we ought to please our friends, ought we not?

"So, what did happen?" I asked meekly.

"Occam's razor, my dear chap, Occam's razor. When assumptions begin to swarm, choose the simplest one."

He must have repeated this sentence at least a hundred times before, in various situations, just as he had told and retold the story of the remarkable William of Occam. Only, what was the good of that, when I had as yet proved less than dexterous in wielding that "razor?" Very well, all the glory belongs to the adroit Holmes. Let us hear the rest.

"Moriarty did send the letter, Watson, but not while dead; he did it while he was still alive. I assume he did the following: he paid someone to deliver the letter to my address on a certain day, namely today, and in an anonymous manner—by sliding it under the front door, so as not to give me the opportunity of questioning the bearer. This arrangement would have been cancelled only if he personally went to the bearer and withdrew the original instruction, which, I surmise, he would indeed have done had he not perished in the lake. Since his arrival in person did not occur for self-evident reasons, the letter was delivered and—here it is. Simple, is it not?"

It really was simple, seen in this *post festum* light. So it always was with Holmes's elucidations. I had indeed good reason to feel sheepish. Reincarnation! Really!

"Splendid, Mr. Holmes," I said sincerely. "The matter is therefore resolved."

"Nothing is resolved, my dear Watson," replied Holmes quietly.

I looked at him, perplexed. "But we know who the sender was, and the method of delivery too."

"Indeed. But these are marginal details. The real problems are only just beginning to appear. We must first discover why Moriarty wanted the letter to reach me only in the eventuality of his death. Then we must establish the meaning of the message."

"You mean—this circle?"

"Yes, but please do not embark upon rash and unfounded reasoning again," said he in a voice that brooked no objection. "The matter is far more serious than one might conclude at a glance."

I had no intention of embarking upon anything. I recalled vividly how he had flared up at my initial comment about the circle. I had no desire to provoke such a reaction again.

"What are you suggesting, then?" I asked dutifully.

"Tell me, what do you know about the circle?" he riposted with a question.

I considered this for a moment. It is strange the trouble one can find oneself in at such times when you are caught out in ignorance about some quite simple matter. What is there to be known about circles, anyway? I attempted to recall knowledge I had acquired a long while ago at geometry lessons, but very little managed to float up to the surface.

"Well...it is a geometrical body...."

"Figure," he corrected me. "Figure, Watson. Figures have two dimensions, bodies have three."

"Figure, of course." I accepted the correction readily. "Well, figure, then...It's perfect, as you said...and connected with it is a constant, signified by a Greek letter...I think it's 'phi' or 'mu' or some such...I am not sure...It is obtained by multiplying something, but surely you don't expect me to remember what? The last time I attended a mathematics lecture was a good forty years ago, and in the meantime I have not had much reason to concern myself with circles, nor is the discipline one of my strong points."

"Pity," replied Holmes tersely, in his usual tone of cold contempt. "A real pity. Can you surmise how many entries related to the circle there are in the *Encyclopaedia Britannica*?"

Of course I could not, but so as not to disappoint him, I ventured a modest estimate.

"Five?" I said in a half-questioning tone, giving him an opportunity to show his superiority by proving me wrong immediately, which he, of course, did not fail to do.

"Forty-three, my dear Watson, forty-three! And only the first three or four are mathematical. The others have nothing to do with the discipline in which you, it is clear, are not well versed. The Greek letter is π, and it happens to be the constant that is obtained by dividing the circumference of the circle by its radius."

"Really?" I asked ingenuously. "I shall have to memorize that. One never knows when it might come in handy. But, what are all those other entries about?"

Holmes's gaze drifted somewhere above me but without really focusing on the upper parts of the walls or the ceiling. It had sailed off to uncharted, distant lands as was usually the case when he was preparing for some philosophical discourse. To me, this pose seemed artificial, even comical, but he clearly enjoyed it.

"You cannot even begin to imagine to what extent the circle is integrated into the very foundations of human history. Its secrets were known even in prehistoric times. Evidence of that is everywhere, even in our vicinity, not far from London."

"You mean...?"

"Yes, Watson! Splendid! Stonehenge!"

I had not thought of Stonehenge at all; something entirely different had been on my mind, something that may not have been prehistoric at all—I wasn't sure about that point—but naturally I did not admit to this. I only nodded my head to suggest that we were in full agreement. Sometimes it can be very useful not to finish one's sentences.

"Everything at Stonehenge revolves around the circle as a symbol, starting with the cyclical chronometer that Stonehenge, among other things, is, and ending with the very shape of that megalithic monument."

"I know, I've been there," I remarked with some self-confidence.

Holmes gave me a look, probably only exchanged by initiates in knowledge of the arcane, and continued.

"The *Encyclopaedia* mentions the circle as the basis of many other sites of ancient civilizations. The Aztec settlements, for instance, were built as groups of concentric circles, the shrines of the first inhabitants of the islands of Japan have a circle—the Sun—as their fundamental symbol, and even the primitive cave paintings of earliest man from equatorial Africa contain strange circular ornaments. Then we cross into historical times...."

But I did not allow him to cross, seizing the opportunity to interrupt him at a moment when he paused for breath; he was, undoubtedly, carried away by the theme, and at such times he would begin to speak faster, even to clip off parts of words, which at moments left him breathless.

"This is all very interesting, Holmes, but I fail to see how it is linked to Moriarty's letter."

He winced, frustrated because by interrupting I had denied him the chance to expound, as was his habit and as all unfulfilled storytellers are wont to do: but his voice was surprisingly conciliatory as he answered.

"I also fail to see it, but some link there must be. Moriarty has sent me the ultimate challenge, one from beyond the grave, and it would be foolish to expect that we shall get the better of him without vast effort. A great task therefore awaits us, Watson, perhaps the greatest and most difficult of all we have faced until the present moment."

"Us?" I asked in puzzlement. "I do not know how I could help here...I mean, my grasp of the secrets of the circle is, to say the least, insuff—"

"Worry not, my friend," replied Holmes cheerfully. "You will not be bypassed in this case above all cases. There are tasks for you, entirely in accordance with your very meager cognizance of these things."

He rummaged absentmindedly through his pockets for a few moments, looking for something. He finally found it not there, but on the writing table where it had been compiled. It was a longish list of books, written in his nervous, cramped handwriting, with many letters omitted and many words abbreviated. It seemed that only I, apart from Holmes himself, could extract any modicum of meaning from those hieroglyphics.

"Here," said he eagerly, "I would ask that tomorrow morning, at the very moment of its opening, you be at the British Museum Library. You will look for Sir Arthur, the director. He will make an exception in my case and allow you to take these books out. Hurry straight back here with them. We have no time to spare, Watson. The Great Clock is striking!"

7. Mattress and Fear

WE'VE GOT A real masquerade going on here.

The toga of the previous arrival is nothing compared to the costume of the new one. A good ten or so milliseconds slipped by before I finally managed to dig it out of my history memory banks: the dress of a sixteenth-century Flemish nobleman, no less!

All of it ever so ornate and frilly—in total contrast to Sri's cotton T-shirts and bermudas, even to the Buddhist robe that he almost never wears now, though Buddha in person is his guest. The Flemish chap has a tricorn hat with some rather revolting feathers curving backwards on it; I wonder which particular bird they had to pluck to get them? The jungle is teeming with exotic birds, but I haven't seen anything quite as lurid as these on any of them.

The silliest part of the latest guest's costume is right below the hat: an enormously wide collar, all pleated and stiffly starched, like the plaster brace hospitals put on people who have broken a neck bone. Because of this, he holds his head unnaturally high in an attitude of extreme haughtiness. He certainly must be very uncomfortable in clothes like that in this hot, moist climate, but it apparently never crosses his mind to take them off. The sacrifices men are prepared to make just to keep up with fashion...

All his other clothes are also oversized and weighty. To begin with, a thick linen shirt, hairy and rough, without a collar; if he's got no under-shirt on underneath it, then I can't imagine how he puts up with the constant scratching it must cause. I get goose bumps just thinking about it. Over the shirt he wears a rough waistcoat of heavy cloth, embroidered and ornamented, with a profusion of small pockets where he keeps a variety of stuff, including a little bottle that he takes out from time to time to sniff at the contents, which makes him shudder a little in obvious pleasure. Recently this has been accompanied by a rather embarrassed expression, probably because no one else at the temple does this.

Over the waistcoat he wears a sort of long jacket or short coat of dark blue, made of some stiff cloth, brocade perhaps, with lots of cloth-covered buttons and puffed upper sleeves; it was probably designed to narrow at the waist but it's hard to tell since the man is about ten kilograms overweight—by the standards of our time, that is—and who knows what was considered appropriate in his. (Clearly he is also a time traveler, like the old Sicilian, but we're agreed: no questions on that point....)

On top of all that he wears a cloak or mantle, with dark red lining, the hem streaked with dried mud. As the monsoon rains are now over, this must be a memento from his own world and era. The man from Flanders takes it off only in the evening when he goes to sleep and uses it as a blanket.

Of course I offered him normal bedding, but an unforeseen problem arose, so that he now doesn't use any bed at all. Thinking he would like it, being a traveler from afar who must be tired, I gave him Sri's favorite mattress with built-in vibrators, which oscillate in a deep-sleep rhythm, but this scared him so badly that he jumped out of bed as if he'd been shot and fled in panic into an empty corner, devoid of technical devices, where he's been sleeping ever since.

There he simply lies down on the bare floor, covering himself with his cloak. At first I found this terribly embarrassing; what kind of a hostess was I if my guests had to sleep on the floor? Later, as our Fleming evidently didn't mind, I decided to play it cool. After all, Sri, as the head of the family, didn't give a hoot. On the contrary, he found it all extremely funny; when our poor guest was first scared by the vibrating mattress, he clapped his hands over his mouth and rushed out of the temple together with Buddha, the two of them fairly doubled up with laughter. Fine behavior for high-minded devotees of Nirvana.

I was almost tempted to do the same on another occasion. When, again thanks to the baby's intervention, I saw the new guest for the first time in the clearing in front of the temple where he and his sort materialize out of nothing, what most caught my eye, not counting the frilly clothes, was his hair. He has a head of hair any woman would envy: long silvery locks down to his shoulders forming a luxurious mane. For this sort of hairstyle, you first need excellent hair, and then to spend hours at the hairdresser's. Only rarely does a woman have the good fortune to look like that naturally, so it's most unfair when a man can boast of that kind of hair.

Just one look at the Fleming after his first night in the temple was enough for me to realize that something was wrong with his hairdo. All right, nobody looks great in the early morning, but with him it wasn't just that. His hair had not lost its wonderful waviness, it lay somehow unnaturally...askew.

And then it dawned on me!

How could I have been so stupid? But of course! The man has a wig! I had a strong desire to laugh. I'm like that sometimes; I think I probably get rid of accumulated tension that way—through unrestrained, almost hysterical laughter. It really gets on Sri's nerves, which in turn makes me laugh even more, which unnerves him further, making a feedback loop—sometimes one very difficult to undo.

Luckily, I managed to stop myself at the last moment. I think the Fleming would have been vastly insulted, not so much because I'd discovered his secret—obviously men were not secretive about wearing toupees in the epoch he comes from—but rather because he would have concluded that I think that that decorative object of which he is so proud doesn't suit him.

Since that first night when he was so distracted he forgot to take off his wig, he's taken the greatest care of it before going to bed on each successive evening and in the morning spending a long time in front of the mirror, titivating and arranging every curl. His natural hair, by the way, is short and already thinning, with a large bald spot on the top of his head. Serves him right—I can't help thinking maliciously.

There have been some culinary problems with the Fleming, too, but quite the opposite of the ones with the old Sicilian geezer. Not only has he made outlandish demands, but I've actually had to beg him to taste the food from my microwave ovens. It's not that he shares Buddha's ascetic convictions on food, no. On the contrary, the man is as hungry as a wolf: he practically drools, watching enviously as the old-timer greedily polishes off dish after dish from my menu, one more exotic than the next.

(I must admit my vanity was flattered when finally, after I'd made something like ten attempts, he mildly praised the quality of the cheese I had synthesized, remarking that "probably nothing better could be expected at such a distance from Sicily": this, though I did it without those all-important pregnant cow droppings....)

In all likelihood, the unfortunate experience with the mattress has caused our man from Flanders to distrust all and any technology, so that he spent a good two days without food, until finally his endangered biology drove him to take a bite, thereby easing the prejudices and fears caused by what seemed to have been a severe bout of future shock which, surprisingly, seems to have missed the Sicilian.

That old chap has been having a lot of fun examining and trying out every device he can lay his hands on, quite undeterred by several sputtering, sparking shorts caused by his inexperienced attempts, or even a minor fire, which Sri put out in time so that no serious damage was done.

He especially enjoys communicating with me, though that began rather slowly, since I was not what you'd call well-versed in classical Greek, although I've been getting better from day to day.

We've started some very interesting and learned debates on various subjects, from ethics to gastronomy, and in these I have to be careful not to confuse him by stepping out of his age into a more recent era. Apparently he isn't even aware that he's been moved into another time; he believes that he died, in fact that he's been killed, and is now in a sort of paradise, or something of the kind. I haven't tried to dissuade him, especially since I myself am not too sure about quite a lot of things.

I think that it was in fact the Sicilian's lack of inhibition in his approach to me—much more than Sri's efforts to persuade him—that finally got the Fleming to come over to my keyboard. This was for some reason very important to Sri, while I must admit I felt a bit embarrassed, at least in the beginning. It looked to me rather as if he were offering me to the guest, to make his stay in our home more enjoyable. As if we were Eskimos, God forbid!

Luckily, it turned out considerably more innocent than that, and I didn't meet with a fate worse than death. What it came down to was that Sri had written a very simple program, to which the Fleming has devoted himself completely. So much so, in fact, that nothing else seems to exist for him.

I don't believe I'll ever understand men. What is it in them that tethers them so fast to some moronic interest of theirs that they completely lose sight of all the other beautiful things in the world? What does this gaudy, jittery Fleming see in Sri's trivial program for computing decimals of the number π, that has made him give up his days and nights to it, practically never taking his eyes off the monitor, across which the numbers march in a slow, unending procession? And how is it, after staring so much at it, that he doesn't develop an ache in that head stuck in that ghastly collar?

8. BLACK CRUCIFIXION

INTO SILENCE AND darkness I sank, though not for long.

From a great distance, far, far away, a familiar voice seemed to be calling me, though I could not recognize whose, nor even if it was a woman's or a man's. When in perplexity I opened my mouth to reply, to ask the many questions still swarming at the edge of my consciousness though eluding my will, a small hand was laid gently on my dry lips to check the vain words at source.

This feather-light touch drove away at once my strange, dreamless sleep, in which my soul seemed to dwell in the forecourts of Hades, and I slowly opened my eyes. As sight returned, my fettered memory awoke at once, and my hand moved quickly to my breast to touch the terrible wound the cross-eyed Roman had dealt me with his deadly sword but a few moments before. But there was no wound: not even a tear in my ragged robe, nor any scar under it on my wrinkled skin.

I looked up in surprise at Marya, for it was her hand on my questioning lips, but received no answer, only that old, double-edged smile, foretelling salvation and disaster. Left to my own poor devices, I glanced around for some explanation of this miracle, which had brought me unexpected deliverance, but found new wonders awaiting me.

We stood in the second circle of Hell, for here was not a trace of those swelling balls that served as stinking prison cells for the worst miscreants. Though no less dreary than the previous circle, as befits the kingdom of the underworld, at least this new place did not seem unearthly, for I at once recognized all that was in it. Had I not known what I did know, I might have thought in my ignorance that we were in the middle of some damp chamber, such as princes are wont to keep in their castle fortresses, to torture their subjects into full obedience, which princes expect to receive by natural right from the lower orders and serfs.

I myself never was, thanks be to God, in any such terrible place although, long ago, my Master received from a depraved prince, known far and wide for his cruelty, a commission to adorn his torture chamber with scenes of the horrors of Hell, so that the wretches dragged thence should before being put to the test lose all hope of an easy or painless deliverance, even did they readily confess to everything. For that cruel lord was insatiable for torture and cared not a whit for confession, be it sincere or insincere.

To my great fright, my Master, the only man capable of faithfully depicting scenes from Hell, as he was later to demonstrate when he portrayed it in all its ugliness in an another place infinitely more inappropriate, refused the commission for reasons unknown to me, refused with hauteur, so that we had to run under cover of night to seek sanctuary in a neighboring duchy. This merciless overlord issued the dire threat that he would one day seize us and force us to do the job, promising us a new reward for our trouble: doing us the special honor of first trying out on us each one of the diabolical tortures that the Master would be made to depict on the walls.

Finding myself in the nether kingdom, remembrance of this past event now chilled me to the soul because for an instant it seemed that the fatal threat of that bloodthirsty mountain prince had finally overtaken us in the worst possible manner and that he would at any moment appear in the shape of Sotona himself to carry out his horrid threat with the greatest pleasure.

And alas, wherever I looked I saw horrid instruments for this exacting of debts; tools that only the most perverse imagination could have invented for exposing the frail human frame to inconceivable suffering. On a blazing hearth were the glowing coals that give to heavy iron its white and raging heat, that it may leave its burning brand on quivering human flesh, the pain of which drives men quite mad. And there, the torturer's table with its iron-winched rack that serves to stretch the body beyond measure and tear its doomed victim apart, plucking his limbs or head from the body. I saw also a great pendulum, its cutting edge finely honed, designed to descend slowly but inexorably from the ceiling, cutting with every fatal arc a deeper slash in the soft body, but so slowly that a seeming infinity must pass before the edge of the pendulum reaches the other side of the poor wretch's frame.

Other devices of torture were there, the use of which I could not begin to divine but of an aspect so loathsome that those I recognized appeared in comparison to be but the harmless tools of some common trade. To what unimaginable anguish is the prisoner exposed in that narrow, coffin-like chest? Does the window in it, placed where the prisoner's face must be, afford the devil an opportunity to feed in cackling pleasure on the convulsions and screams of the hopeless sinner? What filth bubbles in that large cauldron, under which no fire burns? And what is that slimy, scaly thing within, which swims up to the surface from time to time to let out a harrowing, hungry shriek that instantly curdles even the bravest blood? And what mutilation is caused by those heavy boots, braced tightly with metal hoops, beside which a pile of human bones lies crushed and gleaming in spectral whiteness?

But of all these dread devices, one in particular, the largest of them all, caused me the greatest perplexity. A huge wheel stood in the center of the second circle of the devil's lair, laid flat like an enormous platter: it had no sharp edges for cutting off a body's extended parts, no sharp spikes to pierce its soft entrails, no raging fire to burn one with insufferable heat.

Moved by a foolish curiosity, I approached this odd instrument, when on my bony shoulder I felt again Marya's hand, from which a current of reinvigoration flowed anew. I started at this light touch, suddenly afraid that she was preparing me for some new horror, pouring new strength into me that I might better endure yet another test, maybe harsher than all I had so far undergone.

But a careful, searching look revealed nothing that might support these black suspicions. The upper surface of the great circle looked entirely flat, even smooth, as if an industrious carpenter had spent many days polishing it; only at four places were there broad leather bindings, to fix the victim's limbs and so deny him escape from an unknown but surely warranted fate. It was easy to see that the arms would be outstretched as our Savior's were on the holy cross, the legs spread wide in an immodest manner, so that the hands and feet touched the very edge of the wheel, where was a shallow groove whose purpose I could not, at that moment, yet define.

When I examined this groove more closely, bending down to aid my failing eye-sight, I saw it was filled with strange patterns, signs beyond my ken, such as those found in sacred tomes or those that the Master put at times along the base of his frescoes. I regretted now that I had not obeyed his wise counsel to learn the secrets of such letters, but I had always thought that this knowledge was necessary only to idle monachs and not to ordinary mortals, such as I considered myself to be.

These signs were drawn on fields of different colors, alternately red and black, and only one of them, quite round, lay on a field of green, standing out in its particularity, as if it were the beginning and end of a closed sequence. Moved by a sudden impulse, I walked around the edge of this massive wheel and counted on the fingers of both hands three times ten and once seven of these symbols. This made me no wiser, for among the marks of neither God nor Sotona could I remember any that would fit that number.

I looked at Marya, who had not yet taken her hand from my shoulder, but had no time to ask her for an explanation. Nor was it probable that

I would get one, even had events not taken a new turn, for this woman of divine countenance but mayhap demonic nature had not yet uttered a word since my first seeing her, as if she knew not how to speak, or thought me unworthy to hear her angelic voice.

Just then, the sharp ringing of a bell filled my ears with deafening noise from all sides, as if I were standing in a great cave and not in the torture chambers of Hell. I turned around this way and that, seeking with my weak eyes the source of this ringing sound, but saw something else, alas, that filled my soul at once with mighty dread.

It was the most peculiar procession that I had ever seen. At its head strode the Master, garbed in a long black cape spangled with stars reaching to the stone floor. On his head was a cap like the pointed donjon of a nobleman's castle, made of the same star-spangled cloth, adding to his normal stature. I could hardly recognize him thus tricked out and only then remembered that I had not until this moment noticed his absence from this second circle of Hell.

The most remarkable thing about the Master was not these strange garments but rather what he held in his hands. In one he held a royal scepter, glinting with golden reflections, and in the other a large orb made of some cloudy transparent substance, the surface of which gave off distorted reflections of surrounding objects. I had no time to wonder at my Master's new, unbecoming accouterments, because my gaze slid immediately, irresistibly, to two other figures walking behind him in the procession.

The first was of such repulsive mien that I would have fled headlong had I not felt Marya's light hand on my shoulder, infusing me with a fresh, steady flow of calmness. It was a huge insect, as high as the Master's chest, with a multitude of legs slender as willow twigs. I could not understand how they bore the enormous weight of that burly body, nor how they moved so harmoniously in a very complex, regular order, as if following with the intensity of a dancer to the sounds of music inaudible to me.

It most resembled a monstrous spider, harbinger of manifold evil and woe—and verily, he dragged a cobweb after him, not at all thin but matching in thickness the size of the strange creature. A rattling sound reached my ears, driving away that illusion as I recognized, in what I had foolishly thought to be a strand of cobweb, an iron chain with links as thick as a man's finger, which led from one of the spider's many legs back to the third figure. For a moment this calmed me, for I thought that this must be a brave tamer holding his terrible beast under strict control on an unbreakable chain, as the bear-tamers lead their grey animals around at country fairs in the autumn. But when this figure stepped into stronger light, I saw two things at once—and my soul filled with utter horror.

The thick chain from the spider's leg reached back to the third participant in the strange procession, yes, but did not end in the tamer's hand; instead, it was joined to an iron collar around the man's neck, put there as on the meanest slave. Here everything was reversed: this monstrous insect led a man on a chain, not the other way around, as would be the only natural state of affairs and pleasing to the Lord—but lo, he was not even a man. For when I looked more closely, I recognized by many unmistakable signs our host in this underground dwelling place: the fallen angel, the one who dared vaingloriously to gainsay the Lord: the Prince of Darkness, who forever reaches out for faltering human souls: Sotona the mighty, who lured my Master by flattering gifts into the worst sin.

Above his high forehead stood two blunt horns, disfiguring a countenance that was otherwise human. A hairy tail, terminating in an ominous arrow head, dragged on the cold stone floor after him. His body was thick and humped, enveloped in a black cloak, its hem streaked with dried mud and lined in brightest scarlet, which his tottering gait, akin to the Devil on goat's hooves, caused to blaze forth from time to time.

Of all this, my gaze lingered most upon his countenance—that of a hopeless convict being led to inevitable execution. A long trail of sweat meandered down his quivering cheek, and his lips pursed in little twitches, revealing vast unrest of the soul. Had this been a poor servant of God, these would have been clear signs of mortal fear besetting the wretch in his most difficult, fatal hour. But the Devil himself this was, who stood beyond all fear from the moment in which the Lord decreed the greatest punishment for him. For what could be worse than his lot, to dwell for eternity in the mud and excrement of the nether world? I could not imagine it but was not destined to wait long for an answer to this question to be revealed in all its hellish wonder.

Although unmarked with the sacred sign of the cross, the great wheel terrified Sotona, causing him to pull back in savage frenzy when it became clear that his guides were proceeding relentlessly toward it. But the strength of the Devil, though it be beyond any human power, was naught to that of the spider, so that he was swiftly dragged to his circular doom despite his cries, so horrendous that even Marya's face twisted in pain for a moment, losing its angelic smile.

When finally strapped by the leather thongs to the smooth surface of the wooden wheel, Sotona fell quiet of a sudden, as if resigned without further complaint to his terrible fate. But his breast heaved rapidly under the black, flame-lined cloak; from his foul mouth a rapid mumbling came in a tongue quite unknown to me, like the last, black prayer before the end that nothing can postpone.

And at that moment, in my perplexity, I felt something that but an instant before I would have held for ultimate blasphemy and that could be counted among the gravest sins: a sudden wave of compassion for this poor creature of the underworld, whom merciless fate had exposed to final torment on a circular crucifix, torment no less than our Savior's on His cross at Golgotha. If it be the will of the Lord to inflict such revenge on the Devil, then they lie who say His mercy is infinite.

These doubting thoughts had no time to take hold of my unfaithful mind because my Master stepped nearer to offer me the gleaming orb that he had been holding in his hands with the golden scepter. I stood not knowing what to do with this wondrous gift, which was not for my rough hands, but Marya's touch on my shoulder became a little stronger, and a clear understanding came to me: the ball was to be placed in the circular, patterned groove, there to spin rapidly, describing a blazing ring around the spread-eagled Devil and seal his doom.

I shrank back from this awful intimation: was I to become his executioner, my ultimate destiny this, to be the instrument of God's harsh vengeance? But why? Why me, poor sinner that I am? I had a powerful wish to escape this heavy burden, but there was no resisting Marya's incorporeal will, which flowed from my shoulder into my mind, and I placed the orb into the groove filled with the signs on fields of three colors.

I gave it no impetus, but nonetheless it began to move at once along the groove, slowly, then faster, and after circling but a few times became a streak of bright light. With each new turn, Sotona's body convulsed more strongly, jerking this way and that, frantically trying to escape, like a wild stallion when a man first climbs upon his back. For a moment I feared that the leather bindings, although they looked sturdy, would not endure such frenzied pulling, that the Devil would free himself from the circular crucifix and punish his unwilling executioner, but it was not destined to be, fortunately or unfortunately for me.

At the climax of its mad gyrations, when the wheel had begun to shake violently, my Master unexpectedly struck his golden scepter on the stone floor. A sharp sound rang out, similar to the earlier echoing bell, and the spinning ball, as if it had hidden ears, quickly decelerated and lost its brightness. With this, Sotona's convulsions lessened, turning to a slight shaking and the quavering whimper of an exhausted soul.

Marya and the awful spider then moved a step closer to the wheel, the better to see the final stopping of the ball—and I understood that the Devil's suffering was not at an end. Only the Master remained at the same distance, gazing askance, as if the Devil's fate did not touch him at all, as if he knew it beforehand.

A moment later, the fateful orb came to a standstill over the round letter on a field of green, and then I had only enough time to register one unearthly sound before an almighty flash, like the wondrous manifestation of the Lord Himself, sucked into its infinite light the entire second circle of the nether kingdom and all of us in it: a throaty chuckle, a thunderous guffaw that gushed forth from the gullet of the spider-like beast....

9. SHERLOCK HOLMES'S LAST CASE (3)
MORPHINE

WHEN I ARRIVED at Holmes's house the next morning, carrying an armful of books that had drawn curious or suspicious looks from many passers-by along the route, his face looked swollen around the eyes. He was also unshaven; clearly he had spent the whole night reading and had had no time—or had simply forgotten—to perform his morning ablutions.

Of course, I could not then have suspected that I would never again see him in a fresher condition. All the indications of the approaching catastrophe were even then staring me in the face, but I failed to recognize them. No wonder: to perceive them, one had to have the keen sight of a Sherlock Holmes, while all I had at my disposal was the rather unpenetrating sight of a humble London physician.

It was a relief for me to unload my burden onto the couch in the corner of the drawing room and wipe the perspiration from my forehead. I could hardly believe how heavy the books were. I had heard a similar remark from Sir Arthur, the director of the British Museum Library, as he, not without effort and with my assistance, deciphered Holmes's list of required books. Actually, when he had called them "weighty," he was referring more to the intellectual level of the books than to their physical properties—but nonetheless, we agreed in principle.

"Weighty stuff," Sir Arthur had said. He was a rather stocky man, balding, with a smooth manner and round reading glasses with metal frames. These he wore low on his nose—apparently leaving them on even when he was not reading—and he watched his interlocutor over them, causing his forehead to wrinkle in a permanent frown. A long golden chain belonging to a pocket watch flowed out of one slit in his waistcoat and into another. The waistcoat was too tight, clearly having been made at a time when the owner was considerably slimmer than he was now.

"Mr. Holmes is about to embark on a major investigation," I had said, feeling a need to justify my friend's choices, "which demands familiarity with some very diverse fields of knowledge."

"It must be an extremely strange case," Sir Arthur had replied, no doubt trying to satisfy his curiosity but in as unobtrusive a manner as possible. "Mr. Holmes frequently borrows books from us, but I do not remember him ever taking so many at once."

"This is not a case," I hastened to explain. "Rather, he is involved in entirely academic research into a strange phenomenon that has apparently manifested itself in all eras and climates."

"How extraordinarily interesting," my interlocutor remarked. "I did wonder what such diverse titles might have in common. See here."

He began sifting through the books, which had been brought to us from various shelves by his assistants; each time he picked up a tome he cast a meaningful glance at me over his glasses. "*Introduction to Advanced Mathematics. History of Chinese Cooking. The Cosmogonies of Early Civilizations. Floral Ornaments in Islamic Architecture. A Compendium of Secret Societies.* And what do you say to this: *God and Music*! Nobody has asked for this book for...let me check...yes, a full century! Mr. Holmes will certainly get dust in his lungs reading this."

"I am afraid that I cannot tell you anything more specific," I replied, hoping to bring the conversation to an end by preventing Sir Arthur from questioning me further. "Not because of any secrecy that Mr. Holmes's research involves but simply because I am almost entirely ignorant concerning it. My role in all of this is quite marginal. That of the errand-boy, one might say."

"You are too modest, Doctor Watson," said Sir Arthur, blinking at me over his glasses. It was clear he did not believe me. "It is well known that you are Mr. Holmes's right hand." He stopped for a moment, as if contemplating something, and then added, "In any case, I am honored to have made your acquaintance. I hope I will have the pleasure of being at your service in the future, too; pray convey my greatest respects to Mr. Holmes."

Though his curiosity was undoubtedly piqued, he observed the unwritten rule of gentlemanly conduct: do not bang your head against a brick wall. He respected my indication that I was not particularly willing to reveal details of Holmes's schemes. But what, in fact, could I have told him: that behind all this lay a slightly unhinged message from one malicious dead man, written on very valuable, indestructible Italian paper, all of which greatly excited my friend? That would really have complicated matters.

I began to recount my conversation with Sir Arthur to Holmes, but he dismissed this with a wave of his hand, plainly uninterested, and threw himself on the books—quite literally. He jumped onto the couch amidst them and started to browse through the old tomes. He was not leafing through them in a normal manner: he was acting, so it seemed to me, like a man who had misplaced something valuable in one of the books and was now trying impatiently, almost in panic, to find it. His movements were so hurried that here and there a page became detached from the weakened bindings.

I knew Holmes's passion well, that mighty inner drive that would force him to attack with all his energies a case that he judged to be a worthy challenge, but I had never yet seen such violence. In his eyes was a stare that would on any other face offer a sure sign of madness. With Holmes it could have been, admittedly, the result of a night without sleep, but now for the first time, I feared that it might be something of a much graver nature.

Since he was paying no attention to me nor had any wish for conversation, I started to look around the drawing room, unsure of what to do. My gaze inevitably fell on the massive table, strewn with books from Holmes's extensive private library. Besides the books, most of which lay open, there were many sheets of paper, covered with drawings and short comments. Holmes had, it was clear, worked through the night; it was no wonder he looked the way he did. I picked up one of the drawings and looked at it more closely.

There were circles of various sizes, which overlapped in places, creating more complicated geometrical forms: a series of concentric rings, a drawing of a flower with six petals, a two-dimensional representation of a ball, a series of belts drawn so that they formed the shape of a cylinder. There were also some very intricate forms such as I had never seen before. They looked as though they could have been some kind of outlandish, twisted architecture from the Orient, full of rounded surfaces and soft intersections based on the circle.

Several annotations accompanied every drawing. At first I only glanced at these, but when I looked more closely, I observed that they contained very few letters of the alphabet. There were many mathematical symbols, quite unreadable to me with my meager knowledge, peppered with Greek letters and some indecipherable abbreviations. I had had no idea until now that Holmes was so well versed in the Queen of All Sciences.

But the biggest surprises were yet to come. On the second sheet of paper that I took from the table, there was only one large circle, similar in size to that in Moriarty's letter. It was divided into twelve equal segments, and in each segment there was one calligraphically ornamented sign, more a figure than a letter. At once I thought of the signs of the Zodiac and decided to return the paper back to the pile, when something lying buried at the back of my mind announced its presence like a tinkling bell.

I kept the paper in my hand to stimulate my memory—which in the next moment flashed with the lightning of recollection. For this I probably owed thanks to the fact that this business was taking place in the morning, when I am at my freshest. A man of my years cannot expect to maintain equal clarity of mind at all times of day and certainly not in the evening when exhaustion from the day's efforts gets the better of him.

These were not astrological signs but arcane magical inscriptions, the symbols of the Cabal, the marks of Devil-worshippers. I knew that Holmes had for a time been interested in the ceremonies of these perverted and mostly gruesome cults, from their invocations of evil spirits to their Black Sabbath celebrations. He had even attended some of them, not allowing me to escort him at such times. I had had the impression, though, that he still rejected, even despised, all that tomfoolery and mumbo-jumbo, but judging by these symbols, my impression had perhaps been mistaken.

I took another sheet of paper, now quite ready for any surprise. On it was written a vertical column of numbers composed of four figures each. Each number ended in zero, so that it seemed in fact that they each had three figures followed by a miniature circle. These circlets were what united them into a chain, a whole. This misled me for a while, so that it was only a few moments later that I realized that the numbers were years ranging from A.D. 1120 to our own, current year, which was also a "round" year, divisible by ten.

Next to each of the years was a written explanation, abbreviated more often than not, so that I established only a few dates with certainty. The first year in the column was the one in which the Crusaders founded the famous Order of the Knights of the Temple in Jerusalem—The Templars. Next to the year 1430 were the words "Est. Ord. Rosicrucians," the year 1570 saw the founding of the obscure Brotherhood of the Rose, while in 1720 the first lodges of the Freemasons came into being. (I wonder why it had got Holmes's hackles up so when I had innocently mentioned them in our conversation yesterday?)

My extremely modest knowledge of secret societies, brotherhoods, orders, and the like prevented me from determining the significance of the remaining "round" years on the list (some thirty in all). Guessing quite freely, I assumed that the marking "Par" next to 1420 may have referred to my colleague Paracelsus, the grand master of alchemy, but I was not sure, not being able to remember in which century he had lived. (The freshness of the morning was apparently slipping swiftly away....)

"C. of S. G." next to 1690 could have been Count of Saint Germaine, I surmised, feeling proud of my insight, although, in truth, I knew almost nothing about him except that he was some sort of adventurer and eccentric around whom a host of legends had been woven, including one that he had lived for centuries, so that even this conclusion remained unsure.

When my gaze drifted to the bottom of the vertical column, I felt a constriction in my throat. Next to our current year there were the initials "S. H." encircled in thick red ink; then, in brackets, the letter "M," followed by something that was crossed out, so that it was now utterly illegible, and a question mark.

Filled with a dark foreboding, I turned to Holmes, intending to ask for an explanation, but he preempted me. It appeared that he had just then become aware that I was holding one of the papers from the table. As if scalded by boiling water, he sprang up from the couch on which he had been tirelessly leafing through the books just brought to him and swooped on me.

He roughly snatched the paper from my hand. "Don't touch that!"

The haggard appearance of his face made him look even more terrible than he normally did when anger took him like this, so that I flinched and shrank back, raising my hands a little to show that I had no wish to touch anything more on the table. I think that was the first time I had ever been genuinely afraid of Holmes.

He must have realized that he had frightened me, for a moment later he approached, put his hand on my shoulder, and spoke in a voice that was very mild, almost pleading. "Forgive me, Watson. I am terribly tired. I am not fully in control of myself. I need help. That letter...."

He seized his head and seemed to sway a little. I took him by the hand and helped him to the couch. I collected the books, which were still scattered over it, and the fallen-out pages too, and while I was stacking them on top of the carved chest of drawers, he stretched out on the couch without taking off his dressing gown or slippers. He stared dully at the ceiling with the look of a desperate man, his chest rising and falling quickly.

I had to help him. Mere advice to rest and relax would not be sufficient in this state. He had already gone beyond that boundary of exhaustion when he would be able to simply fall asleep. He needed to be induced to sleep, and I knew full well how I could do that most effectively, although everything in me cried out against a new injection of morphine.

Holmes was already on the edge of addiction. Nobody except me, of course, knew about this problem of his; if it ever became public knowledge (God forbid), I, as an accomplice who facilitated his vice, would lose my license to practice and would be struck from the registry of the Royal Medical Society, while his reputation as the most famous English amateur detective would be in shreds. I could be accused of vanity, but I think the possibility of the latter consequence weighed more heavily on me. After all, a small portion of Holmes's glory belonged to me. Hadn't Sir Arthur suggested that he saw me as Holmes's right hand?

Medical reasoning finally prevailed, and I injected him with a mild dose of the narcotic. On this occasion I did not have to wrestle with my conscience; this was a matter of helping a patient to overcome a state of severe exhaustion and not of satisfying the deadly demand of an addict.

The morphine acted with celerity. As soon as I removed the needle from his vein, the spasm of desperation passed from his face and was replaced by an expression first of relaxation, then of bliss. I knew those phases well, and every time I observed them, I had the impression that I myself was also beginning to feel better. A few moments later, he closed his eyes.

There was nothing further for me to do. Holmes would sleep for several hours now, perhaps until evening. I took the slippers off his feet and covered him with a blanket, which I had taken from the largest drawer of the chest. In the meantime, he had turned on his side and drawn his knees up to his chin, assuming the fetal position. He looked somehow fragile, childlike, not at all like a grown person. I would not have been surprised had he put his thumb in his mouth.

Before leaving, I looked around the drawing room, guided by some dark sense of foreboding; though it appeared that all had been taken care of, an inner voice was telling me that nothing had been settled, that everything was in disorder, just like this room in which I was leaving Holmes. In what condition would I find him when next I saw him? And would morphine then be sufficient to soothe him?

I shook my head to rid myself of these disturbing and gloomy thoughts and opened the door to leave the drawing room. I was startled to encounter Mrs. Simpson; in fact I almost ran into her. She had obviously been standing there for some time, eavesdropping. Probably she had been attracted by Holmes's brief shout; most likely she had been disturbed earlier by his noisy night's work.

She murmured something to the effect that she wished to inquire when to serve breakfast to Mr. Holmes. I told her that Mr. Holmes was asleep and that he would not wake up until late afternoon, when he would be fairly hungry, so that she should prepare a large meal for then. Her curiosity unsatiated, the old woman tried to continue the conversation, hoping to draw from me something more about this unusual disturbance of the daily routine, but I suggested that I had urgent obligations to attend to, said goodbye, and left hurriedly.

10. Gambler and Rake

WE HAVE A slight overcrowding problem.

With two new arrivals, there are seven of us in the temple, and this is beginning to make accommodation somewhat difficult. Five people at most can live here in any comfort. Acting the host for once, Sri unhesitatingly took his hammock out to sleep under the roof of the porch, ostensibly to make as much room as possible for the guests, but I know well he was putting himself first. With the hot season now upon us, it's actually more pleasant out of doors at night than inside, where the stale, muggy air is inclined to linger. And in fact, Buddha soon chose to join him.

It's no wonder. Both of them are people of this climate, they know how to deal with it, and they know they can rely on my efficient protection from insects, whereas the rest of the company has been gathered from entirely other parts of the world with very different climates, so they spend most of their time huffing and puffing, unable to adjust.

Understandably, the old Sicilian puts up with this close weather best of all because of his Mediterranean origin. He is now quite used to wearing a light T-shirt and bermudas, does not overdo the cold drinks, and is in any case one of those people who don't perspire much. Since the appearance of the second guest, he's actually given me the least trouble. He suddenly lost all interest in his dogged drawing of circles in the sand and even saw to it personally that all the dirt he had brought into the temple was thrown out. Maybe this was more my job as hostess, and Sri did pass a couple of remarks on the subject, but the old gent certainly acted gallantly and considerately.

The most difficult housekeeping chores for me are created by that obstinate Fleming. Granted, he's finally taken off the heavy garb in which he arrived—the smell of it all was simply dreadful—but he still dresses very inappropriately. Of all the items from Sri's wardrobe offered to him, he chose a thick, lined tracksuit, perhaps because of the polo-neck, which was the only thing that reminded him a little of his collar; in consequence, he's at a constant low simmer, poor thing. I'd be quite happy to wash his clothes every evening, but he's kept his bad habit of not undressing before he goes to bed—still on the floor in the corner: having gotten used to it, I suppose—so that several days go by before I manage to persuade him to exchange his set of clothes for an identical one. It takes four washes to get all the encrusted dirt and perspiration out of them.

By the way, I added several pockets to both tracksuit tops so that he could transfer all his stuff from his waistcoat, items that he obviously sets great store by, among them the tiny bottle with the sharp-smelling fluid, which he constantly sniffs. However, I think that he's still deeply unhappy because of the simplicity of his new clothes, so plain and modest in comparison with his own frilly outfit.

The one object he would have died rather than part with was the wig. Since he's been here, it's gotten all mangy and tatty, losing all its curl, but he obstinately insists on wearing it, paying no attention to the occasional ironic glances of the other guests. The man has obviously grown so attached to it that parting with it would be like amputation.

The taller of our two new guests also has trouble with his dress. No, he didn't arrive disguised in some antediluvian costume like our man from Flanders, not at all. If not quite up-to-date, his sort of suit can still be seen among older folk, especially those born in the last century. It's of classic cut, double-breasted, with a discreet stripe. In the twentieth century, it used to be the dress uniform of the middle classes.

However, middle-class fashions are not the most appropriate for life in the jungle. Stuffy, with stiff collars and all buttoned up, they demand air-conditioning units, but we never had any because Sri didn't like them, though it would have been nice for me. But who asks me anything....

When I looked through Sri's wardrobe for a suitable replacement for that old-fashioned three-piece suit, an unexpected difficulty came up. The new guest is taller by a head than Sri, so that everything's too short. The trouser legs of the track-suit reach only to the middle of his calves, and the T-shirts stop somewhere above his navel.

Sri's clothes make him look really funny, but he doesn't seem to mind in the least. I think that my special liking for him began to develop the moment I understood his good-hearted but superior attitude. Or perhaps I like him simply because of the weakness all women have for tall, distinguished men.

He's about Sri's age, very slim, even lean, his bearing dignified and reserved. We conversed mostly in German, which he speaks well, though something in his accent tells me it isn't his mother tongue. I was too embarrassed to inquire any further, so that his origin remains unknown. As if it mattered.

Of all the inhabitants of the temple, only he has no reservations or prejudices where I'm concerned. Though computers probably did not yet exist in the part of the twentieth century from which he comes, he accepts my existence as something quite natural. What's more, I am, for him, a genuine character, a person worthy of due respect and consideration—in a word, a lady. Once he even brought me a bunch of flowers of many colors, after a walk in the vicinity of the temple, and left it in a small pot of water near the keyboard. Sri would never have thought of that....

And, of course, as might have been expected, I fell in love. Oh, I didn't realize this straight away, and even when it became obvious, for a while I didn't want to admit it to myself. One day I was deliberately rude to him for no reason, like a capricious teenager, which probably puzzled him, but he behaved like a gentleman. He withdrew without asking superfluous questions or behaving like Sri, who would have responded to my attitude by sulking all the more.

I had only a brief attack of conscience on Sri's account, before realizing with some relief that I have nothing to blame myself for: it's all his own fault. If he hadn't neglected me so much, been so rude to me, reduced me to mere cook and washerwoman, if he hadn't blackmailed me with the baby, if he had known how to treat me as might be expected from the man who made me.... But he doesn't. Sri just doesn't know how to deal with women, and that's the crux of the matter.

They say a woman in love easily overlooks the vices of her heart's choice. I very soon experienced the truth of this myself when it turned out that my favorite guest has a hidden passion: he is a gambler. In another situation, I might have been horrified by the knowledge, but now it struck me as romantic. It brought back to me all those love stories in which handsome poker players clean up not just the chips but also unsophisticated female hearts. That's the reading on which I was raised, and there's no getting away from it. Oh, Dostoyevsky did cross my mind, but in his books everything ends so tragically, and what I yearned for most of all at that moment was a happy ending....

The man I've chosen is no poker player; he plays roulette. He's brought with him, from his own time, a miniature version of the game made from finely polished mahogany, a green baize table cover with decorative stitching round the edges and large ivory balls, all obviously handmade. He did not at first reveal any of this but kept his set in a capacious leather bag with corners of hammered brass, which he stowed under his bed so as not to attract attention. I thought it was for keeping his private affairs in.

Only after a few days in the temple did he get it out. At first, this looked like a shrewd gambling tactic: he cased the joint, sized up his possible rivals, adjusted himself to the circumstances, and only then decided to make his move. I didn't connect his delay to another event that occurred just before the first session of roulette.

The Flemish chap's obsession with the screen, where a procession of numbers marched in slow file after the figure three and a decimal point, building up to the endless number π, came to a sudden end after a full seven days. The automatic counter, which I had turned on, now indicated that this happened after the 3,418,801st decimal, though I couldn't make out why the interruption occurred just there. In any case, his guttural exclamation brought everybody crowding round the monitor for a short while; they looked at it carefully, then some of them patted the Fleming on the shoulder. He was bathed in perspiration, but I wasn't sure whether it was due to his polo-neck, which he kept turned up in the middle of a hot day, or over-excitement.

The matter didn't end there. Sri unhesitatingly took the diskette with a very compact recording of the computed decimals of π and walked over to our satellite transceiver through which we maintained our connection with the world. I noticed that something unusual was going on as soon as he switched on the transmit mode and chose an elevation and an azimuth on which, quite certainly, there was no satellite. This could mean only that the message was for outer space. This really confused me. I never even suspected that Sri was into flying saucers and all that....

It all lasted only a few seconds. The entire recording from the diskette flew into the skies in one powerful, high-frequency impulse, and then Sri redirected the antenna toward the usual satellite and returned it to the receive mode. I had no time to find out where the signal was aimed. It could have been any one of literally many thousands of nearby stars that fill a largish sector of the sky. And that one broadcast had almost exhausted our entire store of energy.

If Sri and I had been alone, I might have ignored that bit of business—what do I care for his cosmic preoccupations anyway—but because of the guests, one of them in particular, I had to ask for some sort of explanation. My dignity was at stake. What would people think of me? That I was only a common housemaid who has to do the chores and hold her tongue? That just wouldn't do. But the problem was not so simple: if I asked Sri anything, I would expose myself to the serious risk of getting a short answer to the effect that it was none of my business (or worse), which amounted to the same thing as far as my dignity went.

My tall knight rescued me from this predicament. Before I had decided what to do, he unexpectedly reached under the bed and pulled out the leather bag with the roulette set. When he opened it, he generated a general enthusiasm in which everything else was forgotten at once. Dear God, I never knew I was surrounded by a gambling fraternity! What was my house turning into? A casino?

I sensed an unusual excitement, via the baby, in the latest guest too, the man with whom I could not have any direct communication. Since his arrival, he's just lain unmoving on a bed opposite the entrance to the temple, apparently interested only in communing with my offspring, while I take care of his physiological needs, like a real nurse.

Once the baby told me that I remotely reminded the guest of one of his previous nurses, some Sarah or other, but when the baby created a picture of Sarah taken from the guest's memories, I shivered. Surely he didn't see me as podgy as that? How terrible. I'm going to have to start watching my figure....

The sick chap arrived together with my tall beloved, who in fact was pushing his wheelchair. At first I felt gooseflesh at the sight. The disabled guest looks terribly deformed, like a creature from one of those horror movies I hate so much. But then I noticed his eyes, the only living part of his body, eyes that simply radiated intelligence and goodness—and compassion rose in me. A man with such eyes simply can't be a monster.

But even if my first impression of him had remained unchanged, I wouldn't dare to show it—not only because I'm prevented by my role as a hostess (one shouldn't find fault with one's guests, should one), but also, and mainly, because of the very close connection that immediately developed between the disabled guest and my child. I would never do anything to hurt my darling's feelings.

The baby had announced the arrival of the previous guests by briefly opening its eyes and setting up a telepathic link to my mind (luckily for me, Sri had no idea), but immediately after, it would sink back into torpor, wholly uninterested in the outside world. I'm beginning to believe that its Down's Syndrome is of a form that has a few odd side effects.

After announcing the arrival of the last two visitors, the baby, to my amazement and delight, did not turn itself off again, nor close its eyes. It has finally found a kindred soul. For a short while I was jealous because a stranger had taken my natural place, and my conscience started to trouble me because when the parent-child relationship starts to creak, it's usually the parent's fault; but the baby's pleasure soon drove all these ugly thoughts away.

It was truly delighted by this tie with the disabled guest: I felt it unmistakably in the baby's every gesture. It obviously had to build a telepathic bridge to him too. That was the only possibility because the poor fellow couldn't physically communicate with the world. This way, thanks to baby's mediation, I'm able to take care of him effectively, to fulfill his wishes and meet his needs, while he in turn spends all his waking hours in the baby's company, obviously just as content.

Only fragments of what they say reach me. I'm not very enthusiastic; oh, it isn't the sort of thing that might corrupt a young person, no, not that kind of talk, but it somehow doesn't seem right to be giving continual lessons in the theory of physics and cosmology to someone of its age. It's as though neither of them knows of any other subject. I could understand the baby's interest in those disciplines if Sri were the father, but, bearing in mind whose genes besides my own have been inherited by the baby, something obviously doesn't click. Well. I've made no objections, not wanting to disturb their happiness.

My gambler laid out the baize with the skillful movements born of long practice, dealt the chips, tested the rotation of the wheel; everybody was staring unblinkingly at his every move, and I felt the communion between the baby and the sick man cease for a moment. At that point, a bell rang somewhere in the murky depths of my mind, but I did not immediately understand that it was sounding an alarm. Then things started to move fast.

Everybody placed their chips on the same number; the croupier, acting upon some unheard instruction, did likewise with the chip meant for the disabled guest, so that five large stakes were deposited together. Only the baby and I weren't playing: the baby—understandably—because of its age, and I because nobody asked me. Which, of course, doesn't matter....

They're obviously playing *va banque* all the way, was the thought that imposed itself. All the money is wagered on one throw only and on one number—and then what happens happens. I looked at the croupier, because my heart trembled at the thought that my chosen one might lose everything in a single moment, but like a true gambler, he showed no trace of agitation. A portion of that self-confidence affected me, and not without a slight dose of malice, I began to study the other players. Their expressions showed excitement, but not fear. It even seemed to me that the face of the physically disabled guest, usually expressionless, was twisted into a new grimace, but I couldn't interpret it.

Then the croupier flung the ball.

A long time before the perfectly round piece of ivory began to plummet down the mahogany slope toward the small numbered partitions, I realized that something was happening. Waves of pleasure started to flow from the baby's mind, quickly growing in strength, establishing a powerful feedback loop. They were just about to reach the point of no return, when I, totally unprepared, finally understood what it was all about.

I glanced desperately at the sick man. That vague grimace on his face had, by now, turned into a clear paroxysm of lust. Disgusting pervert! Freak! Monster! Pedophile! How could he do it to the baby? It was still a child!

But then the orgasmic rise, coming through the telepathic link, passed completely to me from the baby, discarding it like the empty cartridge out of a charger, like a used tool, driving out of my head every thought except one: this thing is meant for me! But why?

This was no time for silly questions. The take-off was so tremendous that I completely lost my mind. No wonder: I had already forgotten when I had last been with a man. This seemed to be much stronger: as if I were making love with five of them at once, everybody climaxing in harmony. God, I had no idea I was so kinky....

The ball rolled relentlessly down the slope and finally stopped, at the right number, naturally. Instantly my consciousness splintered in a fierce flash of white, all-engulfing light. Just before ultimate oblivion, I saw for a split second a small figure, its tail tucked between its legs, outlined in the brilliance pouring from the entrance into the temple. He was holding his elongated, hairy hands above his head, thumbs and index fingers clumsily touching in the shape of a circle, while under his feet were those two revolting little turtles.

My scattered being streamed irresistibly towards that circle and soared through it, and then there was nothing except the absolute void and the darkness of an alien, starry night.

11. THE FRUIT OF SIN

I CLOSED MY eyes at the mighty blaze of light.

But the strength of it lingered under my wrinkled eyelids, so that I continued to see the manifestation of the Lord in this most unlikely place: amid the dirt and stench of the Devil's lair. A strange, deceptive feeling came over my disordered mind: that I had plunged headlong into a bottomless abyss and was plummeting dizzily and relentlessly downward, as off a cliff. Surprisingly, I felt no fear, though I had always dreaded heights, even the modest ones reached by the Master's wooden scaffolding.

I seemed to feel Marya's cheering touch, imparting an additional infusion of vigor to help me endure this new trial, but then I knew that her small hand was no longer on my bony shoulder—and fell instantly prey to despair in the conviction that I had been thrown into the deepest hole of Hell, where only the most guilty are condemned for time everlasting, to expiate their immeasurable guilt among the terrible vipers who breed there.

I opened my eyes to face my dread destiny with humility as a true penitent should, knowing that repentance will not bring forgiveness but only a modest peace with God. But a new miracle stood revealed, banishing the sick plunging feeling. Although my vision still danced with points of whiteness, I saw clearly that I had arrived at a place more different from the pit of horrors I had been imagining than day is from night.

Long did I stand there, staring unblinkingly around me at the country into which I had mysteriously arrived, unable to determine whether I really had, through some unknown, undeserved mercy, left the Devil's filthy den for the Elysian fields, or whether this was only another satanic illusion to cruelly rouse my hope only to replace it with infinite despair.

I stood in a green luxuriant meadow, carpeted with a profusion of flowers of many colors redolent of the perfumes of Eden. The meadow stretched in all directions, to the very horizon, without a hill to interrupt the flatness of the ground. Only at a very great distance did I spy a lonely tree, the thick, leafy crown of which towered high above the surrounding plain.

When the excited beat of my heart stopped pounding in my ears, sounds began to reach me: the monotonous voice of the wind, sprung from the tender, bowing blades of grass; the humming speech of countless beetles, which made their homes among the soft verdure; and a muffled noise, which at first I did not recognize. But a distant memory of it returned to me: I had heard it long ago, shortly after I entered the service of my Master, when we traveled to a monastery that stood by the sea—the murmur of waves breaking on the rocks of the shore.

And while I was still looking around, hoping to discover the source of this sound in a place that bore no trace of the sea, I noticed that which I should have first seen: that I was quite alone amid a strange, empty field—without Marya, to give refreshment to my body by that gentle touch which drove all fearfulness from my soul; without the Master too, to be my guide through the Third circle of the underworld, if this indeed be it.

Denied the sure guidance of their wise judgment that had so far saved me many times from going astray, I stood undecided for a few moments, not knowing what to do in this beauteous meadow, so lovely but deserted. Then I realized, even without the Master's directions, that but one path lay before me, leading toward that distant tree, the only thing that stood out from the surrounding monotony.

At a tardy pace I moved toward that far point, beset by dark forebodings that an evil fate lurked there, waiting for me. Then my frightened wits turned in another direction. First my attention was attracted by the springiness of the grassy cover: I seemed to walk on a thick carpet that sprang back, erasing my traces the instant my bare foot left it to take a new, cautious step forward. Nothing, not even the smallest sign, remained behind to show my unsure passage through this land of Eden.

Glancing ahead to divert myself from this disquieting erasure of my tread, which did but add to my deepest apprehensions, I saw a new marvel in the vault of heaven: resting low above the horizon, bathing it in dark colors, I saw not one sun, but two. At first I thought one of them was but the silvery moon because the moon will sometimes rise betimes for its nightly journey before the sun has fully set. But this orb's powerful light made me doubt this: never in all my days had I seen the moon rival the sun itself in brightness.

I had no time to cudgel my poor wits with this new mystery because a creature with an eccentric, hopping gait, more like an animal than a man, approached me. And indeed, when the unknown creature came nigh enough for my weak old eyes to see clearly, I discerned that it was a frightful behemoth such as none had ever seen on the face of the Earth, nor yet, mayhap, in the dread kingdom that lies beneath it.

Had it not six legs, it would have been like unto a great dog without a tail, going by the thick, long-haired, motley fur that hid its face completely. From the invisible mouth below the fur came sounds of barking, similar to the yapping of a fox, but not of savage fury, as I at first, stiff with fear and expecting to be torn to pieces, had thought. Nay, it was straining, instead, to tell me something.

Although I did not understand its inarticulate language, it was not difficult to perceive its impatience—and indeed, the strange beast, after trotting a few circles around me, barking all the while, rushed off again with its hopping gait toward the tree. I stood perplexed for a few moments, then set off myself in the same direction at a swifter pace.

Before I reached it, I saw what previous distance had not allowed me to see: around the thick bole sat hunched forms, arranged in an unfinished circle. I was startled for a moment to see that these too were six-legged beasts. One of them came to meet me and spoke briefly in his strange tongue, and then returned to his pack. And then I spied Marya and my Master sitting huddled in the same manner, heads bowed, at the place where the circle was broken, like stone sentinels guarding the entrance to some invisible shrine, and my frightened soul took heart a little.

I moved toward them gladly, expecting mild words of greeting, or at least a gesture betokening welcome; but there was none of that. They remained motionless, like statues carved from living rock, as if heedless of my arrival or not seeing me with their downcast eyes. However, a commotion broke out among the huddled beasts as I approached their broken circle, and their utterances became harmonious as a crude chant swelled from their rasping throats.

The moment I stepped into their circle—for there was nothing for it—passing between the yet unmoving Marya and the Master, the chant rose to a bloodcurdling yell, and their long-furred bodies began to glow with a radiance like that of the moonlight in a dark night, though here it was still daytime, lit by two suns. This sight, intensified by such a roar, would have frozen my soul and sent me in headlong flight, but another apparition made me stop as if turned to stone. From behind the broad, gnarled trunk, a girl, passing fair, stepped out before me in a gentle motion. She wore nothing but her long, thick hair, which fell to her rounded hips as the last defense of her angelic nudity.

Smiling kindly at me, she kept her hands behind her back, while I, sorely confused, was unable to interpret the purpose of this miraculous appearance. Was it a belated reward from God for my hitherto ascetic life, deprived of all carnality, or a last temptation of Sotona, who could see into my most secret, licentious thoughts?

Silence suddenly reigned, for the monstrous, howling pack had hushed on seeing the girl and returned to their former huddled quietude, their bodily radiance now much reduced. Perplexed, I gazed dully before me. Long stood we thus, as if in some grotesque fresco of my Master's, before the girl made another movement, endowing the scene with unexpected, ancient meaning.

Her hand, until then hidden behind her back, moved forward in front of her abundant breasts to display an apple, fresh and ruddy on her white palm. Her unblinking gaze aimed a clear message at my eyes, but I was still not willing to understand, hoping for yet another impossible turn of events, like a man in sleep who tries to find escape from nightmare in swift awakening.

But this was no idle dream: she extended her slender hand to me to offer this fruit of age-old sin and exile. Exile, yes, but whither? The unnamed answer came the moment I involuntarily took the proffered gift in my trembling hands, as if some other will controlled my mind.

With the sharp sound of thick bark splintering, an inconceivable door began to open in the great bole of the tree before which I stood, revealing a passage into the interior. My frightened gaze saw nothing but total blackness, as if I stood on the doorstep of a dark cellar in the brightness of day. I looked up at the maiden again, but she was already vanishing behind the tree; for a moment I saw her body from behind, full naked, for all her hair hung down in front—and as she disappeared finally, the broken circle around me came abruptly to life.

First the divided ends united, for Marya's hand now firmly clasped the Master's, denying me any retreat from the exile to which I was sentenced. Then the horrible chant thundered forth again, gaining in strength with each new breath, soaring to a high climax. The links of this living chain began to press closer together around my wretched self, their bodies shining strongly once more. This, however, was not the earlier radiance, which had shone out from beneath their fur, but the glow cast by a third yellow sun that at that instant rose opposite the first two, now hastening toward sunset.

I stepped back in confusion, lacking the time even to marvel at this latest miracle, but there was nowhere to retreat. One way only gaped before me, and I unwillingly took it. I did not at once step through the wooden portals leading into the bottomless dark, but paused on the earthen threshold to look back one more time at my Master, with whom I had spent almost half my life. His face, distorted by the grimace of that alien chant in which he now joined, responded only by a blank gaze in which I discerned nothing: no sorrow, no joy, not even a distant memory. At this total void, something in me broke and I took one fateful step and went out from the light into the darkness.

Went out and saw the stars.

12. Sherlock Holmes's Last Case (4)
Flames

I HAD ALREADY begun to climb the nineteen steep stairs toward the drawing room in which I had left Holmes that morning, when Mrs. Simpson called me.

"Doctor Watson!"

She was standing at the door of the dining room. The weak light of the late afternoon, which came from behind her through the large windows, silhouetted her plump figure. Her face remained in shadow, so that I could not look on it for confirmation of the undertone of unease that I thought I heard in her voice.

"Mrs. Simpson?"

Although we had, through force of circumstances, long been acquainted and frequently encountered one another, Holmes's housekeeper and I had almost never had a conversation of any length. Aside from the inevitable remarks on the weather, our communications consisted mainly of her tales about the minor health difficulties that come with advanced years. She mostly complained of rheumatism, which made her movements progressively more difficult, but lately she had not so much been demanding my advice on how to alleviate that illness—as if it could be alleviated in this damp climate—as trying, in roundabout ways, to find out if her difficulty of movement bothered Holmes. I had tried to put her mind at rest, assuring her that Holmes probably did not notice it at all, but she only shook her head and mumbled that "that 'un notices everything."

"I believe Mr. Holmes wishes to be alone," said Mrs. Simpson.

"Oh?" was my irresolute reply. I lifted my gaze to the upper floor. Under the door of the drawing room spilled the orange light of the table lamp, although no sounds could be heard. The induced sleep had, therefore, lasted less time than I had expected.

"I took his luncheon up to him, as you instructed me, as soon as I thought he was up, but he had the door locked from the inside and just told me, 'Later.' Now it's all gone cold. I put in all that work to prepare something tasty for him, and then it all goes to ruin. Look at these carrots, they're like wood, and the eggs have gone all crusty." She paused, as if shy of me, and then added in a low, almost conspiratorial voice, "You're his friend and a doctor too; he might listen to you if you tell him that he is living in a more and more disorderly fashion. I've tried to warn him about it, but he doesn't care much for my advice. In the end, his health will suffer if he doesn't eat regularly. There has to be some sort of order."

I stood there for a moment, not sure of what to do, and then concluded it would be better if I too respected Holmes's wish for solitude. Besides, I was hoping it was simply that he needed a little more time than usual to bring his appearance into order following everything that he had had to endure in the last twenty-four hours. This morning he had looked rather desperate, and though he may have slept enough in the meantime, the effects of the drug would have worn off, thus reducing his anticipated freshness.

I followed Mrs. Simpson into the dining room. Only when I entered the large room, did she start lighting up the lamps. It was strange how that woman liked to be in the dark. When Holmes was not at home, she virtually never lit the lamps. Initially, the darkness in all the windows had frequently led me to the erroneous conclusion that there was nobody at home; on several occasions this could have had serious consequences. Fortunately, Holmes, who missed nothing, soon called my attention to this odd inclination of Mrs. Simpson's. "Darkness within, darkness without," he had said once, without bothering to explain to me in more detail what he meant by that.

"When did Mr. Holmes wake up?"

"Oh, as early as four, I believe," Mrs. Simpson replied. "Though, it could've been earlier...I don't know. Anyway, around four I heard something heavy fall on the floor. A book, more than likely. There are so many of them up there, now." She glanced at me reproachfully and continued. "It gave me a real turn, did that bang. My nerves are getting too tense lately. And no wonder. D'you think I should go on holiday somewhere? At the resorts down south it's pretty cheap now, and the sea air always did do me good. It's not just my nerves though—rheumatism too. Oh, and just lately something's been giving me flashes of pain in the small of my back."

It seems that people can't talk to doctors about any topic other than their own health. They only differ from one other by their degree of persistence in this. Mrs. Simpson was of the more persistent sort.

"Has anyone come in the meantime?" That was my attempt to change the subject: without much delicacy, but without much hope of success either.

"No. No one except the postman. He stopped by for a cup of tea. Brought me a letter from my cousin in Essex, he did, on my father's side, she is. I don't remember if I ever told you about her. She's a bit older than me, poor soul, a martyr to sciatica for years now. Tried everything; none of it did any good. Even went to the continent, to some French doctors, who smeared her with mud.... Imagine that! Ugh! But she only improved for a little while, and then the pains came back." She paused a moment, to give me a meaningful glance. "What would you recommend for sciatica, Doctor Watson?"

I was on the verge of thinking that I was cornered and that there was nothing for it but to agree to a medical chat of the kind I generally avoid as much as possible, when Providence itself came to my rescue. From above came a muffled sound, which made both of us look wordlessly up at the ceiling.

The violin!

It had been years since I had last heard Holmes play. I had convinced myself that he had hopelessly mislaid the instrument to which he had been so devoted in his younger days. Then, playing had helped him to relax, to concentrate. He claimed that his brain worked best listening to the violin. He was capable of spending hours drawing the bow across the strings, endlessly repeating the same theme in a circle, which would finally induce in me, the only person given the privilege of listening to him, a decidedly dizzy feeling. When I consider everything now, I recall that it was precisely my annoyance at Holmes's excessive passion for making monotonous music, which had grown as time went by, that had ultimately motivated me to propose a more effective and certainly much quieter means of auto-hypnosis. My only mistake was that I had believed, not at all profession-ally, that I would always be the one to determine the dosage.

Mrs. Simpson looked me over meaningfully. "What did I tell you?" she said quietly, as if not to disturb the simple theme that was drifting down to us from the floor above. "His health will be ruined!"

She must have read the expression of puzzlement on my face because she immediately started to explain. "Well, of course! When a gentleman of his years suddenly gets it into his head to play, just on a whim, and on an empty stomach at that, it bodes no good. I expect you read about that grocer from East London, a perfectly ordinary person, who suddenly, as he was getting on in life, took to painting—so much so that he soon neglected everything else, his work, family, home, himself too. He would just shut himself up in his room and start smearing canvases with dark colors. He painted nothing but gruesome monsters, ghastly things, God save us, and then he tried to give these paintings to people in his neighborhood as presents, but of course nobody would take them. Who would want dreadful things like that? He took it hard and cut himself off even more, stopped going out of the room altogether—they say the stink from inside was terrible, which wouldn't surprise me at all—and finally they found him dead: choked by a brush that he'd shoved down his own throat! Can you imagine! And that's not all. When they did the autopsy, they found he had a brain tumor the size of an apple!"

Her hands made a circular motion, describing a figure more suitable to a small watermelon, rather than an apple. "Poor wretch," she continued. "Must have suffered from terrible headaches. Just think: such a large foreign body in your head...." She felt the top of her head with her fingers, smoothed the graying but still fairly thick hair, and then said, inevitably, "I also seem to have been feeling some pressure here lately. I thought it was because of the draught, but it has lasted too long for it to be that. Are you of the opinion that I should have an examination? I'm not saying, of course, that it's necessarily something serious, but one never knows, though my way of life is perfectly orderly...."

I had no time to give her another piece of medical advice free of charge because the sound of the violin from above suddenly stopped. It was not just an ordinary discontinuation of playing as when the bow is lifted from the strings; there was first a rough, screeching tone that violated the melody. We looked up toward the ceiling once again in puzzlement.

The quiet lasted for only a few moments, and then events began to develop quickly. First it seemed to me that Holmes was dragging some heavy object across the floor of the drawing room, perhaps the carved-wood chest of drawers, from which books were falling. A moment later I realized that something much more serious and more difficult to believe was taking place. A fight had started up there!

But with whom, in the name of Heaven, could Holmes be struggling? "You are sure Holmes admitted no visitors?" I asked the bewildered Mrs. Simpson. At the same time I jumped to my feet and sprang from the dining-room table to the door. If she answered at all I failed to hear it, because the next moment there was a violent crash, followed by an inhuman, horrific scream. As I rushed up the stairs, I felt adrenalin flooding into my veins and the hair on the back of my head bristling. What was going on? What in the name of God was happening to Holmes?

I reached for the door handle, forgetting in my hectic excitement that Mrs. Simpson had told me that the door was locked. It was still locked and I could not enter, but the sounds from within demanded the utmost expedience. Something ghastly was happening in the drawing room: Holmes's rapid breathing and occasional painful outcries were mingled with some appalling gurgling or snarling sound. In utter confusion, not knowing what to do, I looked for Mrs. Simpson, but she was of no use: she stood at the bottom of the staircase, petrified with fear, helplessly wringing her hands.

"Call someone!" I shouted to her. "A constable! He was on the street when I was on my way here. If you do not find him, go to the police station! Quickly!" As she was still just standing there, immobile, staring at me, her eyes full of fear, I had to shout at the top of my voice, "In the name of God, woman, move! Do as I tell you! Now!"

This shook her out of her paralysis, and she hurried in a small, old-woman's run towards the door, waving her hands in panic above her head. Her hobbling progress and those upflung hands caused me to burst into brief laughter, although this was completely at odds with the circumstances. This involuntary reaction immediately shamed me, and I turned once again to the door of the drawing room and started to shake the handle violently.

Upon this announcement of my presence, the clash in the room stopped at once. For a while the only sounds that could be discerned were heavy breathing and some quiet crackling. It reminded me of something, but at first I could not recollect what it was.

"Holmes!" I said agitatedly. "What is going on? Open the door!"

Several long moments elapsed before my friend replied. His voice was very excited, almost on the edge of hysteria, and accompanying it, the growling sound began anew, only somewhat quieter. It resembled the purring of a large cat.

"Go away, Watson! I must...There isn't any more...."

A thud was heard, and an outcry of pain from Holmes; then the sounds of fighting resumed. I could hear heavy objects flying all over the drawing room, and the sharp crashing sound of breaking glass. The battle between Holmes and the unknown adversary soon became so violent that the whole floor vibrated. The crackling, which I had not recognized a few moments ago, now grew into an ominous roaring, and at that moment I realized what it was.

Fire! There was a conflagration in the drawing room!

I stood back a little, to gain what momentum I could, and charged with my shoulder into the door in an attempt to break it open, but it seemed to be buttressed from inside by some object. At my third attempt, when for a moment it seemed to me that the door might yield after all, the fracas in the drawing room rapidly quieted down again. The only remaining sound was that of burning, but this too was somewhat quieter.

Confused by this new development, I stood there, hesitating. The wish to help a friend in trouble was forcing me onward despite all danger, but parallel to this wish, fear began to rise in me: the kind of fear I had not tasted since when, as a very small child, I was extremely frightened of the dark. Although I belonged to those who hold to common sense and reject superstition, a grim sense of foreboding began to gain a hold over me—a feeling that something unnatural was developing here...something from beyond...that Holmes had entangled himself in matters that surpassed even his dazzling mind. What sort of peculiar...forces...had been disturbed by his sudden obsession with the circle?

But there was no time for such contemplation. Or more precisely, such thoughts were suddenly confirmed in a spine-chilling manner because the voice that came from the drawing room at that moment could have only come from the grave.

"Be off, Watson! Disappear, you little louse, or Holmes's fate shall befall you too! Do not test my patience!"

There was no doubt, none whatsoever. I would have recognized that voice unmistakably among thousands of others, although I had heard it only a few times in my life. Moriarty! But how....?

Suddenly I was struck hard by the symptoms of blind panic: complete paralysis, cold sweat, a sensation of oxygen starvation, trembling weakness in the legs, and a painful prickling that was now crawling up my spine. The worst was that my mind, too, seemed to have been paralyzed. Try as I might, I could not think of any course of action. I knew that I had to do something, that I could not simply continue standing foolishly in front of the drawing-room door, behind which the only person in the world for whom I truly cared was fighting to the death with a...ghost...but nothing came into my head.

Who knows how long this petrification might have held me had it not been shattered by the most horrendous scream my ears had ever heard. It came from Moriarty's throat, of that I am sure, because it had, at least initially, an undertone of humanity, albeit perverted. But it soon grew into the roar of a ravening beast, into the thunder of the furious ocean, into a satanic shriek of pleasure from the very depths of Hell....

This roar finally crushed my will and narrowed my consciousness, so that I yielded in total, helpless fear to the primal instinct for retreat that flooded my being. As I rushed down the stairs, taking them two or three at a time, heedless of the risk that I might trip and fall headlong, I was aware for an instant of a reproach from my suppressed conscience, which told me this was cowardice, that I was, at a fateful moment, turning my back on a man who was more than a friend to me. But my mobility was now governed solely by the blind terror that implacably urged me to escape from this accursed place.

I did not get far, though. At the bottom of the stairs I ran into the constable whom Mrs. Simpson had, in the meantime, managed to call. The impact of our collision was of some force, so that we both fell down; probably our foreheads had collided because as he rose to his feet, he clasped a hand to his head and rubbed a quickly-growing lump above his eyebrow, while I also felt a dull pain in the front of my head. Upon seeing my face, he drew back slightly; he must have perceived on it an extremely unhinged expression. Mrs. Simpson, who arrived after the constable in her hobbling run, confirmed this: seeing me, she covered her mouth with both hands, to choke back an outcry of terror.

We stood like that for a few moments, staring at one another. It was clear that they expected some sort of instruction or at least information from me, but I was still in the throes of panic, so that no words came to my lips. What finally released me from this state of immobility was an awareness that only slowly and with great effort penetrated my mind: there were no more sounds from above, nothing except a very quiet crackling. No more sounds of fighting, no inhuman roars, nor the breaking of things.

"Up...there...fire," I managed to stammer, pointing with a shaking forefinger up the stairs.

The policeman, now fully on his feet, gave me a hand up as well and then started up the stairs. His gait was not very resolute; twice he stopped and turned to Mrs. Simpson and myself, who remained at the bottom of the staircase, but he did not receive much help from us. Quite the contrary; had he gone by our looks and attitude, he would most likely have rushed back downstairs.

When the constable had finally reached the door of the drawing room and grasped hold of and turned the handle, the two of us exchanged looks of incredulity, for the door was no longer locked, and he stepped in without obstruction. A few long moments passed, filled with dreadful uncertainty; the only sound from above was that of crackling, now slightly louder. The fire, it appeared, was still burning in the drawing room, but it sounded nothing like the earlier roar of a full-blown blaze.

Finally the constable reappeared at the door. Observing him from below, we saw only his silhouette around which danced the flickering reflections of the flames. Under normal circumstances, no encouragement would have been necessary: we would immediately have come to the rescue, to help extinguish the blaze. The circumstances, however, were not such, and so several seconds elapsed after his invitation to us to join him before we snapped out of our immobility and began to act.

To my disgrace, Mrs. Simpson managed to do so first. "Oh, what a mess there'll be in the house!" she exclaimed, hurrying to fetch something from the dining room, while I, after a further moment of hesitation, ran upstairs. It seemed to me that I faced many more than nineteen steps, an ascension without end, but this did not bother me. Impatience urged me to climb as quickly as possible, to find out what had happened to Holmes, but on the other hand, an evil presentiment as to his fate dampened this urge of mine.

Inevitably, though, I found myself at the open door, which only a few moments ago I had been unsuccessfully attempting to break down. As I had expected, the drawing room was a shambles. The carved-wood chest of drawers was overturned and the books from it now lay scattered and mostly torn. (What would Sir Arthur say? the thought passed through my mind.)

The couch stood unnaturally slanted to one side (causing me to reflect on how much strength would be needed to move such a heavy piece of furniture), and shards of broken glass from a ripped-out window-pane and two devastated glass cabinets glinted in the carpet, giving the impression of a multitude of small pearls mixed with pieces of smashed chinaware. Shards of glass also covered Holmes's violin, which lay broken in one corner, apparently having served as a convenient weapon. Liquid dripped from an old-fashioned pharmaceutical flask that lay on its side on the edge of the fireplace, accumulating in a small bluish puddle on the floor. I could not identify the substance, but if the contents of the flask were the source of the stench of sulfur, which had filled my nostrils as soon as I stepped into the drawing room, it could not have been anything pleasant.

Of Holmes there was no trace, of Moriarty even less. The only person in the drawing room, except for myself, was the constable. He had seized the brocade cover from the couch and was now using it to swipe at the fire, which was still flickering in the center of the room, in an attempt to extinguish it.

It was only then, watching his panting attempts to put it out and not knowing what to do to assist him, that I became aware that the chaos around me was not, after all, complete. In the very center of the general disorder, as at the eye of a powerful tornado, all was perfectly calm.

The fire, which had consumed a number of Holmes's papers and pages torn from books, had formed a perfect circle on the floor of the drawing room—a circle that could not possibly have been created by pure accident in all this chaos. The constable's blows with the heavy dark red cloth were slowly but surely putting it out, but on the carpet remained a singed, sooty trace that, miraculously, retained its perfectly round shape. In the middle of this flaming circle lay a single sheet of paper, one which could not be harmed by ordinary fire. The unique creation of the maestro Murratori of Bologna, with the dark initial of Holmes's demonic rival who had been summoned to this place by some secret knowledge from the other side of nothingness, a knowledge on which my medical learning was wisely silent. Summoned—but to what purpose? And where was Moriarty now? Above all, though: where was Holmes? What had been the cause and what the consequence of their fierce duel? To begin with, why had it been necessary to accept this ultimate challenge, to venture on a search that extended to the other side of the rational?

The questions began to pile up, but I suspected that I would never obtain answers to them. Who was I, after all, that ultimate mysteries should be revealed to me? A humble London doctor who had neglected his medical practice, private life, and everything else to become the shadow of his remarkable friend, hoping in his vanity to receive a share of his friend's glory.

Now, with Holmes's disappearance, that vainglorious hope vanished at once, making me even more insubstantial than the shadow I used to be. What course of action was left open to me? The faint hope that Holmes would return? It really was not much—in fact, it was infinitely little, but I could find no firmer base to stand on.

And so I helped the constable put the fire quite out, and when Mrs. Simpson timidly appeared, out of breath and carrying a pail of water, I had to invest great effort in subduing her compulsive tendency to put all things in order. Everything in the drawing room had to remain as it was, without alteration, particularly this burnt circle on the carpet, in the middle of the room. I had a presentiment, for which I had no rational explanation, that that circle was especially important for Holmes's return.

All I could do now was to wait. It might turn out to be a long wait, but I felt certain I would not be bored. Mrs. Simpson would be with me, and the *Medical Encyclopedia* was an inexhaustible source of topics with which to while away the time pleasantly.

EPILOGUE

WHO ARE YOU?
I am Rama.
Are you a spirit?
No.
Then how is it that I do not see you or hear you, and yet I speak with you?
I am in your head.
Why would you be in my head?
To help you, among other things.
Do I need help?
Yes. You are as helpless as a newborn babe.
But I am an old man....
You were.
And what am I now?
Something new....
What?
Be patient. You will find out when the time comes.
Am I...dead?
Dead? You're not dead. There's no dying, in The Circle.
In what Circle?
In the final one.
I do not understand you.
I'm telling you to be patient.
I want to, but I am afraid. It is so dark and quiet here. Like the grave.
Or the womb.
Why did you say that?
Because it's closer to the truth.
Are you, then...my...mother?
No; you will be my father.
Father? How?
Miraculously. You will give birth to me.
How could I give birth to you?
From your head.

You will come out of my head?
Yes. Don't be afraid, it won't hurt.
But I...cannot....
You'll be able to, quite easily, when the moment comes.
What happens after? I mean, I will not...be able to live...alone.
You won't be alone. The others will be with you.
Which others?
Well, the Master, Sri...Everybody. They'll take care of you.
Oh. Where are they now?
They're watching us and waiting.
Waiting for what?
For you and me to fulfill the purpose.
What purpose?
The purpose of the Circle.
You mean...that I give birth to you?
Yes.
And you? What happens to you after that?
I'll not be here any more.
Where will you be?
That I can't explain to you. But I'll be safe.
Will I see you after you...are born?
No. I will come into the world in another place, very far from here.
I would like to know what you will look like.
What would you like me to look like?
I do not know...Like Marya...perhaps.
All right, I'll look like Marya.
What should I do, in order that you...come out of my head...be born?
Oh, that's not difficult at all. This darkness is bothering you, isn't it?
Yes...It frightens me.
Summon light, then.
How?
It's simple. Say it.
You mean...like....
Yes.
But I am not...I cannot....
You can. Believe me. Please.
I believe you, but....
Say it, Father. Now is the moment.
Let there be light!

CIRCLE THE FOURTH

1. VISITOR

THE BRASS KNOCKER on the front door sounded thunderously, like the first crash of a summer storm. Mrs. Simpson and I had just sunk into the kind of silence that ensues when all possible topics for conversation have been exhausted. We sat in silence, each preoccupied with his or her own thoughts, surrounded by the semidarkness of the early evening. Preferring darkness, the old woman had no intention of lighting the lamps; I did nothing to encourage her to, since the gathering gloom was quite congenial to my somber state of mind.

It was the fourth day after Holmes's enigmatic and violent disappearance. As soon as I had dispatched my medical obligations—which I endeavored to do as quickly as possible—I hurried to 221-A Baker Street, led by a still living, but increasingly idle hope that some miracle might transpire, that I would once again set eyes on the dearest friend I had ever had—that unique man whose vain and irrepressible thirst for forbidden lore had brought upon him a fate far beyond my ability to comprehend (and his also, I suspect).

Mrs. Simpson, whose previous attitude toward me had been rather reserved, if not cold—obviously for some reason disapproving of my close association with Holmes—now went to the other extreme. She welcomed me not merely eagerly, but with unconcealed joy, undoubtedly finding in my presence a consolation such as relatives can sometimes give to mourners.

This insight at first angered me because Holmes, as far as we knew, was not dead, though, on the other hand, one could hardly have claimed that he was alive, at least in the usual sense of the word. But my anger soon dissipated when I realized that our feelings were identical and that I also found her company pleasing: in Mrs. Simpson I saw the only living link to my missing friend, a link that began to mean more to me than all the familiar objects in this house, much as these reminded me of him.

And yet, although we shared the same pain, it was our tacit agreement never to mention Holmes, not even by allusion. It was as if we both feared not only that we would, by mentioning him, commit some kind of desecration, but also that we might awaken the mysterious forces that had once worked in this place to claim their evil due.

For the same reason, we made no mention of the odd scene in the drawing room above us. On my advice, Mrs. Simpson left everything as we had found it in the room from which Holmes had vanished, although this went deeply against her almost perverse tendency to put the house in order. She did not even demand an explanation as to why the drawing room should be left untouched. She simply accepted my suggestion with relief and gratitude, being loath in any case to meddle in things that she did not comprehend and that frightened her.

I locked the drawing room and took the key with me, which suited her well, because she could now pretend that the room did not exist. Thus was her stay in the house made easier, particularly at night when she remained alone, but of these periods I knew very little because she, respecting our taboo on any conversation about the extraordinary event and anything associated with it, never mentioned them.

Only once—on the second day, I think—I noticed, by her visible agitation when I arrived, that she had experienced some strange unpleasantness, but although I gave her an opportunity to tell me more about it, she hesitated and considered and finally avoided saying anything. I did not press her much on the subject, so that the matter remained unexplained; even more so because the old woman soon, in my presence, pulled herself together. Why did I not do so, despite the curiosity that was gnawing at me? Because I was unready to face what she might have said? Because of cowardice? Perhaps. I do not know.

We did not report Holmes's disappearance to the police. What could we have told them anyway? That behind all this was that madman Moriarty who, purely as a matter of interest, happens to have been dead for several weeks? That the greatest detective genius London had ever known had simply vanished into thin air from a closed room? Of course they would never have believed us, even though, for them, an aura of other-worldliness had always existed around Holmes. This would have been too much, even where Holmes was concerned, so that questioning would have inevitably followed, becoming increasingly awkward for us as we became more entangled in unsuccessful attempts to offer at least a minimally reasonable and acceptable explanation of something that we ourselves did not understand.

As for the constable who had assisted us in putting out the fire, there were no great difficulties there, either. He readily accepted my explanation that the cause of the fracas was my clumsiness and lack of skill in handling Holmes's laboratory equipment, which had almost caused an explosion and a much larger fire. He rebuked me mildly, saying that I might be scientifically trained, but that I shouldn't interfere in things that were beyond my skill; and when I discreetly let him know that I would appreciate his keeping the whole affair a secret, especially from Holmes, he nodded understandingly and even offered to help me to tidy up the drawing room. I somehow diverted him from that and thanked him profusely, assuring him that I could deal best with the matter myself.

When I met him the following day on the street, while I was on my way to the house, he asked me quietly, almost conspiratorially, whether Mr. Holmes had noticed anything and when I gave him a negative answer, he gave a brief sigh of relief. Clearly in the meantime he had begun to regret that he had agreed to hush the matter up, fearing that if the damage were extensive, he might have to share responsibility with me. The trouble with London constables is that occasionally they find themselves in a dilemma between excessive zeal and certain gentlemanly considerations—especially if they happen to have a treacherous lump on their forehead, a lump similar to one that adorns that of the first on the list of suspects....

Mrs. Simpson had prepared lunch for me, glad that she finally had someone who adhered to house rules and ate at the proper time. Holmes almost never did that; he ate only when hunger began to gnaw at him in a really serious way, which could happen at any time of day—or, not infrequently, of night. This irregular behavior created a great many problems for his housekeeper, and she complained increasingly about the matter, but Holmes acted as though he didn't notice.

My problem with Mrs. Simpson's cooking consisted only in the ampleness of the meals she prepared for me. Although, unlike Holmes, I am one of those people who enjoy their food—which could be plainly seen from my waistline—the luncheons that awaited me in the home of my vanished friend were well in excess of my usual measure.

I refrained from telling my new hostess this, however, since it was bound to hurt her feelings; it was clear, from the way she regarded me while I ate, that she was enjoying herself almost as much I was (or at least, as she presumed I was): finally she could prepare meals for someone who appreciated her culinary abilities and did not just mechanically ingest food as if it were some unpleasant, though ineluctable, chore.

The immediate consequence of the overabundant meals I was receiving from Mrs. Simpson was an inevitable drowsiness after lunch, which she was not slow to take advantage of. She would begin long monologues, which consisted mostly of the histories of the illnesses of her various relatives and friends; what was expected from me was not so much to give medical advice as to pronounce my general agreement with her views regarding the diagnosis and the treatment.

Although my attention would begin to flag because of the rush of blood to my overloaded stomach, I recall extensive monologues concerning the discomfort of internal hemorrhoids, the woes of people who had suffered from ulcers for many years, the pitfalls awaiting women of advanced years in first childbirth—"Especially in Wales, where the air is so full of coal dust..."—and inflammation of the sinuses in children, which could be best cured by inhaling the vapor from tea brewed from Scottish highland elder; then there were the horrendous and often lethal diseases brought by the colored people "who are pouring into England like rats from the overseas colonies...."

Once or twice I dozed off, but Mrs. Simpson ignored this, never halting the flow. This was not primarily out of considerateness. The torrent of words pouring from her compensated for the lack of opportunity for female conversation, which she obviously missed greatly, so that my attention, in fact, was not essential. My mere presence sufficed, even if I was asleep; the main listener was herself. That could be discerned by the specific sort of dialogue that she, not rarely, had with herself, asking questions and then answering them.

It was only when I would, thoughtlessly, begin to snore, that she would give a discreet cough, but she would then continue her story immediately, saving me the embarrassment of apologizing for this awkward lapse. The flood of words would begin to abate only at teatime; by then, my stomach would have won the battle with the over-copious food, and my concentration would have fully returned, accompanied by a certain alertness characteristic of the period following an afternoon nap.

Our communication could have become a real dialogue, and yet it did not. Put simply, it became clear that we had no interests in common. The most obvious potential topic was Holmes and what had befallen him, but since we avoided that area, little else remained. Mrs. Simpson would have liked to begin again with the medical anamneses, but she lacked fresh material, having used so much in the earlier monologue. (Though by the next day she would have armed herself with a plentiful supply of new cases.)

On these occasions, I would try to interest her in unusual cases from forensics, or tell her some anecdotes from my younger days on the cricket field, but the former was too distasteful for her, even disgusting (for which I do not blame her), while the latter left her totally indifferent (which peeved me considerably).

And so, after we had taken tea, we would sink into silence. My thoughts would return to Holmes, and hers too, I assume—since the hour of my leaving was slowly approaching, and with it, her utter solitude. At first I had toyed with the idea of suggesting to Mrs. Simpson that I move into the house for a while, but I realized that my doing so would have evoked the suspicions of the neighbors who were accustomed to Holmes's sudden absences but to whom my unexpected residency in Holmes's house would give rise to much unpleasant conjecture and gossip.

On the fourth day after Holmes's disappearance, we were once again sitting at the dining-room table, in the silence that settled on us after the tea had been drunk. The muffled noises of passing hansoms and the infrequent voices of passers-by reached us from the street. Children could be heard as they ran squealing towards the nearby park. The thin cries of evening birds came from the bare tops of the horse-chestnut trees. All of a sudden I remembered, who knows why, the strange paper of *Signore* Murratori, with which this whole sad story had begun. The paper still lay in the locked drawing room, in the center of the enigmatic circle perfectly drawn by fire on the carpet. If I were to go upstairs, perhaps, and take it....

But I was not destined to do this. The hammering of the door-knocker sounded so sharply and unexpectedly that both Mrs. Simpson and I started from our seats. She quickly put a hand to her mouth to choke back an involuntary scream. We remained motionless for a few moments, looking wordlessly at each other, with expressions more eloquent than any words spoken at that moment could have been, while the thunderous sound of the brass knocker echoed through the dark house, seeming to come from all directions at once. Somebody was clearly in a great hurry to be admitted. Could it be, perhaps...This belated thought, which glimmered simultaneously in Mrs. Simpson's eyes, sent a cold shiver through me, but also jerked me from my immobility, and I strode quickly, almost at a run, to the front door, in the process clumsily knocking over the dining-room chair on which I had been sitting.

2. THE BOOK

IT TOOK ME a fraction of a second to recognize him. No wonder: I had previously seen him only once in my life. Moreover, at that time he had been wearing glasses low on his nose, which he did not have now, and he was the last person whom I would have expected to see at the front door of 221-A Baker Street. I think he noticed my momentary confusion, but politely ignored it, because he, too, saw that his unannounced arrival must be something of a surprise.

"Good evening, Dr. Watson," said he, in a voice in which an unsuccessfully suppressed shortness of breath could be heard. At that moment something caught my eye: a long trail of sweat, which came from somewhere behind his right ear, meandered down his massive neck and disappeared under the high, stiff collar of his shirt like an underground stream. Had we not been in twilight, likely a certain flushed hue could have been discerned on the visitor's face. He had come here in a great hurry, perhaps at a run.

"Sir Arthur," said I finally. "What a surprise."

In normal circumstances, the obligations of polite behavior would have demanded a speedy apology and explanation for this 'surprise.' But the circumstances, clearly, were not normal—generally speaking, very few people came to us for normal reasons—so that he omitted all formalities and proceeded at once to what had brought him here with such conspicuous haste.

"Mr. Holmes...I have to see him right away. He is at home, I hope?"

"Well...no. He is not. I mean, he is away."

I have never been a good liar. That is mainly why I chose forensics: I did not have to conceal from patients the truth about the state of their health, because they were beyond caring.

"Oh, no!" exclaimed Sir Arthur, putting a hand to his mouth. "So, it's happened already! I've come too late!"

His voice rose into near-hysteria. This jerked me out of my confusion. At the moment there was nobody on the street, but at any instant somebody might come along, and in view of what Sir Arthur had just uttered, this was the last place I would wish to discuss the matter.

"Please, do come in, Sir Arthur. We will be much more comfortable inside."

I expected him to rush past me, but he hesitated for a moment, as if wondering what the point might be of entering the house if the man he wanted to find was not there. Then, apparently at a loss for what else to do, he shrugged his shoulders, nodded curtly, and came inside. Before closing the door behind us, I looked first left then right, down the street—more out of precaution, because I believed that Holmes would have done so in a similar situation, than out of any expectation that something might be gained by it. All I managed to observe was a quick movement of the curtain in one large window near the front door of the house next door: inquisitive neighbors.

Sir Arthur did not advance very far down the corridor but stopped only a step or two in front of me, the reason for which became quite clear when the door closed completely and we found ourselves in almost total darkness. Mrs. Simpson and her absurd habit of not lighting the lamps!

I mumbled something by way of an apology and hurried forward, overtaking Sir Arthur. I approached the lamp in the middle of the corridor while groping in my pockets in search of a lighter. I did not find it at once—on such occasions, one never finds anything at first try—and this unhandiness had a strange consequence. As I stood under the lamp, impatiently touching this pocket and that in the darkness, I lifted my gaze involuntarily, as people are wont to do when they are at the end of their patience or nerves.

Two things then happened simultaneously. I finally found the lighter—in the place where I should have searched for it first, because that is where I always keep it, in the right hand pocket of my vest. And just before I hastily struck the flint, I noticed for an instant a pale band of milky radiance in a place where it had no reason to be: in the narrow gap between the door and the threshold of the drawing room above.

Fearing that Sir Arthur might notice it too, I quickly lit the lamp, flooding the corridor with bright light that entirely did away with the ghostly radiance from above, so that I wondered if perhaps it had been only a hallucination. The eyes are a very unreliable guide in the darkness.

In any case, this was not the moment to verify my impression—and it is questionable whether I would have gone upstairs without a great deal of hesitation, not to say fear, had we not had a visitor. I took Sir Arthur to the dining room, in which Mrs. Simpson had, only a moment after myself, also lit the lamp. She then beat a hasty retreat into the furthest corner of the room, visibly shrinking from the unknown and unexpected guest.

I opened my mouth to make the introductions, but Sir Arthur was faster. "Mrs. Hudson, I presume? Sir Arthur Conan Doyle, director of the British Museum Library."

"Mrs. Simpson," I corrected him. He turned to me and looked at me perplexedly.

"Simpson? Is not the name of Mr. Holmes's housekeeper Mrs. Hudson?"

"I assure you, Sir Arthur, our housekeeper is called Mrs. Simpson, is that not so, Mrs. Simpson?"

The expected support, however, was not forthcoming from her. The woman stood wordlessly in the opposite corner of the dining room, nervously wringing her hands and gazing distractedly at the new arrival, as if his appearance had deprived her of the faculty of speech. To help her regain her composure, I asked her to make tea for us, a suggestion that she accepted with relief, hurrying off at once into the kitchen. Passing by Sir Arthur, she murmured something, I did not discern what.

I picked up the chair that I had overturned in my rush to answer the door and sat down, first offering Sir Arthur the seat at the opposite side of the table, Mrs. Simpson's customary place. He spent a few moments gazing after her toward the open kitchen door, from which came the muffled clink of the metal and porcelain tea things, then shook his head once or twice and turned to me.

I looked back at him, without a word, at a loss for what to say. The behavior of this man was so unusual that it required an immediate explanation. However, as I had half expected, instead of explaining himself, Sir Arthur had more questions.

"Dr. Watson, you must tell me everything! It is imperative that I know. What has happened to Mr. Holmes?"

I countered with a question: "What gives you the idea that something has happened?" trying to keep my voice as calm as possible, though aware that pretending, like lying, was not my strong point.

"You said he was absent, is that right?"

"Yes. He is away on a new, unexpected case and...."

"Very well, very well," Sir Arthur interrupted me impatiently. "If so, may I have back the books you borrowed for him a few days ago?"

This demand startled me, and I did not try to hide it. The books, or rather the pitiable remains of them, were in the drawing room above us. If I went to fetch them, I would be forced to rapidly invent a convincing story that would explain the state they were in, but I had failed to invent such a story these four past days, although I had tried strenuously. I had known that this moment, when I should be obliged to return the books, was inescapable, but I had not expected it to come so soon.

The seconds ticked away, and I continued to stare at him helplessly and dully, like a child caught in some kind of mischief. On his face it was clearly written that he knew perfectly well what was bothering me, besides something deeper. It was this circumstance that finally shook me out of my immobility. Why had he mentioned the books? What did this man, in fact, know? What was his connection with the entire mysterious affair?

These questions could rescue me from the plight in which I found myself. Sir Arthur certainly owed me an explanation. Not even the police would have burst like this into a respectable home and proceeded with an interrogation from the very doorstep. The moment had come for me to pass from the defensive to the offensive.

"You will of course get your books back," said I finally, in a tone intended to sound slightly reproachful, though I suspect that Sir Arthur did not heed it. "But I would venture to say that at this moment they are not of paramount importance. I should much appreciate it if you were first to—"

Once more he broke into my sentence, heedlessly, almost rudely. "You have no idea how important they are. Especially...."

He did not finish that thought. Probably the strangeness of what he had to say was in total contrast to the look of incredulity on my face. He took from an inner pocket of his jacket a lace-hemmed handkerchief with an embroidered initial on it and nervously wiped the sweat from his forehead. The underground stream still glistened on his neck. He shook his head, as if to rid himself of evil spirits. "Forgive me, Dr. Watson. My conduct...I am aware...I must seem like a real madman to you. But if only you knew the things I've been through these past few days...."

"You are telling me?" I thought to reply, but it would only have complicated the matter even further. We might both have started to confess simultaneously, which certainly would not have been good; only women manage to listen to their companion and carry on talking to her at the same time. In the end, their conversation is reduced to two vast interruptions.

"Sir Arthur," I said instead, not really knowing how to continue and wishing to calm him a little. Mrs. Simpson came to my assistance by entering with the tea on a large silver tray. The tea service was made of old-style Japanese porcelain, particularly dear to Holmes because on the cups and teapot were ornate Oriental writings, which spoke of cherry blossom, the reflection of the moon on the surface of a lake, spring breezes, and frogs croaking in the darkness. On one occasion Holmes had given me a poetically high-flown translation of it. He had always had bizarre tastes, but save for the inelegant pictographs, the service was very pleasant to use.

We each took, in silence, a few sips of the hot beverage produced from the pleasant-smelling Ceylonese plant. Mrs. Simpson did not leave, as might normally be expected from a housekeeper. Nobody asked her to— who had the right? She had been for quite some time now up to her neck in this affair, and deeper, if Sir Arthur's unusual method of address was any sign. Since her place at the table was occupied, she retired once more into the corner where she had originally awaited us, even though that meant standing behind Sir Arthur's back.

The tea seemed to have a remarkable calming effect on our unexpected visitor; better, certainly, than all the words that I could have used. When he spoke again, having drunk perhaps half a cup, his voice was far more composed than before.

"I think it would be best if I told you everything from the beginning, so you may understand my state, and then...I do not know. Possibly...we'll see." He turned briefly to Mrs. Simpson, not because her presence annoyed him but because he wanted to give her to understand that she ought to sit down. All the signs were that the story would not be short, but she did not budge, choosing to remain standing in the place that she herself had selected.

"The event with which everything started," Sir Arthur continued, with a small shrug of his shoulders, "happened four days ago."

I choked and coughed violently, spattering my waistcoat and the lapels of my jacket with droplets of tea. This made a considerable noise, which partly covered the exclamation by Mrs. Simpson. Since she was behind his back, Sir Arthur did not see that she had covered her mouth with her hand. I murmured a few words of apology, ascribing this accident to my clumsiness, and he, after only one suspicious glance, continued.

"In our Library, in the department of rare and antique books, one volume inexplicably turned up, a volume that absolutely should not have been there, a new book, just printed, in mint condition, so that my assistant who saw it first—which was not very difficult to do, against the background of ancient manuscripts and incunabulae—first thought that somebody had misplaced it. Such disorder, however, is quite untypical of the British Museum Library. We are, as you know, proverbially thorough, particularly in the department of rare and antique books."

He paused as if expecting me to confirm this proverbiality; a moment later I nodded and said: "Oh, indeed."

"When he pulled it out of its place and observed it more carefully, a new surprise lay in store for him. Perplexed, he hurried to my office to demand an explanation where he thought he could most naturally obtain it—from me—not because a brand-new book happened to be found among ancient tomes, but rather because my name was given as the author's."

"You?" I asked bewildered. "But you do not write. At least not as far as I know, I mean, not publicly...."

"Not publicly, and not in secrecy either. I do not publish under any pseudonym, if that is what you are thinking. But, on that book was no pseudonym. It was my full name and title: Sir Arthur Conan Doyle. It is not impossible that someone else in Britain or the colonies shares the same name, but it is quite certain that we do not share a knighthood. It could only, therefore, have been me."

"How very strange!" I exclaimed involuntarily.

"Indeed," he agreed. "Especially since I knew for certain that I had never written the book. At first I thought that someone was playing a game with me, that it was somebody's misguided joke, or worse, a deliberate misrepresentation. A man in my position, you know, must always be on the alert. One never knows who might be plotting one's death. Oh, not literally, of course, metaphorically speaking. Careers are, you know, very flimsy things...."

Sir Arthur paused to take another sip of tea. He drank it rapidly, without savoring the beneficent liquid, as if drinking ordinary water. This was in a sense an insult to Mrs. Simpson, who fortunately did not notice anything, since the visitor now sat with his back half-turned to her.

"I looked at the name of the publisher; I was of a mind to contact him immediately and clear this matter up. Such things are not done in decent, ordered societies, you know, but it were better that I had not looked. On the title page there were two things that quite bewildered me."

Sir Arthur paused again, and I thought at that moment that it was a pity that the man really was not a writer; he was undoubtedly a born storyteller, gifted in postponing the denouement, in creating tension, in interrupting the narration at the most exciting places, though that sort of thing generally irritates me.

"First, the publisher," Sir Arthur continued. "I am, because of my profession, naturally familiar with the publishing world, so that there was no need to look up any source of information to verify that such a firm does not, nor ever did, exist in London, or in fact in the length and breadth of the British Isles. At that moment I had not yet thought of the third possibility."

"The third possibility? What do you mean by that?" I asked, puzzled.

"The third possibility, yes. The year of publication clearly pointed to it: a full forty-three years from now. In the future. The publisher who brought out that mystifying book is yet to come into existence."

I stared incredulously at him and opened my mouth to say something, but not a word came out. The only sound was a brief, wheezing cough from Mrs. Simpson in the opposite corner. If this was too much for me, I can only imagine what effect it must be having on her. Only Holmes, perhaps, would have enjoyed this.

"I don't understand you, sir. What—future? You do not mean to say...."

"Exactly that. Yes. But don't demand an explanation, please, I haven't any. It is a complete mystery to me too. I probably should have visited Mr. Holmes at once, as soon as the book came into my hands. Perhaps he could have taken some action, then."

"Certainly you should have. I am convinced that Holmes would have found some...er...natural solution to the entire matter. You yourself mentioned the possibility that it might be a tasteless practical joke, did you not?"

"Nobody invests such effort in a bad joke, Mr. Watson. To write a whole book—and a book of superb quality at that—just for the sake of tomfoolery.... No, that is quite improbable. Oh, but the contents of the book are such that I could not visit Holmes. Haven't I mentioned its title?"

"No, I think not. Am I right, Mrs. Simpson?" I looked up at Holmes's housekeeper. If there are faces that eloquently express the state of the soul, hers was such. Fear, confusion, disbelief, an impulse to retreat—all this could be clearly read in the small wrinkles around her eyes and in the slight trembling at the edges of her lips. The old woman shook her head briefly.

"That's because of excitement, Mr. Watson. In such a state, I sometimes omit the essential. The title of the book was—*The Adventures of Sherlock Holmes*."

3. VANISHED

"*THE ADVENTURES OF Sherlock Holmes*," I repeated stupidly, for lack of anything more intelligent to say. There are circumstances in which a man feels that he must say something but knows that whatever he says will sound foolish.

"Precisely," replied Sir Arthur. "I quite understand your puzzlement, Dr. Watson. You can imagine how I felt upon taking into my hands for the first time a book of which I was supposedly the author and which spoke of the adventures of a man whom I happen to know well. I cannot say we are intimate friends, but Mr. Holmes has frequently visited our library, and I have always been at his disposal, so that in time a relationship developed between us, one which is more than mere acquaintanceship."

He paused, in the manner of one who had sunk into his memories. The silence was now disturbed only by the tiny tinkling of porcelain. A moment or two later I realized that it was caused by the trembling of my hands in which I held a saucer and a cup of tea.

"Most extraordinary," I said finally, hurriedly placing the cup on the table. "A book purporting to be yours, about Sherlock Holmes, appears inexplicably in the department of rare and antique books in the British Museum Library, looking as if it is from the future—"

"And that's not all, Dr. Watson," Sir Arthur interrupted me. "It is true that the year of publication of this enigmatic volume is one which is yet to come, but this is not its first edition. By studying the title page, I found that the original first edition had appeared in—this year!"

"This year? Then you ought to be able to trace it. As far as I know, one copy of everything printed in Britain is obligatorily sent to the British Museum Library, is it not?"

"Certainly, certainly. But nobody has published such a book this year, and so we do not have it on our list."

"The year is not finished yet," said I, trying to be clever. "There are two and a half months to go, so possibly...."

"Nothing will happen in the remaining months of this year, Dr. Watson," replied Sir Arthur with assurance. "A firm that does not exist is stated as the first publisher, but there is something else, more momentous.

On the back folder of this future publication, a short biography of the author, Sir Arthur Conan Doyle, is given. Could you make an assumption as to his profession?"

"I have a feeling that he is not the director of the British Museum Library."

"True, he is not. He is a doctor."

"Then it is not you?"

He eyed me suspiciously. I used to get that sort of look from Holmes when some remark of mine irritated him, who knew why. Fortunately, Sir Arthur's reaction was more restrained than Holmes's.

"It would seem so," he answered in a mild voice. "By the way, the biography is accompanied by a photograph. We do not look at all similar."

"Do you, perhaps, recognize that...other...Doyle?" asked Mrs. Simpson unexpectedly. Her voice sounded somehow distant, muted. Sir Arthur had obviously quite forgotten about her: he jumped a little when she spoke up.

"No, he is completely unknown to me," replied Sir Arthur after a short hesitation, turning for a moment to her.

"I thought it might be some cousin of yours. You know, relatives are sometimes capable of making mischief, out of envy...jealousy...Worse than complete strangers, more ruthless. For instance, I have a nephew in Devonshire...."

"But, how is it possible?" I said, quite puzzled. My words prevented Mrs. Simpson from gathering momentum. "You said that there is no other Sir Arthur Conan Doyle."

Sir Arthur did not answer at once. He looked down at his half-empty cup of tea, in which he turned the spoon. He was deep in thought, and he did it unconsciously, making a small monotonous tinkling. When he spoke, it was in a deeper, quieter voice.

"Indeed there is not. At least not in this London."

"Not in *this* London?" I repeated, understanding nothing at all. "To the best of my knowledge, there isn't another. Admittedly, there have been proposals that some towns in the colonies be named 'London,' or rather 'New London,' but—"

"I do not mean the colonies, Mr. Watson," said Sir Arthur impatiently. It was becoming his habit—an unpleasant one—to interrupt me. He was beginning to acquire Holmes's manner. "I mean another London...in another England...on another Earth...."

He fell silent, leaving me in a dilemma as to whether he had finished the sentence or left it dangling; in any case, it was an unfinished thought. What "other London?" "Other England?" What could the words "other Earth" possibly mean? There was nothing "other" in these matters. London and England and the Earth especially, are each unique.

"What nonsense is this, Sir Arthur?" I asked, intending to give my voice a rough undertone, but it came out somewhat shrill and timid. "Of what 'other' places do you speak? There is no other London, far less another England. Or, God forbid, another Earth."

There was no answer, at least not immediately. He continued to make circles in the tea with his spoon, first in one direction and then in the other; this motion undoubtedly had a hypnotic effect on him, making him seem somehow lost, displaced. One could see that he was finding it hard to continue, that he was struggling fiercely with evil spirits inside him. The underground stream on his neck still glistened, although the original flush of his face had long passed.

The silence was broken by Mrs. Simpson. "Sir Arthur...Would you like to eat? You must be hungry. You can't have eaten anything for ages. I could quickly make you something tasty. Perhaps some nice scrambled eggs...."

Turning once again, he gave her a short, vacant look, as if only the sound of the woman's voice and not the meaning of her words had reached him. "Don't you understand?" he said, turning to me. "There is no alternative explanation. None that I can see, at least."

"Oh, there is," I said enthusiastically, like a man to whom all had been suddenly made clear. "And a perfectly visible one. Occam's razor!"

"Occam's razor?"

"Yes. In solving his complicated cases, Holmes often relied on the wise instruction of William of Occam, a Dominican churchman of the fifteenth century. 'When assumptions start to multiply, choose the simplest one.' And I have already mentioned the simplest solution: in all likelihood, someone is playing a joke on you, a stupid joke. You said that nobody in his right mind would invest so much effort, the writing of a whole book, just for a joke. That is true, but who says this is a normal person? If I have learned anything in my years of association with Holmes, it is that a twisted mind is willing to undertake any and every effort in order to fulfill its schemes. In this case, we are dealing with such a mind. Somebody picked you as a target, Sir Arthur, somebody slightly unhinged but also very industrious and as you yourself said, endowed with literary talent. He wrote a book on Holmes—which, by the way, Holmes certainly deserves: it is a wonder that nobody has ever thought to write one before; I would very much like to read it—and then had it printed with false, misleading data on the title page. Small printing shops in the East End will do that for an appropriate sum of money, although this kind of forgery is liable to severe penalties. And then he managed to place it in your department of rare and antique books. This would involve quite an effort, but it would still be incomparably simpler than your idea of...another London, on another Earth.... Wouldn't it?"

I said all of this in one breath, triumphantly, incontrovertibly, like Holmes used to do when concluding a case. Everything fitted, everything was in place, there was a reasonable explanation for everything. If my friend could only see me at this moment! I was proud of myself.

Not for long.

"I would probably have reached that conclusion myself, Mr. Watson, had I not been holding in my hands that—volume. To begin with, it was made in a manner that is not in use anywhere in this country or, almost certainly, in any other. Every aspect of it was somehow...different, more perfect. The work, the binding, the luxury of the covers, the typeface. It simply does not belong to our time. No modest East End printer would be able to produce anything remotely similar. Not even the luxurious editions of the Royal Printing House can compare with this. Then there's the paper—"

"There is extraordinary paper in our time also," I interrupted him, straining to rescue my daring assumption, which had suddenly begun to wobble though it had looked so steady, at least to me. "In Bologna, Italy, a *signore* Murratori...."

I stopped in mid-word, struck by an idea that seemed quite mad. The thought of Murratori had started a long chain of associations, at the end of which stood one name: Moriarty! If all that Sir Arthur was saying were true, then behind the mysterious appearance of the book chronicling Holmes's adventures was not some idle prankster who had spared no effort to carry out his lunatic idea; no, the perpetrator of such a convoluted and twisted hoax centered on Holmes and not on poor Sir Arthur, could only have been the shadowy genius of Moriarty! But...how?

He was just about to ask me something, but Mrs. Simpson spoke first. "I'll go and prepare a meal. You'll feel much better after you've got some scrambled eggs inside you. I've got some fresh eggs, you know, and—" As she walked out of the dining room and into the kitchen, she continued to discourse on the advantages of evening scrambled eggs and the importance of regular nutrition in general for a healthy mind. We watched her go in silence, in which there was something conspiratorial, as if both of us were tacitly glad that the conversation that was to follow would be without a witness.

When we were left alone, I spoke first. "Sir Arthur, does the name 'Moriarty' mean anything to you?"

"Moriarty? You mean that arch-criminal who was recently, I think a few weeks past, found dead in a lake?"

I nodded, but before I could continue, Sir Arthur raised his head, looked me piercingly in the eye, and added in a voice reduced almost to inaudibility:

"Except that he did not perish there."

I stared at him, my jaw dropping. This was too much. Not even his batty hypotheses about books arriving from the future and other Londons on other Earths had shaken me as much as this simple statement of a secret that I had thought nobody else besides me knew or could ever know. Only my ears had heard that horrendous, inhuman voice behind the locked door of the drawing room. Suddenly, I felt as if the rug had been pulled from under my feet. Everything around me seemed to sway.

"How...how do you know?" I stammered.

"Elementary, Dr. Watson," replied Sir Arthur in a tone now more brisk and energetic, as if my involuntary admission of the correctness of his statement, which he had barely dared to whisper, now gave him heart. "I read it in the book."

"In which book?" I asked, aware of the stupidity of the question.

This was confirmed by another penetrating glance from Sir Arthur, but his reaction was not violent this time either. "In *The Adventures of Sherlock Holmes*," he said mildly. "I have read the book, naturally."

"Naturally," I repeated mechanically, like an echo.

"Exquisite reading matter," he continued enthusiastically. "I would not be in the least ashamed to be its genuine author. Quite the contrary."

"But you are not?"

"I certainly am not because among other things, I have never had much of an imagination, you know. I am a man with both feet firmly on the ground." He paused for a moment and added in a somewhat crestfallen manner: "At least I was, until recently."

"What do you mean, imagination? Is it not a book about the real experiences of Sherlock Holmes, something like a romanticized version of his diaries? I thought...."

"Oh, no, you had the wrong idea. As far as I can judge, nothing in it is real. Not one of the cases described in it has really happened. It's all fictional."

"But why would someone go to the trouble of inventing Holmes's adventures when those that have actually happened are more than sufficient—in excitement, in mystery...."

"I can only guess, Mr. Watson. And the simplest assumption, fully in the spirit of your beloved Occam's razor, tells me that the writer...whoever might be my mysterious namesake...simply did not know of Holmes's real adventures. What is more, he probably had no idea that Holmes exists. I mean, this Holmes, here...."

His voice tailed off again. The sudden silence was penetrated only by the muffled noises of the preparation of food in the kitchen. This time Mrs. Simpson had not left the door open behind her, as she had done when she went to fetch the tea. It was obvious that she did not wish to hear anything more of the dialogue in the dining room.

"Well, is there another Holmes? Are we returning to your extremely...er...strange idea of another London?"

"I am afraid it is an inevitable idea, Mr. Watson, though I agree that it is certainly not the simplest possibility. On the contrary."

A thought crossed my mind, filling me with a strange wave of anxiety, such as I had never before experienced. "Am I mentioned in the book? I mean, does another Watson go with the other Holmes?"

"Oh, certainly. You are present in every story. Holmes's steady follower and assistant. His right hand, just as you are here."

Although the cold fingers of dread had penetrated my chest, I was simultaneously flooded with a feeling akin to pride. I could not resist the urge to ask: "That other Watson...How is he described?"

He did not answer at once. It seemed to me that he was taking some time to find the right words. When he spoke again, a smile played briefly on his lips. "Well...quite true to life, I should say. There are some minor differences, though. You, for instance, do not sport a moustache, while the other Watson does, but you are, for the most part, represented as you are: a good-natured man, loyal, useful, simple in spirit...."

Sir Arthur fell silent, but his smile widened, as if he wanted to add something, but refrained at the last moment. "You would not be disappointed, Dr. Watson, especially in view of the fact that the character was not, of course, modeled on you. As far as I can judge, Mrs. Hudson is also represented with verity."

"Mrs. Simpson," I corrected him.

"Yes. Mrs. Simpson. I keep making that mistake because in the book her name is Hudson. Similarly, your address is given as 221-B Baker Street, while this is 221-A. That's why on my way here today I first knocked on the house next to yours, convinced that it was Holmes's. You see, these minor, seemingly unimportant discrepancies ultimately persuaded me that this book on Holmes's adventures is not from...this world. I first noticed it in the descriptions of London. Yes, it was the London we know, the Houses of Parliament, Big Ben, Trafalgar Square, Tower Bridge, Piccadilly, the West End—but everything seemed somehow misplaced, wrong, out of true, real and unreal at the same time. You could recognize things, but there was always some jarring inaccuracy in the details, something which did not fit, conspicuous to a greater or lesser extent. Then I asked myself what possible reason the author could have had for introducing such a multitude of differences, which would only confuse the reader. Do not these mistakes discredit him from being a reliable guide through plots of detective stories in which every smallest detail must be in its proper place? How is anyone to believe that the narrator holds all the threads of the dramatic action in his hands, if, for instance, Tower Bridge is quite needlessly shown to be a good two miles upstream?"

The question was, of course, not directed at me, but as Sir Arthur had fallen silent for a moment, I felt it my duty to say: "I don't really know."

"The answer was there, in front of my eyes," he continued, ignoring my remark. "But very hard to accept, precisely because of a prejudice emerging from respect for Occam's razor. Oh, by the way, Occam is frequently mentioned in the book, but as a Franciscan monk from the fourteenth century and not a Dominican one from the fifteenth, as he is here. Another discrepancy, you see. So, in fact there are no mistakes. London is, like everything else, shown with perfect fidelity; however, not this, our London, but another, different one."

"Sir Arthur," I said, having thought of something I should have demanded much earlier, as soon as that unfortunate volume was mentioned. "Would you show me the book? *The Adventures of Sherlock Holmes*? I would like to see it myself. You brought it with you, I hope?"

His gaze again drifted to his teacup, which had been empty for some time. He was still making circles in it with the teaspoon, clearly unaware that he was doing so. The monotonous clinking sound spread through the room like the distant, but ominous tolling of a bell.

"I cannot show it to you, Dr. Watson," he said finally, looking up at me. "It has vanished."

4. THE LAST CHAPTER

"WHAT DO YOU mean, vanished?" I asked with incredulity. "Somebody took it? Stole it?"

"Oh, no. I literally mean vanished, right before my very eyes. I was actually holding it in my hands at the time, and then—a sudden flash of white light, searing, blindingly bright. Every hair on my body stood up, my skin tightened into goose pimples...I sensed that sparks of some sort were crackling everywhere around, dancing on the surfaces of the surrounding objects in my study, on my clothes and uncovered parts of my body. There was no discomfort, no pain, quite the opposite. I experienced something akin to delight, exhilaration. As if I were...flying...in a trance. Everything was rattling around me, like an earthquake. It lasted—I don't know—fifteen seconds maybe, no more. When the flash died down and my eyes grew accustomed again to the usual light at my desk—which took some time—the book was just not there. My hands were still in the same position, as if holding it, but the book had disappeared, I simply don't know how. I felt nothing, no motion...."

I stared at him for a few moments wordlessly, filled with a mixture of disbelief and anxiety. Everything that this man had said since he set foot in Holmes's house sounded absolutely incredible and unreal, and reason was telling me that it was devoid of any sense, that it was lunacy...However, another part of my mind, that which kept reminding me of what had happened to Holmes in my presence, kept emitting signals that tightened my throat, sent shivers up my spine, accelerated my breathing...Being a doctor, I easily recognized the symptoms of catatonic fear.

"Er...when did this happen?"

"Oh," said Sir Arthur, taking his watch from the pocket of his waistcoat. It was a massive watch, on a thick gold chain; when he lifted the lid, the first few notes of "God save the Queen" sounded. "Exactly one hour and twelve minutes ago. The wall clock in my office was just striking four when the—event—occurred."

"But, that was now! I mean, this afternoon."

My talent for stating the obvious was again evident. This time he did not look suspiciously at me. The man seemed to be getting used to it.

"That's right. I made my decision promptly. I simply had to see Holmes about the matter. All the reasons that had previously prevented me from doing so had become immaterial. I left immediately; I tried to catch a hansom along the way, but unsuccessfully. You know how it is, a free hansom is never at hand when you need it most. I lost count of how many passed me, but every one was taken, as if to spite me, so I was forced to walk all the way from the Library to here, which is, I am sure you will agree, quite an accomplishment for a man of my age and stature."

I nodded in agreement, remembering my own suffering in similar situations. Sir Arthur was approximately my age and build, so we shared similar problems.

"It seems that I do not partake of sufficient exercise. I was quickly out of breath and managed to keep going only because I so strongly desired to see Holmes. At times I thought my heart would leap out of my chest. Besides, I was burdened by the foreboding that I would not find him here...that I was too late. As in fact turns out to be the case."

My gaze drifted involuntarily to the underground stream of sweat on his neck. It had dried up, leaving only a dry meandering trace. I felt sorry for him, knowing what an effort he had put into getting here, but I did not quite understand the hurry. There were several incomplete or undivulged elements to his story. For one thing, I did not understand why he had not come to Holmes immediately after the discovery of the book. He would have been too late, of course, since the book's mysterious arrival had, apparently, coincided with Holmes's equally mysterious disappearance, but he could not have known that. He had mentioned something from the book's contents in this regard, but nothing that he later told me of the book, strange though it might seem, could have explained the delay. Quite the opposite: knowing Holmes well, he could easily have imagined that he would be delighted with the entire matter which, to him, would surely have posed the case of all cases, more challenging even than those Moriarty had created for him. And then, after four whole days of restraint, this great, almost panic-stricken urgency at the hour when the key item of evidence had vanished, leaving one with no choice except to trust or not to trust Sir Arthur's word. On top of everything else was his feeling that Holmes would not be here. On what might that have been based? Something did not fit.

Either Sir Arthur was not telling me the whole story, or he was inventing the whole thing. But why would he do the latter? Oh, I could think of several fairly convincing reasons. Adhering to Occam's razor, I would gladly have plumped for some of these, rather than the more fantastic possibilities, if Holmes really had absented himself for some new case. In light of what really had happened to my friend, however, Occam's razor was no longer a reliable guide. Hence I had to assume that he was telling the truth, however incredible it sounded, but also that he was holding something back. He had left out some key element. I did not know why—perhaps because the entire affair was too unbelievable, and he feared I would not accept it. Or was it because of his unfulfilled storyteller's tendency to delay the denouement, to build up the tension? If it were the latter, I had to let him know that I did not hold much appreciation for that sort of thing. In literature, perhaps, I can tolerate it, though it irritated me there too—so that I frequently read the end of a novel first, which usually made Holmes angry—but in reality, certainly not, and least of all in a situation like this. His last remark gave me an opening to clarify matters.

"What makes you think that you are too late, Sir Arthur? And in what sense too late? If the volume has already...gone, then I see no cause for hurry, particularly as I do not anticipate Holmes's early return. He is, as I say, traveling...out of London, so that...."

"I know where Holmes is," said he in a tone of quiet confidence that brooked no disagreement.

"You do?" I said dully.

"I do...He is out of London, all right, very far outside London. So far, actually, that I myself refused to believe it until the expression on your face at the front door when I asked you if Holmes was at home confirmed for me, finally and fully, that the book was telling the truth."

"The book? I do not understand."

"Aye, the book. The last chapter of *The Adventures of Sherlock Holmes*. The book is so coherent, so unified, except for that closing chapter, which differs completely, in style, point of view, genre, as if written by another writer with an entirely different intention, and not by Sir Arthur Conan Doyle—I mean, not by that other Doyle."

He paused, losing track for a moment at the thought of this strange duality of his person, which gave me time to accustom myself to the new turn of events. The bristling of short hairs on the back of my neck told me clearly that this was not just another divergence. I knew the symptoms: I had experienced it many times while working with Holmes. The unraveling was about to begin; the case would now be solved. The time for unnecessary postponements was finally over. It was then that I envied Sir Arthur: he had had the opportunity to read the whole thing in advance, the end first and then all the preceding chapters; he had not had to exert himself unduly, like me.

"The final section is titled 'Sherlock Holmes's Last Case,'" he continued. "Unlike the rest of the book, it is narrated in the first person: Holmes himself describes his last and most marvelous adventure, a case that is not at all of a detective nature, at least not in the sense that the others are, the ones about which Doyle writes."

"Not of a detective nature?" I asked perplexed. "Holmes was...I mean...is the greatest detective genius of our age. What other occupation could he have?"

He gave me a look in which there was a hint of rebuke, perhaps even anger.

"How odd that you should ask that, Dr. Watson. One would expect you to know better the man in whose company you have spent so much time. Hasn't it ever crossed your mind that he might be deeply dissatisfied by the fact that he was squandering his unique talents—his intelligence, ingenuity, education, exploratory enthusiasm—on something as trivial as sifting the dregs of human society? And that is what he has been doing, is it not—investigating criminal cases, the most debased expression of human nature, behind which stand such low passions as avarice or sick perversion or pathology. They may have been complex cases, beyond the range of the ordinary police intelligence, but unraveling them soon ceased to give him pleasure, lost the magnetism of challenge. Admittedly, he continued this work but without enthusiasm, by inertia, because it was expected of him."

"You are mistaken, sir," I said energetically, feeling a new wave of anxiety and unease. Sir Arthur had touched a very painful and well concealed place. "Holmes took on new cases with excitement and enjoyed solving them...."

"Because you...helped...him, Dr. Watson." The rebuke in his eyes turned into open accusation.

"Oh, do not overestimate me, Sir Arthur. I was only his companion and assistant, and should not be credited with—"

"I don't mean that sort of assistance. I mean morphine."

He said it flatly, as if stating an ordinary fact. The simplicity of the statement disarmed me completely, so that I did not even try to pretend or to defend myself.

"How...do you know?" I stammered.

"From the book, of course, from the last, confessional chapter. Holmes describes how he sank into ever deeper depression, even hopelessness, from which he was rescued by your injections. They were all that kept him from falling headlong into the abyss of utter despair, which yawned all around him. Time slipped away inexorably, and his life was getting more and more bogged down in the monotony and grayness of banal criminal cases: an occasional mysterious murder, an inexplicable disappearance, a cunningly planned theft, and similar petty matters. Despite the fame he gained by solving them, he began to loathe them, longing for true spiritual challenge. He desired to face some of the great, ultimate questions because they were his match. He felt terribly misused and slighted, and even thought of suicide."

Of course, this description of Holmes's condition fit the truth perfectly, although Sir Arthur could not, should not know it. How did he—I had the most awkward feeling he saw through me. And then, as the icy fingers of panic tightened around my chest, a thought occurred to me, and I clutched at it like a drowning man at a straw and said: "But the book...it is not about this Holmes, you said it was about that other...." I halted, surprised by my own readiness to accept, when in dire straits, this hypothesis that I had thought only a moment ago to be insane.

"Only partly, Dr. Watson. Most of the book does indeed refer to the 'other' Holmes, the one that flowed from Doyle's pen. But the last, confessional chapter was written by your friend personally—by 'this' Holmes, as you say."

"How do you know? How is that possible?"

"I do not know how it is possible, but I know for certain that it is so. To begin with, there are no discrepancies, everything fits reality as we know it. There is no other London; our London is depicted, this one in which both of us are now. Besides, events are mentioned that we both know truly happened here. For instance, your visit to the Library with Holmes's instructions to fetch certain books for him."

"That does not prove anything yet," I said, interrupting him again but for the moment not caring about courtesy. There was no more time for beating about the bush—open discussion was unavoidable. "I mean, with all due respect, even without this supposed...confession...by Holmes, you knew I came to the Library. If you wish to persuade me that it is genuine, you must describe some event...some phenomenon...about which you could not have known anything."

This time Sir Arthur's look was conspicuously pitying. That was precisely the way Holmes looked at me when I dared to doubt some of his extravagant theories merely because they sounded impossible to me. I was noticing in general an increasing similarity between the two men—at least in the range of looks at their disposal.

"Gladly, Dr. Watson. Do you wish to start from the very beginning—from Moriarty's epistle containing the circle? On Murratori's paper?"

5. LIGHT

OF COURSE I surrendered at once. It was the gesture of an experienced chess-player who knows when the game is over and respects his opponent too much to waste his time with superfluous additional moves. I decided not to interrupt Sir Arthur with any further suspicious and inappropriate questions, but nodded briefly and became all ears.

"In fact, we must go back another step," he began. "To Moriarty's death in the lake several weeks ago. It was not, as officially declared, an accident. Oh, no, don't worry—Holmes did not kill him, as has just occurred to you, judging by your face. It was a premeditated suicide."

I barely repressed an exclamation; only my firm decision not to interrupt stopped me, but not before my mouth had gaped open. The sight must have been rather comical since my companion smiled briefly before continuing.

"It seems that Moriarty, who—you will agree—was no less intelligent or astute than Holmes, suffered from the same ailment as his rival. The initial pleasure in carrying out perfect crimes soon faded, leaving behind a void, which could only be filled by greater intellectual challenges. Unlike Holmes, who sank into moodiness and hopelessness and waited for such challenges to come knocking at his door, Moriarty was more enterprising and went looking for them, and in the right place—the British Museum Library."

The "Ah!" that escaped from me was quite involuntary. I pulled a penitent face, which drew another brief smile from Sir Arthur.

"It was only from Holmes's confession that I managed to piece together what had in fact happened right under my nose. About half a year ago I noticed a steep increase in interest in some of our ancient volumes. Various people of both sexes began to visit the department of rare and antique books, always studying the same few titles. I did not attach any great importance to this, thinking it was part of the recent fad for esoteric subjects. How could I have known or even suspected that it was always the same person, the proven master of disguise—Moriarty. Whatever it was that he was trying to find in the ancient tomes, he wished the search itself to be as inconspicuous as possible. Not long after, the interest suddenly waned, and this attracted my attention, but by then it was too late. The only remaining trace was the fact that several pages had been torn out the disappearance of which could not be explained, because we strictly scrutinize every user of rare and antique titles. Of course, the puzzle would have been much easier to understand if we had known who, in fact, had been visiting us."

I nodded mutely, to show my full understanding. I remembered how many times I myself had been a victim of similar tricks of Moriarty's. On one occasion, he deceived me by disguising himself as a statue in a park, from whose hand a jet of water was flowing. Luckily, I had taken an oath of silence, so I was not tempted to reveal this embarrassing incident. To think I had so gladly quenched my thirst from that fountain following a hard chase after Moriarty....Holmes shook with laughter for a good fifteen minutes when I told him the story, and he had explained to me the nature of my "fountain."

"I tried to find out by reconstruction what was on the missing pages that was so important that somebody should act with such vandalism, but I failed, of course. It would have been an act of vanity to expect success. Who am I, after all, to measure myself against the genius—dark though it be—of a Moriarty? Only now, from Holmes's confession, I have an idea, though incomplete, about it."

The sudden sound of the wall clock in the dining room striking six o'clock interrupted Sir Arthur. We both looked for a moment at the great pendulum under the clock face. It was swinging hypnotically. I think that the unexpected sound startled him a little more than me. He was obviously one of those people who "lived" their own story as they were telling it. For him, it was as if Moriarty were somewhere near, in the room with us, disguised maybe as the wall clock, or even as me....

"Apparently, Moriarty accidentally came across this idea about the existence of another world. The other Earth, with the other, differing London and all the rest. It was, at last, the great challenge, the ultimate adventure of the spirit, something that he had yearned for and would never share with his main rival—if he did not have to. But the powers he possessed, though great, were nevertheless not great enough to carry out the plan that inevitably followed from the discovery of that parallel world: an attempt to communicate with it."

"Communicate...with...." I whispered.

"Aye. All the more so because, as Holmes claims, the stolen pages indicated that from the other side too efforts to establish such contact are constantly being made—known for some reason as 'completing the Circle,' a metaphor no doubt that somehow infiltrated into our world, or grew here parallel to it. I do not know. In any case, the trail Moriarty began to follow, the signpost concealed in some ancient book, the founding stone on which he was to erect this entire edifice, was this: a circle."

I remembered at that moment my conversation with Holmes regarding the circle from Moriarty's letter and his excitement at the time. How angry he had been with me when I had failed to see in the message of his arch-rival anything more than just a circularly drawn line! But how was I to know? To me it was just a plain, ordinary circle. I have always been one to take things at face value.

"However, to open such a channel," Sir Arthur continued, "it was essential to jettison certain hindrances, certain items of ballast, the first of which was one's own corporeality, materiality. You see, nothing material can penetrate the barrier between the two worlds. Holmes, in his confession, explains in detail why this is so, and mentions some discoveries that are only to be made in the future; unfortunately, my familiarity with physics is really very modest, so that I did not understand much. What I did comprehend was, that there are some tiny particles that rotate in opposite directions and have opposite electric charges—but why they cannot mingle with each other, I cannot explain."

There was in his voice an undertone of dismay, almost as if he were ashamed. I hastened to encourage him.

"You may omit the technicalities, Sir Arthur. I do not know much about physics either."

"Thus, Moriarty had to fulfill the necessary condition. To divest himself of his own body...to die...at least, in one sense."

"How does one die 'in one sense'?" In my voice there was no surprise. My capacity to be surprised had long since faded in this conversation.

He shrugged. "Well, the body dies, but the...soul...does not. I am aware that in other circumstances this would sound like mere babble, religious mysticism, but do not forget that these are special circumstances, very special."

The warning was quite superfluous. Even had I wanted to, how could I forget?

"Holmes was most impressed by Moriarty's achievement, although in fact Moriarty succeeded not so much through his own ingenuity, as through his experiences in the Orient, where he learned some extremely bizarre techniques from Tibetan monks: astral projection, levitation...."

Holmes's intuition had been correct, then. One enigma in Moriarty's life had finally been explained: he had reached the Dalai Lama and had not fallen into the trap of becoming a radish or a ladybird. But how had he got them to reveal to him their most precious secrets? Then I thought of Holmes's ominous warning that the man should never be underestimated, not even when dead, let alone alive.

"So, Moriarty 'died' in the lake," Sir Arthur went on. "Accidental drowning after his boat overturned was the official report, and you did indeed identify the body, but the body only. His spirit was, in the meantime, preoccupied with the greatest of all challenges—an attempt to establish contact with the Others. However, the first attempt failed. Moriarty alone was just not enough to achieve this. He was, thus, faced with a terrible dilemma: to abandon the entire project at the moment when he was so near to accomplishing it, or to ask for assistance."

The sound of the kitchen door opening interrupted him. A moment later Mrs. Simpson came into the dining room, carrying a laden tray. The smell of fresh scrambled eggs and onions roasted in oil filled the room.

"You will soon feel much better, Sir Arthur," said she. "Nothing like a good bite to eat for overwrought nerves. Dr. Watson will tell you. We've often spoken about it, and just today I mentioned to him a cousin of mine in Kent who...."

I looked at her crossly, and she stopped talking. The old woman coughed a little in embarrassment, placed the plate on the table in front of Sir Arthur and added, "I made this for you too, Dr. Watson, in case you're hungry. Now if you'll excuse me, I have to tidy up the kitchen."

She left hurriedly. In her movements I recognized a mixture of emotions: she was glad to leave the dining room because then she would not have to listen to things unpleasant to her, but she was also angry because I had not allowed her to expound her views on medicinal matters.

Sir Arthur waited until the kitchen door was closed, then continued. "Moriarty's predicament was truly horrible: he simply could not abandon everything, but on the other hand, only one man existed who was in every respect able to help him complete the project: his sworn enemy, his eternal opponent, Holmes."

He paused and glanced at the food. He must have decided to suppress for the moment his animal appetites and give priority to the story, which he too was obviously enjoying and which was nearing a climax, for he gently pushed the tray toward the middle of the table. It occurred to me that it was fortunate that Mrs. Simpson had gone out.

"In the end, he decided, with the deepest reluctance, on the latter. He now had to win Holmes over to the idea. This was facilitated by one action which had initially been motivated by sheer malevolence. Moriarty meant for Holmes to follow in his steps and reach the same goal, but only as runner-up and not as an equal. Without that, Moriarty's sense of triumph and gloating would not be complete."

Knowing Moriarty's nature well, I could easily believe that. I have long been puzzled by the conspicuous incongruence between Moriarty's extraordinary intelligence and his equally extraordinary baseness of character. Only after one of Holmes's casual remarks did I realize that in fact there was no contradiction at all. "It is just a common prejudice," Holmes had said, "that great intelligence must be accompanied by great goodness. All prominent criminals in history were very intelligent. The opposite case is much rarer."

"This is why he arranged," continued Sir Arthur, "that after his 'death' Holmes should get a letter on Murratori's paper, with a circle drawn on it; he believed that this would be sufficient encouragement to Holmes to embark on the same course, but to hedge his bet, he also arranged that crucial pages, which he had torn out of the ancient books, arrive soon thereafter, under separate cover."

"Holmes did not mention that other letter to me," I said. Even as I said this, I was aware that by these words I was finally confirming the veracity of Sir Arthur's story. There was, now, no return. There had been no return in fact for some time. The game of hide-and-seek was over.

"Holmes did not have an opportunity. The second letter was delivered to him in your absence, after you had injected him with morphine and left him apparently resting. The postman gave the letter to Holmes personally, as instructed, while Mrs. Hud—Mrs. Simpson was making tea for him."

"Apparently?"

"Apparently, yes, because the morphine played a key role. Instead of helping him to sleep, as you had intended, it woke him up. It drove away the exhaustion and cleared his mind, enlightening it. Under that influence, but also with the help of the missing pages, everything began to fall into place. Voids were filled, blunders eliminated, falsities dispelled. Borne on an artificial tide of enthusiasm and delight, Holmes rushed up an ascending line towards the light, which was beginning to appear before him, toward the closing of the Circle."

"But it did not go all that smoothly. There was a clash, a struggle. I heard Moriarty's savage yell, a madman's roar, in fact. And the destruction in the drawing room...."

"Oh, yes. The union could not be accomplished painlessly, without strife, but that was just a marginal episode."

"Union? You do not mean...."

"Integration, yes. It could not have been done in any other way. Holmes alone would not have succeeded, nor would Moriarty alone. Only by a uniting of the forces of those two sworn enemies could the ultimate step be taken—the lifting of the barrier between the two worlds. Moriarty had tried alone and failed. This is why he took the union much harder. He felt like a loser, a man who had to share with somebody the spoils that he had almost grabbed for himself. Hence the rage that you could hear through the door of the drawing room. For Holmes, however, this joining was an exotic adventure, an exceptional new experience. It is not every day that your mind gets—quite literally—merged with the mind of someone who was your chief enemy during the course of your life."

"But that means," I said, taken by a new, sudden, terrible thought, "that Holmes is also dead...at least in the sense that Moriarty is!"

"I should rather say that he made a transit into...a new form...of existence, though in every practical, earthly sense you are, I think, right. Yes, technically he is dead, although of course his body, or corpse, is missing."

"What happened to his body?" I said in a trembling voice. The concept of a "new form of existence" was certainly comforting, but nevertheless I felt as if I were standing in a morgue.

Sir Arthur shrugged. "I don't know anything about that. In Holmes's chapter there is no mention of it. Perhaps it will turn up somewhere, as Moriarty's floated up in the lake."

He said it as lightly as if we were discussing some misplaced trifle or wrapping. I shuddered involuntarily at the thought.

"Is that the end of the chapter? I mean, is there any mention of events after Holmes and Moriarty broke through the...barrier, as you describe it?"

"Well, there is a brief part remaining. Four, five pages at most, but I understand very little of it. The narration switches back to the third person, since it is clearly no longer Holmes. I thought perhaps that it might be a new being, created when Moriarty and Holmes were made into one, immediately before the breakthrough, but that is quite uncertain. Be that as it may, he is now on some...planet...if I understand correctly. The planet seems to be without any atmosphere, but that does not currently create any difficulties for him, totally unprotected though he is. He is steadily walking in the direction of a destination that he calls 'The Circle.' He is racing against the rising of a sun, one of three suns that shine in the sky of that world, but it is not clear even to him why he is there or what will be when he steps into that 'Circle.' He is dressed in a priestly robe with a hood. Occasionally he thinks he hears music. The story ends at the moment before he steps into the 'Circle,' so that the meaning of the whole business remains pretty unclear."

He fell silent, clearly having nothing more to say, but I continued to stare at him; I had an odd sensation that the silence was gradually thickening around us, becoming almost palpable, substantial. From this silence, a tense foreboding seemed to grow, increasing the evil sense of anticipation created by the unfinished story. Naturally, in such circumstances my ability to think was totally paralyzed. And what could I have thought, faced with a history so fantastic, so unreal? Yet, one question did form slowly in my mind.

"So we do not know if the contact was made. I mean, if the 'Circle' is the barrier that separates the two worlds—"

"Oh, we do, we do. Have you forgotten?"

My gaze told him eloquently that I had no idea what he was talking about.

"The book, for God's sake! The first artifact that came from the other world into ours." I think this was the first moment in conversation with me that his patience failed him. Which was remarkable—Holmes's would have given out long since....

"But you said nothing material...."

"I did. I can only surmise how the book...got through. Perhaps the barrier is...impenetrable...for material objects only at first. Bear in mind the coinciding of the arrival of the book with the probable arrival of the united Holmes-Moriarty being in the 'Circle,' if that is what the last chapter speaks of. Perhaps the book did not pass through as an object."

"What do you mean?"

"It might have materialized here."

"Materi—"

"Holmes does mention the word, in his explanations of physics, remember? Particles which spin in opposite directions and all the rest? There is an analogy with a mirror there. You put some object before the barrier—an image is reflected here, an identical image. Not a mere reflection, however, but real, material. Though as I understand it, a vast expenditure of energy is involved. This might be the case, but of course I cannot be sure. My grasp of physics is, as I mentioned, fairly poor."

"All right, let us suppose that something of the kind did happen and that the volume really was from another world. How do you interpret its vanishing? Why did it disappear? What is the purpose of an artifact, as you call it, if it is soon to, to...melt into thin air?"

Sir Arthur did not immediately answer. For some time now he had been absently picking with his fork at Mrs. Simpson's scrambled eggs sitting in the center of the table. It was plain to see that he was not aware of this. I remembered at that moment how he had just as mechanically mixed the dregs of his tea in the cup. These absent, hypnotic movements probably soothed him, preparing him to say something that was gradually building up inside but could not find a suitable vent. So it was this time.

"The purpose," said he, repeating my word. "Maybe the only purpose of the book was to warn us, to prepare us. To announce."

"To announce what?" This sort of simple-minded question often made Holmes lose his temper.

"Not what, *whom*." In Sir Arthur's voice this time there was no reproach; it was mild and subdued, prophetic, perhaps. "Our...envoys, Holmes and Moriarty, have arrived in the other world, but not suddenly and not unexpected. As I understand it, their transition was anticipated, there was a group of...a group of those who waited, knowing that they would arrive. There is no such welcoming committee on this side, or there was not, until recently, but now...."

"Who would make up a welcoming party of that sort? Nobody knows of this, except us: you and I and, partly, Mrs. Simpson. You surely do not mean to say that...."

He only shrugged his shoulders; I felt my hands tremble. After a moment or two, the tremor spread to my entire body and a few seconds later I realized that the vibration was not produced by my shaken psyche. Sir Arthur was shaking too, and all the objects around us in the dining room also: the crockery in the corner cupboard, the small ornaments in the glass cabinets, the tray with the now cold scrambled eggs in the middle of the table, the chairs, the lamp hanging from the ceiling.

The pendulum in the wall clock was forced out of equilibrium; losing its rhythm, its swing reached a point previously unattainable—the side wall of its wooden casing. A hollow, crunching noise of ominous origin was coming from the upper floor and I thought I also heard the sounds of furniture moving in the drawing room. At the same time, from the kitchen erupted the crashing sound of pots and pans falling from their wall hooks to the floor, accompanied by Mrs. Simpson's scream.

"An earthquake!" I exclaimed in panic, jumping to my feet and running for the door.

"No, in God's name, not an earthquake, Watson!" Sir Arthur shouted after me. He was on his feet too, but standing still, his wild gaze riveted to the ceiling. "It is beginning! Don't you understand? This is exactly how it shook when the book disappeared! Now there will be light...."

And, indeed, there was light.

When in two strides I found myself in the corridor, I was blinded by a powerful white radiance streaming down from the upper floor. I remembered then that milky band that I had noticed in the darkness when Sir Arthur arrived and that had vanished when I lit the lamp. But now the feeble spark of the lamp in the corridor was entirely lost in the mighty blaze from above, a glare that engulfed and absorbed everything. Although of unimaginable intensity, it was in fact the very negation of light, because as in a dark night, everything was lost in it, invisible, flooded by the core of the noonday sun.

Instinctively, I put my hands over my eyes, but the brilliance went right through the soft tissues, unobstructed even by the bones, which were noticeable only as stripes of slightly dimmed light. And so, with my eyes tightly closed and hands pressed firmly over them, I continued to see.

I saw her first as an amorphous entity that materialized at the top of the staircase leading to the drawing room. As she moved down a step, limbs became visible in the elongated ovoid, limbs long and fragile—and I knew a woman was treading towards me.

The second step down revealed her hair, long and wavy, falling in cascades behind her shoulders and out of sight. The third step in her slow, graceful descent brought a distinctness to her curves, soft and gentle, emphasizing breast and loins.

When at the fourth step her face became visible—virginal, of amazing grace—the shock of recognition stopped my heart for a moment. Of course I had seen her before, innumerable times—and she had always smiled down on me from on high as now, serenely, chastely. On me—and all others who, as believers or just out of curiosity, visited cathedrals or the humblest little churches in the remotest places, wherein she dwelt, on walls or in icons, her child in her arms, or more rarely alone.

Mary!

I put my hands down and opened my eyes. The brilliance was still there, but it no longer distressed me. Now I was seeing with another, altered vision that reached beyond light, seeing deeply, through, all the way to the barrier and beyond.

And there, across the rim, I finally saw them gathered in The Circle. All of them: Holmes/Moriarty, and the old man, Mary and the Master, and Sri, Buddha, the monkey, and the others, and Spider, the spheres, and the pack. All the builders were there together, creators of the link, contact makers, smiling and waving to me. I smiled too and waved a hand briefly at them. Then I stretched out my arms to Rama, helping her to descend the few remaining steps between us.

ACKNOWLEDGMENTS

The author would like to thank L. Timmel Duchamp for her close reading of *The Fourth Circle* and many precious suggestions.

AFTERWORD
A Brief History of *The Fourth Circle*

I WAS 45 when I wrote *The Fourth Circle*, back in 1993. By that time, I was the author of several books dealing in various ways with science fiction, all of them non-fiction. My sole previous excursions into the realm of fiction writing were a play, "Project Lyre," and a short story—nothing worth mentioning, although "Project Lyre" was published in a Japanese magazine.

Why would a scholar, with an MA and a PhD in science fiction, suddenly decide to turn to fiction writing, deep into middle age?

When, in 1990, after an entire decade of truly hard labor, I published *The Encyclopedia of Science Fiction*, a two-volume set so large and heavy it could almost have been used as a blunt instrument, I realized a simple fact: there were no more challenges for me in that direction. Indeed, what goal more ambitious could I have set for myself, as a writer of non-fiction, than an encyclopaedia?

Yet I was intellectually far too young for retirement. The solution to the problem was to find a new challenge elsewhere, outside of non-fiction writing. One possibility was to embark on an academic career. I could have accepted an offer to deliver a course on the history and theory of SF genre for the Department of Comparative Literature, Faculty of Philology at the University of Belgrade. I declined the position, however, deciding that it wouldn't be very different from early retirement.

The key factor which led me to try my skill at fiction writing was my editorial experience. In 1982 I founded "Polaris," one of the first privately owned publishing houses in the former communist countries. "Polaris" was basically a one-man show. I performed almost all the duties, from selecting titles to packaging copies to be sent to subscribers. I didn't mind this diversity, until one of the duties finally became a burden too heavy for my increasingly older shoulders.

Editing translations and original texts was never a job I much liked. It's very time consuming and largely unrewarding. Maybe I wouldn't have found it so difficult to do, if the works I dealt with hadn't seemed to me of poorer and poorer literary quality. It was inevitable that I would eventually ask myself a fundamental question. Why was I wasting my two most precious commodities—time and a certain talent—to contribute to the promotion of other writers, when I could invest them in my own writing? I could surely write better than the majority of authors I published in "Polaris." There was a certain arrogance in this stance, I don't deny it, but without it I probably would never have dared to launch myself into the turbulent sea of fiction writing.

Although rather voluminous, *The Fourth Circle* was written in less than four months in early 1993 while a civil war was in full swing all around me. It was a very peculiar experience, quite different from the writing of any of my non-fiction books, when I knew precisely what I wanted to do and how to do it. In the case of my first novel, there was no plan, no preconception whatsoever. Although it might sound incredible, when I typed on my monitor the simplest possible first sentence—The Circle.—I hadn't the slightest idea what would follow.

But somewhere beneath my conscious level, quite unknown to my rational self, a critical mass was gathering. My knowledge of literature in general and science fiction in particular, accumulated over previous decades, gradually transformed into a new quality. As soon as it had a chance to be released, it erupted almost like a volcano. Actually, the eruption would probably have been even stronger, had it not faced an unexpected technical obstacle: the velocity of my typing. I type, namely, (mis)using only my right hand index finger, which, after many years of such abuse, has become rather thicker and more gnarled than its left hand counterpart.

What I went through at that time was almost a personality-split. I was simultaneously a writer, mostly unconscious of what he was doing, and a reader more and more impatient due to the slowness of the writer's typing. It became particularly frustrating during the closing chapters of *The Fourth Circle*, the Sherlock Holmes pastiche, when I could hardly wait to see whether and how several seemingly unrelated structural threads would eventually merge to form a consistent tapestry.

In the end, the reader was rather satisfied, although somewhat reluctant and embarrassed to state it openly, due to his very close ties with the writer. The writer, for his part, was also pleased, although he remained as blissfully ignorant of what was happening as he had been in the beginning. Yet, he learned maybe the most important lesson about the holy mystery of artistic creativity: one doesn't have to know exactly how something functions as long as it functions.

The Fourth Circle was originally published in late December 1993. The following Spring it won a prestigious Serbian literary award—"Miloš Crnjanski." Curiously enough, it was a mainstream, not generic, award. The unquestionable SF elements in my novel were neglected, purposefully or not. It was primarily credited for its "literary values." One eminent critic hailed it as "a postmodern rhapsody."

I should have been more than satisfied. My first foray into literature had already proven quite a success. Alas, the limitations of that success were all too evident. As one cynic rightfully remarked, when you write in Serbian, you don't write at all. Indeed, your work is available to a theoretical maximum of about ten million native speakers, although the real number of potential readers is far, far inferior. The initial print-run of *The Fourth Circle* was only 500 copies, with an additional 500 printed after it won "Miloš Crnjanski." And that was it.

If I didn't want to remain first in the village, but to try my luck in the city, I had to provide an English translation of my novel. Once in English, it would become readable not only in the English-speaking countries, but throughout the world. It was easy enough to see that. To make it happen, however, was by no means straightforward and inexpensive. I confess I have always envied authors who write originally in English. First, they don't have to bother at all about providing translations of their works. Second, they never pay their translators. Their publishers gladly do that for them. But, as we all know, the world isn't a just place, particularly if you aren't among its privileged inhabitants.

Quality English translators from the Serbian are a rare breed. It's no wonder, therefore, that they are in strong demand and appropriately expensive. So, even when you manage to engage one, you are not quite certain whether you should be glad because your work will be properly translated, or sad because it is going to cost you a fortune. Sadness usually prevails, since it is an investment that very rarely if ever pays off. What you eventually get for your money is a mere chance to get to where any English speaking author is when he has just completed his work. There are no further guarantees whatsoever even of recouping your investment, let alone of making a profit. You really have to be quite a gambler to agree to such terms.

I certainly felt like one when Mrs. Mary Popović agreed to translate *The Fourth Circle*. And like any over-optimistic gambler I tried to see only the bright side of the whole enterprise. First of all, if there was someone able to cope with the translating challenges of my novel, it was Mrs. Popović. These were rather numerous and demanding. To start with, the four separate narrative lines needed to be distinctive in tone, which was probably the hardest task to achieve. In order to accentuate the differences between them, in the Serbian original I used four different fonts, one of them created particularly for that purpose. It referred to the episode taking place in a Medieval monastery, for which I almost invented a new language. Then, there were many intertextual references, ambiguous allusions, puns...It wasn't going to be easy money for the translator.

Indeed, the translating lasted almost six months. I spent a substantial part of that time with Mrs. Popović, assisting her in finding her way through the complex labyrinths of *The Fourth Circle*. I remember some moments of real trouble, almost desperation, when we struggled to find proper English equivalents for some of the subtler points in the original. I knew from my own experience (more than 50 translated books, mostly from English) that a translator's life is by no means a bed of roses. Yet, only now, working on my own novel, did I fully realize what a martyrdom it could be. Had I not written it myself, I would have been tempted to find the author and explain to him, mostly in a non-verbal way, what I thought of his linguistic and other virtuosities. By the end, Mrs. Popović and I were in full agreement: she had been shortchanged for her labour.

In my naivety, it seemed to me then that the worst part was behind me. I had a—hopefully—good novel, very professionally translated into English. What else could be needed in order to place it with an American or British publisher? Well, first I discovered I needed an agent. That came as a total surprise, since the institution of literary agents simply didn't exist in the part of the world I lived in. A writer dealt directly with publishing houses, without any intermediaries. Some American publishers, to whom I sent *The Fourth Circle* in late 1994, returned it unopened, briefly stating that they would only consider manuscripts received through agents.

Eventually, I managed to find an agent to represent me, although right from the start he wasn't very enthusiastic, and understandably so. At that time, with Sarajevo under siege and horrible bloodshed throughout the Balkans, anything with the prefix "Serbian" was automatically and indiscriminately identified as suspicious, to say the least. Indeed, soon one rejection slip followed another. The fact that none of them had anything to do with the literary qualities of my submission was scant consolation.

Under these bitter circumstances there were also a few amusing incidents. One publisher, for example, happened to like my novel quite a bit. Alas, he concluded that, however good, it was, at least at the moment, "unmarketable." (That was the very first time in my life I met this term used in what I thought was a predominantly literary context.) Yet, I got a counter-offer from him. Could I deliver, he asked, a 100,000 word novel about the civil war in Bosnia, preferably in three months. I shouldn't restrain my vivid imagination in any way when it came to atrocities, serial rape, concentration camps and other similar pleasantries so much admired by the mass audience. Such a novel would be not only marketable, but very probably bound to hit the best-seller lists. The gentleman was rather confused and disappointed to hear that I simply wasn't interested in hiring myself out as a writer, regardless of the advance he might have been willing to offer me.

When apparently there were no more publishers to whom my agent could submit *The Fourth Circle*, he stepped forward with an ingenious proposal. I should change my name. What do you mean, I asked incredulously. He meant I should choose a pen name, preferably something that would sound American. Like what? Well, we could try to find an analogous version of your original name. What would that be? After a brief etymological consideration, he boldly suggested: Donald Livingston. Why would I be Donald Livingston instead of Zoran Živković? Can you really imagine, he asked, that anyone called Zoran Živković would ever be able to publish anything in the USA? I could. He couldn't. So, inevitably, we went our separate ways.

I first received notice that, against all the odds, one of Zoran Živković's works of fiction (not *The Fourth Circle*) had been accepted for publication in the USA in the Spring of 1999, during the NATO campaign against my country. It happened between two air raids, in the short period when the electricity was on long enough to pick up my emails. My first thought was that it was another example of the irony of fate. After many years of futile attempts I had finally achieved my goal only to become another regrettable collateral victim in the next bombing. Fortunately, fate wasn't that ironic, although I managed to escape it only by a narrow margin. I happened to live just across the street from the Chinese Embassy which was hit, allegedly by mistake....

In 2004, exactly a decade after it had become available in English translation, *The Fourth Circle* will at last be brought out in the USA by Ministry of Whimsy. And not only this novel, but all my fiction works:

Impossible Stories (an omnibus of five related mosaic-novels: *Time Gifts, Impossible Encounters, Seven Touches of Music, The Library* and *Steps through the Mist*; also Ministry of Whimsy) and *The Book/The Writer* (Prime Books). With some luck, I might even see my latest, just completed novel, *Candid Camera*, published in the same season.

So, as you have seen, esteemed reader, *The Fourth Circle* had a very long journey to make before finally reaching you. But, please, pay no attention to all the troubles it has seen. They are irrelevant. In the solemn world of literature, troubles don't count. The only thing that matters there is what an author has achieved against them.

Zoran Živković
Belgrade, early September 2003